Through My Eyes

by

Suzanne Rossi

Through My Eyes

Cover Art by *Kim Mendoza*

The Wild Rose Press, Inc.
PO Box 708
Adams Basin, NY 14410-0708
Visit us at www.thewildrosepress.com

Publishing History
First Crimson Rose Edition, 2015
Print ISBN 978-1-62830-848-8
Digital ISBN 978-1-62830-849-5

Published in the United States of America

The muscles of his jaw flexed as he clenched his teeth. It dawned on me his chin was several inches above the top of my five-foot-four-inch height. In the close confines of the tiny elevator, I also realized he possessed a lean body. I shook my head.

For the love of God, get a grip.

My anger drained away, and I was left with his emotions swirling in my mind. The man was worried and more than just a little frightened. I also caught a sense of desperation along with something else.

A vision flashed in front of my eyes. I saw him crouched next to something in a dark alley. Other people stood staring at what I instinctively sensed to be the body of a woman. Reed McIntyre had been a homicide detective.

He was also angry.

I opened my mouth to tell him goodbye when another picture sliced through my mind. I saw a woman with long hair walking and clinging to a man as though needing support. His expression was one of such twisted hate it distorted his face into a malevolent mask. I almost gasped out loud. Then, I realized I viewed a moving picture. Was this the couple of last night?

I came to an abrupt decision.

Praise for Suzanne Rossi

"I found [*ALONG CAME QUINN*] entertaining and a quick read. It's a fun road romance with a twist on the treasure that I think is different yet believable. And it just goes to show that sometimes you can't see what's right under your nose."

~*Dear Author*

~*~

"I couldn't wait to turn each page to see what would happen next. Suzanne Rossi has definitely been added to my must-read list. The terrific twist on the run of the mill mob story makes [*ALL IN THE FAMILY*] a definite keeper."

~*Theresa Joseph, The Romance Studio*

~*~

"[*A TANGLED WEB*] has to be THE BEST romantic/suspenseful/mystery novel that I have read to date. The love scenes were perfectly timed with the plot, the suspense kept me turning the pages, and the mystery was superbly developed."

~*Happily Ever After Reviews*

~*~

"[*NEARLY DEPARTED*] is the BEST ghost story I have read in a long time. The wacky cast of characters is so colorful and fun that they bring the story to life."

~*Night Owl Reviews*

~*~

"I really got a good laugh out of [*HEAR NO EVIL*] and enjoyed the plot immensely which draws you in from the beginning… This author has done an incredible job penning this amazing tale."

~*The Romance Studio*

Dedication

I have a fabulous Crimson Rose editor in Johanna Melaragno. She has led me through the sometimes tortuous road from good book to really good book eight (nine counting this book) times. She's more than an editor, but a friend who isn't afraid to tell me I need to make changes. Her advice has always been spot on.

~*~

Romantic suspense is my natural writing niche, but one day a paranormal story popped into my head. *Nearly Departed* was born. My Faery Rose editor for that book was Sarah Hansen. She also kept hammering at me about details until I was ready to scream. But like Johanna, she was right, too. I owe her another paranormal, and I swear I'll get one to her as soon as possible.

~*~

Since this book has elements of both romantic suspense and the paranormal, I want to dedicate *Through My Eyes* to both of these ladies for all their wonderful help. Without their guidance, I'd have never succeeded.

Thank you, Johanna and Sarah.

Prologue

Gravity no longer existed. The spirit of Kathy Watson hovered above the murder scene watching in horror as her boyfriend Gerald's arm, a bloody knife clenched in his fist, rose and fell. Blood gushed from her perforated body, soaking into the ground. Kathy died with the fourth stroke, but the man continued to stab.

This can't be happening. It's a nightmare. So, why do I feel pain? I wouldn't feel pain in a dream, would I?

Gerald's frenzied motions ceased. He staggered to his feet, viewing his work with a twisted smile. Blood saturated his clothing. His fly distended.

He dragged her body to the river and heaved it into the water. She bobbed like a cork until the current swirled her downstream. Thunder rumbled in the distance.

Kathy knew this river. She and her grandfather had fished here when she was a kid. Numerous snags dotted the shoreline and shallow bottom. Days could pass before anyone discovered her remains.

Gerald laughed and flung the knife far out into the flow. The gore-stained clothing followed. His erection had not withered. Naked, he waded out a short distance, took care of the problem, and then washed the blood from his body. Finished, he returned to his car, donned clean clothing from the trunk, and whistling a cheerful tune, drove away.

A light at the end of a yawning tunnel beckoned in front of her. So, it was true. The comforting glow urged her to enter. She floated in air, refusing to make the final journey. She couldn't. Not yet.

Dark rage spun in tight circles like a whirlpool. *I didn't know the dead had emotions. The experts must have missed that one. But then, I've never been dead before.*

At any other time, she'd have considered the moonlight sparkling off the water beautiful and romantic. Never again. The little clearing where she had expected a declaration of love was now cold and blood-covered.

Kathy saw no reason to linger. She needed help. She demanded vengeance.

Chapter One

I hate being psychic. Some people claim it's a gift. I've always considered it a curse. Sometimes, images pop into my mind without warning—-like last night.

The vision had shaken me so much that early this morning I called Marilyn Anderson, my best friend since grade school. She agreed to meet me for breakfast at a coffee emporium near her office. She's a psychiatrist with a small practice in East Memphis. I'm one of her patients.

"Geez, Sasha, you look awful," she exclaimed. She set her coffee cup and plate containing a cranberry muffin in front of her before slipping into the chair across from me. "What happened?"

"God, Linnie, it was terrible. I was at Le Bistro with Phillip Casey when suddenly I did my thing. There we were sipping wine, talking about his work and—-wham—-before I realized what was happening, a presence filled me. I usually have some kind of warning—a dimming of my vision or flashes of light, but this time it just came."

Why was I babbling? Fear coupled with a desire to disbelieve what I'd seen?

I raised the cup to my lips with trembling hands and sipped the strong, hot brew. A burst of energy surged through me. Maybe all this caffeine wasn't such a good idea. I should have opted for soothing herbal tea.

"What did Philip do?" Linnie asked.

"Freaked, of course. He thought I was having some kind of seizure and called the paramedics. When I came to, I'd been slapped on a gurney and strapped down like a prison escapee. I'll never be able to show my face in that restaurant again."

Linnie slathered butter on her muffin and frowned. "Are you sure you didn't have a signal? You could have been distracted."

I shook my head. "No, I'm sure. He was telling me about his job. Do you have any idea how boring investment banking is? I seriously doubt Phillip will ever call again. And I wasn't about to tell him the truth. The fewer people who know about my abilities, the better."

"I understand," she said, taking a bite of the muffin. "But you're being evasive. I asked about the vision."

I paused. She was right. "There's something else."

I took another swig of coffee trying to dig up the courage to tell her. Last night's vision had frightened me, and I wasn't sure how to deal with it. I closed my eyes, letting the rich aroma of French Roast swirl up my nose. Maybe it would help me find the words.

Linnie leaned forward and said in a low voice, "Well?"

Confused and at a loss, I replied, "I'm sorry. I don't know how to explain it. My visions center on objects or places. I can find lost jewelry, wallets, or items like that, but it's after the fact. Last night was different."

"Different how?"

I raised my cup, taking another fortifying gulp. "I saw it all—-beginning to end. I watched a man murder a woman. He stabbed her over and over, and then dumped her body in the river."

Linnie sat back and gazed around the crowded coffee shop before shoving her half-eaten muffin away.

"Are you saying this happened in real time?"

"I'm not sure."

Wadding up her napkin, my friend tossed it onto the plate and pushed back her chair.

"We can't talk here. Let's go to the office. My first appointment isn't until nine. That'll give us an hour or so to tackle this. Did you call the police?"

"And tell them what? I have no idea who was involved or where the murder took place. I don't even know when it occurred." I wanted to cry, and pushed the coffee aside. "You're right. Let's get out of here."

I followed Linnie in my car to her office just off Poplar on Ridgeway. She used her swipe card to enter the employee garage while I parked out front and rode the elevator to the third floor. I often had appointments either before or after hours. Linnie refused to charge for her services, claiming she owed me.

Several years ago I "saw" her fiancé for what he was—a scum-sucking abuser. My vision had shown him hitting a woman. Even my best friend hadn't believed me, but when the son of a bitch used her as a punching bag, Linnie filed charges. She'd been lucky; he killed his next girlfriend. He was presently doing two-to-ten in the Mississippi State Penitentiary for manslaughter. In my opinion, Parchman, as the prison was called, was too good for him. He should have been shot.

We met at her office door. Linnie fumbled through the key ring for the office key while I waited. A man passed us, and then paused in the hallway.

"Good morning, Dr. Anderson. You're in early today."

"What? Oh, yes, I guess I am." She found the key and inserted it in the lock, then looked up and smiled. "Busy day ahead. Have a good one."

"Will do. I'll talk to you later." He nodded at me before moving on.

Linnie walked in first, flipping on lights. Not even her receptionist, Janine, had arrived yet.

"And who was that?" I asked.

"Oh, his name is Don Something-or-other. He works for the engineering firm down the hall. I've spoken to him a few times. He asked me out a few months ago, but I declined. Not my type."

"Not your type? He's good-looking and interested enough to ask you out. Since when isn't that your type?"

Linnie dropped her purse on her desk. "He's one of those people who are always first in and last out of the office. That tells me he's either a workaholic or has a shitty marriage, probably both."

"And he asked you out?"

"Okay, I don't know about the married part and have to admit he might not have asked me out if he had a wife stashed in the closet. Ask Janine. She's had lunch with him a couple of times." She pointed to the sofa. "Have a seat. We're here to talk about you and this vision."

I took a seat on the sofa and chewed my fingernails.

"Stop it," she said. "You don't do that anymore. Remember?"

I lowered my hands and clasped them together in my lap. I no longer smoked either, but that didn't stop me from wanting to light up.

"Now, tell me about this vision from the beginning," Linnie said, sitting in a chair.

"I already have, at least as much as I can remember. Only this time…" my voice trailed off. I still didn't know how to describe what I'd seen.

"Sasha, take a deep breath and close your eyes."

I obeyed.

"Now, think back to the vision, and tell me what you saw. Take your time."

Suddenly, I wanted to leap to my feet and run like a rabbit to a hidey hole. Instead, I took several more deep breaths.

"It wasn't like anything I've experienced before. Normally, I see images like a series of photographs in a slide show. They're still—-nothing moves. But last night, it was like watching TV. This man had a woman on the ground. He straddled her legs and kept plunging a knife into her chest. Blood flew everywhere. Then he stood, dragged her body to the river, and threw her in."

I gulped and shivered, then wrapped my arms over my churning stomach. Linnie rose and handed me a bottle of water from the small fridge in the corner of the room. I opened it and drank. My entire midsection seized in a hard cramp before relaxing. I breathed easier and set the bottle on the table.

"Can you identify the victim or the killer?"

I shook my head. "I viewed it from above. He was in shadow and his body prevented me from seeing the woman clearly." I rubbed my temples to ease a small ache. "I think she had long hair-—maybe brown. I wish I'd seen their faces, especially when he dragged her to the river."

"What river? The Mississippi?"

"I don't know," I said, my voice rising.

"Think, Sasha," she insisted. "Was it wide? Was the current swift? What kind of terrain led to it? Did the killing take place in a field or the woods?"

I closed my eyes and remembered. "I—I don't think it was the Mississippi. It wasn't wide enough, but trees surrounded it."

"Okay, good. What about the killer? What did he do after he threw her in the river?"

"He tossed the knife in, too, and then his clothes."

"He was naked?"

"Yes."

"Logic says he couldn't have walked too far through the woods naked as a jaybird. Did you see a car or a road?"

I shook my head. Fear squeezed my heart. "I don't remember. I think there was more to the vision, but it's not coming through."

"Do you want me to hypnotize you?"

"Not now. Let's see if I can remember on my own."

"Sasha, we should report this to someone."

"Who? I don't know where the crime took place. Woods are woods and it's April. For all I know, this occurred in Kentucky or Iowa. Hell, there's no evidence it happened in the United States." I hoped my abilities hadn't gone global.

Linnie sat back, her forehead furrowed. "Why

don't I make a few discreet inquiries of local authorities to see if they've had any missing persons reported in the last twenty-four hours?"

"No. Remember the last time I contacted the police?"

Several years ago, a bank robbery netted the criminals a cool hundred grand. In my vision, I saw a suitcase wrapped in garbage bags being buried on the edge of a cotton field. I used local landmarks to lead the Arkansas State Police to the area. They dug for several hours and found nothing. I'd felt like Geraldo when he opened Al Capone's safe.

"And I still say that by the time the cops decided to believe you, the thieves had come back and retrieved it," Linnie said.

"Let's wait and see if a body turns up. According to my vision, the woman is dead and in the river. Sooner or later, she has to surface."

I bit my lip. I hadn't meant for my words to sound so callous. I didn't want to think about the victim. I may not have been able to see clearly, but her emotions had tapped into mine. The talons of her terror had clawed deeply, leaving me shredded and breathless.

I re-played the vision again in my head. The scene wavered and blurred as if viewed through a pair of glasses with an outdated prescription. Why, I didn't know. If it would clear—-just for a moment—-maybe I'd be able to see the killer's face.

The outer office door opened, and then closed. A glance at my watch showed it was almost eight-thirty. The newcomer had to be Linnie's receptionist. I finished my water and stood.

"I've got to get to work, Linnie."

"Why don't you call in sick today? You've witnessed a murder, for crying out loud." She also rose.

"No, I want to stay busy." I slung my purse over my shoulder and gave her a hug. "I'll be all right, and if I remember anything else, I'll call you. I promise."

I exited her office.

"Hello, Miss Bellwood. I didn't know you were coming in this morning," the receptionist said with a smile.

"Good morning, Janine. It was a last minute decision." I glanced at my watch again while she gathered several file folders from her desk. "Oops, gotta run. Have a good one."

I waved and left. I liked Janine Henderson. She'd been with Linnie for the last two years, and even though this was her first job out of secretarial school, she'd managed to bring order to a chaotic office. My best friend may have been able to organize her patients' minds, but couldn't keep a scrap of paper where it belonged.

Settled in the car, I tapped my fingers on the steering wheel. Had my vision taken place nearby?

On impulse, I grabbed my cell phone and called Dr. Clarke Pennington, my boss, the Dean of Paranormal Activities in the Psychology Department at the University of Memphis. He'd hired me as his research assistant because of my strong ESP abilities, but I'd kept the vision thing to myself. Author of several books about the paranormal, he wasn't above using the experiences of the people who came to him for help as the basis for one or more chapters. I had no intention of becoming a statistic or contributing to his royalty checks.

Of course, I wasn't above peeking into his files now and again to see if I could find anyone else with powers like mine. I'd discovered a few people with varying degrees of true psychic ability. It helped to learn I wasn't alone.

Far too early for Dr. Pennington to be in the office, I left a message complete with moans and groans about food poisoning, saying I'd be in tomorrow.

Slipping the car into gear, I swung out of the parking lot and headed for I-55. I needed more information—-more details. Instinct told me the murder had occurred close by. I turned south for Mississippi.

****

I entered the elevator in Linnie's office building and jabbed at the third floor button. I'd spent the better part of the day driving the back roads of northern DeSoto County and seen nothing familiar. I should have known better. What a silly waste of time. I'd gone off half-cocked—-like I was going to drive straight to the crime scene and solve the whole thing. And why Mississippi? I had no idea.

Hypnotism was the only answer. I'd tried calling up the vision by myself when I returned home, but failed, finally phoning Linnie to request a session after her last patient of the day.

I knew in my bones I was dealing with true evil. The realization sent cold chills up and down my spine, scaring the crap out of me.

Entering the empty outer office, I spied a sign stating, "Please Wait" on Linnie's office door. Since it was after six, Janine had gone home. I flopped into a chair and crossed my legs, my foot jiggling in the air while I scanned a magazine. I didn't have long to wait.

Within a couple of minutes the inner door opened, and Linnie stood on the threshold.

"Come on in, Sasha."

She looked worried and distracted, a frown marring her brow. Her blue eyes held a hint of wariness. Even a few tendrils of her thick, dark brown hair had escaped from the usually immaculate French twist.

"Are you all right?" I asked, slipping past her.

She nodded and gestured. "Have a seat."

I turned and stopped to stare. A man sat in one of the chairs.

"Sasha, I'd like you to meet Reed McIntyre. Reed, this is Sasha Bellwood."

The man rose, extending a hand. Politeness and tradition had me accepting. His large, warm hand engulfed mine. I scanned his craggy face and had the feeling those sharp blue eyes missed little.

"Miss Bellwood." Apparently a man of few words, he was brief and to the point.

"Mr. McIntyre," I reciprocated.

The handshake lasted all of two seconds. He released me and gazed into my eyes as though trying to read my mind. It gave me the creeps. I turned to Linnie.

"What's this all about?"

"Sit down, Sasha."

I obeyed, as did McIntyre.

"Reed is a former member of the Memphis Police Department and I asked him here to…"

I leapt to my feet in anger and disappointment. How could she?

"Dammit, Linnie, I said no cops and you're my doctor for crying out loud." I heard the accusatory words and assumed my face mirrored the disbelief surging through me.

"Calm down, Sasha."

"No!"

I slung my purse over my shoulder and headed for the door only to have that warm hand close around my arm. My skin burned at his touch.

"Please, Miss Bellwood, no doctor-patient confidentiality has been breached. I promise."

He spoke gruffly, and I decided he didn't often use the word "please."

"If it's any help, I was Dr. Anderson's patient three or four years ago, too. And I'm not officially a cop anymore."

He dropped his hand from my arm with a smile. The harsh contours of his face softened. Fine lines spread out from the corners of his eyes. Not the world's handsomest face, but the kind a person felt inclined to trust. I wasn't the trusting sort.

"Sasha, Reed doesn't know anything about your situation. He's here for your abilities," Linnie said. "Please, hear him out."

I returned to the chair, sitting on the edge, ready to flee if necessary.

"My abilities?"

McIntyre cleared his throat. "I understand you claim to have certain psychic abilities. I was wondering if you could help me."

Not liking the sardonic phrase "claim to have," I shot a glance at Linnie who bit her lip and shrugged, then turned my attention back to McIntyre.

"Have you lost your wallet or some jewelry, Mr. McIntyre?" I'd meant to come off sounding in control, but the words had a nervous ring to them.

"No, a body. Two to be precise."

I sprang from the chair again.

"That does it! Linnie, I'll call tomorrow, assuming I've forgiven you for this."

I practically ran from the room, slamming the door behind me, and raced for the elevator. Tears welled in my eyes. I had never expected my best friend, not to mention psychiatrist, to betray me to a total stranger. I punched the down button, and then jumped when that warm hand once again closed over my arm. The scorched sensation returned. The man moved like a cat. I'd never heard him coming.

"Miss Bellwood, don't blame Dr. Anderson. I called this afternoon and asked for her help in contacting someone who has whatever it is you have."

"I do not have a disease, Mr. McIntyre. I have highly developed ESP skills and can occasionally find things that are lost. So far, that does not include bodies. Goodnight."

The elevator doors opened and I marched inside. To my dismay, so did McIntyre.

"Allow me to explain. Can I buy you a cup of coffee? I really do need help."

"Try the yellow pages. Look under the heading of psychics. I'm sure you can find one that meets your criteria." I jammed my finger on the first floor button and held it there.

He ran his hand through his overgrown dark brown hair. It curled in the nape of his neck and over his ears. He needed a trim. Even so, I found it attractive, and then kicked myself for noticing. I wanted him gone.

"Miss Bellwood, I don't have much in the line of social graces, nor do I have the gift of gab. I've always considered psychics charlatans, one step ahead of the bunko squad. The fact I'm even thinking about consulting one shows my desperation."

He wanted to use *my* abilities he didn't believe in to find a couple of bodies? Was he kidding?

"And how does this make me want to help you?"

"I put that badly. I'm not suggesting you're a con artist. I know you don't take money from gullible people, gaze into a crystal ball, and tell them what they want to hear. I just don't know where else to turn."

The frown on his face once again deepened the lines in his forehead and from nose to mouth. The muscles of his jaw flexed as he clenched his teeth. It dawned on me his chin was several inches above the top of my five-foot-four-inch height. In the close confines of the tiny elevator, I also realized he possessed a lean body. I shook my head.

For the love of God, get a grip.

My anger drained away, and I was left with his emotions swirling in my mind. The man was worried and more than just a little frightened. I also caught a sense of desperation along with something else.

A vision flashed in front of my eyes. I saw him crouched next to something in a dark alley. Other people stood staring at what I instinctively sensed to be the body of a woman. Reed McIntyre had been a homicide detective.

He was also angry.

I opened my mouth to tell him goodbye when another picture sliced through my mind. I saw a woman with long hair walking and clinging to a man as though needing support. His expression was one of such twisted hate it distorted his face into a malevolent mask.

15

I almost gasped out loud. Then, I realized I viewed a moving picture. Was this the couple of last night?

I came to an abrupt decision.

Chapter Two

The elevator doors opened and I stalked out, leaving McIntyre to trail after me.

"I'll give you exactly one cup of coffee, mister, so you'd better hone your social skills and your gift of gab real fast. Café Au Lait is only three blocks from here."

Ignoring him, I whirled and strode from the building. I took time to clear my emotions before arriving at Café Au Lait and found Reed McIntyre already seated, sipping a cup of coffee. He didn't rise when I approached. Pulling out a chair, I sat and called out an order for a chocolate mint latte to the waitress behind the counter.

"I thought maybe you'd changed your mind." The lines in his face deepened as he frowned.

"If I had, I wouldn't be here now."

"I'm sorry. I'm not used to dealing with people like you," he muttered.

"People like me?"

He had the grace to look embarrassed. "Another apology due. I told you I have few social skills."

"I suppose you're one of those cops who think crime labs and forensic science is a bunch of hooey, too."

"Nope. Forensic evidence is crucial to solving crimes. Most people don't realize what can be learned from a single hair or a cigarette butt."

The waitress brought my latte. He paid the tab while I sipped the minty mocha. I stared at him before commenting, "Psychics have solved cases when forensics was at a dead end."

He shook his head drawing in a deep breath. "DNA doesn't lie. Neither does ballistics. It's science. Psychic visions are often revealed as 'bodies of water,' 'alleys,' or 'a large field.' They're vague and imprecise."

"So, why do you want my help? I'm liable to be vague and imprecise, too."

I couldn't keep the sarcasm from my voice. He closed his eyes and rubbed his temples with his fingertips. I picked up on his frustration. It was my turn to be embarrassed. He was only being honest.

I reached across the table and laid my hand on his arm, stilling the movement. He opened his eyes. For reasons I couldn't understand, compassion swept me.

"Forgive me, Mr. McIntyre. I didn't mean to be bitchy." I removed my hand and picked up my latte, taking a generous gulp. "Why don't you start at the beginning? I'm not sure I can help, but I *can* listen."

He raised his cup and drained it. "I'm not sure where to start."

"You worked Homicide, didn't you?"

"How did you know?"

I gave him a look.

"Yeah, right. Sorry." Sighing, he broke off a piece of the empty Styrofoam cup and played with it for a second before dropping it on the table.

"It all began eight years ago. My partner and I were assigned to investigate the murder of a woman found in an alley near an East Memphis mall. She'd been strangled. We interviewed family and friends, including her ex-boyfriend, but came up with zilch." His brow knit. He snapped another piece of Styrofoam from the cup. "After a while, the case went cold. I hate cold cases."

"Must be lots of unsolved murders out there. Why did this one bother you so much?"

"The crime scene was too clean. She'd been killed somewhere else and her body dumped. The murder itself was savage. The killer had struck her on the head from behind. Then, the son of a bitch used a bicycle chain to strangle her." His lips snaked into a thin line.

"Did you ever find where she'd died?" I asked before taking another gulp of my latte. I stared into the light brown liquid, preferring it to the angry look on McIntyre's face. He didn't exactly scare me, but I couldn't suppress the shiver that raced down my spine. I sensed a multi-layered man whose emotions ran deep.

"No. Carpet fibers on the front of her dress didn't match those of her apartment or the residences of anyone else we questioned. The killer was clever. Most of the forensic evidence was from the alley."

"What about the ex-boyfriend?"

"He had an alibi. Both he and her family had the impression she'd met someone new, but no one could come up with a name or a description." He paused and dropped the now crumbled Styrofoam into the growing pile on the table. "Mary Alice Maghee. That was her name. Have you ever heard of a more clean-cut, All-American name than that?"

I sensed the remnants of his anger and sorrow after all this time.

"Mr. McIntyre, I don't understand how I can help.

You said something about finding a body. You *have* Mary Alice's body, and I doubt I can tell you anything about the killer at this late date."

"Reed, call me Reed."

"I'm Sasha. I repeat, I don't see how I can help."

He quit fiddling with the battered cup and looked me straight in the eye.

"She was the first."

I clenched my teeth to keep them from chattering as unearthly cold rolled over me. My breath caught in my throat, and I prayed the blackness on the edges of my vision would encroach no further.

I tried to convince myself the reaction had nothing to do with his last sentence, but with low blood sugar due to lack of food. I didn't succeed, and once again I saw the sword of evil poised above my head.

"The—the first?"

"Are you all right? You're white as a sheet."

I raised my cup to my lips with trembling hands and drained it. "Yes, I'm fine. Too much caffeine. What do you mean, the first?"

"About six weeks later, another murder with the same M.O. occurred. Nice girl, new boyfriend no one else had met, but instead of a bicycle chain, the killer used the cord of a computer mouse."

My vision cleared and the freezing cold abated. "How bizarre. Was she also found in an alley?"

"No, the middle of a construction site about a mile from the first scene."

"Then how do you know the two are connected?"

"The same carpet fibers showed up."

"How many bodies have you found so far?" Queasiness rumbled my stomach. I needed food, real food, not the sugary stuff offered at Café Au Lait.

"Seven. The last one was discovered in Olive Branch over two years ago. The Desoto County, Mississippi, cops cooperated with us, but the case is considered cold."

"Let me guess, strangulation and the same carpet fibers."

He shook his head. "The killer changed his M.O. Added stabbing to the list. This girl was stabbed fifteen times in the neck and chest." Reed broke off another chunk of Styrofoam and proceeded to shred it.

"Somebody must have had a very messy house or apartment, not to mention clothing." My mind snapped back to my vision, the huge volume of blood, and the killer stripping naked. "Couldn't the police connect any of her friends or acquaintances to the crime?"

"Nope. She and three friends went barhopping on Beale Street. They'd been drinking heavily. When it came time to head home, they realized Susan Parker, their designated driver, was missing. A couple of hunters discovered her body in a field two days later."

"No leads at all?"

"A bartender at Jammin' recalls her talking to a guy at the bar, but it was Saturday night and the place was packed. He had no idea if she left with him or her friends. The friends were too drunk to remember."

My stomach rumbled and the queasiness returned. I gazed around the coffee shop. We were the only two patrons, and yet I had the most absurd impression we were not alone.

"So, there haven't been any new murders in two years?" I asked. "Any kind of sexual assault in all of this?"

"Not a sign."

"The killer could have used a condom."

"The women showed no indications of recent sexual activity."

No, there wouldn't be. A missing piece of the puzzle slipped into place. The man of my vision waded into the water and jerked off. A cold chill raced over my body. I wanted a quick dinner and a warm bed. It had been a helluva twenty-four hours.

"What do missing bodies have to do with this?"

"Bridget Connor disappeared three years ago. Her family in Poplar Bluff, Missouri, said she called a few days earlier singing the praises of her new boyfriend. His name was Scott. That's all they knew. We never found him or any indication he ever existed."

He stared at the table as though seeing it for the first time. The little pile of destroyed Styrofoam had grown steadily. Grimacing, Reed swept the tattered heap into the remains of the cup.

"Eleanor Gayle vanished a few weeks later. She and some friends went on a weekend junket to the Tunica casinos. They stayed at The Winning Touch. When it came time to go home, Eleanor was nowhere to be found."

"Casinos have surveillance cameras everywhere except the johns. I know. I was a cashier at The Lucky Dog for a while. Didn't they show anything?" I asked.

"She played blackjack, roulette, and pulled a few one-armed bandits. She talked to her fellow players and downed her fair share of drinks. The security camera from the east entrance showed her leaving alone at three o'clock on Sunday morning."

He rose, gathered his mutilated cup and my empty

one, then tossed them into the trash can. He returned and stood next to the table.

"Sasha, I don't know if you can help me. I'm not even sure the missing girls are dead. I have this gut feeling they are, and an even stronger fear our guy is about to strike again. I'm desperate."

I had no idea how I had gotten dragged into this or why. I suspected his hunch was right. My vision posted too many similarities to be a coincidence. But before I divulged anything, I needed to know more. I'd call Linnie later and have her hypnotize me tomorrow morning. I couldn't face doing it tonight.

"Give me a number where I can reach you," I said abruptly. "We'll meet at Linnie's office tomorrow morning. I'll call with the time. Bring a photo or an item of the women's clothing if you have them. I won't guarantee the results."

"Thank you," he replied, handing me his business card.

For someone who questioned my abilities, his face bore an odd expression of relief.

"Don't thank me yet. I may not be able to help."

"Then I'm no worse off than I am now."

Without saying goodbye, he turned and walked out.

****

I stopped at a Chinese take-out joint on my way home. I still had this queer impression I was not alone, like someone was staring at me. Another shiver raced down my spine as though invisible breath blew on the back of my neck. I kept looking over my shoulder to see if someone hid in the backseat.

Back home, I called Linnie between mouthfuls of Kung Pao Chicken.

"Sasha, I didn't tell him anything specific. It took a while for him to admit he wanted to consult a psychic."

"You had no business telling him about me—period."

"When you called, it seemed like a perfect solution to his problem. I only told him I'd found someone."

I wanted to rant and rave. Then, that vision of Reed McIntyre standing over a woman's body in an alley swam in front of my eyes.

"Okay, I guess I forgive you."

"Did you talk to Reed?"

"Yes. What can you tell me about him?"

"I can only say he's a former cop who is still helping the police as a consultant on cold cases."

"Why is he a former cop? He seems kind of young to be retired." I shoveled another forkful of spicy chicken into my mouth, and then chased it with a long swallow of ice-cold beer.

I didn't want to admit it, but Reed's stories about the murdered and missing women intrigued me. I'd tell him about my vision if, and when, I had something concrete.

"Let's just go with health reasons for the moment," Linnie answered in a professional voice.

"Health reasons? What health reasons? He looked pretty damned healthy to me."

"Sasha, if he wants you to know, he'll tell you." She paused before continuing. "Did you tell him anything about your vision?"

"No. Why should I? I don't know if it's related to anything he's seeking. Besides, I don't have enough information. I refuse to look ridiculous again."

"Are you going to help him find the missing

women?"

I left her hanging as I let the spices from another mouthful of my dinner roll over my tongue. My eyes watered. This was a good batch tonight. I grabbed the beer and chugged.

"Yes. I'll do it in your office in the morning. After he leaves, I want you to hypnotize me. I can't swear that what he's talking about and what I saw are connected, but I have to make sure."

"All right. I'm not sure about the timing of my first appointment. Is seven o'clock too early?"

"Yes, but it'll have to do."

I hung up and called Reed McIntyre. The devilish imp inside me hoped he found the time Linnie chose horrific.

"Seven's fine," he said, dashing my hopes. "I'm an early riser."

"Okay, I'll see—"

He'd hung up.

I shrugged. He was abrupt and rude—-so what? I could be the same way when I felt like it.

I finished off the rest of the edible Chinese blow torch and popped the cap on another beer to put out the fire.

With any luck it would help me sleep.

****

Kathy Watson had never given the term "undead" much thought. Not a fan of ghost stories or horror fiction, she refused to question whether the word was even valid. So, finding herself in that peculiar space between living and dead confused the hell out of her.

It had taken a while after her vow of vengeance to conclude she'd reached out and touched someone. One moment, she floated, watching the tail lights of Gerald's car disappear down the road, and the next, she was in an ambulance *and* the head of a woman named Sasha. Then, she realized this woman had viewed everything through *her* eyes.

Kathy wished she had more experience or the ability to ask advice from others in her predicament. If she did, she'd be able to tell Sasha exactly who had killed her. Unfortunately, she had no clear concept of how to get her message across. All attempts to communicate directly ended in frustration.

I'm too new at this ghost thing.

At least Kathy had managed to stick with her host. It wasn't easy. Being in someone else's head proved tiring—-kind of like having several TVs in the same room on different stations. The experience was not unlike a crowded sports bar on a busy night. Not only did she hear Sasha's words and thoughts, but was forced to listen to the voices of other people. It was much easier to vacate the head and float nearby with others present. The downside to that was she lost the ability to hear. It was like being in a vacuum.

Kathy was surprised Sasha knew Dr. Anderson. She had gone to see the psychiatrist with her self-esteem in tatters after that rat-bastard, Jack Santana had dumped her. Kathy chose the first female shrink in the phone book. Four sessions restored her confidence.

But apparently not my judgment in men.

She wanted to guide Sasha to the murder scene, but failed. Instead, her host had driven into Mississippi, not Northern Shelby County.

Kathy's frustration built when Sasha tried self-hypnosis. She'd been flung from her head and all attempts to re-enter had met with failure. Now, she was in some coffee house with a man. The experience must have clogged her pipeline into the living world because she saw neither person clearly. They looked like bad surveillance tapes with fuzzy images, and since Kathy was no longer in Sasha's head, she couldn't hear their conversation. *Perhaps I'm still under the influence of the drug Gerald must have slipped into my wine.*

Her vision improved with the Chinese food. Maybe it was the MSG. By the time Sasha went to sleep, Kathy had reestablished a fragile contact. Obviously, not all the information about the murder had been absorbed.

Maybe she's as confused as I am. How do I get through? Then, she had an idea. *I'm dead. If I appeared to Sasha while she was awake, why can't I do it during sleep? A lot less brain clutter that way.*

She had no clue how to do this and no time to search for instructions, so even though the contact was tenuous, Kathy forced her way further into Sasha's head.

****

I jerked awake, fighting with the covers clinging to me like cloth fingers. Finally free of the cotton and down grasp, I sat upright clutching my chest and struggling for breath.

Oh, my God, I hurt. The pain was deep and burning everywhere in my torso, but even as I came to full consciousness, the torture receded, and I realized I'd been dreaming. And not just any dream. I'd dreamt the vision.

I sat like a stone for several minutes until my pounding heart and ragged breathing returned to acceptable levels. I dragged the sweat-saturated tendrils of hair from my face and shoved the comforter aside, then ran for the bathroom where I threw up.

Afterward, I brushed my teeth and gazed at my reflection in the mirror.

I looked like hell. My black, chin-length hair hung in stringy rat tails, the perspiration already hardening the strands like a perverse mousse. Terrified brown eyes stared back. They filled with tears, which soon overflowed, trickling down pale cheeks. I resembled a ghost.

Gripping the sides of the pedestal sink, I gulped and breathed deeply, trying to regain control.

I hadn't expected a vision in my dreams. That had never happened before. And this time I didn't hover over the scene. This time, I was the victim. I saw the flashes of moonlight glistening off the plunging blade, felt the searing pain as the metal cut into my body, and heard the flesh ripping along with crunching bones. I smelled the coppery scent of spewing blood.

I'd looked into the face of the killer and mentally cursed him. Unfortunately, I didn't see him. My mind had been sluggish and my vision blurred.

I wiped the tears from my face, drank a glass of water, and staggered back to bed. Shivering in the freezing cold room, I crawled in, pulling the covers up to my chin. A slow mind coupled with blurred vision. Had the killer drugged his victim? I closed my eyes and remembered the dream.

The snippet I'd viewed earlier in the elevator of two people walking had started it. The victim and her killer staggered along a winding path in the woods until coming to a small clearing near a riverbank. I saw it all through the victim's eyes.

In the dream, my eyelids sagged and I had a hard time remaining awake. Lowered to the ground beneath a tree, my companion laughed and straddled my thighs. Then he spoke.

"You're a slut, Kathy. Just like all the rest of them. It's my duty to eliminate sluts."

The voice came through raspy as though electronically altered. He reached into the front pocket of his jeans and removed something. Slowly, the man extended a knife blade, and laughed again before raising his arm.

I struggled to cry out and throw him from my body. My muscles refused to obey. I realized the danger, but could do nothing to stop what was about to happen. This was the terror the victim had transmitted, shredding me last night.

The blade flashed when the knife descended, striking me to the right of the breastbone. Pain clawed and ripped. Blood spurted and drenched my chest, then flowed down my side in a hot river.

I wrenched my eyes open.

"No!" I screamed, forcing the image from my mind.

Oddly enough, the rejection worked. My pounding heart slowly returned to normal. The temperature in the room warmed. I swallowed hard and once again fought nausea. It took a minute before that, too, disappeared.

I flung back the covers. No more sleep for me tonight. I stumbled into the living room where I turned on the TV, staring at old movies for the next six hours.

****

Sasha's scream ejected Kathy from her host's mind with a violence she'd not expected. Caught by surprise, she careened around the room, bouncing off the ceiling and walls. With each rebound, her speed accelerated like a crazed dot in the computer game, Jezzball.

The last ricochet catapulted her toward the open bedroom window. Unable to stop her momentum, Kathy Watson sailed through the screen and into the darkness, breaking her frail connection to the only person who could help her.

Chapter Three

I was late. Seven o'clock, even to a person who'd been up all night, was an outlandish time of day for anything. Another ten minutes wouldn't make any difference. I'd do the best I could with Reed, then get down to business when he left.

I rapped on the doors to the building until the security guard, Bob, let me in. In his early thirties, he'd been the daytime guard for a couple of years and knew me on sight. Pleasant and jovial, he always had a smile on his face. Linnie saw to it he received a special envelope on Christmas.

"Good morning. You're here early," he said, his brown eyes crinkling. "Must be the day for it. I've opened up for several people."

"I have a special session with Dr. Anderson." I glanced at my watch. "What time do you get here anyway?"

"I'm on duty from six in the morning until four in the afternoon."

"There's no guard after four?"

"They let the nighttime guards go a few months ago. Economy's bad. We have a patrol car come through several times a night. Cleaning crew has a key." He shrugged. "At least I have a job."

I rode the elevator to the third floor and exited. The

man from yesterday was in the hall just outside Linnie's office. He had an ear to the door and his hand on the knob as if about to enter, then turned to face me.

"Oh, hi. I was just wondering if Marilyn was in yet." He stuck out his hand. "I'm Donald Duckworth."

Was he kidding? *Donald Duck*worth? He must have seen the expression on my face for he laughed.

"I know. Happens all the time. The kids in school had a ball with it. Makes it hard for women to take me seriously, but I'm a nice guy once you get to know me."

I shook hands. "I'm Sasha Bellwood. Nice to meet you, but I have to run. I'm needed inside."

"Sure, see you around."

He sauntered down the corridor, whistling a tune off-key. I turned and entered the reception area.

The door to Linnie's office stood open. I heard voices and hurried in only to pull up short.

Reed was ensconced on the sofa studying the contents of an open file folder on the coffee table. Linnie sat in a chair opposite him talking with a second man seated next to her. The stranger rose when I entered.

"Good morning, Sasha," she said, also rising, but continuing to stare at the man. "Would you like a cup of coffee?"

When I didn't answer, she finally turned toward me. The expression on her face changed.

"Are you all right? You look freaking awful."

I didn't need to be told I looked like the bride of Frankenstein. I'd seen that for myself this morning. Not even copious amounts of concealer and blush hid the dark circles under my eyes or my pale cheeks.

"I didn't have the best of nights, and I'd prefer

tea," I replied. I turned my gaze to the stranger. "Who are you? Somebody else who wants me to find something?"

I couldn't keep the tartness from my tone. No sleep and another stranger didn't make me happy.

Reed looked up from the file. "This is my former partner, Detective Jeff Hammond. I asked him to join us."

"Why?"

"Because I want to find this guy as much as Reed," Hammond said. "And you, of course, are Sasha Bellwood. I'm pleased to meet you."

He looked young, maybe mid-thirties. His sandy hair was cut in a conservative style, and he smiled while extending his hand. The gaze emanating from his gray-green eyes oozed friendliness. Not as tall as Reed, he possessed a sturdy body. I doubted an ounce of flab could be found anywhere. The image of a bulldog ran through my mind.

"How do you do, Detective Hammond?" I shook his hand and searched his eyes. They still looked friendly. "I gotta tell you, I don't need another skeptic. One is enough."

"On the contrary, I have the highest respect for people with ESP and psychic skills. As a cop, I always look toward the unconventional when the conventional doesn't work. I wanted to do this a couple of years ago, but was overruled."

I had the impression Hammond had just taken a jab at Reed and glanced in his direction. He remained hunched over the file, ignoring us. Had he been opposed to bringing in a psychic? Probably.

"As I told Reed last night, I can't guarantee I'll be

of any help. You may be disappointed."

He smiled and winked. "Meeting two beautiful women at seven in the morning is never a disappointment."

I found myself charmed and realized he still held my hand. A derisive snort from the sofa had me slowly extricating it.

"Don't pay any attention to old Reed. He was born surly. He flunked cop charm school," Hammond said.

"Whereas, you aced the course, and then took an advanced degree," Reed replied, turning a page without looking up.

Linnie returned from the make-shift kitchen area carrying a tray with coffee for three and tea makings for me. She placed it on the table near Reed's folder.

"Cream and sugar, Jeff?" she asked the detective, arching her eyebrows.

"No thanks, doc. I take it strong and black."

"You know, I have a theory about coffee and how people drink it," she said, resuming her seat. Hammond also reclaimed his chair.

"What's that?" he said.

"The more complicated the personality, the more additives go into the coffee. For instance, women's personalities are often very complex. They tend to use sugar and cream, sometimes the flavored kind. On the other hand, men gravitate toward black, sugar, or cream, rarely flavored. When they do use both, I know I'll have to work harder to extricate their problems."

I sat on the sofa next to Reed and poured the hot water over the tea bag, dunking it in and out of the cup while Linnie flirted with Hammond. I'd heard this theory line before. Sometimes it involved wine or liquor. It depended on where she flirted.

"Is there any French vanilla creamer around?" Reed asked, emptying a sugar packet into his coffee.

I choked back a laugh. The two of them ignored us.

Hammond grinned at Linnie and took a gulp of the hot liquid. "And what about those who add nothing?"

She grinned back. "In my professional experience, those people are straightforward, down to earth, uncomplicated. How they drink their coffee is also very telling. Sippers take things slowly. It gives them time to arrange their thoughts before they speak. They frequently have something to hide. Gulpers are quick and decisive."

A loud slurp from next to me had me stifling another laugh. Maybe Reed McIntyre had a sense of humor after all.

"Where do slurpers fit in?" Reed asked.

"They're right up your alley with bad manners," his former partner replied.

"If the two of you are finished with the coffee foreplay, could we get down to business?" Reed said, gulping from his cup and making a face.

A blush tinted Linnie's cheeks.

"I'm ready whenever you are," I told Reed. "Did you bring a picture or an item of clothing?"

From the file he produced a snapshot, handing it to me. It depicted a young girl in a cap and gown. Her smile was wide and her eyes sparkled with good humor. Long dark hair cascaded over her white clad shoulders and a fringe of bangs peeked out from beneath the mortarboard. Reed then read off a sheet of paper.

"This is Bridget Connor, twenty-one years old, a junior at The University of Memphis. She disappeared between Friday afternoon and Sunday evening on the weekend of April 15th. Her roommate had been out of town and reported her missing Tuesday morning. Her car was later discovered in the parking lot of The Wolf Chase Galleria Mall. This photo was taken at her high school graduation."

I stared hard at the image of a bright, vivacious young woman. An intrusion I couldn't pin down wormed its way into my perception.

"She was an optimist and took life in stride," I said. "She liked people and people liked her in return. I sense a warm, trusting nature."

"Even I read that in the photo. She majored in Sociology and enjoyed helping others," Reed said in a clipped tone. "Do you get any sense of her whereabouts?"

"Not from this. If this is a high school graduation picture, then it was taken three years before her death— if she's dead. Sorry, no bad vibes are grabbing me."

"That's what I figured."

"Reed, don't be so sarcastic. This is not an exact science," Hammond said in rebuke.

"It's not science at all," he replied.

"I'm sure Sasha is doing the best she can," Linnie said, tossing me a glance.

"For someone who wants my help, you're being damned negative. Negative vibes can block positive waves. Be a little more open-minded," I snapped, trying to control my temper. "Do you have a piece of clothing from the victim? Something she wore when she died would be nice, but then you don't have that, do you?"

I took a couple of deep breaths. Anger was also negative. I needed to clear it from my head.

From under the coffee table, Reed produced a brown paper bag and extracted a white, zip-up cardigan.

"This was found in the front seat of her car."

I felt her the instant I touched it. The image popped into my mind clear and sharp.

"She met him in the parking lot. She was wearing jeans, a pink T-shirt, and sneakers. She brought this, too, but forgot to take it with her when she got into his car. She's excited. He's new in her life—-two weeks, no more. Not even her roommate has met him yet."

Silence overwhelmed the room. The ticking clock on the credenza sounded like a jackhammer. I'd never experienced something like this before and was terrified. I couldn't make eye contact with Linnie.

"What's he look like?"

"I don't know. I'm not seeing like that. It's emotional. I'm feeling."

"Then how do you know what she's wearing?" Reed asked in a hard tone.

"I can't explain it. I just *know*."

"You know, but you can't see the killer?"

I wanted to hit him and curse at Linnie for having put me in the position of defending my abilities to people I barely knew. I swallowed hard, trying to keep my thoughts positive.

"That's right, I can't. What did her family say?"

"According to her parents, his name was Scott and he met her in a bar near campus. She told them he was a social worker from Jackson, Tennessee, taking a couple of refresher courses at the university. The only description we got was that he had blond hair, gorgeous eyes, and a killer smile—-Bridget's words to her folks when she called on Thursday evening. Nobody recalls having seen him on campus and there were no courses for what he claimed being offered that semester."

"Well, for what it's worth, I'm certain she's dead," I told him. "I just can't tell you where. Sorry."

"Maybe it's been too long," Hammond said.

"Maybe. I don't know."

Reed said nothing, but took the sweater and the photo from my fingers and replaced them. He then handed me a second picture.

This woman was older, closer to late twenties, with short dark hair, cut in a very hip style-—all spikes and glued in place with hair gel. Her eyes held a look of experience Bridget's had not. This girl had known her way around the block.

Once again, Reed read from a sheet of paper. "Eleanor Gayle, twenty-eight years old, from Memphis. She and two friends treated themselves to a weekend at the Tunica, Mississippi, casinos. They stayed at The Winning Touch, checking in about ten-thirty on a Friday night, and hit the tables. The couple with her said they split from Eleanor. The last time they saw her, she was sitting at a blackjack table around midnight on Saturday. When checkout time rolled around on Sunday, no one could find her. She was officially listed as missing on Wednesday."

I rubbed the photo, and then traced the image with my finger. As with Bridget's picture, I sensed no life force of any kind. My fingertip grew cold. The intrusive feeling returned, stronger this time, as if the women were trying to tell me something.

"I'm sorry. I'm not getting anything. I think she may be dead, too," I said. I handed the photo back to Reed.

He said nothing, but tucked it back into the file, and then produced a plastic bag from under the coffee table. From it he pulled a black, spandex mini-skirt.

"This was taken from her room at the casino."

I held the garment, closed my eyes and stroked it against my face. Eleanor's personality came through loud and clear.

"She loved coming to the casinos. She played a pretty good hand of blackjack and hoped to meet up with someone who could show her a good time. Was this the woman seen leaving the casino alone at three in the morning?"

"Yes. We pulled surveillance tapes of cameras at other entrances to see if we could find someone leaving about the same time. It's a popular casino. Lots of men came and went."

I stared off into space as more energy from the skirt crackled along my nerves. My heart thudded in my chest. Never had I gleaned so much from a vision.

"She was generous with her favors to men. She had lots of partners and boyfriends." I handed the clothing back to Reed. "That's about all. What did she do for a living?"

"Receptionist for an insurance company. Her bosses loved her, but the women had reservations. Eleanor flirted with anything male, and it built resentment. Several months before she disappeared, she had an argument with the girlfriend of one of the salesmen. Eleanor kept her job because she was organized and gave good phone."

"The other woman could be responsible," I said.

Reed shook his head. "Airtight alibi. She was the maid of honor at her sister's wedding in Houston,

Texas."

"Do you get any sense of where either of these women could be?" Hammond asked.

I shook my head. "I know Bridget probably met her killer at the mall, but I get no sense of how Eleanor died. If she had been wearing the skirt..." I let the sentence trail off.

Reed packed up the items and rose from the sofa.

"You didn't tell me anything I didn't already know or suspect," he said. "I didn't really expect you to. Thanks for trying."

He stepped past me and strode out the door. Detective Hammond also stood.

"I apologize for Reed, Sasha. He's not the most diplomatic of people. He doesn't mean to be rude. Don't take it personally."

He shook my hand, and then turned to Linnie who had remained silent throughout the session. I knew that wouldn't last long.

"Be seeing you, Dr. Marilyn," he said. He took her hand, too, but instead of shaking it, raised it to his lips. "I'll be in touch."

He left the room, closing the door behind him.

"Do I smell a conquest?" I asked.

Linnie turned away from the door with a shrug. "Maybe. I don't know yet. He's a good-looking devil, isn't he?"

She had a gleam in her eyes suggesting she'd told a little white lie.

"Oh, he's that all right, and then some. Charming and probably great in bed, too. So, are you going to ask him out or be traditional and wait for him to call?"

"I haven't decided. I'll give him a couple of days

and if he doesn't pick up the phone, I will."

"Linnie, be cautious. Remember the last charming, good-in-bed man you dated? What was his name—Jake? It turned out all he wanted was free analysis. And the jerk before him, that actor, Danny? You got all starry-eyed and bought bridal magazines only to find out he was gay. He was using you to prepare in case he got a role as a romantic lead."

"I know, I know. My tip-off with him should have been when he didn't even try to get me into bed. I thought he was being old-fashioned and considerate. I found it unique," my best friend lamented. "Actually, I found it…"

"Don't you dare say charming," I interrupted.

She grinned. "Charming."

"And of course, let's not forget good old Brian. He gave you a black eye, broke your jaw, and was responsible for the six stitches in your busted lip."

Linnie heaved a huge sigh. "I should have listened to you when you told me about your vision of him pounding on another woman."

"You're damned lucky not to have ended up dead like the next girlfriend. Is he still in jail?"

She picked up the cups from the morning's session stacking them on the tray, and carted them back to the kitchen area.

"As far as I know. He has another two years to run on his sentence."

"What do you mean, as far as you know?" I didn't like the sound of that. "You testified against him at his trial. I thought the authorities had to notify you if he was released early."

"They are and they haven't, so I guess Brian is still

choppin' cotton on Parchman. What has all this got to do with Jeff Hammond?"

"Probably nothing. I'm just saying, take it easy. He seems like a fun kind of guy. Go out. Have a few laughs. Enjoy dinner and a show. Just don't buy any bridal magazines." I paused for a moment. "I can't see how anyone as easy going as Detective Hammond ever had a successful partnership with Reed McIntyre. That must have been like partnering with the dark side of the moon."

"Reed is all business when he's working, and this morning was work to him."

"He was rude and insulting." My mind drifted back to our conversation the night before at the coffee house. "He didn't come out and say it, but I know he thought my answers to be little more than the generalities of a carnival huckster."

"Not necessarily. I think he may have been pinning his hopes on what you had to say and was disappointed he couldn't go dig up a body."

Linnie had a point, but his abrupt departure still rankled. I had failed to live up to his expectations and that's what irritated me. I had worked hard over the years not to let my inability to always provide answers morph into guilt.

A tap on the door interrupted my thoughts. Janine poked her head in.

"I'm sorry. I didn't know you had a patient. Really, Dr. Anderson, you have to leave me a note or something when you schedule people out of hours," she said in an exasperated tone.

"You're absolutely right. I'll try harder to remember. When's my first scheduled appointment today?"

"Ten o'clock."

"Good. Please put Sasha down as a hypnosis session."

Janine nodded, and then closed the door.

"How can a psychiatrist be so disorganized?" I murmured.

"I have no idea. I'm a good listener and can give advice to people who need it, but every morning I check to make sure I remembered to wear panties. Do you know I keep an extra toothbrush and deodorant here at the office—-just in case?"

We both laughed. Then, Linnie sobered.

"We've stalled long enough. Chit-chat time is over. You look like hell, Sasha. What happened?"

I sighed and rubbed my forehead with my fingertips.

"I had a nightmare. It was horrible. For the first time in my life, I was afraid to sleep and scared of the dark. I stayed up watching old movies from midnight on."

Linnie turned on her tape recorder. "Go ahead. Tell me. I'll need to know before I hypnotize you."

I sucked in a shaky breath and relived the nightmare. Even now, in broad daylight, it gave me the shivers. When I finished, I stared into Linnie's shocked face.

She turned the tape recorder off. "Holy cow. No more 'grandpa-buried-the-life-savings-under-the-front-porch-in-a-mayonnaise-jar' for you. You've graduated. Your abilities just took a giant leap forward. You actually became the victim and saw everything through the woman's eyes?"

I nodded. "Every last movement. God Almighty, I felt the pain, heard the knife slicing. I'd never been so terrified in my life. After puking my guts out, I went back to bed and tried to remember so I'd have a clear idea of what to tell you, but couldn't handle it. That's when I abandoned sleep and decided to keep company with Fred Astaire and Ginger Rogers."

"Sasha, maybe it's time for you to seek out other psychics and talk to them. Get an idea of what it is you're experiencing."

"What? I'm supposed to knock on Madame Zalinski's Psychic Parlor door and say, let's have a convention?" The frown causing my friend's forehead to furrow worried me. "Wait a minute. Are you saying you can no longer help me?" My heart plummeted somewhere past my stomach.

"I honestly don't know. Maybe you need to consult a parapsychologist. Let's put you under and see if you can draw more details from the vision."

"I'm not sure I should. After last night, I've had just about all the details I can stand."

"If it gets too upsetting, I promise to bring you out. This involves murder, Sasha. Somewhere a young woman is dead. She has a family who wants answers."

"Or at least, closure," I replied, thinking of Reed and his photographs. Those families must be in agony not knowing their loved ones' fates. "Okay, let's do it."

I took up my usual hypnosis position prone on the sofa, ready to revisit the most frightening vision of my life. I moistened my dry lips and shivered. I usually looked forward to these sessions. They cleared the cobwebs after having used my abilities. But this time, I was scared to death.

Chapter Four

I wiggled my hips deeper into the sofa cushions, propping up my shoulders and head with a throw pillow. Linnie closed the blinds, bringing the room into a comfortable semi-darkness. Water trickling from the small fountain on the credenza behind her desk and the scent of eucalyptus emanating from several strategically placed aromatherapy beakers always helped me relax. A few seconds later the soft kiss of air on my face told me she'd turned on the ceiling fan. It was a familiar routine.

I closed my eyes and took several deep breaths to clear my mind of the recent, unsettling events. I heard the telltale click of the tape recorder re-starting.

"Are you ready?" she asked.

"Not really. I'm still wound up from earlier."

"Take a few moments to visualize. Put yourself on a sailboat, the breeze in your face. Listen to the gentle slap of water on the hull as it glides through the placid water."

The visualization worked. Within a few minutes, my muscles released the tension that had built during the session with Reed.

"Okay, I'm ready now," I told Linnie.

"Open your eyes and gaze at the ceiling fan. Watch the blades. Breathe in through your nose and out through your mouth. Slowly...slowly. Watch the blades. Concentrate on the blades. Feel the air wash over your face."

I stared at the ceiling fan twirling in slow motion and listened to Linnie's voice grow softer with each word. Soon it was hard to keep my eyelids from closing. Now, instead of seeing the fan, I heard a gentle swish as the blades pushed the air out into the room.

Languor crept up my body from the toes. With each whoosh my muscles grew limp. My mind tumbled from consciousness and into that nether realm of twilight sleep.

"Sasha, can you hear me?"

"Yes," I heard myself murmur.

"Good. Are you comfortable?"

"Yes. I'm floating."

"Excellent. I want you to think back to the night before last. You were having dinner with Phillip at Le Bistro. What happened?"

"He's boring me to death. I'm wondering how fast I can eat and get back home without being rude."

"How is he boring you?"

"All he talks about is his job. I'm tuning out most of what he says. I pretend to listen, but find my eyes drawn to a painting on the wall."

"A painting? What kind of painting?" Linnie asked.

"It's a river scene."

"I see. What happens next?"

Even under hypnosis, my breath caught in my throat and for a moment I had trouble answering.

"Everything gradually goes silent. I no longer hear the babble of conversation, the clink of silverware on china, or the music from the piano bar in the lounge. I'm staring at the painting when I suddenly feel as though I'm being filled. It's an invasion I can't avoid."

"Concentrate on my voice, Sasha. Listen and allow your mind to drift into another dimension."

She spoke soft, soothing words until I slipped from twilight sleep into a deeper trance. I no longer consciously heard Linnie asking questions or my answers, but knew both occurred. Time was suspended and my mind would not remember what I recalled.

****

I opened my eyes and drew a deep breath. The ceiling fan still rotated. I had returned to the real world. Linnie got up and readjusted the blinds as I pushed myself into a sitting position.

"Did I do good?" I asked.

She turned off the fountain and the fan, and then gazed at me with a troubled expression. "You did very well."

"Can I listen?" I said, nodding toward the tape recorder.

"Yes. I think you should, but take a couple of minutes to freshen up first. I'll get us both a cup of tea."

A slight wave of dizziness washed over me as I stood—-not an unusual occurrence after a hypnosis session. I made my way to Linnie's private bath. A quick glance in the mirror showed I hadn't lost the dark circles under my eyes. I looked like a clown with the blush on my cheeks highlighting my pallor. I washed my face. Better to look like a ghost than Bozo. The action also gave me time to regain my sea legs. When I emerged, the tea was ready. I curled up on the sofa and sipped.

"How are you feeling?" Linnie asked in a quiet voice.

"A little tired and shaky, but that's all. Go ahead and play it back. I want to hear."

"Are you sure you're up to it?"

I wasn't, but had to know. I nodded. My insides tightened. I listened to the tape twice.

"I remember that painting now. It was similar to the murder scene in my vision. And I also remember how the killer disposed of the knife and his clothes. I just wish I could identify where it was. The killer took a chance. No one drove by and saw his car."

"I find it interesting the vision occurred in silence, yet you *heard* everything in the nightmare."

"I find it more interesting that in the nightmare, I became the victim." I placed my empty cup on the table with shaking hands, my heart thumping hard in my chest. The dizziness returned, and I fought for control. "Linnie, what's happening to me?"

"I think the victim, this Kathy has contacted you."

"You mean like—like *possession*?"

"I know it sounds frightening, but yes, that's what I think."

I could take no more. In the past two days, I'd been scared out of my wits on numerous occasions, making me suspect I was psychotic, and now, my shrink was suggesting I was possessed?

I stared and tried to suppress the bubble working its way through my chest into my throat. I failed, and burst into tears. Linnie ceased being my psychiatrist and became my friend. She leaped to her feet and sat beside me.

"But why? Why possess me?" I sobbed.

"I don't know. I'm not a parapsychologist. You do have certain abilities and maybe, at the time of the murder, you were open to reception."

"You mean, at the time she died, because I was bored out of my skull, staring at a painting of a river, this Kathy person kind of rode the beam into my mind?" I said, hiccupping.

"Maybe," Linnie answered, handing me a tissue.

Nausea churned my stomach and I gulped in an effort to erase it. Dammit, I had been violated and didn't know whether to be angry or frightened. God knows, I didn't want to accept it.

"Linnie, am I going crazy?"

"No! Absolutely not! And don't use that term!" She rose, striding to her desk where she opened a drawer and removed a large notebook.

"Do you think my vision is in any way connected to the murders Reed is pursuing?"

"If it is that means a serial killer, silent for two years, has struck again. Are you going to tell him?"

"I don't know." Why should I if he didn't believe in my abilities? I didn't need his skepticism along with everything else.

I tried to pull myself together by taking deep breaths, focusing on the vague theory that while I might not be completely normal, I wasn't nuts either.

I mopped the tears from my face while Linnie leafed through the book, muttering to herself. I blew my nose and rummaged in my handbag for make-up to repair the ravages of the last few minutes. I finally gave up. No amount of cosmetics was going to make me human. I looked like hell and felt like crap.

"Here," Linnie said, rising from her desk and

returning to the sofa. "Dr. Roger Silberstein has been working with psychics and doing paranormal research for close to twenty years. He's not some crackpot or pseudo-shrink like your boss. Dr. Silberstein is highly respected in our field. If you want, I'll make the appointment for you."

I took the slip of paper and tucked it into my purse.

"Let me think about it for a couple of days, okay? I need to absorb this…this new wrinkle."

"Don't take too long. The sooner you talk to him, the better."

I grabbed my purse and rose. "I won't. I promise. What time is it?"

"Almost nine-thirty. Why?"

"I'm late for work," I said, heading for the door.

"Take the day off, Sasha. Pennington is like a barracuda. He'll take one look at your face and know something's up."

"I can't. I called in yesterday saying I had food poisoning. If he notices, I'll just say I'm still feeling rocky." She followed me to the door, where I stopped and kissed her cheek. "Thanks, Linnie. Breakfast tomorrow at Café Au Lait?"

She nodded and I left. Only nine-thirty? It was going to be a long day.

****

I walked into the Psychology building on the University of Memphis campus with no memory of how I arrived. Needless to say, my mind had been otherwise engaged.

I entered the office and saw my boss, Dr. Clarke Pennington, standing at my desk, the phone in his hand.

"Sasha, thank goodness. I was beginning to worry

about you. How are you feeling?" he said in a pompous voice that matched his expression before replacing the receiver.

He lied. Clarke Pennington didn't care about me or anybody else. He was *numero uno*. I spied a large stack of files on my desk. That's the reason he worried. He was afraid he'd have to do his own filing.

"I'm still a little shaky, but I can function."

"Good. I'll be out of the office this afternoon and need you to pull some files for me. Mrs. Westover had a dream the other night about finding a lost treasure. Since she believes she has been reincarnated, this could be a breakthrough. I'm going to interview her at one o'clock."

I slipped behind my desk and sat down. "I'll have her file in a few minutes."

He smoothed his blond hair in a practiced gesture, no doubt checking daily to see if any gray had dared appear. He looked younger than his fifty-three years and kept his medium build fit at a gym not far from campus. Other than that, he looked unremarkable, standing a tad under six feet. Golden-brown eyes could slice and dice if he so desired. Some people considered the color exotic. I considered it just weird enough to give me the creeps. His face reminded me of a ferret, all sharp and pointed.

"Fine. Bring it in as soon as possible." Without another word, he entered his office and closed the door.

I didn't like my boss and didn't need the job, only having applied several years ago for something to do. I stayed because the subject matter was relevant to my life. To the best of my knowledge, he'd been at the university some ten years after having left private practice somewhere on the west coast.

Last year, Linnie met Pennington when he spoke at a seminar and had formed an instant dislike. According to her, he pontificated for an hour and a half on nothing, and then had the audacity to pat himself on the back with a self-satisfied smirk at the following reception. Her voice had dripped with contempt. The letters behind his name were academic, not medical. She thought his books were bullshit and frequently urged me to quit his employ.

Unfortunately, he'd found her fascinating and had called frequently suggesting they collaborate on a book. Linnie hadn't been interested and told him where to go.

I alphabetized the files on my desk and leafed through one on a new client. The subject matter was precognition. It sent my mind in a whole new direction. Suppose I wasn't possessed by this Kathy person. What if I had seen the future? Did I hold some unknown woman's fate in my hands—or my mind?

I dropped the folder and crossed to the file room next door. The Rolodex on top of the first set of drawers contained cross references. I quickly looked up precognition and discovered six files in the past year on the subject.

I searched them out and read two. One was a simple case of knowing who was on the other end of a telephone call before answering. Pennington had dismissed the woman after two interviews on the theory she could not add anything new to the subject. Besides, caller ID had blown holes in that premise.

The second one dealt with dreams and was still an open case. My boss had documented several instances of what the woman dreamed with the reality. She was bang on most of the time. It gave me goosebumps. Imagine having that kind of responsibility. If I was seeing the future, how on earth would I ever find and warn Kathy?

"What do you think you're doing?" Pennington asked from the doorway.

I jumped, almost dropping the file. Damn, I'd been so engrossed I'd never heard him approach. He'd caught me snooping.

I snapped the file closed and hugged it to my chest.

"Oh, Dr. Pennington, you scared me to death."

"What are you doing?" He took the file from my trembling hands, read the name, and then gazed at me with raised eyebrows.

"I...I saw a file on my desk and thought I remembered the name from another time."

"All you had to do was check the Rolodex. There's no need to pull a file." His eyes narrowed as he looked at the file again. "Precognition. Are you interested in the subject?"

"No, not really." My voice sounded nervous. To cover my actions, I moved to the "Reincarnation" file drawer and withdrew the Westover folder. "Here, I believe you needed this."

He smiled and tried to look sincere, but failed. "Forget the filing. Come into my office. We haven't had a talk in quite a while."

I followed him into the inner sanctum with shaky legs and a thumping heart. I wasn't a very good liar, but given enough time, I could come up with something plausible. I hoped this was one of those times.

"Sit down, my dear." I obeyed. He sat in a leather chair behind his ornate walnut desk. "Tell me, have you had any more luck in finding things? I believe the last time we talked you had been contacted by a former student of mine who was searching for a lost ring belonging to her grandmother. Did you find it?"

"I indicated the general area where she should look and yes, she found it."

"Wonderful. Do you ever see things not in photographs?"

"Like what?" I asked, struggling to prevent my hands and my voice from shaking.

"Have you ever had something—-a vision, if you will—-just pop into your mind?"

Heat suffused my body and a droplet of sweat inched its way down my spine. I remained in eye contact with him. The sudden warmth intensified the scent of my perfume, and I wondered if he smelled it, too.

"You mean, like I see a wallet or a ring in my mind and know instantly where it is?"

"Yes. Could your ESP abilities have sharpened over the last couple of years?"

"I don't think so. I don't recall any visions."

He tapped a pencil on the blotter in front of him. "I see." His sharp ferret eyes bored into me. "You wouldn't withhold information, would you?"

Thump, thump, thump. My heart beats pounded in my ears. I licked my lips.

"Why, no, of course not. If things had changed, I'd have talked to you immediately, Dr. Pennington." I tried to inject sincerity into my voice, and then jumped when his private phone rang.

With a frown, he answered. "Dr. Clarke Pennington...yes, Mr. Walters, I have you down for next Monday at three o'clock."

I used this opportunity to rise from my chair.

"Could you hold for a moment, Mr. Walters?" He covered the mouthpiece with his hand, "We'll talk again later, Sasha. Go ahead and finish the filing."

I nodded and left the room, closing the door behind me. I leaned back against it. That had been close—too close. With any luck, he'd forget about continuing the catechism and concentrate on other matters, like Harriet Westover, her past life, and how he could incorporate it into his next book.

****

I finished the filing and transcribed the notes my weasel boss had dictated over the past couple of days. Mercifully, he remained behind the closed door.

About halfway through my chore, the door to the corridor opened. A man stuck his head inside.

"Hello, gorgeous. Got a few minutes?" Jeff Hammond said with a cheeky smile.

"Hi. What are you doing here?" I pulled the headphones off and stopped the machine.

"My, you're suspicious. Can't a guy just stop by and say hi to a beautiful woman?" He sauntered into the room and perched on the corner of my desk. "All right, I'll come clean. I wondered if you'd like to have lunch with me."

"Lunch?" I leaned forward. "H-m-m, may I remind you whose hand it was you kissed this morning?"

He grinned. "Busted! You're right. I want to pump you for information about Marilyn Anderson. But that's only part of the reason I'm here. I read the riot act to Reed back at the station. I told him he'd been rude, insulting, and owed you an apology."

"I'll bet that went over big."

"Big enough. He growled and snarled, telling me to mind my own business. Actually, I think he kind of likes you."

I snorted. "Couldn't tell it from the way he acts."

"I know. He's not much of a people person. The roles were well-defined whenever we played good-cop-bad-cop."

"Linnie says he was very dedicated."

"Still is. Hates unsolved anything. In these cases, though, I think he's way off base trying to connect the dots and come up with a serial killer. Now, how about lunch? You name the place, provided it's not the student union."

I wagged my finger. "I'll have you know they serve a mean meatloaf."

"God forbid," he groaned.

We were both laughing when Pennington emerged from his lair. He stared and from the look on his face I knew he expected an introduction.

"I'm going to lunch, Sasha, and then on to Mrs. Westover's. Don't expect me back this afternoon," he said, continuing to gaze at my visitor.

I had no choice. "Jeff, I'd like you to meet my boss, Dr. Clarke Pennington. Dr. Pennington, this is a friend of mine, Jeff Hammond."

"Mr. Hammond, a pleasure," he said, offering his hand.

"Actually, it's Detective Hammond," Jeff replied.

Aw, shit!

Pennington's eyebrows rose and he shot me a calculating look. "Detective? Don't tell me our fair Sasha is in some kind of trouble?"

Hammond laughed. "Not at all. My partner and I met with her this morning on a police matter."

Double shit!

The good doctor did more than shoot me a look this time. He swiveled his head and glared. "Oh, really." His soft voice masked the irritation in his eyes.

I thought fast. "Yes, that's true. Would you believe that even the police lose things? Some urgently needed open case files were misplaced. A mutual friend suggested they contact me."

"Indeed," my boss said, arching his eyebrow, skepticism written all over his face.

"Uh, yes. Someone accidentally chucked them into a box, and they ended up in the cold case file drawer. Sasha put us on the right track. I dropped by to thank her and ask her out to lunch. Hope that's all right with you," Hammond replied.

I breathed easier. He'd recovered fast and sounded truthful.

"Of course, by all means, go and enjoy your reward. I don't require Sasha to account for every minute of her time. All work and no play, you know."

Pennington smiled and tried to be charming, but I think Reed's former partner knew snake oil when he saw it.

"If you'll just give me a couple of minutes to freshen up, I'll be ready."

"Yes, I must be going, too," my boss said taking the hint. "We'll have to continue our chat at a later date, my dear." He nodded to Jeff and exited the room.

"What was that all about?"

"I'll explain over lunch. Give me five minutes, okay?"

I grabbed my purse and hurried to the ladies room down the hall. When I returned, he was gazing at the photos on the walls.

"Strange place to see photographs of old houses and cemeteries," he commented.

"Old *haunted* houses and cemeteries," I corrected. "It's Pennington's way of impressing the easily impressed. Shall we go?"

Hammond smiled and took my arm. The simple action lifted my spirits. It had been a long time since I'd been out with an *interesting*, good-looking man, even if he was after information on my best friend.

****

I slid into the booth at the Campus Bar and Grille. It nestled on a side street just off Southern Avenue. Small, but popular with both students and faculty, they served the best chili in town. Their fries weren't bad either.

A waitress appeared immediately. She had waited on me numerous times and knew how to get an order in and out.

"Hi. Whatcha gonna have?" she asked me while eyeing my companion with a not so subtle appreciative glance.

"Iced tea, sweetened, and the chili," I answered.

"What would you suggest, darlin'," Hammond drawled, giving her a slow smile.

Swell, Reed's searching for a serial killer while I'm having lunch with a serial charmer.

Smiling back and half closing her eyes, the waitress responded, "Everything on our menu is first class."

"In that case I'll have a burger, medium rare, fries,

and iced tea."

"You know, it's a good thing I'm not the jealous kind," I remarked as his gaze riveted on her rear end sashaying back to the kitchen.

"Don't mind me. I just like women, all shapes, all sizes, it doesn't matter. Don't take me too seriously."

"I won't, Detective Hammond."

"Call me Jeff. What was that byplay between you and your boss?"

I gave him the lowdown on Pennington and his propensity for using the experiences of others to his advantage.

He shook his head. "I had him figured for a smooth operator."

"He is."

He sat back and smiled. "Before we go on to more interesting topics, I do have a couple of questions about this morning."

"Such as?"

"When you hold a photo, how do you feel?"

"What?"

He shifted in his seat, leaning his elbows on the table. "What do you feel when you're holding a picture? Is it a tingle, a throb, a vibration? What happens?"

The waitress brought our tea, winked at Jeff, and moved on. I took my time squeezing the lemon into the glass. I'd never been asked that question before by anyone other than Linnie and was surprised by it. Stirring my drink, I tried to answer.

"I'm not sure I feel much of anything. I usually deal with inanimate objects. I stare at the photo. If there's something to see, the edges kind of blur.

Sometimes my peripheral vision dims bringing the picture into very sharp focus, or I see flashes of light."

He didn't need to know that occasionally images that had nothing to do with photographs popped into my head holding me in a trancelike grip. Up until the other night, those had been few and far between.

"But how do you know where to find things?"

"It's never exact. I see a room or a house—something connected with the object. Sometimes I fail to see anything. Until this morning, I never tried to find people. I'm sorry I couldn't help. Why do you want to know?"

He chugged a long swallow. I did the same and let the icy combination of sweet and sour slide down my throat. I hadn't realized how thirsty I was.

"No reason, it's just that every once in a while I…Aw, who cares? Let's talk about something more interesting, like your psychiatrist. I need details. And remember, lady, I am a cop and this is an official investigation." He wiggled his eyebrows up and down.

I laughed. "What do you want to know?"

"Just the facts, ma'am."

"Linnie and I met in the fourth grade. My parents moved here from Shreveport during the school year. That made me the new kid. We were seated alphabetically, so I sat behind her—Anderson-Bellwood. She hung with me during recess and lunch. We've been friends ever since."

"Why psychiatry?"

"She always wanted to know what made people tick. If a classmate did something silly or illogical, she had to know why. Even at twelve, she was psychoanalyzing."

Our food arrived and the waitress departed with a disappointed look on her face when Jeff didn't acknowledge her smile.

I snatched up the hot sauce from the condiment tray, dumping several shakes into my chili. Jeff slathered mayo on his hamburger bun along with the lettuce and tomato. The onion stayed on the side.

I spooned a huge portion into my mouth, then grabbed for the iced tea. Damn, it tasted good. The heat sent chili smells straight up my nose and into my brain. My taste buds may have burned, but my olfactory sense loved it.

Jeff apparently had no problem with his burger. He wolfed half of it down quickly.

"Any men in her life?" he asked, wiping his mouth with a napkin.

I hesitated and shoved another spoonful of chili in before answering. I tried to keep it light. "Past, present, or future?"

"Present and past. I plan on being the future."

"To the best of my knowledge she is footloose and fancy free at the moment."

"How about the past?" He didn't look at me as he shoveled a couple of French fries into his mouth.

"You'll have to ask her about that." I had no intention of revealing any of the men in Linnie's past. Given Jeff's flirting nature, I couldn't figure out why it mattered anyway. He was definitely a hit and run dater.

"Sounds ominous. Guess I'd better be on my best behavior. Did she talk about me after I left this morning?"

"That is so girlie—just like in high school," I told him with a chuckle.

"Hey, guys have the same insecurities women do."

Jeff finished his meal, but I took my time. I was in no hurry to return to the office until I was certain Pennington was safely ensconced in the Westover living room. I knew he'd question me sooner or later. I preferred later.

"What's your story, Jeff? Are you a native of Memphis?"

"Nope. I was born in a small town just outside of Mobile, Alabama. My parents died in a fire when I was eight. I went to live with my uncle."

"That must have been rough, losing your parents so young." Compassion washed over me.

He shrugged. "I guess. When I turned eighteen, my uncle gave me a check for five grand along with some good advice to get out of a dinky, dead end town like Lockerville. I took it and headed for Mobile." Jeff drained the last of his iced tea, rattling what was left of the melting cubes in the glass.

"Were you always a cop?"

"I worked a variety of jobs for a while before going to a job fair. The Mobile Police Department was recruiting, and I thought I'd give it a try. I liked it."

I rested my elbow on the table, cupped my chin in my hand, and gently tried to probe his mind. Oddly enough, I came up with zilch. It happened sometimes with forceful personalities.

"Why did you leave Mobile?"

"Itchy feet. I moved to Birmingham for a couple of years. I didn't like it. Nine years ago, I took a chance on Memphis." He shot a glance at his watch. "As much as I'm enjoying this, I have to get back to work. Can we do it again sometime?"

It was twelve-forty-five. Pennington should be well on his way to Collierville by now. "I'd love to."

If he ever connected with Linnie, the proposed lunch date would never materialize.

****

I spent the next three hours finishing the dictation left by my boss. I laid the folders on his desk so he could review them for changes and decided to call it a day. Two nights of very little sleep had taken its toll. I would go home, pop a frozen dinner into the microwave, and hit the sack. Who knew, maybe I'd even sleep uninterrupted for a change.

Whew! Life in the fast lane.

I was almost to the door when the office phone rang. I was tempted to ignore it. The fourth ring had me dumping my purse on the desk. The caller ID was unfamiliar, so I knew it wasn't Pennington. I picked up.

"Clarke Pennington's office."

"I've been told I owe you another apology," Reed stated without so much as a hello, how are you, or kiss my foot. A lifetime of politeness kept me from hanging up.

"Yes, you do, but then I have the suspicion you spend half your life apologizing for something or other."

"You're right, I do. I'm used to it." He paused, and then continued in a hesitant voice. "I really am sorry if I offended you this morning. Jeff was all over me about what a pain in the ass I can be. Let me make it up to you. How about dinner tonight? A nice place out in East Memphis. Have you ever been to Giovanni's?"

I couldn't have been more surprised if he'd suddenly crawled through the phone line and popped out in front of me stark naked.

"Once."

"How about it? Can you meet me there at say seven-thirty?"

My tiredness disappeared, and I answered in a crisp tone. "If you want to improve your social skills, Mr. McIntyre, I can suggest you start by picking me up. That's what a gentleman does."

"Does that mean you'll go?"

How dense could one man be? "Yes, although why I don't know. You're paying, right?"

He actually chuckled. "Yes, my treat."

The chuckle did me in. I found it endearing. It humanized him. And the hesitancy I'd heard earlier made him just a tad vulnerable. I remembered Jeff's comment at noon about men having the same insecurities as women. I gave him my address and hung up.

Weaving my way through the heavy Midtown traffic, I marveled at how someone who, with the exception of Philip, hadn't had an honest to God date in over six months was suddenly as popular as Susie Cheerleader.

Chapter Five

Giovanni's was an intimate restaurant tucked away in the center of an upscale shopping center. They boasted a well-stocked bar, an even better wine cellar, and the best Italian food outside of Italy. Linnie had treated me for my birthday one year.

I scrutinized my wardrobe before finally settling on an ivory silk pantsuit. Reed arrived on time dressed in tan slacks and a light blue knit shirt with a navy sport coat. While he hadn't had his hair cut, it was neatly combed.

"Good, you're ready," was his only comment when I opened the door. I wanted to smack him given the time I'd spent selecting the clothes and applying the make-up.

"Good, you're on time," I shot back. "Let me get my purse."

I didn't invite him in. Instead, I grabbed the tiny gold evening bag that matched my sandals from the foyer table, slung it over my shoulder, and joined him on the front stoop.

He said nothing as we walked to his car in my driveway. I opened my own door and slid onto the seat. I couldn't let the opportunity to needle him slip past as he backed out, then drove away.

"This is going to be a short evening," I said.

"Why is that?" He shot me a questioning look.

"For starters, when a gentleman picks a lady up for a date, he compliments her on how nice she looks. He doesn't say, 'good, you're ready.'"

"I see." He braked at a stop light, and turning, let his gaze rake me from head to foot. "You look very nice. Is that what you needed to hear?"

Oh, brother. I bet this guy hadn't had a date in years. Compared to him, I was Miss Popularity.

"Your sincerity overwhelms me."

The light turned green and he focused his attention back onto driving. "Is there anything else I neglected to say?"

"Not say, but do. You could have opened the car door for me."

His lips twitched, but whether in irritation or fun, I wasn't sure.

"I thought women frowned on that sort of thing these days. I was under the impression they wanted to be considered independent and one of the guys."

"Equals. We want to be treated as equals. However, common courtesy is never taken off the menu."

"That's good and confusing. And women wonder why men never understand them. Since I've already admitted my social faults, why don't you teach me the finer points? I'm sure with your expertise, I'll become a much sought after escort."

"You know, if you weren't driving, I'd hit you."

He laughed. The deep, rich timbre filled the car and sent a jolt of something along my nerves. I shot a covert glance at his profile. No, he wasn't handsome or charming like Jeff, but I recognized the something as old-fashioned desire.

I sucked in a long breath, turning my gaze back out of the windshield. God, I was in bad trouble. I'd known the guy twenty-four hours and had this irresistible urge to jump his bones. I wasn't even sure I *liked* him.

Sasha, you are *a nut case.* The man would probably run for the hills if he knew the direction of my thoughts.

In an effort to pull the conversation and my mind into less dangerous territory, I asked, "Where do you live?"

"When I retired from the force, I bought a small fixer-upper in Germantown. I like working with my hands and keeping busy. I've repaired and remodeled. I use the pool every day during the summer."

"I did a lot of work on my house, too. I had to call in the experts for the electricity and plumbing, but I'm not bad at painting and drywall."

Good grief. Have we found common ground?

The conversation for the remainder of the drive revolved around houses. By the time we arrived at Giovanni's, I realized something unexpected. I was enjoying myself. At least, he didn't talk about investment banking or my psychiatrist.

After being seated and giving our cocktail orders to the waiter, an awkward silence fell. Reed fiddled with his napkin and silverware before finally looking me in the eye.

"I guess I should get this out of the way. I'm sorry about my attitude this morning. I'm not sure what I expected. Maybe I thought you'd take a look at the photos and say, 'sure, she's buried at X marks the spot.' Maybe I was curious about this psychic thing. *Maybe* I got exactly what I expected—nothing. At any rate, I was rude and I apologize."

He drew a deep breath as though glad to have finished an unpleasant task. A tinge of pity tweaked inside me.

"Apology accepted. I'm sorry I couldn't help. I always feel badly when I can't give the answers people want to hear. A missing ring or money is one thing, but the families of those women need closure."

"At first, I stayed in touch with them, but as time passes, the phone calls get fewer. If I could only find something for them to bury, to mark with a headstone, I'd feel better."

Our drinks arrived, a vodka and tonic for him, and a glass of Cabernet for me. The next several minutes involved intense menu perusal and discussion. The waiter returned and took our food order. We settled in to sip our cocktails.

"I'm not sure how much of this psychic stuff I'm willing to believe, but Jeff says it's there and Dr. Anderson agrees with him. When did you first experience it?"

"I was six. One of my schoolmates had misplaced her book bag. I saw it plain as day sitting beside a telephone pole at the school bus stop. I didn't find it at all strange, so I told her."

"You have a sad expression on your face. Why?" he asked.

I sipped some wine, allowing the full rich flavor to swirl over my tongue before answering. "She told her friends and soon kids were asking me to find all kinds of things. Eventually, my teacher got wind of it. When I told her how I found the items, she said I shouldn't lie or hide things, and then pretend to find them as a joke.

She punished me."

"What did your parents have to say?"

"They agreed with my teacher until a few weeks later when my mother lost an heirloom locket. I saw it in the pocket of a skirt. The clasp was loose. She'd taken it off and forgotten about it. As more incidents occurred over the next few years, my folks warned me never to talk about them. They said people would think I was a freak."

"But you did talk about them, didn't you?" he asked, drinking some of the vodka and tonic.

"Only to Linnie. It wasn't until we were in college that she suggested I go into therapy. If I helped someone, I did it through her. She and I would meet with the person who either described the lost object or had a photo of it."

"And you found it?"

"Most of the time." I was sick of me as the subject matter. "How come you're no longer a cop? You look too young to be retired."

"I'm closing in on the big four-oh in November." He swigged another gulp of his drink. "I'm no longer officially on the force because I was wounded in the line of duty five years ago."

"You mean, like, shot?" I squeaked, my heart giving a huge thump in my chest.

"Yes. Once in the shoulder, once in the leg, and twice in the chest. A fifth bullet grazed my head."

"Oh, my God! You're lucky to be alive," I said, gasping. "How did it happen?"

"Jeff and I had been tracking a murder suspect for months when we got a tip. We pulled up in front of a house in North Memphis and saw our man sitting on the couch through the living room window. I went around to the rear while Jeff called for backup. I'd just entered the back yard when the kitchen light went out. Then, the back door burst open. The next thing I remember was being drilled with a red hot poker in my shoulder and chest. Then *my* lights went out. I woke up three weeks later in Intensive Care with a broken femur and a portion of my left lung removed."

"What went wrong?"

"Jeff said the guy looked out the window, saw him, and took off for the back of the house."

"Why turn out the lights?" I gulped the rest of my wine. Forget about savoring the flavor of fine Cabernet. I was listening to a real life *Law and Order*.

"Never said the perp was a dummy. He knew if there was anyone out back, they'd see him silhouetted in the light."

"So, how did he see to shoot you?"

"I hadn't gotten behind cover yet, and the next door neighbor had his back security light on. It all happened so fast I never had a chance to throw myself on the ground."

"So you ended up being silhouetted. What happened to the suspect?"

"Jeff shot and killed him."

"So, how come you're still on these cases?"

"When I failed the physical to be reinstated, I haunted the Chief's office for months. We struck a deal. Told him if I solved twenty percent of his cold cases, the department would hire me as a consultant. If I didn't, I'd never darken his doorstep again. He agreed. I put thirteen out of twenty-five to bed."

Our salads arrived and we spent the next few

minutes eating. It gave me a chance to mentally digest what I'd learned. As usual, Linnie had it right. Reed was dedicated and had damned near given his life for that dedication. He reminded me of a pit bull who, once its jaws were clamped onto something, refused to let go.

He also had the soul of a manipulator. He'd maneuvered the Chief of Police into handing over cold cases, including the ones Reed suspected were the work of his serial killer.

"So, how did you meet Linnie?"

"That was part of the agreement. I would attend therapy sessions." He shrugged. "Okay, I admit I was depressed about losing my job and obsessed with finding a serial killer."

"You're still obsessed," I commented as the waiter removed the salad plates and served the entrées.

I leaned over to inhale the aroma of sauce, mushrooms, and artichokes. My mouth watered. Veal Sinatra was one of my favorites.

Reed didn't do anything so obvious. He simply cut off a slice of lasagna and shoved it into his mouth, then smiled as he chewed. I followed his example. My taste buds exploded in culinary rapture. Neither of us spoke a word.

While I ate, I made a decision. I would tell Reed my powers were a bit more involved than just gazing at a photograph. I channeled my mind into his, but detected nothing except enjoyment of the meal. Whatever worries or anxieties he had, they were not at the forefront of his thoughts at the moment.

We refused dessert, but accepted coffee. When the waiter left, I took a cautious sip and a deep breath. I was about to reveal a secret to a man who was little more than a total stranger and a skeptic to boot.

"Reed, you said the last victim of this possible serial killer was stabbed. Did she die where you found her?"

"No. She'd been moved and moved carefully. There was little forensic evidence to go on. No hair or fingerprints showed up. We found blue fibers on her clothes and matched them to the carpet of a Ford Taurus. There are a lot of those around. We never found the car."

A sudden flash skipped in front of my mind's eye. "The car was stolen and later dumped in a lake or a river. I'm not sure which."

He stared, then sipped his coffee and smiled. "We figured as much."

Now was the time. "Reed, I have something to tell you. My abilities go a bit further than divining lost items from photographs."

"I wondered how you found a schoolbag, a locket, and all those other items with no picture as a guide." His face bore a noncommittal expression. He drank his coffee without breaking eye contact.

"I have visions. I see things. Sometimes, I see a sharp picture of an item and where it's located. At other times, it's more like a slide show with a series of photographs. The other night, a new wrinkle was added. I saw something in motion. I'd never done that before. It scared me to death, and that's why I was at Linnie's last night. I wanted her to hypnotize me to see if I could remember more."

"Given my attitude toward psychics, why are you telling me?"

"I saw a murder. A man killed a woman. He stabbed her repeatedly and dumped the body in a river."

He sat still as a statue with the coffee cup suspended halfway to his lips. His hard, ice cold eyes bored a hole through my body.

"Can you identify or describe the man?"

"No. There were too many shadows."

He set his cup down. "All right, tell me about it."

I leaned forward, giving him the full account of my vision at Le Bistro. When I finished, I sat back and waited for his reaction.

"That's graphic. So, this guy got sexual gratification from the killing? Wouldn't be the first time. But when you get right down to it, your information is vague. There's nothing to grab a hold of."

Skepticism clouded his eyes, and I could tell he wasn't buying it. "That's not all. I have a name to go with the victim." I told him about my nightmare. "It was the most freakish thing I've ever experienced. The man called her—me—Kathy."

The expressions on his face had changed from noncommittal to skeptical to inscrutable during my narrative. Now, he sat with his sharp, angular features frozen in a mask of disbelief, his eyes wide and staring.

"If you became the victim, then you must have seen the killer's face," he said through stiff lips.

I shook my head. "No, I think he drugged her because the images were blurred—out of kilter."

"And he called her Kathy? You're sure?"

"Yes."

He picked up his coffee cup and clasped it until his knuckles turned white. I thought the thing would shatter. Reed drained the dregs and set it back down with a precise movement.

"Before I left for your place, I got a call. A missing persons report has been filed on a Kathy Watson, age twenty-two, five-feet-three-inches, a hundred and ten pounds with blue eyes and brown, shoulder length hair."

My heart plummeted to my toes and my breathing stopped. I literally had to gasp for air. My ears reverberated with a loud buzzing. I clapped my hand over my mouth to suppress the nausea welling from my suddenly cramping stomach. A tremor worked its way from my toes upward.

"Breathe, Sasha. In through your nose and out your mouth," Reed ordered, sounding eerily like Linnie this morning.

I obeyed. Within a few seconds my breathing returned to normal. The buzzing receded. My stomach continued churning, however, and the trembling refused to stop. I may have been in shock.

"Don't faint on me. Okay?"

I nodded and reached for my water glass, shaking so badly a sizeable portion splashed on the tablecloth. I managed several small sips until the dryness in my mouth allowed me to speak.

"Sorry. Oh, my God."

"If what you saw is true, then the serial killer may have struck again," Reed said in a grim voice. "And you have no idea where this vision occurred?"

"No, but what makes you think it's the work of your serial killer?"

"My gut tells me."

Tears filled my eyes, threatening to overflow.

"How come you know about it? It's not a cold case."

"I have several friends in homicide who keep me informed. They know about my obsession."

I swallowed hard, muttering under my breath, "Why me? Why pick on me?"

"What do you mean by 'pick'?"

I waved him into silence and blinked the tears away. "Reed, can we go? I need to be alone. I'm not handling this very well."

He signaled the waiter for the check while I slid out of the booth, heading for the ladies room. I slammed the stall door and waited for my stomach to either reject its contents or calm. When I didn't lose my dinner, I exited, walked to the wash basin on wobbly legs, splashed water on my face, and then stared at my reflection in the mirror.

My complexion was pasty white. Dark circles under my eyes made them appear to recede into my head. With my sunken cheeks, I resembled a cadaver. I didn't even try to fix my make-up.

I patted my face dry with paper towels and rejoined my date. Reed rose, placing his hand on my elbow to guide me out of the restaurant and to the car.

"Are you sure you're all right?" he asked in a low voice.

"I will be once I'm home."

"What did you mean by the word 'picked'?"

I shook my head. "Not now, Reed."

I couldn't bring myself to discuss the hypnosis with him. Not yet. I didn't think he was ready for Linnie's possession theory.

And all those lascivious thoughts of earlier in the evening had vanished. My date with Reed ranked right up there with Philip's. I was batting a thousand.

****

"Oh, crap, Sasha. I can't believe any of this is happening," Linnie said when I met her the next morning for breakfast.

I gulped some of my double shot. "At least, I got a good night's sleep thanks to one of those sleeping pills you prescribed."

"I'm sure Reed now realizes you aren't some flake in a turban and flowing robes."

"No, just a flake."

"Did he say anything about another consultation?"

"Nope. He just dropped me at my place and said he'd be in touch. I think he may have been as shaken as me."

She bit into a muffin. "Did you tell him anything about the hypnosis session and my theory?"

"Hell, no. He really will think I'm a freak then."

"I wish you wouldn't use that word," Linnie said in exasperation. "So, what are you going to do?"

"I have no idea. What can I do? I've already driven the back roads of northern Desoto County. Do I expand to Marshall, Tate, or Tunica Counties? That's insane. And do I add Tennessee and Arkansas to the list?" I set my cup down and stared into its black depths. "I guess I just have to wait for another vision."

"If you're being used as a channel, why didn't this Kathy visit you last night? After telling Reed, you'd think it would be a primetime opportunity."

"I don't know. Maybe because of the pill. All I do know is, I almost tossed a really fine meal and Reed, who has possibilities, will never ask me out again."

"Do you want him to?"

I stroked the cup with my fingers before picking it up and taking a generous gulp of the bitter brew.

"He's had an interesting time of it. Imagine being shot and almost killed in the line of duty. And you were right about his dedication. Now, if only he had some manners."

Linnie grinned and shoved the rest of the muffin into her mouth. "Manners don't count when you're sweating up the sheets," she mumbled with her mouth full.

She had just struck a little too close to home.

"Oh, for Pete's sake, who said anything about going to bed with the man?" I needed a change of subject. "Guess who I had lunch with yesterday?"

"Don't tell me that weasel boss of yours put a crowbar in his wallet and took you out."

"Phfft! Hardly. I had a very nice lunch with Detective Jeff Hammond."

Linnie wiped her fingers on a napkin and chugged the last of her latte.

"Oh, really? And what was the topic of conversation?"

"His sole purpose was to pump me for information about you. You have definitely made a conquest. Do you want the lowdown on what he asked?" Linnie had that cat and the canary smirk on her face. "What?"

"Jeff called, and we had dinner last night at a Brazilian steakhouse in Peabody Place."

"That man doesn't let any grass grow beneath his feet, does he? Your grin resembles the Cheshire Cat's. Please tell me you didn't sleep with him on the first date."

"Of course not," she replied in an indignant tone.

"But I can tell you he's one hell of a kisser. Curled my toes and sent my hormones racing."

I had the distinct impression I'd never find out if Reed could curl my toes. I already had firsthand knowledge regarding the hormone part.

Linnie grinned. "Now, fill me in on what he asked."

I gave her the lowdown on his probing questions as to her availability. "What did you talk about at dinner? You've already used the coffee-personality analogy."

"Oddly enough, we talked about psychic phenomena, the cold cases, and the session yesterday."

"You talked about me?" I asked.

"Not specifically. Jeff is very interested in ESP and psychics. He also thinks Reed should return to therapy. He claims his partner is still obsessing about serial killers."

"Reed could be right," I ventured.

"I told him that, but on the other hand, Jeff could be right, too." She glanced at her watch. "Oh, geez, I've got to get out of here. My first patient is due in fifteen minutes."

She gathered her purse from where she'd slung it over the back of her chair. I laid my hand on her arm.

"Take it easy with Jeff, okay? I think he's a natural born heartbreaker. I'd hate to see you stung again."

Linnie laughed. "Yes, mother. Don't worry. Even I can see fun is at the top of Jeff Hammond's list of priorities."

I sighed and watched her walk out as I finished my espresso. A cold chill rippled along my spine and for the life of me I didn't know why.

****

I sizzled like a burger over the coals from the grilling my boss was giving me.

I'd arrived at work a full half hour early and was stunned to see Pennington in the office. He never showed up before ten. At first I thought he wanted to review the notes I'd transcribed from yesterday, but it soon became apparent I was the center of his attention.

"And what kind of help are you giving the police?" he asked for the third time.

"Dr. Pennington, I told you. They misplaced some files, that's all."

"Have you known this detective long?"

"A couple of years," I lied.

"How did you meet? At a crime scene?" he persisted.

"No, at a bar. We were both trolling and made the connection. After a few dates we decided to remain just friends. Do you want me to transcribe your notes from Mrs. Westover's consultation?"

I tried to ignore his beady eyes boring into mine without flinching. It wasn't easy.

"Later. You know about the book I'm writing, don't you? I would hate to lose a possible chapter on advanced ESP because you failed to answer my questions. I expect loyalty from my employees, Sasha. I can't tolerate not having it. We've worked together for over four years and I'd hate to see that come to an end."

The slimy little bastard was threatening me with dismissal if I didn't cooperate. I was tempted to tell him what he could do with himself. At the moment, however, I needed the job to keep my mind off of my other problems.

I swallowed. "Why, of course, Dr. Pennington. I'm

very loyal. I just haven't got anything to tell you. Honest."

He stared a few more seconds, and then smiled that smarmy smile he gave people when he tried to be charming.

"All right, my dear. I'll organize my notes on Mrs. Westover's session. You can transcribe them this afternoon. Put them on my desk when you finish. I have a luncheon engagement with the university president and some potential endowment donors to the psychology department at noon. I may not be back."

I nodded. He swept from the room into his office, closing the door. I breathed a sigh of relief and picked up a few folders, then marched to the file room.

That had not been pleasant. I shoved a file into a drawer. He suspected I was holding out and had the brains to realize he'd get nothing more from me on the subject today. But I knew Pennington. He'd give it a rest for a while before homing in again.

I spent most of the morning keying notes into the computer files on various cases. While I worked, I pondered the future. My days with Clarke Pennington were numbered. A sizable inheritance from my grandmother ensured I didn't have to work, but I liked the routine of a schedule. I had to have structure. Maybe it was time for a change. I wondered if the local discount store was hiring. It would be something different.

Pennington left for his luncheon, giving me a short nod as he passed. It was his way of showing his irritation at my silence. The door had barely closed when the phone rang.

"Sasha, are you busy for lunch?" Reed asked in my

ear.

"Now?"

"Yes, I'm a couple of blocks from campus. I could be there in ten minutes."

At least, he wanted to see me again. "All right, I'm in the psychology building, room 312."

He hung up without saying goodbye. Annoyed, I replaced the receiver with a hard click. A simple "see ya" would have been nice.

I dashed to the ladies room and freshened up, then returned to the office a few seconds before Reed knocked and entered.

"Are you feeling better?" he asked.

"Yes, thanks. I had a good night's sleep. That helped. I guess my confession didn't totally send you running in the opposite direction."

"What do you mean?"

"You're asking me out again. I take that as a positive sign."

He smiled. "After I got home, I went over what you told me. I wanted to pick your brain for more details about this vision you said you had."

It wasn't much of an answer, but it would do. *So much for my scintillating personality.*

He looked rested, and although the lines seemed permanently etched in his face, his eyes were a clear, steady blue. In spite of myself, those pesky hormones danced through my body, and my desktop *was* fairly clear of clutter. I wiped the image from my mind.

I reached for my purse. We'd better leave before I did something I wouldn't regret. We were almost at the door when Reed's cell rang.

"McIntyre here…When…I see. Any ID yet…Can

you tell how long it's been...Right. I'll leave now."

He disconnected, his mouth set in a grim line, his eyes hard and cold as ice.

"Reed? What is it?" His expression scared me.

He didn't answer for a moment, and then turned that chilling gaze onto me.

"That was Lieutenant Dyson. This morning two fishermen hooked the body of a woman out of the Frog River. She has multiple stab wounds."

Chapter Six

"I'm coming with you," I said.

Not giving Reed a chance to refuse, I grabbed my purse and hurried out the door. Reed followed, but said nothing.

The oddly named Frog River carved its way across the northwestern portion of Shelby County before merging into the Mississippi. It wasn't overly wide or deep, but the current had been known to escalate from mild to swift after a rain. It also tended to overflow. On its more placid days, fishermen drowned worms from the banks.

Years ago, environmentalists and conservation authorities succeeded in having a large chunk of wetlands on the north side of the river declared a nature preserve. Located on slightly higher ground to the south, residents of the county enjoyed Frog Park.

"Is it Kathy?" I asked to break the silence. We had been speeding northward for the past several minutes.

"No ID yet," he replied tersely, running a yellow light.

I held my breath as it changed to red. Reed ignored the blaring horn of an irritated motorist crossing behind us.

"Who found her?"

"I told you—a couple of fishermen. That's all I

know."

His tone was sharp. I shut up and used my skills to concentrate on his emotions.

His fear that it was Kathy sliced deep into my mind. I also read frustration and uncertainty. The frustration was in not being able to prevent another death. The uncertainty centered on me and my abilities. His prejudices against psychics were crumbling. I sensed both rejection and relief warring in his mind. He didn't like it.

I pulled my thoughts away from Reed as we drove through the gates of Frog Park and followed a winding road to its northwestern corner. Police cars and ambulances crowded a small parking area. Trees obscured the river.

I exited the car. Reed remained silent, striding down a sloppy path. I hurried to keep up, my shoes squishing in the mud. Most of the cops and paramedics congregated on the riverbank. He finally slowed his pace, then stopped and stepped aside. Several yards away, a blue tarp covered the body. It looked lonely. A pang of compassion settled in the pit of my stomach. I turned and joined Reed who approached the attending officers.

"What happened?" he asked. "Any ID?"

"No, not yet," one of the officers replied.

"These men were fishing when one of them thought he'd hooked into a big catfish. He brought it to the surface, took one look, and called 9-1-1," the second policeman said, jerking his chin in the direction of two men standing well out of the way.

In their fifties, the men paced and smoked, gazing everywhere except thirty yards downstream.

"I don't suppose you found anything in the line of evidence on the bank?"

The first cop shook his head. "No. Tipton County had a heavy thunderstorm a few nights ago. Sucker dumped a couple inches of rain. The Frog overflowed. I guess when the water receded, the body caught on a snag."

Another official-looking man joined Reed and the officers.

"What can you tell me, doc?" Reed asked.

"Preliminary COD is stabbing. She was probably dead before she hit the river. I'll know more when I get her on the table."

"Any idea how long she's been in the water?"

The doctor shrugged. "Two days, maybe three."

Reed turned away, cupping my elbow in his hand. "Think you can stand to look at a body?"

My stomach turned over, and I licked my lips. "Do I have to?"

"You wanted to come along. The least you can do is tell me if she resembles the woman in your vision."

"Uh, I don't want to keep you from your investigation."

"Not my investigation. I'm tolerated as an observer provided I stay out of the way."

I didn't have much choice. He steered me along the sodden riverbank to the deceased where he crouched and lifted the edge of the blue tarp revealing the woman's features.

I'd never seen a dead person before other than at a funeral. This was raw and unpleasant. At first, I thought it couldn't possibly be the Kathy of my vision and dream. From the little I'd seen and remembered the woman had possessed an oval face. This apparition at my feet had a round facial structure.

As though reading my mind, Reed said, "She'd be a lot thinner in life. She's bloated from decomposition and being in the water."

My stomach clenched. I drew a deep breath, and then wished I hadn't. The stench almost knocked me off my feet. I recognized it as part river smell and part rotting flesh. I gagged, swallowed, then closed my eyes and turned my head.

"I…I'm not sure."

"Sasha, please," he said softly. "I know it's tough, but I need your help."

He needed my help? I hadn't expected him to admit it. I swallowed again and opened my eyes, forcing my gaze onto the pitiful remains of a human being.

I shuddered as I tried to picture the face of the young woman in my vision. I hadn't seen it clearly and what I had seen had been twisted in terror. This was infinitely worse. Fish had fed.

Brown hair hung in limp strands over her shoulders. Numerous cuts shredded her T-shirt. Faint reddish-brown stains splotched the now waterlogged white material. I concentrated on the vision.

"Yes. I think that's her. The face was never clear, but the stab wounds look right." I didn't mention they also felt right. "Can I go now?"

Reed flipped the plastic back over her face and torso, and then rose to once again cup my elbow with his hand. As he led me away, I threw a glance over my shoulder. Poor thing. She'd loved, not to mention trusted, the wrong man and had died for it.

"I'll take you back to the car. You said in your vision that the killer stripped and tossed his clothes into the river, too?"

"Yes, along with the knife, and I don't want to sit alone in the car. I'll just stay here out of the way," I said, pointing to a fallen tree.

"It'll be wet. Just a minute." He disappeared and returned a few minutes later with a sheet of plastic. "Use this to sit on. I'm going to assist the officers in trying to find more evidence. I won't be long."

I spread the plastic on top of the log and sat, relieving my shaking legs of their burden. I needed the break. I'd gotten strong vibes from the corpse I suspected was Kathy. She had been a real flesh and blood person. I no longer thought of her as a body.

She'd been dead when the killer had tossed her into the muddy water. In an eerie sensation, I felt more than saw her drift downstream, and then experienced the slow sinking. She swirled in the current ten feet below the surface until the branch of submerged tree trapped and held her immobile.

The rising floodwaters from the storm had dislodged and carried her on. If it hadn't been for the fisherman and his hook, she'd have continued on into the Mississippi where discovery would have taken longer, if at all.

I shivered even though the day was warm and humid. Low clouds scudded across the sky promising more rain later. Reed and the others walked along the riverbank, probing the bushes and the refuse in the water. I couldn't bring myself to look at the forlorn Kathy lying wet and cold on the ground. Blinking my eyes, I tried to stem the gathering tears.

"Sasha? What on earth are you doing here?"

Startled, I jerked my head. Jeff was coming down the path. "I was with Reed when he got the call about a body being found."

"But why are you here? Only police and authorized personnel are allowed at a crime scene."

"Because I can identify her."

He frowned and gave me a stern look. "You? But how would you know..." he stopped in mid-sentence and drew a sharp breath. "My God, you knew about this, didn't you? Your psychic powers uncovered something, right?"

The harsh countenance of a moment before was replaced with astonishment and a strange, eager glow in his eyes. Maybe because I was heartsick and scared, I could no longer hold back the truth. Besides, he had been on my side from the beginning. I trusted him.

"I'm afraid so."

I told him everything about the vision, the dream, dinner last night, and the connections, but kept silent about the hypnosis. As with Reed, I wasn't ready to discuss the possibility of possession.

Unmindful of the wet bark, Jeff sat beside me. "Are you sure this is Kathy Watson?"

"Pretty much. Her face was never very clear, but the location of the wounds tells me it is."

"That's thin. What about the killer? Can you see him? Make any ID?"

I shook my head. "No, not really. What wasn't in shadow was blurry. I just have an impression of very light colored hair and a solid build."

Even as I spoke, there was something about the light hair that bothered me, but the answer proved elusive.

"Think, Sasha, did he use his right or left hand? What kind of a knife was it? What was he wearing? Did the crime take place here? Describe the surroundings."

His rapid fire questions left my head spinning. "Not so fast, Jeff. I can't think straight."

"You must! Come on, concentrate. It's important."

I rubbed my forehead with my fingertips. "Please, Jeff, not now. I'm upset."

Before he could argue further, Reed strode up carrying a soggy piece of cloth. He unfurled the dripping material and held it gingerly by the top edges. It was a sweatshirt. Like a flash of lightning, I recognized it.

"He wore it. The killer. It was his," I stated in a flat tone.

"The stains on the front must be the victim's blood. I'll send it to forensics and see if they can make a match," he replied.

"For DNA purposes, the sample is hopelessly contaminated, but it's worth a shot," Jeff said. "Where did you find it?"

"Caught under a branch along the bank." Another officer arrived with a large plastic bag. Reed slipped the sweatshirt inside. "Are you all right, Sasha?"

"As right as I can expect to be. I've brought Jeff up to date on my involvement," I confessed.

"What about the rest of the clothing?" Jeff asked.

"Nothing yet."

"I doubt if you'll find it. He secured his sneakers by tying the legs of his slacks around them. The sweatshirt was tied around the entire bundle," I told them. "I guess the sleeves weren't long enough to hold the knot."

Jeff turned. "Let's get back to those questions I asked. Think hard. Did he hold the knife in his right or left hand?"

God, didn't he ever let up? I wanted to cry. "Leave me alone."

To my surprise, Reed crouched in front of me and cradled my hands in his.

"Sasha, I know this has been a shock, but anything you can tell us could put this animal away."

I couldn't fight the two of them. I closed my eyes, recalling the vision and the dream. Biting my lips, I opened them again and stared at Reed.

"He's right handed. He reached into his right hand pocket and took out the knife," I said, and then drew in a breath. "No, not slacks. Jeans. He was wearing jeans."

"What kind of knife was it?" Jeff asked.

"I don't know. A knife. It had a handle and a blade."

"Did he have to open it?" Reed said.

"Yes. He straddled her legs and made her watch as he pulled out the blade."

"How long was the blade?"

"Shit, I don't know, Reed. Four, maybe five inches. I'm not an expert on knives." My irritation level rose. What did they expect? I had psychic powers, not magical.

"Did he kill her here?" Jeff probed, his expression intense.

I heaved a deep breath, quelling the urge to flee, and then gazed at the surrounding trees and bushes. "No, it wasn't here. I see a clearing at the edge of the riverbank. I think they walked along a path. Her gait is

unsteady, faltering, as though she's drunk or drugged."
I felt a little drunk or drugged myself. "I'm sorry.
That's all I can come up with. I'm tired. Maybe I can be
more helpful later. I need rest."

Both men rose. "Thanks, Sasha," Jeff said.
"You've been a great help. I'm going to see what I can
find further along the bank. Coming Reed?"

"In a moment." Jeff left, and Reed pulled me to my
feet. "Come on. Let's get you into the car. Curl up on
the back seat and try to take a nap. I may be a while."

I was too tired to argue. He assisted me up the path,
opened the car door, and waited until I had scraped the
mud from my shoes.

"I stiffed you for lunch. Would you settle for
drinks and dinner when I'm done?"

"That's the best offer I've had all day and, I might
add, a nicely worded invitation." I tried to joke.
Anything to relieve the tension of the last few minutes.

"See, I'm trainable." He smiled and ran a finger
down my cheek.

My heart thumped for a couple of beats before I
crawled into the back seat. He closed the door, smiled,
and headed toward the path. My gaze didn't leave his
broad back until the trees and bushes hid him from
view. Kicking off my shoes, and using my purse as a
pillow, I laid down.

He was still skeptical, but his attitude had softened.
I guessed that as a cop he couldn't afford *not* to
consider all possible angles. And I qualified as an
angle, or at least my powers did.

Linnie had been right on another count. My
psychic abilities had undergone a dramatic
metamorphosis and my life an irreversible change. I

wasn't sure I could face it all yet.

On impulse, I sat up and yanked my cell phone from my bag, then dialed Linnie's office.

"Dr. Anderson's office. How may I help you?"

"Janine, this is Sasha Bellwood. Is Dr. Anderson available? I need to talk to her."

"Yes, she has a few minutes until her next appointment."

I waited impatiently while I was put through.

"Sasha, what's wrong?"

I gave her the whole story. "Linnie, I'm not handling this very well. I never expected my abilities to change or increase."

"Do you want to come in this evening and talk about it? I have time at seven-thirty."

"No, Reed and I are going out to dinner. Besides, I'm not sure this is something you can make better. I have to deal with it. I don't even know why I called."

"Because you wanted to talk. That's why I'm here. Are you sure you don't want to come in? I can clear an hour later this afternoon."

I hesitated. I'd love to pour out my feelings to Linnie. Then I remembered I had no idea when Reed would finish.

"No, I'm sure. I'll be fine."

"Have you called Dr. Silberstein yet?"

I heaved a sigh. "No."

"Call him, Sasha."

"I…I can't just yet. I feel more comfortable with you."

"Then, come in tonight. Bring Reed and we'll talk."

The last thing I wanted was to discuss this with

Reed in attendance. "That's all right. I'm sorry to have bothered you. I guess I wanted to let you know a body had been found."

"If you change your mind, give me a call," she said. "At least, you no longer have to wonder if your vision was true."

"Small consolation. I'll talk to you tomorrow. Lunch?"

"McCauley's at one?"

"Deal. See you there."

I hung up and reclined again. I felt better for having unloaded the horrible events of the last couple of hours, and wondered where I headed.

****

"Sasha, wake up."

I opened my eyes, disoriented for a second until I realized I was still in the back seat of Reed's car, an odd dream swirling in my subconscious. I sat up trying to blink the sleep from my eyes and gazed out the window, surprised to see the car at a stoplight near campus.

Reed glanced over his shoulder. "There's a bar not far from here—The Regulator. It's nothing fancy, but they have a decent menu."

I'd been there on several occasions. The name came from the numerous antique Regulator clocks hung on the walls.

"The Reg is fine. But I need to get my car. I don't want to leave it unattended too long. The campus police will have it towed after nine o'clock."

"Where did you park?" he asked.

"In the lot behind the psychology building."

Still trying to clear my head, I slipped on my shoes

and gave him directions. A few minutes later we pulled up next to my car, the only one remaining.

"What time is it?" I asked.

"Close to six."

That late? No wonder I felt groggy. I got out and followed him in my car to the bar. We slid into an empty booth in a back corner, ordering a pitcher of beer and burgers.

"Did you find any other evidence?" I asked when the waitress had left.

"No, but something can still turn up, especially if we find the murder scene. Talked to the medical examiner just before we left. He found a driver's license and a credit card in her jeans pocket. It was Kathy Watson. Her parents have been notified."

A lump formed in my throat. I swallowed hard and shivered. At least I hadn't developed precognition. Even so, I still wished I could have helped more. If only I could see the killer's face!

"God, I feel so sorry for them. I've never lost someone I loved to violent crime. They must be heartbroken."

"Devastated. She was their only daughter."

The lump broke. Tears welled, and then overflowed my eyes. I grabbed a napkin from a holder on the table and tried to dry my cheeks. I blew my nose and crushed the wadded paper into the palm of my hand.

Reed allowed me to regain control, and then clasped my hands in his. "Are you all right?"

I nodded. "It's been a lousy day. Did the doctor say anything else?"

"The autopsy is scheduled for tomorrow morning,

but he did say he thinks some of the wounds are post-mortem."

"You mean he stabbed her after she was dead? That's sick."

"Show me a serial killer who isn't."

The waitress brought our pitcher and two frosty mugs. Reed poured. I raised the cold container to my lips and chugged half of it down in a few gulps. Heavy on the hops, the bitter liquid slid down my parched throat. I rubbed my hand across my forehead.

"Headache?" he asked.

"No. Just trying to make sense out of a dream I had."

"The one where you saw things through the victim's eyes?"

I shook my head. "I was having this crazy dream when you woke me."

"About the murder?"

"No, just a silly dream."

"I wish I could remember my dreams. Tell me about it."

I never related my dreams to anyone except Linnie, but Reed had an expression on his face that made me feel I could tell him anything. Before I thought twice about it, I talked.

"I'm in a forest, and I know it's summer because I'm hot and sweaty, but all the leaves on the trees are dead. There's no real path to follow, so I keep wandering a twisting course. I'm thirsty and have the feeling water is near—I just can't find it. Bushes snag at my clothes like they have hands, not wanting me to continue.

"Suddenly, I come to a clearing. The vegetation is

scorched as though it had been in a fire. I want to leave, but can't seem to move."

"A frequent dream reaction. Something to do with anxiety, I think," Reed said.

"Possibly, because I *am* scared. I'm also no longer hot, but cold. I can see my breath. A bird flies into the clearing and settles on the branch of a tree for a few seconds. Then, the poor thing falls to the ground—dead. I'm scared—really scared. My heart pounds and I try to run, but can't. There's something evil in that clearing. Then, you woke me."

Reed refreshed his mug and wrinkled his brow before answering. "The forest could represent the woods you were just in. And while it's not summer, you were sleeping in an enclosed car. Only the front windows were open. That could explain why you felt hot."

"I suppose," I said, taking another drink.

"It's not surprising you dreamed of death. You'd just seen a dead body. And Lord knows Kathy Watson didn't die a benevolent death. It was evil through and through."

His lips thinned, and the look in his eyes hardened. I understood. She hadn't deserved to die like that, betrayed by love.

"Dream analysis never interested me. I had enough problems in my life without screwing with my sleep, too."

The why and what of the dream depressed me. In view of the last couple of days, I figured Linnie would add that analysis to the expanding list of things to discuss.

Reed drained his mug and poured another. His

brow knitted into lines. I sensed his confusion.

"Is something wrong?"

"In a way, yes." He drank more beer. "I hate to admit it, but there may be something to this psychic stuff. Unless you're the killer or saw the murder from behind a bush, you must be telling the truth about having powers of some sort."

It wasn't the nicest way of putting it, but I gave him points for saying it at all.

"Reed, I'm not sure I can help any further. I can't identify the killer or find the bodies of those missing women. Are you sure you're dealing with a serial killer? I mean, how many ways are there to commit murder?"

"You'd be surprised. And yes, I'm sure he's a serial killer. There are too many similarities to be dismissed as coincidence. The carpet fibers, for example. They link the first two victims. And the savagery of the stabbings can't be ignored. Susan Parker had dozens."

"Reed, you have no evidence linking all of the murders. Carpet fibers, strangulation, stabbing, that's it. Has he shot anyone?"

"Not that I know of." He drained his mug again. "He's got to be stopped!"

"But it's been two years since the last murder."

"He has a pattern. The first two occurred within weeks of each other. Then there was a gap of almost two years until Elaine Banks was found strangled in a Mid-town house being re-habbed. Jennifer Randall followed two weeks later."

"Was the forensic evidence consistent?"

"No. Victims three and four had identical carpet

fibers, but not the same as one and two."

"So, if this is a serial killer, then he moved—assuming he killed in his own house or apartment."

"Bridget and Eleanor came next three years later. By then, I was no longer on the force. As soon as the cases went cold, I jumped on them. A year later, Susan Parker was killed, but the pattern broke."

"How?"

"No second murder—that we know of."

"But why stop?

He shrugged, refilling his mug. "Maybe his blood lust, his urge to kill is satisfied. Kathy begins the pattern again." He slammed his fist on the table, causing the newly poured beer to slop over the side of the glass and splatter onto the table.

His lips had compressed further, and he breathed heavily through his nose. The blue eyes shot sparks of laser ice. I'd never seen a more intense look on a man's face.

I laid my hand on his arm. "Reed, you have no definite proof of anything along those lines. I thought serial killers left some kind of gloating message to show how smart they are for the police. Isn't that what Son of Sam and the Zodiac killer did?"

"Yes, but Ted Bundy didn't. I think we're dealing with another Ted Bundy. Someone too smart or too psychotic to draw attention to himself. I've lived and breathed this for years. I refuse to give up."

"You're obsessive and have to face the fact you may never find him."

"No. I'll get him. Even when I'm on my deathbed, I'll still be thinking about him."

His words troubled me. Determination was one

thing. Letting the situation control your life was another.

"Have you considered returning to therapy?" I asked.

"Funny, Jeff asked that yesterday. He thinks I'm spinning my tires on black ice."

Black ice. The ice formed on sidewalks and roadways when the temperature hovers just below freezing. Disguised as a damp patch of concrete, it waits to ensnare the unobservant pedestrian or motorist.

"It's something to consider," I said.

Reaching into his jacket pocket, Reed took out two photos and placed them between us on the table.

"Bridget and Eleanor—I owe them, Sasha. I owe their families. I can't let them go unavenged."

I sighed and picked up the photo of Bridget Connor. Her smile, so carefree and animated, reminded me that here was a young woman who genuinely loved people. I wished I could help find her. I wished—

My peripheral vision dimmed and the picture dropped back onto the table from my suddenly numb fingers. Reed was saying something, but his movements had taken on the elements of a movie being run in slow motion. His voice became muffled and indistinct. Even as I watched, my dining companion receded into a foggy background and was replaced by a frightening, clear image of murder and its aftermath.

Chapter Seven

I experienced the same sensations as at Le Bistro a few nights ago—the odd tingle of being filled from toes to head and noise reducing itself to a faint buzz. The vision would be next, blotting out all other sights.

I was still cognizant enough to realize Reed knew something out of the ordinary had happened. He called my name twice and shook my arm. When I didn't respond, he leaned over the table and grasped my shoulders, giving me a shake that should, and probably did, rattle my teeth. I hoped he didn't panic and call the paramedics. Twice in one week could land me in the psych ward.

Then, the vision grabbed my consciousness. The restaurant, Reed, and everything else surrounding me faded.

I wasn't sure what I viewed, but it scared me to death with the kind of fear that left me listening to my own heart hammer away much too fast, gasping for breath, shaking, and sick to my stomach. In spite of all that, I tried to be observant about details, and then wished I hadn't. The photo triggered something, because I witnessed Bridget Connor's death. It wasn't pretty.

I have no idea how long I remained in the trance, but gradually the vision diminished and the sounds of the restaurant returned. Reed's worried, stunned expression swam into view. He looked like he'd been hit on the head with a two-by-four. His trembling hands held my wrists and, still psychically aware, I read his emotions. He was scared and about to become a believer.

"Sasha? What the hell happened? Are you all right?" he demanded in hushed tones.

I blinked and licked my dry lips. I couldn't answer. My stomach churned and cramped. I pulled my hands free and slid from behind the table. I needed to find the ladies room fast. My legs refused to cooperate and I sagged, grasping the table just in time to prevent myself from hitting the floor.

Reed leaped to his feet, supporting me.

"Sasha, where do you think you're going? You're pale as a ghost. Sit down."

"I can't," I said, gasping. "I'm going to throw up. Help me to the ladies room. Now!"

He didn't argue, just slung his arm around my waist, guiding me through the crowded bar to a back hallway and a door marked "Dames." Other patrons stared, probably assuming I was drunk. I didn't care. Reed tried to follow me inside. I pushed him back. No way in hell would I allow him to watch me hurl.

The bathroom was neither the cleanest nor the most fragrant I'd ever been in. It looked as though a mop had occasionally been swept through, but the dirt accumulated in the corners of the stall and in back of the toilet told me it hadn't been done lately.

It was the odor of some floral disinfectant, which didn't quite mask the scent of urine and other smells that made me bend over the bowl, gagging, until I finally vomited.

When I finished, I staggered out of the stall to the lone basin and turned on the tap. Cupping the cold water in my hands, I rinsed my mouth and bathed my face. Only then did I realize I'd been sobbing the entire time. I couldn't bring myself to gaze into the mirror. I knew I looked like hell.

Someone pounded on the door. "Sasha, are you all right?" Reed shouted, and then paused for a few seconds. "Answer me, dammit. If you don't, I'm coming in."

"Yes, Reed, I'm-I'm all right. Just give me a second."

In spite of the noxious restroom odors, I inhaled several deep breaths, walked unsteadily to the door, and opened it. Reed stood on the other side, both hands braced against the door jamb, his body filling the entryway.

He said nothing, just put his arm around my shoulders and helped me back to the table. I slid into the booth and took a sip of beer, then pushed the glass away.

The waitress, undoubtedly a witness to my stumbling rush to the restroom, stopped next to our table.

"Water, please," I said.

She nodded and left, returning a few seconds later with a large glass, the obligatory lemon wedge stuck on the rim. I squeezed the fruit into the water and sipped, the tart liquid soothing my dry throat. *Much better*.

"All right, what the hell was that all about?" Reed demanded.

"You know. You just don't want to admit it."

He picked up the photos of Bridget and Eleanor. "You had a vision?"

His slow speech indicated I was right. "I'll say."

He fingered the pictures and shoved them back into his pocket. I sensed the conflicting emotions warring within him, including skepticism and an almost desperate desire to believe.

"Which one? Tell me," he finally said.

I drew a shaky breath. "It was Bridget Connor. She sat in the front seat of a car, a paper cup in her hand, her vision blurring. The man with her asks if she'd like some more wine. She doesn't, but he fills her cup again, urging her to drink."

"Are they parked or driving?"

"Parked."

"Any idea where?"

"No. It's an empty parking lot."

"Do you see any lights?"

I shook my head. "It's dark, but there's enough light from the dashboard to see by. The radio or CD player is on."

"You can hear things? I thought the last vision was silent."

"It was, but the dream wasn't. Maybe I'm branching out." I didn't mean it as a joke. This entire business was getting out of hand, scaring the tar out of me.

Reed apparently didn't find it amusing, either. He never so much as cracked a smile. "Okay, go on. What happens next?"

"He-he scoots over next to her, puts his hands on either side of her face, and kisses her. 'Bridget, has anyone ever told you you're too trusting? For all you know, I could be a very dangerous person.'"

I gulped some more lemon water and let the tangy flavor swirl around my dry mouth before swallowing. Reed's gaze never left my face. A muscle in his cheek twitched.

"She laughs and says she's not afraid. Her words are slurred and her vision blurry. Her eyelids feel heavy. She realizes something isn't right, but can't do anything about it.

"'But you should be, my dear, you should be,' he says, and then slides his hands around her throat. He strangles her." My hand strayed to *my* throat. "I felt his fingers squeezing, digging into her neck, his thumbs pressing on her windpipe." I gagged and shivered, my hand dropping back to the table. "Whatever he used to drug her is effective, she can't fight back. I'm not going to go into the terror and pain she feels. I can't."

Reed's hands covered mine. "Don't try, Sasha. I don't want to hear it, either. You were out of it for a good five minutes. Is there anything else?"

"I felt her die, and then the images changed. I watched the son of a bitch bury her. His final gesture was to pour the rest of the wine over the grave and laugh." I hiccupped and bit back a sob.

"The sadistic bastard."

Anger and revulsion replaced my fear and sickness, but were nothing compared to the icy rage rolling off Reed. I glanced into his face. It was impassive. His eyes were not. They were hard, cold, and furious.

"Did you see the killer's face?"

"No, the drug kept everything blurred and it was dark. What I saw was in shadow."

"I wish this vision had begun when she got into the

car with him," he muttered.

"She wasn't afraid then. She didn't realize the danger until it was too late. Maybe that's how this whole mess works. Maybe I can't see anything until the fear or uncertainty begins."

"How about his voice? Would you recognize it again if you heard it?"

"I doubt it. It sounds funny, maybe because of the drugs. I'd *heard* through her just like I saw."

Reed released my hands and ran his fingers through his hair. "Okay, you can't identify the man. What about the location."

"Let me think for a moment." I paused to collect my thoughts. "There's more to the burial part. He wrapped her body in a hunk of plastic, kind of like the tarp covering Kathy, slung her over his shoulder, and then carried her through the woods. I saw a triangle of trees—two are shagbark hickories, I'm not sure about the other one. There's a hole in the middle of the triangle with mounds of dirt piled beside it. He must have selected the burial site and dug it earlier."

"Does he have a shovel with him? Can you see his face now?"

"No. When his back isn't toward me, the—her body blocks my view. He's carrying the shovel in his hand. He rolls her into the grave and piles the dirt on top. Then he does the wine thing and leaves."

"What about the plastic and the shovel?"

"He takes them."

Reed started to ask another question when the waitress arrived with our food.

"Do you feel like eating?" he asked.

Oddly enough, I did. Now that I had talked about

the vision, the nausea vanished and as unfeeling as it seemed, I was starving. To prove it, I slathered mayonnaise on the bun, mashed it down on top of the lettuce and tomato, and took a huge bite. Grease dribbled down my chin and I hurriedly wiped it with a napkin.

"I guess that answers my question," he murmured, following my actions and chomping on his sandwich.

I was well into my burger and fries before we continued the conversation.

"Sasha, think hard. What can you remember about the woods? You said he wrapped her in a sheet of plastic?"

I nodded and slowed my chewing, finally putting the half eaten burger down.

"He spread it out on the ground next to the passenger side of the car and laid her on it."

"Can you identify the car?"

"No, I'm not good at things like that. Besides, it was dark out and the car was also a dark color."

"So, there could be upholstery fibers on whatever clothing is left," he said.

I had no idea. "He's parked on the side of the road just beyond a curve." I sat up straighter. "There's some kind of hill off to the left."

"A hill? In this area?"

I ignored him, concentrating on my memory. "No, not a hill. It's too uniform. More like a large berm, a sound barrier. It's definitely man-made."

"Does the killer carry her over it?"

"No, he goes in the opposite direction. He looks funny."

Reed finished his sandwich and shoved the last of

his fries into his mouth before asking, "Funny? How?"

"His hair is all shiny, so are his hands," I replied wishing I could see through the darkness more clearly.

"Shiny? As in light reflecting off of plastic gloves? Where's the light coming from?"

"Moonlight. It's dappling through the trees." In a flash, I recognized the origins of the shininess. "A cap! He's wearing a shower cap! Like those you get in hotels along with the shampoo and soap."

"It makes sense. We never found any hairs."

I pushed my plate away.

The waitress stopped by and slapped the bill on the table. Reed looked at me with sharp eyes.

"Are you ready to leave?"

I drained the last of my water, nodding. I felt better, but the exhaustion of the vision and remembering everything had taken its toll. I was operating on fumes.

Dropping some money on the table, Reed helped me out of the booth and escorted me to my car.

"Can you drive?"

"Yes. I'll be fine."

"I'll follow you home, just in case," he said firmly.

I knew better than to argue. My fingers trembled, and it took three tries to get the key into the ignition. In a way, I was glad he followed. His presence gave me a strange sense of well-being. I stopped short of thinking protected.

At my house, he once again held my elbow, walking me to the front door. He took the key and opened it.

"Do you want me to come in for a while?"

Of course, I did. "I've been told I make a mean cup

of coffee."

"Funny, I've been thinking about coffee since we left the restaurant," he said, smiling.

He settled on the sofa while I filled the coffee pot. A few minutes later, I carried two steaming cups into the living room.

"This is nice," he said, eyeing the furnishings.

"I give you full credit for being a fast learner."

"What do you mean?"

"I don't think floral prints and peach-colored walls are quite your taste, but at least you were being polite."

He grinned and lifted the cup to his lips. Now, I laughed outright.

"What's so funny?"

"You. I was thinking about the session at Linnie's. You dumped all that sugar and cream in your coffee when you really like it black."

"That's because Dr. Anderson and Jeff were flirting like a couple of high schoolers. Sometimes, I enjoy playing the smart ass."

"You're good at it."

"So I've been told."

I drank some coffee without really tasting it. "Reed, did I help at all tonight?"

"Some. Your description is vague, but I'll check out any new subdivisions in the tri-state area that may have used an earthen embankment as a sound protector. That would indicate a highway, maybe an interstate nearby."

"The Nonconnah Parkway still has some undeveloped area between Germantown and Collierville," I said, using the old name for the expressway spur. It had been renamed after some politician several years ago, but most people still called it by its original designation. "There are trees and bushes growing on the hill."

"How big?"

"Different heights."

"It could be the land across from the berm has been developed since then. I hope I don't have to dig up someone's yard or a golf course to find her." His forehead wrinkled in a slight frown.

"I don't think you will. She's still where he left her, untouched for all this time."

"How can you be sure?"

I shrugged. "I can't. It's just a gut feeling I have. The grave isn't deep—no more than three or four feet. If the land had been developed, I think her body would have been discovered and you would have heard about it."

"You're probably right. I'm tired. It's been a long day and my mind is slow." He drained his cup. "Would you like me to bunk on your couch tonight?"

I hesitated. I'd long ago given up the illusion of depending on a man, yet the thought of Reed sleeping on my floral print sofa and covered with a pink afghan made me want to smile. First of all, it was a silly image, and second, depending on him didn't feel as unsettling as it once might have.

He took off his jacket. "You're giving it too much thought. I'll stay. Got an extra toothbrush?"

The decision had been made, and the fact that I had not controlled the situation didn't upset me.

"Brand spanking new from the dentist two weeks ago. I feel fine, but the last time I had a vision, a nightmare followed. I guess a shoulder to lean on wouldn't be such a bad idea."

He grinned and slid his hand around my neck, then pulled me forward.

I didn't have time to think, only react as his lips covered mine. A zing zipped along my nerves and my arms snaked around his neck. Before I knew it, our bodies were glued together.

I hadn't expected a Reed McIntyre kiss to be gentle. I was right. It was hard and demanding, sending my blood pressure, not to mention my hormone levels, to an all-time high. I could have stayed this way forever, maybe even kicking it up a notch or two a la Emeril, but Reed pulled back, a look of mild surprise on his face.

"I think you'd better get that toothbrush now. Otherwise, I may not stay on the couch," he whispered, stepping back with a smile.

"Yeah, I think maybe you're right."

I walked toward the bathroom on wobbly legs. Holy cow. My nerves jingled, and I had to remind myself I wasn't even sure I liked him.

Liar. You like him just fine. In fact, you'd love to drag him into bed and see if he's as good in other areas of acute turn on as kissing.

I resisted the urge and found the toothbrush along with a small tube of toothpaste. Laying it on the vanity, I detoured to the linen closet for a couple of sheets and a pillow.

"Here you go," I said, returning to the living room and quickly making up the sofa. "You should be comfortable."

"I'll be fine."

A half smile played on his lips. "Good night,

Sasha. I'll see you in the morning."

I had no choice but to nod, murmur a faint echo of his words, and disappear down the hall. I brushed my teeth, and then slipped into my nightgown. Pulling back the covers, I made a mental note to tell Linnie my toes had not only curled, they'd damn near fallen off.

****

The past twenty-four hours had confused and frustrated Kathy Watson.

After being ejected from Sasha's mind, she traveled through time and space, unable to stop her momentum. Along her journey, she encountered other entities also on unknown pilgrimages. They all bore sympathetic expressions. Some smiled. One touched her and Kathy instantly experienced a jolt of something she could only describe as "knowing." She and this female apparition had a bond. What, she couldn't begin to imagine.

"Who are you?" she asked.

The woman smiled. "My name's Bridget. Thank you."

"Thank you for what?"

She received no answer. Bridget moved on.

Kathy stopped in the middle of the stream of ghostly pedestrians like a clot in an artery.

"Will someone please tell me what's going on?" she pleaded. No one did. "Please!"

Finally, a man paused. "We're all searching for our others," he said.

"Others? What others?"

"Our connections. Our links to the earthly world."

Before she could ask anything else, he rejoined the flow.

Had all these souls lost their connections or were they just searching? And how did she go about finding Sasha again? The most sensible way sounded like joining the river of beings, but in which direction?

Kathy paused for a moment, and then made a decision. She'd head back the way she'd come. Not sure of how to accomplish this, she literally jumped into the stream on her right.

"This isn't so bad," she murmured as her spirit flowed quite easily with the others. In fact, it was rather pleasant. It sure beat the hell out of her morning jog.

Having no idea when or where to reenter the real world, she floated like flotsam, then noticed some of the other presences exiting at what to her resembled holes. She took a chance and projected herself through one.

She had come out in an unfamiliar rural setting. Men on horseback fought with swords.

"Nope, not this one."

She thrust herself back through the hole and into the stream. *Maybe I need to concentrate on where I want to go.*

It took two more tries before she found a location she recognized. Unfortunately, it was near where she'd been killed. But at least she had a fix. She wondered how long it would take to reestablish contact with Sasha.

And who the hell was Bridget?

Kathy shook the question off. She had to find Sasha. Gerald was still out there. Who knew when he'd prey on another unsuspecting woman?

Forget about Gerald for now, too. Concentrate on relocating your connection.

She should have paid closer attention to *where* Sasha lived. As it was, she had no idea. Should she return to the coffee house? No, what good would that do? Sasha might not be a regular customer.

Sighing, Kathy drifted like a feather on the wind. Surely there had to be a way to accelerate her speed. She concentrated and willed herself to go faster. To her surprise, it worked. She zipped along through space, only pausing to inspect likely neighborhoods, but found nothing familiar.

The sun rose and Kathy continued searching. Strange, she had always associated ghosts with night and darkness, but here she was circling the rooftops in broad daylight. None of the residents going about their daily routines in the streets had any idea she was above them. In a way it was fun.

Then, Kathy rounded a corner and gasped. This was it! This was the street. And there was Sasha's house! She'd found it.

Oh, thank God.

Now what? She couldn't very well go up and ring the doorbell. Circling around to the back of the house, Kathy experimented. She stretched her hand out toward the back door and drifted forward. Her hand disappeared through the wood.

Well, I'll be damned.

She pushed the rest of her presence into the kitchen. Turning, she stared at a gooey substance running sluggishly down the door. She remembered the movie *Ghostbusters*. So, ghosts *did* leave some of themselves behind. Interesting.

Kathy shrugged and wafted through the rest of the house. Sasha wasn't there. What a letdown. After searching all night and a good part of the morning, the one person who could help her wasn't home. Damnation!

Kathy hung suspended three feet from the ceiling. It wasn't like she had any place else to go.

Sooner or later Sasha had to come back.

Chapter Eight

I sat at my desk transcribing the notes Pennington had dictated the day before. It was almost ten o'clock, and I'd been at it since eight-thirty. Reed had proven to be an early riser, making enough noise banging pots and pans to wake the dead.

"Do you know what time it is?" I demanded, giving up any further attempts at sleep and wandering into the kitchen.

Reed looked at his watch, holding a frying pan in his hand. "It's six o'clock."

"That was a rhetorical question. I know it's six in the damned morning. What are you doing?"

"Making breakfast."

He received big points for that answer. He also received points for pretty good bacon and eggs. After eating, we left the house together, he to his place and me to the office.

No nightmares had disturbed me, but that didn't mean I'd had a good sleep. Maybe that's why it was so hard to concentrate this morning.

I shrugged and resumed typing, only to sigh and hit the backspace button to correct yet another error. At this rate, it would take all day to finish a simple five-page report.

My frustration was interrupted when the office

door opened and Reed entered.

"Am I disturbing you?" he asked.

"Yes, thank God. I seem to be all thumbs today. What are you doing here?"

He toyed with a fluffy stuffed flamingo sitting on my desk. Linnie had given it to me years ago, a souvenir of a trip to Florida. Its mate sat on the mantel at her house. We'd named them Ken and Barbie. I owned Barbie. They were silly and completely out of character for both of us, but I loved mine.

Reed set it down and grinned. "Cute. I didn't know you were into stuffed wildlife, especially in Pepto Bismol pink."

"Never mind. Why are you here?"

"I just wanted to make sure you're all right. Last night was…" he hesitated. "Eventful for both of us."

I assumed he referred to my vision and not the kiss.

"I'm okay. Are you a believer now?"

He raised his eyebrows and shrugged. "I don't know. Maybe. Let's just say I'm not as skeptical as I was two days ago." He paused. "I'm going to follow up. I've already done a search of recent subdivisions in the tri-state area that may have used an earthen berm for noise abatement."

"I wish I could be more specific about where she's buried."

"It's more than I had yesterday. I'll concentrate my search in Northern Shelby and Southern Tipton Counties. Maybe into Fayette County a ways. Since she disappeared from The Wolf Chase Mall, it seems logical the killer wouldn't travel too far to dig the grave, drug, kill, and then bury her."

I drummed my fingers on my desk. "You know, I

just can't help feeling her grave site is still undisturbed."

"I hope you're right. Noise abatements are usually found between homes and roads. My guess is the houses are on the other side of the hill."

Something nagged at the corners of my mind like a shadow just out of reach. Maybe I would catch the image later. I turned my attention back to Reed.

"I'd love to go with you, but I have work to do. You'll call if you find anything, won't you?"

"If I find this needle in a haystack, I'll let you know. I don't expect..."

He was interrupted by the office door opening and turned, coming face to face with my boss.

"Good morning, Sasha." He glanced at me, then at Reed, and held out his hand, the smarmy smile in place. "Hello, I'm Dr. Clarke Pennington. Are you waiting for me?"

Reed gave him the Reed McIntyre Universal Greeting of a brief handshake and a one word response. "No."

Pennington looked taken aback. "I see. Then, you must be another one of Sasha's friends." He turned to me. "I've been meeting quite a few of my research assistant's acquaintances lately."

His eyes narrowed, and I read suspicion in his eyes, silently demanding an introduction.

"Dr. Pennington, this is Reed McIntyre."

"It's a pleasure to meet you Mr. McIntyre. The last friend of Sasha's I met was a police detective. Are you in that line of work, too?"

"Used to be. I'm retired."

"I see. The other gentleman—what was his name,

dear? John? James? No, Jeff. He said something about finding missing files. Are you also seeking missing files?"

"No. Sasha, I have to go. I'll let you know if I find anything. Dr. Pennington." Reed nodded to my boss and left.

"He was certainly abrupt. What's he looking for?" he asked with a frown.

My mind was on Reed, the vision, and our steamy, almost had sex kiss. I spoke before I thought. "A body."

"A body! Whose? What's going on here and why haven't you told me?" Pennington demanded.

Oh, shit. My lack of concentration and daydreams about Reed had tripped me up. I tried to correct my mistake.

"I worded that badly. A gravesite. He's looking for a gravesite. He's doing research on his family."

My boss stared, the suspicion in his eyes deepening. "You're lying. I can see it in your eyes. You're helping the police in a murder, aren't you? Your skills *have* become more advanced, haven't they? I demand you tell me everything immediately."

A red flush slowly crept up his neck, tinting his cheeks, and finally his forehead. I half expected to see smoke curling from his ears. I had no idea what to say.

When I remained silent, Pennington slammed his fist on my desk, causing me to jump.

"Answer me, dammit!" His lips drew back over his teeth. "You've been holding out. Tell me whatever it is you know. Everything!"

I leaped to my feet. I'd had it. Maybe my careless response to his question had been a Freudian slip. I opened my mind and tapped into his. Fury, avarice, the desire to control, and oddly, his literary agent's phone number popped up in my brain.

"No!" I shouted.

He straightened. Add shock to the other emotions in his mind. He was surprised to find his docile research assistant not as docile as he thought.

"What! How dare you? I pay you a good salary and expect something in return besides typing my notes."

"You pay me dog shit and the only reason you want to know anything is so you can write a book." I rattled off the phone number I'd envisioned. "Your agent, right?"

I didn't think his shock could deepen, but it did.

"My God, your abilities have improved."

Freudian or not, my slip of the tongue set into motion what I'd contemplated yesterday. I gathered my purse and stuffed as much as I could into it, including the flamingo. Luckily, I carried a big handbag and didn't keep many personal items at the office.

"What are you doing?"

"I quit, Pennington. You're a sleazebag. Always were, always will be. I don't need you or this shitty job."

He glanced at the door as I swung around my desk. For one panic-stricken second I thought he'd try to block my exit. I walked quickly, reaching for the doorknob.

"You owe me, dammit. I hired you with the understanding you'd confide in me. I had plans."

I opened the door and turned. "I know. You planned to use me like you've used so many other people who came to you for help. Well, I'm not going to be a chapter or the subject matter of your next book.

If anybody writes about it, it'll be me!"

"Why, you two-timing little bitch…"

I slammed the door on his comments and strode down the hall toward the staircase. Out in the parking lot, I slid behind the wheel of my car, heaved a huge sigh, and pumped my fist in the air. Yes! I was free.

I had to celebrate. I whipped out my cell and called Linnie.

****

Patience had never been one of Kathy's virtues. Her often exasperated mother had told her so on numerous occasions. She floated around Sasha's house while she waited.

Her host had strange taste. She approved of the floral print sofa and the soft pastel walls, but found the chrome and glass coffee table and the modernistic floor lamp with its long arching arm out of place. She considered eclectic decorating another phrase for garage sale. Kathy was more of a country fan.

The phone rang for the fifth time in the last few hours. The same guy, a man named Pennington, left another message.

"Sasha, I know you're there. Pick up." The caller paused a few seconds. "Call me. You can't just walk out like this. I need you. Collaborate with me and I promise to split the advance and the royalties fifty-fifty." He hung up.

From the other messages, Kathy deduced this Pennington was Sasha's boss and that Sasha had just quit.

Good for you, Sasha. This guy sounds like a creep.

So, if Sasha no longer worked, where the hell was she?

If I'd just told my boss to go to cram it, I'd come home, open a bottle of wine, and celebrate.

Maybe that's what she'd done. Maybe at this very moment she was in some bar with a bunch of friends hoisting a few. Damn. Why couldn't she have found Sasha's house earlier? No telling when the woman would return.

Kathy sighed, glancing at the clock on the mantel. It was after two. She'd been waiting for close to five hours. Suppose Sasha didn't come home? That was silly. She lived here. She had to return.

The only problem was Kathy didn't feel like waiting any longer. Her need for answers grew with each passing hour. She thought about the spirit named Bridget who had thanked her in the stream.

There's a bond of some sort. I know it. She's the person I should be seeking. There's more to this than just Sasha.

It made sense. Sasha was just as confused as Kathy, but this Bridget seemed to have knowledge of something important. But where to find her? Hurtling herself back into the stream of souls sounded like the best choice.

The phone rang again and Sasha's former boss left another message. Kathy was amused. He'd started out brusque and demanding, and then turned more conciliatory. Pretty soon, he'd beg. Kathy wished she could be around for that part. She bet Sasha wouldn't mind hearing her boss grovel, either.

The clock chimed two-thirty. Her patience snapped. Time to go. She'd find this Bridget and demand answers.

Kathy eased her way out the back door, most of the

gooey mess she'd left upon entry coming with her.

Later, Sasha.

Kathy launched herself back into the air. A hole opened in front of her as another spirit shot past. She took advantage of it and rejoined the stream of restless souls.

****

Linnie breezed into Ribs and Ribs and gave me a high five before sitting down. I'd spent the last couple of hours on a shopping spree at a nearby mall.

McCauley's seemed a little upscale for this kind of celebration. As any pig and sauce lover knows, when barbeque calls, ye must obey. It called to both of us.

"Thank God, you are no longer working for that creep, Pennington," she crowed. "What happened? I crave details with my barbeque."

I laughed. "I'd finally had enough and told him to stuff it. Between Jeff and Reed's visits the last couple of days, Pennington had most of it figured out anyway."

A waitress arrived and took our order. When she left, Linnie continued. "Details, Sasha, details. Including what Reed was doing there."

Giddy with my new found freedom, I laughed again and gave her the details of my abrupt termination.

"Whew! Did he really try to stop you from leaving?"

"No, but it crossed his mind. I was still tapped into his emotions. I never realized how scary he could be."

"Well, you're done with him now and that's what counts."

During our conversation, the waitress had brought our iced tea. Linnie sucked hard through the straw and winked.

"Okay, now tell me why Reed was in your office at ten in the morning. Are you two becoming an item?"

I ran my hand up and down the sweaty glass before grasping it and taking a sip. "Maybe."

"Sasha, 'maybe' is an evasion. Come on, what gives?"

"Reed stopped by to see if I was all right. We'd been out the night before, and it was not a pleasant experience. I had another vision."

"Oh, my God. About one of Reed's missing women?"

I nodded. Linnie had seen and heard damned near everything in her line of work, but shock was plainly visible on her face and in her eyes.

"What was his reaction?"

"He didn't want to believe, but did. Kind of shook him up."

"What did you see?"

"I felt Bridget Connor die, and then kind of hovered overhead while the son of a bitch buried her."

I told her the whole story. When I finished, Linnie sat back, gazing at me with a puzzled expression.

"And you didn't call me?"

"No, I was with Reed and didn't need…" I broke off my sentence realizing what I was about to say.

"You didn't need me," she finished. "Sasha, do you understand the importance of this?"

"I'm transferring trust?"

She nodded. "I'm more concerned with the fact you saw another murder through the victim's eyes. I think it's time you called the parapsychologist. You *are* experiencing a kind of possession."

That was not what I wanted to hear. "Linnie, I

123

can't deal with paranoia and evil spirits right now."

"Not all possession is evil spirits. It isn't always Amityville. Call. Let Dr. Silberstein hypnotize you."

I shook my head. "Not now. Maybe in a couple of days."

"You might not have another couple of days. How many body finding visions are still to come?"

That thought had crossed my mind, too, yet I still hesitated. "If Reed finds Bridget's body, I'll call."

"Promise?"

"Promise," I replied, crossing my heart.

Our food arrived. I took a moment to lean over and inhale the aroma of perfectly cooked ribs. There's no place in the world like Memphis for barbeque. Sorry North Carolina, Kansas City, and the rest of the South, but Memphis wins. I didn't even count Texas. They barbeque beef and everybody knows real barbeque is pig. Famous as he was, Elvis stuck around all those years for it. Well, that and the fried peanut butter and banana sandwiches.

I tore off a rib and chomped down, ripping the meat from the bone. The sauce dribbled down my chin. I wiped it with my finger, and then popped it into my mouth, the tangy flavor tickling my taste buds into overdrive.

Linnie wasn't doing a bad job with her slab, either. In fact, she was two ribs ahead of me and had reduced her small pot of baked beans by half. I prefer cole slaw. We ate like a couple of pack animals for a while until the lack of conversation got on my nerves.

I tossed another denuded bone onto the growing pile and asked, "So, are you and Jeff becoming an item?"

She stopped gnawing and smiled. "Maybe."

"Dr. Anderson, 'maybe' is an evasion."

Linnie laughed and sucked barbeque sauce from her fingers. "Okay, I saw him last night. He came over to the house, and I fed him spaghetti."

"I can top that. Reed spent the night."

She dropped the rib, staring, her eyes wide. "You and Reed did it?"

"He slept on the sofa and made breakfast this morning." I picked up another rib and nibbled.

"And that's all?"

"Well, he did kiss me."

"And?"

"My toes are singed and still tingling."

I felt like I was back in high school playing kiss and tell, and then realized I wouldn't be engaged in the silly game if my relationship with Reed hadn't taken a turn for the serious. For me, relationships were few and far between.

"Okay, I told. It's your turn."

Linnie laughed. "Jeff and I made out like a couple of teenagers, but that's all. Actually, he was kind of upset about finding the woman's body in the river. He talked a lot. He's worried about Reed. He thinks this latest death is fueling the serial killer theory. *I* think he's concerned Reed may be right, and a serial killer is on the loose."

"He was surprised to see me at the scene. I told him about the vision."

"I know, he mentioned it. He asked me a lot of questions regarding you and your abilities. I reminded him I couldn't tell him anything. He said he wanted to talk to you privately soon."

"I don't like so many people knowing. It makes me feel like a freak."

"Will you stop using that word? You have a power some people consider a gift from God. Think of all the parents of missing children who would love to have the ability to find their kids. I think you should make yourself available to the police. They have a lot of unsolved crimes on their books."

I polished off the last rib and drained my iced tea.

"You could be right. When this is over, I'll think about it."

"Just like you're going to think about calling Dr. Silberstein?"

"I said I would." My voice rose. I didn't like being nagged, even if it was for my own good. "Linnie, let's not argue. You may be my friend and shrink, but you're not me. I have to work up the courage—even to admit the truth."

She used a wet nap on her fingers. I gave up trying to clean my hands. No matter how many washings with soap and water or wet naps, the barbeque smell clings for days—thank goodness.

"I'm sorry, Sasha. I know this isn't easy. Jeff was upset, too. I guess finding a dead body floating downstream is traumatic even for police officers."

"Please, don't refer to her as 'the body.' She has a name, Kathy Watson. She lived, she died a horrible death, and I feel like I know her."

The waitress brought the check and Linnie slapped a couple of twenties down on the table with a frown. Her actions irritated me, as though she disapproved of my words.

"What's the problem? Am I wrong to regard her as

a human being? I'm sorry. I can't think of her as a statistic. Maybe that's why I never assisted the authorities. To them, they're *all* just another dead body."

Linnie didn't answer. A furrow crept across her brow. "Kathy Watson, Kathy Watson. Why does that name sound familiar?"

"I may have mentioned it. Or perhaps Jeff did."

"Maybe." She paused. "No, it's something else. Give me a while. It'll come to me."

We slid from the booth and out the door into the parking lot. Why is it some people have all the luck? Linnie had found a space near the front of the restaurant. My Saturn was on the end of the outer perimeter. She stood like a statue next to her car, her face blank, making no effort to get in. Then she turned to gaze at me.

"Kathy Watson," she murmured again, biting her lower lip. "Sasha, I may have known a Kathy Watson. A couple of years ago, I think I had a patient by that name."

Chapter Nine

"Good God, Linnie, are you sure Kathy Watson was a patient?" I asked, thunderstruck at the idea.

"No, but it's so familiar. What else could it be? Kathy Watson isn't an unusual name. Maybe I'm thinking of another woman."

I ran around to the passenger side and jumped in. "Come on. Let's check your files. If it's true, then Reed needs to know."

Linnie slid behind the wheel and took her time inserting the key in the ignition, then fastening her seat belt. She started the car and hesitated.

"Shouldn't I contact the police instead of Reed, assuming Kathy Watson was a patient?"

I sat up straight with surprise. "Linnie, what are you saying? That Reed shouldn't be told? That's crazy. He's desperate to find the killer."

"Reed is obsessed with finding a serial killer, has been for years. Not everybody buys into his philosophy."

"I thought you were on his side."

"Sasha, it's not about taking sides. Reed may be right, but if Kathy was my patient, the police need to be notified first."

"Well, there's nothing to stop *me* from telling him," I exclaimed with some heat.

"Are you sure you're not letting Reed's obsession rub off on you? Don't forget, you're involved with her death, too, even if it is in a cerebral way."

"How do you explain my connection to Bridget Connor? Or am I possessed by more than one entity?" I tried, but failed to keep the tartness from my voice.

"Sasha, don't get angry." She jammed the gear lever into reverse. "Let's head back to my office and see if we can find Kathy Watson. This whole argument may be moot."

Linnie was right. If Kathy had been a patient, then the police should be called first. I'd take care of informing Reed. He may have been obsessed, but in my opinion, he was right.

We caught all the lights green and pulled into Linnie's spot in the parking garage.

"Hello, gorgeous," Jeff said as we entered the office.

He sat on the edge of Janine's desk, a grin on his face. I glanced at the receptionist. Her cheeks glowed bright pink. I assumed Jeff was being Jeff and flirting. I wanted to tell Janine she was out of her league.

"Jeff, what are you doing here?" Linnie asked.

He stood and lightly kissed her lips. "I was feeling kind of low and thought the company of a beautiful woman would cheer me up. The fact I've found three is a bonus."

Janine blushed pinker, I snorted, and Linnie rolled her eyes.

"Come on, Casanova, into my office before Sasha dies laughing and Janine self-combusts."

Jeff and I followed her through the door while Janine resumed typing. Linnie tossed her purse onto her desk and asked, "Why are you so down?"

Jeff ran his hands through his hair and sat in a chair. "I had to interview Kathy Watson's family today. They came to claim the body. It wasn't pleasant."

"No, I don't imagine it was. Why don't you tell me about it?"

"Why don't I leave the two of you alone?" I murmured, turning toward the door.

"No, stay, Sasha. You're involved in this, too," he said.

I glanced at Linnie who shrugged and sat on the sofa while I took the remaining chair.

"What's wrong, Jeff?" she asked.

"Reed may be right. I had a long talk with Kathy's parents and brothers. There are disturbing similarities between her death and the deaths of several others."

"How?" I leaned forward, gazing into his gray-green eyes. "Have you talked to Reed today?"

"No. I haven't contacted him yet." He shook his head. "Her mother said Kathy had been dating a man from work. She thought it was becoming serious, so was surprised when her daughter broke it off a few weeks ago."

"Let me guess, she found a new guy?" I said.

"Her sister-in-law told me Kathy called last week full of news about her new boyfriend, a guy named Gerald—no last name. Said she sounded in love and happy as a lark."

"Oh, dear, that does fit the pattern, doesn't it?" Linnie murmured. "What else did they tell you?"

"According to her father, his daughter was making plans to bring this guy home to meet the family. He kind of assumed that meant this was more than just a casual relationship."

"I'd say that sounds familiar," I stated. "It follows the rest of what the girls told family members and friends. Now what?"

I jumped with surprise when my cell rang before he could answer. I fumbled in my purse, found it, and flipped it open. "Hello?"

"Hi, Sasha, it's Reed. I just wanted to know if you're available for dinner tonight. It's been a long day and I could use some company."

"Dinner? Sure, I guess so. How goes the search?"

"Not good. I'll tell you about it when I see you."

"All right, but there have been developments here as well," I told him.

"Who is it?" Jeff asked.

"It's Reed," I answered.

"Who's with you? Where are you?" Reed asked.

"Jeff. He and I are with Linnie at her office."

"What kind of developments?"

"Let me talk to him," Jeff demanded.

Trying to carry on a three way conversation was confusing. I relinquished the phone to Jeff.

"Reed, I talked to Kathy Watson's family today. It looks like you may be right. There are way too many similarities…I agree. Let's get together…Marilyn and I can join you two for dinner if that's all right with Sasha." He tossed me a glance and I nodded. "It's okay with her…All right, we'll meet you there. So long."

He handed the phone back to me. "He suggested The Welcome Mat at six-thirty. Is that okay with the two of you?"

"Fine with me," Linnie said.

"Me, too," I echoed. "He sounded tired. He's been

searching for hours."

"Searching for what?" Jeff asked.

I told him about my newest vision and the unsettling consequences. "I just wish I could have been more specific."

"Marilyn, hypnotize her. Sasha could have stored up information we need."

"No, Jeff. I can't. I've had two gruesome visions in the last few days, plus I just quit my job. I can't handle any more stress. I'd never go under."

"Are you sure? Try! It might work," he urged.

"No, honey, I have to agree with Sasha on this. We'll try tomorrow or the next day. In the meantime, we have news for you. Kathy Watson may have been a patient."

"What! When?"

"I don't remember when or even if." She picked up the phone and punched one of the buttons. "Janine, would you come in for a moment, please."

A few seconds later, her receptionist walked through the door with a steno pad and a pencil in hand.

"Janine, does the name Kathy Watson mean anything to you?" Linnie asked.

"Not off the top of my head. Why?"

"She was murdered a few days ago. The name sounds familiar and I thought perhaps she was a patient, but if you can't remember, then I guess she wasn't."

"How long ago would she have been here?" Janine asked. "If it's been over two years, then I wouldn't recognize the name."

"I'm not sure. It could have been a while."

"Let me search the computer and the old files. It shouldn't take but a few minutes."

"Wait a minute, Janine," Jeff said. "Marilyn, do the names Mary Alice Maghee, Melissa Tallmadge, Jennifer Randall, Susan Parker, or Bridget Connor ring a bell?"

"Only Bridget's, and I heard it for the first time the other day. Why?"

"You see a lot of people. If any of those women came for a consultation, you might not remember. Janine would you please check on those names as well?" he asked.

He repeated the information, his brow furrowed as if in thought as Janine wrote.

"Mary Alice Maghee, Melissa Tallmadge, Jennifer Randall, Susan Parker, and Bridget Connor. I'll be as fast as I can," she repeated leaving the room.

A sudden shaft of fear sliced through me.

"Jeff, what's on your mind?" Linnie demanded.

"I don't know. Just a hunch. Let's see what Janine turns up." He glanced at his watch. "I need to touch base with the station. I'll be back in a few minutes."

He exited the room, leaving Linnie and me staring at each other.

"I'm getting a really bad feeling about this," I said.

"So am I." She lifted the phone again. "Janine, cancel the rest of my appointments for the day. Thanks."

"You didn't have to do that."

"It's only two people and I'd make a lousy psychiatrist today. You're having visions, Reed's off searching for a body, I may have known one of the victims, and now Jeff is acting all mysterious and cop-like." She worried her lower lip.

"Why don't I make us some coffee? Or would you

133

prefer tea?"

She smiled. "Tea would be wonderful."

While I put the kettle on and arranged the cups, Linnie pawed through her desk. Not finding what she sought, she moved on to the credenza. From one of the drawers she yanked out a large notebook.

"What's that?"

"One of my old appointment books. Maybe I can find Kathy's name in it."

She ran her finger down the pages, and then flipped them over, pausing every now and again at one of the names listed.

"Damn, what did I do before Janine arrived?" she muttered.

"You forgot appointments and transcribed your own notes. You worked sixty-hour weeks, lived on junk food, and used what free time you *did* have to hang out with the wrong men. I was there."

"I was also struggling to build a practice."

"You had a good practice. You were just too cheap to shell out for a receptionist. If I hadn't contacted the secretarial school, you'd still be floundering in paper."

"I can't believe how disorganized I was. I can barely read some of this."

She reached the end of the ledger, tossed it back into the drawer, and pulled out another one.

"How old are those books?"

"Four years. So far I haven't seen anything familiar, except for you and Reed."

The kettle whistled. I poured the hot water over the tea bags and carried one to her.

"Here. Forget searching for a while. Janine's ten times more organized than you. If there's anything to find, she'll do it."

"I suppose you're right."

We took the next ten minutes to drink and discuss the eventful day. We were verbally abusing my former boss when Jeff returned. He refused tea, but accepted a bottle of water. A few minutes later, Janine opened the door. She held three files in her hand.

"I found Kathy Watson. She was a patient a couple of months before I started working here." She handed one of the files to Linnie. "I also found something on Jennifer Randall and Susan Parker."

"What?" Linnie yelped. "I don't remember them at all."

"Well, technically they were your patients, but they never had an office appointment."

"How can that be?" Jeff asked.

"In my early years, I did a lot of work at clinics and rehab. I quit about three years ago when my practice started growing."

"You mean they were in group therapy?" I asked.

"Is that the case, Janine?"

"Yes. There are just a few notes." She handed over the rest of the folders and left. Linnie read quickly.

"Jennifer Randall was in a rehab group almost six years ago. I can't remember a thing about her. According to my notes, she kicked her coke habit and was released." She laid the folder aside and opened another. Jeff picked it up and read while Linnie continued. "Susan Parker was in group therapy three and a half years ago. She shoplifted. I do kind of remember her. She dealt with stress by stealing."

"What about Kathy?"

Linnie flipped through the file notes. "She was

only here for four visits. Self-esteem problems. It says here she ended her sessions in a better frame of mind and able to cope with her feelings of inadequacy. That's it."

"Did she also attend group therapy?" I asked.

"Yes. Office visits were on Mondays and group was held on Thursday nights."

Jeff took the folder and leafed through it, a frown furrowing his forehead. "Marilyn, you know what this means, don't you?"

"What?"

"It means the killer could be one of your patients."

Her eyes widened. "You can't be serious."

"But I am. He could have been in a group or have access to your files."

"No way, Jeff. First of all not all groups have the same make up. Jennifer was addicted to cocaine. Susan stole. Kathy had self-esteem problems."

"He still could have had contact with Kathy through group," Jeff insisted.

Linnie shook her head. "No. While men have self-esteem problems, and there are mixed groups, Kathy's group was all women who had a history of getting dumped or beat up by their boyfriends. Sorry, you'll have to look elsewhere."

"I still say it's a patient. One who is accessing your files, looking for vulnerable women."

"Only Janine and I have the passwords to the computer, and the file drawers are locked."

"Any dedicated hacker can sneak past codes and keys can be duplicated or stolen. We're dealing with a highly intelligent killer," he reminded her.

"There's more than one password and only Janine

and I have the keys."

"Jeff, if that's the case how come not all the victims are Linnie's patients?" I asked.

"I don't know. Maybe some are people he just met, like that bimbo at the casino. Who knows? Honey, I'm going to need your patient list."

"I can't do that," she protested. "These are confidential files."

"I'm not talking specifics. I don't care why they're seeing you, I just want the names."

"No. End of discussion." Linnie snatched the files back from his hand. "You shouldn't have seen these."

"What does it matter? The women are dead."

It was the first time I'd heard Jeff sounding so cold and insensitive.

"Jeff, I'm not sure I want you to read my file. And I think Reed would rather his information didn't go any further than Linnie," I told him.

"I could get a court order," Jeff said.

"Then get the fucking court order," Linnie replied in a hard tone.

A wave of energy, not unlike that when I'd first viewed the photos, pulsed through the air. Fear? Anxiety? Anger? It vanished as quickly as it came before I could identify the source. Linnie? Jeff? Or one of the dead women in the files?

Jeff ran his hand through his hair and clenched his jaw. "Okay, you win for now. I've got to get back to the station. I'll pick you up at six-fifteen, all right?"

Linnie nodded. He kissed her and left the room.

"Brother, what a day," I said.

"Are you kidding? What a week. I feel like I've been run over by a steam roller. And we still have to get through tonight."

"Why is this happening now?"

"What do you mean?"

I finished my cooling tea. "Would Kathy have tapped into my mind if I had paid more attention to Philip and investment banking instead of gazing at that painting?"

"I don't know. The reality is it happened."

"Then how come I haven't…" I paused seeking the right words, "…heard from her in over forty-eight hours?"

"I can't answer that, either. Maybe, because her body's been found, she had some sort of closure. Maybe because Bridget Connor appeared."

"Swell, spooks are taking numbers and forming a line."

Linnie sighed. "Call Dr. Silberstein. He can delve into this better than I."

"I will. Honest. I'm just too tired to deal with much else other than dinner tonight." I massaged the back of my neck. "Jeff was forceful, wasn't he?"

She nibbled on the tip of her pen. "He certainly was. He should know about the doctor-patient privilege. I'm sure he's run into it before. This is the first time he's been anything other than charming."

"He was on the job and you…we got in the way. He'll probably be back to normal tonight."

"He'd better be, because I'm not giving him or anyone else my patient's names," she said with a frown, tossing the pen on the desk. "Oh, hell, I'm exhausted. I'm going home, have an adult beverage, and soak in the Jacuzzi. I might even be human by dinner time."

I looked at my watch. "It's almost four. I should

get back to my place. I wouldn't mind a little downtime myself. Can you give me a lift back to Ribs and Ribs? My car's there."

We stopped by Janine's desk on the way out.

"Janine, finish up those notes and put them on my credenza, and don't forget to re-file the ones you pulled. Then, call it a day and go home."

"Thanks, Dr. Anderson. I'm almost done. By the way, I rescheduled Mr. Jenkins for eleven o'clock next Tuesday and Mrs. Hardaway for two-thirty Wednesday."

"Thanks, Janine. Have a good evening. I'll see you in the morning."

"Same to you. Goodnight, Miss Bellwood."

"Good night, Janine."

As I got in Linnie's car, a ripple of concern flowed through me. I suppressed a shiver. Something in the air just didn't feel right. I had no idea what or why.

****

The minute I walked into The Welcome Mat, I sensed the night would be a disaster. I was the first to arrive, requesting a table for four. Reed had called earlier to say he was running late and asked me to meet him at the restaurant.

The Welcome Mat was one of the few moderately priced restaurants in Germantown. After being seated, I took a moment to look the place over. The large room accommodated booths along the perimeter with tables in between. The bar was located along the back wall. Muted lighting set a pleasant ambiance, and the upholstered chairs were soft.

A waiter stopped by. I ordered a glass of Pinot Grigio from a well-appointed wine list and sat back to wait.

Reed walked through the door ten minutes later, making a beeline for me. I deliberately tapped into his emotions. He was discouraged and depressed. The search had not gone well. He was also dog tired, not a surprise considering the last couple of days.

"Sorry to keep you waiting," he said, pulling out a chair.

"No problem. You look bushed. Bad day?"

"Depressingly uneventful."

"Tell me."

"Might as well wait until Jeff and Marilyn get here."

"They're here now," I said, nodding toward the doors.

I didn't have to tap into emotions to know the two had been arguing. Linnie's smile was tight and Jeff's movements stiff. My first impression of the evening was right on.

"Sorry we're late," Jeff said. "I got tied up in traffic."

"That's all right. I just got here," Reed replied.

The waiter appeared and took the rest of the drink orders. Linnie, a wine drinker, demanded a martini, and Jeff a draft beer. Reed opted for his usual vodka and tonic. When our server left, an uncomfortable silence descended.

To break it, I asked Reed, "Tell us about your search. I take it you didn't find anything."

"Not a damned thing. One subdivision with an earthen berm was located next to I-40. Definitely not in your description. Another was adjacent to a golf course and had no road running next to it. Also not in your vision. The third and fourth were recent construction, and the fifth was an office complex with no wooded area in sight."

He spoke crisply as though it was my fault. Guilt rose like it always did when I was unable to help, but this time I put his words down to frustration and didn't allow the guilt to remain.

"Maybe it has nothing to do with houses or noise abatement," Jeff said. "Maybe it's just a hill. There are some around, you know."

"You think we're over-analyzing the vision?" I asked.

"That's a possibility."

"Your visions are usually clear, but then we're moving into uncharted territory," Linnie offered.

The waiter arrived with our drinks. Linnie immediately ordered a second and took a huge gulp of her martini. Jeff bolted down half his beer, while Reed took a long swallow of his drink. I sipped. I had the feeling I was the only one in emotional control.

"Well, Linnie and I had an interesting day," I said.

"How?" Reed asked.

I told him about quitting my job along with the news three of the murder victims had been Linnie's patients.

"And I still say turning over your patient list to the police will do no harm." Jeff glared at Linnie.

"And I say, no way in hell." Linnie drained her martini and set the glass on the table with a hard click.

"We're talking murder. The killer has to be someone you've treated. May still be treating. For all we know this maniac has a record of violence toward women."

The waiter brought her other drink. She picked it up and gulped. The rest of us ordered seconds, too.

"Have you guys been arguing about this all the way here?" I asked.

"Pretty much," Jeff said.

"You were fifteen minutes late picking me up," Linnie countered.

"I told you, an accident on Walnut Grove had traffic tied up."

"You could have called."

Jeff drained his beer. "This has nothing to do with my being late. You're pissed because you know I'm right about the killer being one of your patients. All I want is a list of names. I'll run them through the computer and see if there are any priors."

"No fucking way!"

Linnie's voice rose and her comment stopped conversation at nearby tables. People stared.

I almost gasped at the sensation of icy rage that pummeled me like a battering ram. Emotions were running so high I couldn't tell from whom the anger emanated. Reed frowned. Jeff scowled, his lips set in a thin line. Linnie's expression resembled a thundercloud, her eyes shooting sparks of lightning.

Then, as quickly as it came, the rage disappeared. Reed spoke first.

"Lower your voices. We're in a public place. Marilyn's right, Jeff. Her patients come to her with an expectation of confidentiality. Even a court order could damage her practice. On the other hand, there's nothing saying she can't go through her list of patients and cross match group sessions. If the same name turns up, she can notify you."

Jeff's tense face relaxed. "That might work."

"Plus, some of the people are dead. Doesn't the doctor-patient relationship end with that?" I asked.

Linnie's expression also softened. "And the law does allow me to break doctor-patient confidentiality if I think lives are at stake."

"There, problem solved," I said as the waiter returned with our drinks. "Why don't we order?"

The time it took to make food selections gave us all a much needed breathing space. By the time we finished, Linnie and Jeff were smiling.

"I'm sorry for nagging you, honey. The Watson case has me tied up in knots," he said.

"I'm sorry, too. You're right. I *am* worried the killer could be a patient." Linnie patted his hand.

"Okay, I think we've talked this subject to death," I said. "Jeff, is there anything new with Kathy's case? Any suspects?"

He shook his head. "None. We do have the results from the lab on the sweatshirt fished out of the river. The bloodstains were probably Kathy's and we got a couple of hairs from the collar. Won't do much good. Any sweat or skin cells remaining could give us DNA, but the water and the silt of the river hopelessly compromised everything."

"Anything about the sweatshirt itself?" Reed asked.

"Nothing special. The label is the kind sold by discount stores across the country and the size, large, is common."

"So, it's a dead end?" I inquired.

"We'll try, but like I said, the river didn't do us any favors. A good defense attorney will get it tossed in a heartbeat."

"Damn, I had hoped," Reed muttered.

Maybe it was the talk about the river that brought an image slashing in front of my eyes. I picked up my glass with shaking fingers and sipped the wine.

"You know, maybe the hill in my vision had nothing to do with noise abatement."

Three pairs of eyes swiveled in my direction.

"What do you mean?" Reed said. His brow furrowed.

I drummed my fingers on the table while I tried to organize my thoughts. I remembered the shadows lurking in my mind from earlier. I hadn't grasped the significance then, but the mention of water revealed them.

"Have you seen something?" Linnie questioned.

"What is it?" Jeff put in.

"The mention of water got me thinking. Other than the bluffs along the Mississippi and Crowley's Ridge down in Desoto County, the terrain is as flat as my Aunt Minnie's chest. Suppose the hill I saw is connected to water."

"You mean like a dam or a levee?" Reed asked.

"Could be." I sipped my wine again.

"Levee as in the Mississippi?" Linnie said.

"I don't know. I don't see water, just the hill. And in my dream I was thirsty. I had the sensation that water was nearby. That's what I searched for."

"There are several manmade lakes in the area," Jeff said.

"And if not a dam, it could be a retention hill. With the land so flat, the water has to be held by something." Reed turned to me. "Sasha, think hard and describe the hill again."

I closed my eyes, taking a deep breath. "All right, keep in mind that I'm viewing this from about ten feet above the action. Yes, the hill is higher than my head. The trees are various heights, but some are quite large." My eyes snapped open. "Of course! The road is dirt or gravel. There'd be no need for any kind of noise abatement."

"So, we should be looking along the river. All kinds of roads follow the levees," Reed suggested.

"Or for a lake or a pond," I said, pausing. "I don't think we're dealing with a Mississippi River levee. Those suckers are twenty-five, thirty feet high. This one's no more than fifteen. It's probably restraining something manmade."

"You mean like Arkabutla or Sardis?" Linnie asked, naming two local lakes.

"There's Lake Enid and Lake Grenada, too," Jeff added.

Reed shook his head. "Too much traffic. Too many campsites. Enid and Granada are too far away. The killer would want to dispose of the body close to the killing site. We're looking for a much smaller lake. Maybe something on private property."

"So, where does that leave us?" I asked. "There must be hundreds of private lakes in the area."

"My guess is the killer used either I-40 or Stage Road to leave the mall with Bridget. He parked somewhere, produced an already drugged wine, killed her, and then buried her close by. He'd have a hard time explaining a dead body in the front seat if he got stopped for a minor traffic violation."

"And the grave was already dug. The less time with a body, the less likely he'd get caught," I said.

145

"I'll search tomorrow in Lakeland, and then move north and east," Reed stated with new hope in his eyes. "First thing in the morning, I'll get online and scope out all the lakes and ponds fitting your description."

"Wish I could go with you, but I'm working a case in South Memphis. I have to interview potential witnesses all day," Jeff said.

Our food arrived: steaks for the men, salmon for me, and seafood salad for Linnie. We ate in silence, and while the fish was delicious, my enjoyment was tempered by the return of the uneasiness I experienced leaving Linnie's office. I tried to dismiss it as the previous gruesome conversation, but finally gave up.

I lowered my knife and fork before saying, "Something is not right."

Everybody ceased chewing to stare with varying expressions from questioning to anxious to fearful.

"What do you mean, not right?" Reed asked.

Jeff gave me a hard look.

Linnie swallowed and said, "Sasha, are you having another vision?"

I shook my head. "Not exactly."

"Not exactly?" Jeff echoed.

"It's more of a feeling than a vision. I'm not sure I can describe it. It's like a disturbance in the…" I paused seeking the right terminology.

"If you say the force, I swear I'll hurt you," Reed told me.

"Well, I'm sorry, but that's what it is. I can't describe what I don't understand. I felt it off and on for the last couple of days, and earlier when we left your office, Linnie. Oh!" I exclaimed. Still pictures like photographs flipped through my mind. "Oh, dear."

"What? Sasha, stop the dramatics and tell us what you see," Jeff demanded.

I ignored him, and gazed at my best friend.

"I see a woman." Before I could say any more, the images intensified. My vision dimmed and my ears buzzed.

I was going under, and there wasn't a damned thing I could do about it.

Chapter Ten

"Sasha!"

"Oh, my God!"

"Leave her alone!"

I heard my dining companions' comments, which told me I wasn't far under. And the images flashing across my mind were still, not moving. I wasn't viewing things through someone else's eyes. Even so, what I saw was scary.

Gradually, the pictures faded and the sounds of the restaurant returned to normal. My vision cleared. Reed, Jeff, and Linnie stared at me with a mixture of expectation, fear, and worry on their faces.

I licked my dry lips and sagged back in my chair.

Linnie reached out as though fearing I might topple onto the floor. "Are you all right?"

I nodded and straightened, then grabbed my wine glass and drained the remains before turning my attention to the water set at my place. God, I was thirsty.

"What did you see?" Jeff and Reed said at the same time.

"Let's get out of here. I'll help her to the car. You guys take care of the check," Linnie said, pushing back her chair.

"No, I'm all right. I just wish these damned things

would quit popping in and out in restaurants. I'd like to enjoy a meal for a change. Besides, I want to tell you what I saw while it's still fresh."

"More about Bridget?" Reed asked.

"Kathy?" from Jeff.

I inhaled a couple of cleansing breaths. "I'm back to photographs. They flipped by so fast I only saw a portion of them. A woman met a man and got into his car. She knew him and wasn't afraid. That much I got. The rest was all a jumble, but I know something bad may have happened."

"*May* have happened?" Reed questioned.

"As I said, the images rushed by. I felt more than I saw."

"What did you feel?" Linnie asked.

"Frustration, relief, fear, rage, and satisfaction all rolled into one. I'm not sure, but I may have made contact with the killer."

Linnie gasped and Reed's eyes went wide.

"Can you ID the woman? Where this vision occurred?" Jeff inquired, his voice sharp.

"The background's dark and dingy. Nothing is recognizable."

I didn't want to go on because I didn't want to believe. Then Reed asked the same question as Jeff.

"Can you identify the woman? Was it Eleanor?"

"No. It wasn't Eleanor." I turned my gaze to Linnie. "Oh, God, Linnie, I'm so sorry. It was Janine."

She sucked in a started breath, and then let it out in a rush. "Are you sure? Janine?"

I nodded, blinking back tears.

"Check," Reed barked at our passing waiter.

Shaking and pale as a ghost, Linnie snatched her

cell phone from her purse. She dialed and waited for several seconds. "Hello, Janine? It's Dr. Anderson. If you're there, please pick up...Janine, *please*, it's important...Okay, maybe you're in the bathroom or taking a walk. Call me back immediately. I *have* to hear from you."

She hung up and bit her lip. "She didn't answer. I'll try her cell, but she usually turns it off at night."

I hoped that was the case when Linnie left another message in Janine's voice mail.

The waiter brought our check. Reed and Jeff tossed several bills onto the table and rose.

"Let's go. Where does Janine live?" Reed asked.

"Bartlett. She rents a small house on Fillmore Street. I'm not sure of the exact address. I drove her home once when her car was in the shop," Linnie replied. "Shouldn't we call the police?"

"Honey, I am the police," Jeff told her.

"And tell them what? That she might be in danger because Sasha had a vision?" Reed said. "For all we know she could have met a friend and is getting tight at the nearest bar. The only danger she may be experiencing is one hell of a hangover. Can you walk?"

He sounded like a man desperately wanting to believe what he'd just said.

I nodded, but he slipped his arm around my waist anyway, and we rushed from the restaurant to his car.

"Marilyn, you and Jeff lead. We'll follow."

Bartlett is due north of Germantown and we covered the short distance quickly. It took longer to find Fillmore Street. We cruised up and down several blocks numerous times until finally stopping in front of a white clapboard house with green shutters and azaleas growing under the front windows.

We piled out of the cars and stared at the darkened home. No outside light glowed by the front porch and the interior was blacker than the night. A streetlamp a couple of houses away provided dappled shadows as it shone through the leaves of the trees.

"Is this it?" Reed asked.

Linnie nodded. "Yes. I remember the azaleas and the walkway from the drive. There's a detached garage around back."

"I'll go check it out," Jeff said, leaving us standing on the sidewalk.

"She's not here," I said softly.

"She could be inside, hurt or…or worse," Linnie commented with a sob.

"Don't jump to conclusions," Reed said. "Maybe she's gone to bed."

"It's barely nine o'clock," I replied.

Reed crossed the yard and mounted the front steps, then knocked on the door. Linnie and I followed. No lights flashed on and no sound came from within. Jeff rejoined us.

"Garage is locked and empty," he reported. "Maybe Reed's right and she's with friends."

Reed tried the front door. "It's locked. Jeff did you check out the back door?"

"Yeah, it's locked, too."

"*Now* do we call the police?" Linnie begged.

"Sasha, think. You said the background of the vision was dark and dingy. Can you be more specific?" Reed questioned me.

"I don't know. It was just dark. Gray and cold. It could have been cement, I suppose, like the side of a building." I paused and held up my hand for silence, then closed my eyes to concentrate. "I sensed other cars nearby."

"A parking garage?" he pressed.

"I don't know!" My voice rose in frustration. "It's possible."

"A parking garage?" Linnie whispered, her hand at her throat. "Oh, no."

"The office," Jeff said. "We're at the wrong place."

We hurried back to the street and the cars.

"Sasha, can you drive?" Reed asked.

"Yes. I'm all right—really."

"Good. We'll go back to the restaurant and pick up our cars. You and Marilyn follow Jeff and me. We'll probably be parting company tonight."

We drove quickly back to the restaurant. Jeff helped Linnie into my car, and then he and Reed took off, following each other at a fast clip. I tried to keep up with them, but my driving skills are more along the little old lady lines. The other two cars rapidly outpaced me. Linnie cried most of the way.

"Come on, honey, pull yourself together. Maybe my psychic abilities are on overload and I've crossed my wires. There could be nothing to this. How much do you know about Janine's personal life?"

"She doesn't have one. She sends most of her paycheck to her family and rarely goes out. I remember her saying her father is on disability and her mother has major health problems. God Almighty, the poor girl drives a ten-year-old Toyota Corolla she bought used. Her budget is so tight she sometimes eats leftovers from a Sunday meal the rest of the week."

Linnie sniffed and blew her nose. If Janine was that

short of cash, then a drinking spree with friends was out of the question. Foreboding pressed on my chest, and I shivered.

We pulled up to Linnie's office building where Jeff and Reed, parked near the entrance to the garage, met us.

"There's no attendant," Jeff said. "How do we get in?"

"We did away with the attendant several years ago and went to swipe cards. There were barely enough spaces for employees, let alone visitors. Now, visitors use the lot and enter by the front doors."

"So only employees use the garage?" Jeff asked.

"To the best of my knowledge. I mean, I don't see how a visitor could get in without the card."

"So, swipe us in," Reed demanded.

"I can't. The card's in my car."

"Did you call this in?" I asked.

Jeff shook his head. "Not yet. Let's see what we find here first. If her car's gone, there's no use in cops showing up."

While we'd been talking, Linnie had fished her keys out of her purse while striding to the front doors. She unlocked it, and we trouped to the elevator. The trip to the third floor was silent.

Linnie unlocked the door and flipped on the light. The outer room was empty, as was her office.

"She's not here," I said, using the same words I had at the house.

"Did you expect her to be?" Reed replied in an impatient tone. "Marilyn, I assume this building has security of some sort."

"I think a car comes around several times a night."

"How about cameras? Any in the parking garage?"

"Yes. One at the entrance and two on each level. Do you think…"

"Call the security company now," Jeff ordered. "I want those tapes removed immediately. Tell them it's a matter of life and death. Reed, let's go check out the garage."

"Right. You two stay here and lock the door."

"Wait a minute," I protested. "Why can't we go with you? Four pairs of eyes can see twice as much as two."

"And two pairs of feet untrained in police procedures can trample evidence. Make some coffee. We'll be back," Jeff ordered, his voice harsh.

They left, and Linnie turned the key in the lock.

"Swell. I'm sick to my stomach, worried to death, and have now been relegated to the level of little woman," she fumed.

"Jeff's right. Evidence in these cases has been almost nil. Come on, let's make coffee and call the security company."

The security company refused Linnie's request. Cursing, she hung up, called Jeff on his cell, told him the situation, and gave him the number. Ten minutes later the two of them returned to the office.

"Are they coming?" I asked.

"Yeah," Jeff replied with a grunt. "I told them this was an official police investigation. A car should be here soon."

"Did you find anything in the garage?" I asked.

"Yes," Reed answered. "One car and a potato."

"A potato?" I hadn't expected to hear that.

"What the hell does that have to do with

anything?" Linnie demanded.

Reed tossed a medium-sized Idaho on her desk, one end black with carbon.

"One of the oldest tricks in the world," he said. "A potato shoved up the tailpipe and your car won't start."

"And you found this in Janine's tailpipe?" Linnie asked, poking at it with a pencil.

"The Corolla was unlocked. The registration says Janine Henderson," Jeff said in clipped tones.

I sensed the anger boiling inside him. I think we all knew we were dealing with murder, but no one wanted to say the word out loud.

"I guess this means she didn't go out for drinks with friends," I murmured, blinking tears from my eyes.

No one replied. They didn't have to. Linnie rose and ran for her private bath. We heard her retching through the closed door. She came out wiping her mouth and the tears from her cheeks.

A loud knock on the outer door startled me, and I couldn't prevent a little squeak from passing my lips. I was even more astonished to see both Jeff and Reed, pull guns as they headed for the door.

"It's probably the security company," Jeff said. He positioned himself flat against the wall behind the entry while Reed cracked the door, his gun concealed along his right thigh.

"Yes?"

"East Memphis Security," came a reply.

The guns disappeared, Jeff's into his shoulder holster and Reed's into his pocket. Reed opened the door. Two men stood on the other side, one in uniform and the other in street clothes. The uniform spoke first.

"My name's Hopewell. I understand you have a

problem on the third parking level."

"Yes," Jeff said, showing the men his badge. "We need the tape from the cameras on that level and from the entrance pulled. We have a missing person and think she may have been abducted sometime after four."

The other man spoke up. "My name's Grayson. I'm the technician. You're lucky. Those cameras have a twenty-four hour loop starting at midnight."

"Then what are we waiting for? Let's get the tape and bring it back here," Reed said.

"Got a warrant? Can't let you have the tape without one," Grayson said.

"Fine, fine," Jeff snapped. "But we can view it."

Grayson shrugged. "Guess there's no harm in that."

"Hopewell, you have a gun," Reed said eyeing the holster at the man's hip. "Stay with the ladies until we get back."

They left. Hopewell closed the door and sat on the corner of Janine's desk.

"How about a cup of coffee," I offered.

He refused. Linnie and I retreated into the inner office to wait. The men returned with three tapes. Jeff popped one of the cassettes into Linnie's old VCR and hit the "play" button.

The image was typical security camera grade, grainy and not quite in focus. The date and time appeared in the lower right hand corner. Jeff fast forwarded to three-forty-five, paused the action, and then turned to face Linnie.

"Walk us through this. What time did you leave?"

"Around four. Sasha and I drove back from Ribs and Ribs in my car. I wanted to check my files, because

I thought Kathy Watson may have been a patient. You were here, remember? Sasha's car was still parked at the rib joint, so I drove her back to get it."

"Sasha, is that how it happened?" he asked.

"What? You don't believe me?" she said with an indignant tone.

"Everybody sees things differently. Sasha?"

I nodded. "Yes, that's basically the way things went."

"Not basically. *Is* that what happened?" Jeff said.

"Yes!" His tone had sharpened, and I wasn't sure I liked being given the third degree.

"Did you see anybody in the hallway? Did you talk to anyone?"

"We didn't see anyone, and we only talked to Janine when we left," I said.

"You talked to Janine. What about?" Jeff continued to use a no nonsense cop voice. It was intimidating.

Linnie tucked an errant strand of hair back into her French twist.

"I asked her to finish transcribing some notes and to re-file the folders we'd looked at. I told her to go ahead and leave when she finished. She said she didn't have much left to do and wished us a good night."

"That's all?"

"That's it," I said.

"Okay, let's watch the tape," Reed, silent until now, requested in a tired voice.

We all sat on various pieces of furniture, our eyes glued to the TV screen. Jeff hit "play."

The garage was open to the outside with decorative wrought iron grills in the openings, and adjoined the offices it serviced. This gave employees the option of

157

parking on the same level as their business. The camera angle aimed down the drive area toward the elevators and stairwell located next to each other. Only the back or front portions of the parked autos, depending on if they were pulled or backed in, were visible. Of the thirty spaces, twenty-six were shown.

Jeff paused the tape again, turning to Grayson and Hopewell. "This tape doesn't cover the entire level. Why not?"

"The cameras were installed after construction. We found if we put them at the far end, one of the overhead beams blocked out the elevator and stairwell. We felt they were more important than a couple of rows of parking spaces, so we located them on the next beam," Grayson explained.

"Yeah, the only thing you're missing is the drive down from the fourth level," Hopewell added.

Jeff resumed the tape. At that hour of the afternoon there was little activity. A woman exited from the stairwell, walked to her car, and retrieved something from the trunk, then returned the way she'd come. A car rolled down from the fourth floor, continuing out of frame to the second level. At three fifty-five two women emerged from the stairs.

"That's us," Linnie said.

If I hadn't been expecting it, I'd have never recognized myself. The film quality was poor, but I saw nothing suspicious around us. Within a few seconds our car drove away, and then we were treated to ten minutes of boring inactivity. I glanced at Linnie, who was taking a long pull at a bottle of water.

"Who the hell is that?" Reed said.

I turned my attention back to the screen. A man, at

least I assumed it was a man, wearing a long trench coat and a baseball cap slithered around the side of a car. He stooped near the tailpipe, and then rose, backing out the way he'd come.

"I'll be damned," Jeff said.

"He put the potato in the tailpipe," Linnie commented, stating the obvious.

"He just happened to have a potato in his pocket?" I asked in disbelief.

"We are dealing with one very intelligent killer," Reed replied.

I noted his use of the word killer.

"But where did he come from?" Linnie demanded.

"The one place the camera can't see. Play it back, Jeff." We all watched the tape again. "See, he knows to stay out of sight by keeping to the side. Then when he has to show himself, he makes sure his back is toward the camera."

"I don't understand. How did he know which car was Janine's?" I asked.

"Because Reed's right. He's one very smart customer. He cased the place. Probably watched Janine arrive or leave and knew she'd park on the third level. A ten-year-old Toyota isn't hard to find."

"But why?" Linnie cried. "Why pick on Janine?"

"She's young, inexperienced, and privy to information that could seal his fate," Jeff replied.

"How would he know?" she asked.

Reed stood, balling his fists in his pockets. "Me. He knows about my interest in these cases. For all I know he's followed me for months or years. I no longer see Dr. Anderson professionally, but when I suddenly begin showing up at her office, he adds two and two, then realizes that sooner or later a victim's name will trigger a memory."

"And if he's that smart, then seeing me up here is another red flag," Jeff added. He hit the "play" button again. "Let's finish this out."

Linnie jumped to her feet. "I can't watch this."

"Yes, you can. Sit. You may recognize a person or a car," Jeff ordered, his tone brusque.

She obeyed and wiped more tears from her face.

We waited fifteen painful minutes before Janine emerged from the stairwell and got into her car. A minute later, she got out again. Even with the grainy image, I saw her shoulders slump and could almost read her thoughts. On a tight budget, she didn't need auto repairs.

Then a dark colored car pulled up next to her and stopped. It was impossible to see the driver through the tinted rear window, but Janine leaned down, opened the door, and got in.

"Oh, God!" Linnie clapped her hand over her mouth and ran for the bathroom again.

The car remained stationary for several seconds, and then backed out of frame. We watched until five o'clock when employees left. Soon Janine's car stood alone.

"Where did he go?" I asked.

"He left with the rest of the employees," Jeff said. "Several dark cars passed. Pick him out. He knows the video's going to be shitty."

Linnie emerged from the bathroom and sat next to me on the sofa. I put my arm around her shaking shoulders.

"Did you recognize the car?" Jeff asked her.

"No. Do you know how many black or dark colored cars there are? Hell, I drive a dark gray Honda Accord."

"We might be able to see his face from the other camera angle," Reed said.

Jeff nodded and switched the tapes. This camera showed the drive to and from the fourth floor and the last four empty parking spaces. He fast forwarded to four-ten, and we watched a figure, the bill of the baseball cap pulled low, hurry down the fourth level drive, then slide off to the side. A minute later, the trench-coated form ran back the way he'd come.

Jeff advanced the tape up to four-twenty. This time we viewed Janine from another angle. A dark car swung down from the fourth floor and stopped.

We all leaned forward. I held my breath. The tape went opaque.

"What the hell!" Jeff shouted.

"The sun," Reed said. "The sun came through one of the west side windows and glared into the lens." He leaned back and ran his hand through his hair. "Damn!"

"Son of a bitch!" Jeff exploded. He kicked Linnie's desk. "I don't believe this!"

"How can we have such bad luck?" I said with a groan.

"Maybe he planned it that way," Reed muttered.

"Nobody's that meticulous," Jeff snapped.

"Actually, they are," Linnie said. "Obsessive-compulsive behavior has many forms. Doing the same thing at the same time every day isn't unusual. If he feared discovery, he'd take the time to know about camera angles and the sun."

"Which leads me back to this asshole being a

patient," Jeff told her. "Who came to see you yesterday?"

"I had a full load in the morning—an elderly man dealing with his wife's death, a college student trying to get through his senior year, and two ladies. One was coping with her husband's infidelity, and the other with her mother's Alzheimer's. I cancelled the last two afternoon appointments when Sasha and I realized Kathy may have been a patient. None of them are homicidal."

"We still have the entrance film," Reed said, his expression blank and his voice resigned. "I doubt if it'll do any good, but let's see it anyway."

The entrance camera was located on the front pillar of the garage. The angle was good, giving the viewer a decent look at those swiping in and leaving. The film quality was also clearer. Jeff paused the motion at every dark car exiting beginning at four-forty-five.

"There! That's him," I cried.

The camera caught the man leaving at five-ten, the busiest time. The bill of the cap was still pulled low and the collar of the trench coat drawn up to shield his lower face. The car hesitated, waited for the safety arm to rise, and then pulled away.

"I'm not surprised. If he's smart enough to evade the other cameras, he's smart enough to cover his face," Reed said.

"But where was Janine?" Linnie asked.

Jeff rolled the tape back and we watched again in slow motion. The front seat was empty.

"We lost sight of him after she got in the car. He could have transferred her to the trunk," Jeff suggested.

"But why didn't she fight?" I asked. "If it was me,

I'd scream like a maniac, kicking, scratching, and biting all the way."

"Maybe he had a weapon," Linnie said.

"Maybe she's still here," Reed answered.

Jeff pulled out his cell and dialed. "This is Detective Jeff Hammond. I need some back up at The Ridgeway Office Complex just south of Poplar. Possible abduction. Reed McIntyre is with me along with a couple of guys from the East Memphis Security Company. We need to search the building. Get out an APB right away. The victim is Janine Henderson, age twenty-three, five feet, three inches, a hundred and ten pounds, light brown hair, blue eyes. She went missing at four-twenty this afternoon."

A strangled noise from Linnie made me tighten my arm around her shoulders.

"She's dead," she sobbed. "I just know it."

"Probably," Reed said.

Reed hadn't had a lot to say in the past hour or so. I tapped into his emotions and felt anger, sorrow, and an odd sense of guilt—all of which I understood.

Jeff finished his call and grabbed the last tape from the VCR. "Sorry, Grayson, but these are evidence now."

"Yeah, I figured. I still need that warrant, though."

Jeff opened his cell again and called asking for a warrant.

"Get all the tapes from all the levels," Reed told him. "This bastard came from somewhere."

"I'll get right on it," Grayson said and left the room.

"Unless he's employed here, he came in the front doors," Linnie remarked through her tears.

Reed sighed. "We can review them at the station. Maybe our experts can enhance the images."

"Let's hope so," Jeff muttered. "I want this guy real bad. Janine was a nice kid."

I wished he hadn't used the past tense.

The squad cars arrived and the search began. I locked the door behind Reed, Jeff, and Hopewell, then put the kettle on. I scrounged in the little fridge and unearthed a small jar of strawberry jam, a loaf of bread, and a container of margarine. I didn't really want anything to eat, but tea and toast kept me busy.

Linnie had regained her composure. She rose and fired up her computer.

"What are you doing?"

"I'm going over files of former patients. I doubt if the killer is someone still with me, but he has to be someone Janine knew and trusted." She banged her fist on the desk. "Dammit, I've never had a homicidal patient before."

"Could a present patient have fooled you?"

"Yes. I'll go through those next." She covered her face with her hands for a moment, and then resumed her typing. "If he's one of mine, I'm going to find him and make him pay."

I curled up in the corner of the sofa while she worked, my mind numb from the evening's events. I wondered how much more I could take. Linnie muttered over the case files, rejecting one after the other.

In spite of Jeff's and Reed's conclusions, I wasn't so sure about the patient theory. It was a four-story building containing offices and employees with knowledge of where the cameras were placed. And anyone who worked here for a long time could easily know the routines of people.

I assumed each floor had the same layout. The third housed Linnie's practice and a CPA firm renting several offices on the far side. A consulting engineer had a similar set-up. The last remaining office belonged to a lawyer. I couldn't see any of them as possible killers.

"Linnie, how many people work at the other offices on this floor?"

"What? I don't know. Why?"

"I was just curious. There are thirty parking slots."

"I take up two, the lawyer has about the same, the engineers laid some workers off last year, so I don't know about them, and the CPA moved in about three years ago. It's tax season. I guess he's pretty busy." She stopped reading and looked up. "Why?"

I told her my theory.

"I suppose you could be right. With the turnover of offices, a stranger in the hallway wouldn't be unusual. And the CPA probably has clients from eight until five."

"How long have you been here?"

"About five years."

We each ate two slices of toast and drank three cups of tea before Jeff, Reed, and the two security men returned. The looks on their faces were easy to read.

"I take it you didn't find her," I said.

"Not a trace," Reed replied. "We searched every stairwell, mechanical room, bathroom, and office in the building. And the only car still in the garage is Janine's. We are fresh out of places to look."

"We did get a warrant for the rest of the tapes,

however," Jeff told us. "They're on the way to our experts. I'll drop these off on my way in." He gathered the cassettes from Linnie's desk. "What are you doing?"

"Going through old patient files," she answered.

"About time."

She glared at him. "Yeah, well, Sasha has an idea that makes sense."

"What's that?"

I told them my thoughts on the killer being an employee of one of the businesses in the building.

"That's a possibility," Jeff conceded. "Grayson, are there any cameras in the hallways or stairwells?"

He shook his head. "No one ever bothered to install them."

"Damn," Jeff muttered as Grayson and Hopewell left. "We'll check out everyone. In the meantime, I suggest you ladies head for home. It's been a helluva day."

"Do you really think I can sleep?" Linnie demanded. "I'm staying right here until I can eliminate or confirm the killer belongs to me."

"I don't want you alone in this building at night," he said.

"I think Hopewell will be holding court until daylight," she replied, ignoring him and pulling up another file on the computer. "I'll lock the door."

"I don't care. Go home. If Janine has met with foul play, you could be next on the killer's list, especially if he *is* a patient."

"Jeff's right, Marilyn," Reed said. "Please? At least until we can check out the people in the building."

Linnie looked up, rolled her eyes, and then

resumed reading.

"I'll stay with her," I volunteered.

"No." Reed spoke with a firm voice. His brows drew together in a scowl. "You could be in danger, too. You've been seen with me and Jeff on several occasions."

I opened my mouth to argue when Jeff's cell rang.

"Hammond. What's up?" He listened for a full thirty seconds, his face set in stone. "All right. Thanks. We'll be there in twenty minutes." He dropped the phone into his pocket.

He had bad news. I sensed his reluctance to share. I also sensed what it was. My breath caught in my throat and I glanced at Reed. His face was also impassive. He knew, too. Linnie ceased reading and stared.

"Jeff?" she said softly.

"That was Detective Brannon. A couple of uniforms making a routine check of an abandoned building on Symons found the body of a female in the alley out back."

Chapter Eleven

"Is…is it Janine?" Linnie asked, her hand at her throat, her voice breathy.

"I don't know. Come on, Reed, let's go." Jeff moved toward the door.

"Wait. I'm going with you," she said, shutting down her computer.

"There's no need for that," he said. "I'll ID the body if need be. You and Sasha go home. I'll call you either way."

"No. If it is Janine, I want to identify her."

"Linnie, it's not a pleasant experience," I told her.

"You don't understand. I'm responsible. If one of my patients is a killer, then this is my fault. The least I can do is save her parents the anguish of having to view their only child in a filthy alley or on a slab in the morgue."

"Then I'll go, too. We all go," I said to Jeff. "Sitting around waiting for a phone call just doesn't cut it. Janine's disappearance has made this personal."

"I agree," Reed replied suddenly. "They should come. Sasha's right, Marilyn. It won't be pleasant."

I silently blessed him. He understood Janine was not Kathy or Bridget, dream entities whose only connection to me was after death. I'd known Janine and had talked to her once a week for over two years. She was flesh and blood. I felt as responsible as Linnie. If I hadn't come to the office with my first vision of Kathy, neither of them would have been involved.

"I don't care." Linnie rose and picked up her purse with trembling fingers. "Let's go."

Symons Street was located in a seedy part of North Memphis two blocks off Watkins, a main drag. Drug and gang activity forced the police to frequently cruise the neighborhoods. The area we sought was lined with stores, most selling cheap merchandise and payroll advances. Many businesses were boarded up.

Linnie and I followed Jeff and Reed. The ride was silent. I intruded on my friend's emotions to make sure she could deal with what lay ahead. I sensed guilt and fear. Could she, even as a psychiatrist, handle this on such a personal level? I hoped that was the case.

We parked in the middle of the block. Police cars and an ambulance clogged the alley entrance. Jeff and Reed walked quickly down the narrow passageway. Linnie and I followed at a slower pace, stopping at the crime scene tape blocking our path. Jeff beckoned us forward, and we passed under it, tiptoeing along the side of one of the buildings to avoid damaging any evidence. Ahead lay a body covered with a tarp.

Linnie sucked in an audible breath, choking a little. I shivered. It was reminiscent of yesterday, and I knew who we'd find under that plastic sheet.

"Are you sure you want to do this?" Jeff asked.

Linnie nodded. I clasped my arm around her waist. Jeff stooped and pulled the tarp back. It was Janine.

"Oh, God!" Linnie said, gasping, her hands covering her face. She burst into tears.

I took one last look at Janine Henderson before

leading Linnie away. Her head was twisted at an impossible angle, but the face showed no trauma other than a couple of scrapes from where she'd hit the concrete.

"Oh, my God, Sasha," Linnie said between sobs. "All the way over I was praying it wasn't her, but deep in my heart I knew it was."

"I know. I was doing the same," I replied, patting her back while she cried on my shoulder.

Reed joined us. "I'm sorry, Marilyn. Are you all right?"

"No, I'm not all right, dammit!" she managed to choke out.

I shook my head at his silly question. "She will be soon." I swung my gaze to Janine and back again. "Her neck was broken, wasn't it?"

"Looks that way. Marilyn, did Janine carry a purse? There isn't one with the body."

I winced at his terminology. Linnie emitted a strangled cry, and then lifted her head.

"Her name is Janine, dammit, and yes, she had a purse. It was one of those huge affairs that hold everything, including the kitchen sink. She carried books, magazines, her lunch, and anything else she might need. It was heavy as lead, and I used to joke she could get arrested for carrying a deadly weapon. Oh, shit, I'm going to be sick again." She turned and lost the toast.

"Get her home. Neither of you can do anything else," Reed said.

"I'll take her to my place."

Linnie straightened and wiped her mouth with the back of her hand.

"Why bring her here? Why not just leave her in the garage or in her own car, for God's sakes?" she demanded.

"People," he answered. "She may have been discovered too soon. The killer wanted to be long gone when that happened. It also raises the question of what a young, well-dressed, woman would be doing in this neighborhood. The first assumption is drugs. Luckily, Jeff got the word out before she was found."

"Her poor parents. What am I going to tell them?"

"You don't have to tell them anything. Let the police do that," I told her.

"But it's my fault!"

"No, it isn't," Reed insisted. "The police will tell them she was abducted from the parking garage at work, robbed, and killed. We have no proof as yet this was in any way connected to our serial killer. The M.O. is different."

"But you believe it is, don't you?" I asked.

He didn't answer. "Go on home. There's nothing more you can do here."

Before I could lead her away, two cops with a teenager in handcuffs motioned from the tape barrier and called out to Jeff. He turned and walked a few paces toward them. Reed, Linnie, and I followed.

"Who's this?"

"Found him on the corner of Liberty and Hamilton. Goes by the street name, Slick. He tried to sell an undercover cop a credit card, a couple of rings, and an ATM card," one of the policemen answered.

The second officer held a large tan faux-leather purse from his fingertips. "We also found this in a dumpster on the corner. Wallet's still inside, minus money and, guess what, credit cards."

"Hey, man, you can't pin nothin' on me," the kid said with a curled lip. "I found that shit."

"Shut up," Jeff said, pulling on a pair of plastic gloves. "Liberty and Hamilton, huh? That's only six blocks from here." He opened the purse and extracted the wallet. "The driver's license says Janine Henderson, complete with an address. Sell that, too?" He turned to one of the uniformed cops. "Call the Bartlett police and bring them up to date. Tell them to get a couple of cars over to 1527 Fillmore Street. Have one of our guys go with them. Check out the house. It's bad enough the poor woman's dead, she doesn't need to be burglarized in the bargain."

The officer nodded, moving away to speak on his radio. Jeff fingered the items handed to him by the other policeman.

"The credit card also has Janine Henderson's name on it. Are you Janine?"

"Fuck off. I know my rights. I want a lawyer," the youth said.

"This is not a court of law, Slick. This is a crime scene, and you're standing thirty feet from a murder victim. How'd you get her purse? Tell me the truth, and I might not arrest you for killing her."

"I didn't fuckin' kill the bitch. She was dead when I found her."

"Sure, kid." Jeff held the rings in the palm of his hand. "Marilyn, can you identify these?"

Linnie moved next to him. "Yes, those are Janine's. The garnet belonged to her grandmother. I gave her the vintage marcasite for her birthday last year." She glared at the kid. "Little bastard."

"Hey, fuck you, bitch. I don't need no 'ho givin' me shit."

Linnie lunged for him. Reed had to pull her back.

"Where'd you get the purse?" Jeff pressed the boy.

"I tell you, you let me walk?"

"Could be."

"Found it."

"Where, Slick?"

"End of the alley. It was just layin' there."

"Try again," Jeff ordered.

The kid glared at him and hawked a loogie two inches from the tip of Jeff's shoe. I tapped into the little wise ass's emotions. He was scared, but I found no traces of guilt—at least, not of murder.

"How about I tighten those handcuffs and arrest you for murder right now? I'll see to it your holding cell is filled with all kinds of rough, tough dudes just waiting to be your new best friend. Like that, Slick?"

Slick sneered and breathed hard through his nose, glaring at all of us. He licked his lips, and then said in a sullen voice, "I was cutting through the alley and found it next to her. She was dead. Didn't see how she had any more use for it."

"So, you found a body, robbed it, stole the purse belonging to the deceased, and then tried to sell the credit cards and personal effects to an undercover cop— is that the drill?" Jeff asked him.

"Yeah, so what?"

"Get him out of here. Book him for theft, suspicion of murder, and anything else you can think of," he told the officer.

"Hey, you don't know who you're dealing with. I'm important." Jeff ignored him and the policeman grabbed the kid's arm. "Hey, I get a private cell, right? No buddies."

Slick was led away loudly proclaiming his innocence with every step.

"Sasha, get Marilyn home. It's late and this is going to take a while. I'll be in touch. I'm sorry, honey," Jeff said, leaning down and kissing Linnie's cheek. "Try to get some rest."

Reed escorted us back to my car.

"Are you staying, too?" I asked, sliding behind the wheel.

"For a while. I really have no business here. I also have to continue the search for Bridget tomorrow. Jeff will keep me clued in." He stuck his head through the window and lightly kissed my lips. "Be careful driving home."

I nodded, started the car, and drove away. A glance in my rearview mirror showed Reed already headed back to the alley.

****

"Come on, Linnie, please take one," I begged. "You prescribed them for me."

"I don't need sleeping pills," she said, batting my hand holding the bottle away. "God, I wanted to kill that little bastard in the alley. I wanted to rip his fucking head off and shit down his neck."

"I know. So did I. I'm sure Jeff and Reed felt the same. Come on, just one. I've got the kettle on. We'll have some herbal tea, and then go to bed. I'll take one, too. We both need dreamless sleep," I cajoled.

"Jeff and Reed have seen dead bodies before. They're used to it. I'm not." She started to cry again. "Especially when it's a friend."

I handed her a box of tissues. She sat curled up in the corner of my sofa, her shoeless feet peeking out from under her skirt. The kettle whistled.

"I'm going to get you a cup of tea and make up the guest room."

I left the tea on the end table along with the pills, grabbed linens from the closet, and made the bed. When I returned to the living room, I found Linnie exactly as I'd left her, the tea untouched. She stared across the room at nothing, but at least no longer cried.

"Bed's ready," I said, picking up my cup from the coffee table and sipping. "Your tea's getting cold."

She sighed and sipped. "There. Happy?"

I picked up the pill bottle and shook it, the contents rattling. "I'd be a lot happier if you took one of these."

"Yes, Dr. Bellwood. If I take one, will you get off my back?" At least she said "if." That was progress.

"Promise."

I shook a pill into her hand and watched like a mother hen until she swallowed it along with half her tea. She stood.

"If I'm not mistaken, these little buggers work fast. I'm partial to falling asleep in bed, not on your hallway floor."

I found another dentist's contribution to good oral hygiene and handed her a T-shirt to sleep in. She brushed her teeth and undressed, then slipped into bed.

"Remind me to call Dr. Garland in the morning," she said, yawning.

"Who's Dr. Garland?"

"My psychiatrist."

"Wait a minute. My shrink sees a shrink?"

"I listen to other people's problems eight to ten

hours a day, five days a week, and I'm on call twenty-four-seven. It can be damned depressing. Why wouldn't I see a shrink?"

"I never thought about it that way."

"Jeff has warts, you know," she murmured, her voice drowsy.

"Excuse me? Warts? Where?"

"Not on his body. On his personality. He can be demanding, and I think under all that charm, he's also controlling. He reminds me a little of Brian."

"Brian was a scumbag who beat the crap out of you because you overcooked his steak. A cop has to be demanding and in control. I take it you are referring to the argument about your patient files," I said.

Linnie made a little assenting noise. "He was really pushy in the car. Said I was insensitive to his needs and the needs of the community. I was selfish and he was only trying to help. Got mad when I told him to fuck off. Said ladies didn't use that kind of language. Can you imagine?"

I chuckled. "I would never have put Jeff Hammond on the list of twenty-first century language prudes. Don't worry. He's just frustrated. Imagine how Reed feels."

She yawned again and settled deeper into the pillow. "Reed passed frustrated long ago. He's into obsession and anger now."

"I can understand that. He wants this killer and is furious the guy's been allowed to continue for so long."

Linnie didn't answer. She was sound asleep.

I turned out the light and tiptoed from the room, cleaning up our tea cups and setting the timer on the coffee maker for the next morning. In the bathroom, I eyed the sleeping pills. God knows my body screamed for a good night's sleep, but what if Linnie needed me? I'd be dead to the world. On the other hand, she wasn't likely to awake until morning either.

I opened the bottle and swallowed one, then crawled into bed, awaiting blessed oblivion.

****

Neither of us had much of an appetite in the morning. I awoke at seven-thirty, refreshed and rested, and was pouring a cup of coffee when Linnie joined me, giving me a big hug.

"Thanks for taking care of me. I appreciate it."

"Feeling better? How did you sleep?"

"It's going to be a long while before I feel better, but I slept well." She poured a cup of coffee and sat at the kitchen table. "I wonder if Jeff has any news? Maybe I should call."

"I'd wait. My guess is he had a long night. He'll call when he can. What's on the agenda for today?"

"I'm going to cancel all my appointments for the next week. I can't deal with seeing people. *Then* I'm going to search my files from top to bottom. If the killer's there, I'll find him."

"I'm at loose ends. Can I help?"

"You can call my patients and pull files no longer in the computer."

"I think I can handle that."

"First, I need to go home and change clothes."

I rose and gathered up the garbage I'd forgotten to take out the day before.

"What the hell is this?" I asked, fingering a slightly sticky residue on my kitchen door.

Linnie came over and felt it, too. "Have you

painted lately?"

"No. Maybe I've got an air leak and this is condensation."

She sniffed her fingers. "No smell. You could be right. Check your weather stripping. It might be loose."

I opened the door, dumped the garbage in the can, and inspected the rubber around the door frame. It looked all right, but then I was no expert.

I dismissed the door from my mind and headed for the bathroom. On my way through the living room the blinking light on my answering machine caught my eye. I hit the play button. Linnie wandered in, and we listened to my former boss bully, demand, cajole, and finally beg my forgiveness.

"Miserable little weasel. I wonder if we could pin the serial killings on him," she muttered.

"Now, there's a thought," I said, erasing the messages. "Too bad he doesn't possess a killer smile. He is definitely not the new boyfriend type."

"Just because you think he looks like a ferret, and he resembles a snake in the grass to me, doesn't mean someone else might not find him attractive."

I snorted. "That little worm as a killer? He might talk a victim to death, but that's all."

"I don't know, Sasha. He thought about trying to stop you from leaving yesterday."

"It was in and out of his mind so fast, it barely registered."

I resumed my interrupted journey toward the bathroom, dismissing thoughts of my ex-boss as a serial killer.

When I exited the shower the sound of voices in the living room told me Reed had arrived. I dressed quickly and joined them.

"Any news?" I asked.

"The man came bearing gifts of caffeine," Linnie answered.

He handed me a Styrofoam cup. I pulled the top off and sniffed appreciatively.

"H-m-m, chocolate mint latte. You are winning big points," I told him, taking a sip. I was flattered he remembered my favorite flavor. "Any news?"

"We found the car the killer used in a Kroger parking lot. It had been hot-wired. The owner, a barge broker, works on the fourth floor. He reported it stolen at six o'clock."

"What about the coat and hat?" Linnie asked.

"Found the coat in the possession of a homeless guy not far from the alley. Says he found it and the cap in a dumpster, but gave the cap away to a friend."

"So, no forensic evidence," I said, a trifle bitterly.

Reed shrugged. "We're sending it through trace, but anything we find is useless until we have a suspect, unless he's already in the system. Somehow, I doubt it."

"What happened after we left?" Linnie asked.

"Things wound down in the alley by two o'clock. I went back to the station with Jeff to look at the rest of those tapes." He stopped and gulped from his coffee container.

"And?" I prompted.

"The guy exited from the fourth floor stairwell, cap pulled low, coat collar up, just like in the car, and proceeded to test car doors until finding one unlocked. He then walked down the ramp to three, did the potato thing, and returned to the fourth level stairwell. At four-eighteen, he jumped into the car and came down the ramp to three again."

"Just as Janine was getting out of her car in disgust," Linnie said. "He probably came back down to three and hid in the stairwell, spying on when she left the office."

"I'd say that's a good bet."

"Reed, did the tapes show anything about Janine after she got in the car?" The fact she hadn't fought still bothered me.

"No, the sun obliterated much of the angle to the fourth level until five-oh-five. My guess is she was already dead," he answered.

"But how?" Linnie demanded.

He sighed and drained the rest of his coffee, not looking at either of us.

"Reed, come on, I'm much better today. I can take it," she insisted.

"We enhanced the tapes showing Janine getting into the car. There was a twelve second gap from the time she got in to the time the killer backed up. The guy leaned over as though to help, and then grabbed her chin with his left hand and the back of her head with his right. One hard, vicious twist did it. She died instantly. I doubt she was even aware of what was happening. When we found the car, we checked the seat belt on the passenger side. Someone had tampered with it."

Linnie closed her eyes and took several deep breaths.

"After he parked, he simply got out and transferred her body to the trunk," he said in conclusion.

"Find him, Reed. Find him and kill him for me, because if you don't, I will. I'll search and search until this sick son of a bitch is no longer a threat," Linnie said in a soft voice.

"Don't worry, we'll get him." He rose. "Sorry, I have to get to work. I need to do research on private lakes with earthen berms." He leaned down and kissed my cheek. "I'll be in touch."

"Have you heard from Jeff this morning?" Linnie asked.

"No, but I figured if he had any more information, he'd have called. It was close to four when I left the station. He was still up viewing tapes. What are you two doing today?"

I told him of our plans.

"That's a good idea. Let me know if you find anything. Jeff is going to start checking out the rest of the people in the building. Keep the door locked."

I saw him out the door and turned to find Linnie behind me, her face set with a determined expression.

"Drive me home, Sasha. I want to change and get to the office. God help this whacko if he *is* one of my patients."

Whacko. For Linnie to use a derogatory word toward someone with a mental problem showed her anger.

She strode out the door, leaving me to grab my purse and rush after her.

****

I pulled into a space near the front doors of the building. Neither of us could stomach parking in the garage. We met Bob, the security guard, in the lobby.

"Dr. Anderson, Miss Bellwood, I heard about Miss Henderson. It's awful, just plain awful." He ran his fingers through his sun-streaked dark blond hair with a disgusted expression on his face. "I warned the building manager and the security company that more cameras were needed if a night guard wasn't here. I wanted to put them in the hallways and the stairwells, but the cost was too high. Maybe now, they'll listen to me."

In her office, Linnie made a huge pot of strong coffee and fired up her computer. It didn't take a genius to see she was loaded for bear. I almost felt sorry for the perpetrator if he was her patient. Almost.

I got down to the business of canceling appointments, giving a family emergency as the excuse. When one woman asked after Janine, I told her the receptionist was on vacation. I had no idea what the police had released to the public.

We had avoided reading the newspaper and watching the early TV shows this morning—assuming Janine's death was important enough to warrant coverage. In a city the size of Memphis, not all murders were newsworthy. There were just too many of them. In the car, Linnie had turned the radio off with a quick flick of her wrist. I didn't blame her. I couldn't stand to hear or read the accounts of Janine's death in cut and dried news reports, either.

I rose from Janine's desk and wandered into Linnie's office. "You're all set for a week from Monday. Your first appointment is Mr. Holcombe at ten. Do you want me to call an employment agency and arrange for a temp?" I asked, pouring myself another cup of coffee.

"Would you mind doing it for a while? Seeing a stranger in Janine's place will be hard to take."

"I suppose I can do it for a couple of weeks, but I don't think it's a good idea for me, as a patient, to work with you."

"I'll be all right by then. Oh, I'm seeing Dr. Garland at three this afternoon."

I sipped the strong sludge in my cup. "Would you like to stay at my place for a few days?"

Linnie shook her head. "No, it's important to get back to a regular routine. I'll be fine."

"So, how goes the search?"

"I'm trying to cross reference every group session I sat in on. Some go back to when I first started practicing. I only keep electronic files for three years. Anything earlier has been deleted from the computer. However, the hard copy files should still be in a cabinet."

"Any luck?"

"Not one name has cropped up more than twice."

"How can I help?"

She tossed her keys across the desk. "Here, get into the file cabinet in the far corner behind Janine's desk. Those are the oldest files. It'll be a pain in the ass, but start searching for names."

I pulled ten files at a time, and then made a list of the names. I'd separate them by gender later. Linnie was right. This would take forever.

Deep into my work, I jumped in fright when the outer office door opened. Linnie and I had both forgotten Reed's warning to lock up. It was hard to imagine the killer strolling in and taking out both of us, but then anything was possible. My fingers tightened on my pen, and I eyed the letter opener at the edge of the desk pad.

A well-dressed man wearing tan slacks and a blue sport coat walked in and approached. "Is Dr. Anderson in?"

He didn't *sound* like a homicidal maniac or serial killer. His voice had a neutral tone.

"I'm sorry, but the office is closed until a week from Monday. Would you like to make an appointment?"

My heart leapt when he reached into his coat pocket. A gun? A knife? I tightened my stomach muscles and braced for an attack. He brought out a wallet and flipped it open. I stared at a badge.

"I'm Detective Richard Brannon with the Memphis Police Department." He returned the badge to his pocket. "I'm investigating the death of Janine Henderson and wanted to ask the doctor a few questions."

This guy looked like a cop. Tall and built like a fireplug, his hair was liberally sprinkled with gray as was his moustache. I imagined the bristling eyebrows could intimidate even the most hardened of criminals when he frowned. I relaxed and lifted the phone.

"What is it, Sasha?"

"A detective is here to see you."

"I'll be right out."

I hung up. "She'll be out in a…"

I didn't get to finish the sentence when the door to her office opened.

"I'm Marilyn Anderson. How can I help?"

The man nodded. "Detective Richard Brannon. I need to ask you a few questions about Janine Henderson. Can we go into your office?"

"Anything you ask can be said in front of Sasha."

He turned and stared with raised eyebrows.

"Sasha Bellwood," I said hurriedly. "I'm a friend of Dr. Anderson's. I also knew Janine."

"I see," was his only comment.

"Sasha was with me last night when I identified the body. Jeff Hammond and Reed McIntyre can vouch for her," Linnie added.

"I remember. Also noticed Reed put in an appearance."

"Do you know him?" I asked.

He nodded. "Worked with him on a couple of cases before he left the force."

"And you believe in his serial killer theory?"

"Yes, although I'm not sure this is one of them."

"Please have a seat, detective," Linnie said. They both sat, he in a chair and she on the sofa. "What do you need to know?"

"Did Miss Henderson have a boyfriend?"

"Not to my knowledge."

"Was she in the habit of picking up men in bars or nightclubs?"

"Certainly not!" Linnie replied in a shocked voice. "Janine was a decent, hardworking young woman with sound values. She didn't indulge in that kind of lifestyle."

Linnie told Detective Brannon about Janine's personal life. I hadn't known Janine on that level, but I couldn't imagine the prim and proper receptionist, a devotee of twin sets, below the knee skirts, and comfortable shoes, suddenly appearing in a nightclub wearing spandex and stilettos. Janine? But the cops had to cover all the bases. For all we knew, she could have participated in *Receptionists Gone Wild.*

"What time did you arrive here this morning?" the detective asked.

"Around nine, I think, didn't we, Sasha?"

I nodded. "That sounds about right."

"I suppose you'd have mentioned it if your office door were unlocked."

Linnie's eyebrows rose. "Of course. Why should my office door be unlocked?"

"Miss Henderson's keys are missing. They weren't in her purse, her pockets, the alley, or a dumpster. We've impounded her car. They weren't there either."

"You think that slimy little street punk sold them, too?" I asked.

"Claims he didn't find any keys, and the police said nobody approached Miss Henderson's house last night."

"Someone could have entered before she was found," Linnie said, her fingers clasped together so hard the knuckles showed white.

Brannon shook his head. "We got in this morning. Nothing had been disturbed. TV, stereo, an old desktop computer—the kind of things a burglar would snatch—were all there. That leaves your office. She had a key, didn't she?"

Linnie nodded and looked at me. "Jeff thinks the killer could be one of my patients. Oh, my God. Is that why she was killed? To steal her keys, so this maniac could get in? Why?"

"The files," I said. "If he's a patient, then Reed and Jeff were right when they said he might figure out we'd come to the patient angle sooner or later. I wonder if he stole his own file."

"Well, he couldn't have deleted it from the computer. He didn't have the password to either mine or Janine's."

Brannon gazed at the screen saver on Janine's

machine. "How did you get in, Miss Bellwood?"

"Dr. Anderson gave me Janine's password."

"I had to have hers in case she was out of the office," Linnie explained, running a hand through her hair. "Oh, God, what a mess. If he hasn't been a patient in three years, we may never know his name."

"Linnie," I said slowly, rising from the desk and crossing to one of the file cabinets. "What if he wasn't after his own file? What if he was after one of those we went through yesterday?" My theory was busted when I found and pulled the files. "Oh, well, it sounded good."

Linnie reached for Kathy's file and opened it, then stiffened; her eyes wide. "Oh, shit."

"What is it?" Brannon asked with a frown.

She laid the folder on the desk. It contained sheets of blank paper. I quickly checked Jennifer and Susan's folders. The original notes were there.

"He stole Kathy's file," I said. "What was in it?"

"Nothing of any consequence," Linnie replied.

"That you know of," the detective answered.

"Thank God, it's still in the system," she said. "He probably stole his file, too. It would take weeks, maybe months, before we'd find it, if at all."

I don't know what prompted me to return to the file cabinet where I extracted two more folders. Not having the guts to open them, I handed both to Linnie.

She opened the first one and let a batch of blank papers fall onto the desk. I bit my lip. I knew the second folder would be identical. I was not wrong.

"Oh, my dear God," she breathed.

Brannon repeated his command of earlier. "What is it?"

Linnie licked her lips, heaved a huge sigh, and

rubbed her forehead. "The killer took Sasha's and Reed's files."

Chapter Twelve

I sat before my trembling legs collapsed, and moistened my dry lips.

"Exactly how up to date was my file?" I asked.

"Janine transcribed your last visit yesterday."

"Wait a minute. Both you and Reed McIntyre are patients?" Brannon inquired.

"I am. Reed was a couple of years ago."

"Actually, Reed was here early yesterday morning," Linnie replied. "He called late the night before. Said he needed to talk."

"What did he say?" the detective asked.

"I can't reveal that. His was one of the files Janine was working on when we left last night."

"Why swipe files still in the system?" I asked.

"Because the killer's desperate to find out how much you know," Brannon replied.

"He doesn't take the time to hack into the computer. The hard copy is easier, and he has the keys," Linnie said.

Brannon's cell rang. He answered, listened for a few seconds, and then hung up.

"I've got to go. I'll need the sheets of paper and the folders. There may be fingerprints. I also want you to come down and get printed so we can eliminate yours."

"Mine are already on file," Linnie told him. "My

apartment was burglarized a few years ago and the police took my prints for that reason."

"Check with the Mississippi Gaming Commission. I worked briefly at The Lucky Dog Casino in Tunica five years ago," I replied.

Linnie opened the bottom drawer of Janine's desk and extracted a box of small trash bags, handing it to Brannon. He ripped one from the roll, and using a tissue to avoid leaving his own prints, bagged the folders and paper, then gave each of us his card. "If you find anything else missing, give me a call."

Several seconds of silence ensued after he left. I finally broke it. "Now what?"

"I have no idea. Reed's right about one thing. This guy's watching and probably following him," she said.

"I feel violated."

"I suppose I should call Reed and tell him." She rubbed a hand over her forehead.

"No, let me handle it," I said. "He'll call with an update on the search for Bridget. I'll tell him then."

The office door opened and Jeff entered. His somber expression was a contrast to his usual brash self.

"And why isn't this damned door locked?" he said. "I can't believe you came into the office this morning."

"What else was I going to do?" Linnie replied. "I couldn't just sit at home. Besides, I wanted to check patient files. I will not quit until this guy is slapped on a gurney with a needle stuck in his arm."

"I know how you feel, honey." He put his arm around her shoulders and kissed her cheek. "I want him, too. Did a Detective Brannon see you?"

"Yes, he just left. His theory on Janine's missing

keys was right. The killer let himself in and stole some files."

"Whose?"

Linnie told him while I watched anger and frustration slide across his face.

"Damn! I think the two of you should get the hell out of Dodge. Hop in the car and go down to Pensacola or over to Hot Springs. Both of you could be on his hit list."

"I can understand why Sasha might be in danger, but why me? Hell, I'm not even sure he's a patient yet."

"Yes, you are or you wouldn't be going through your files. Face it. You treated him. Eventually, you'll put a name with a face. Please, honey, for me?"

"He got what he came for. He's probably taken his file, too. No. I refuse to cut and run. If there's anything to find on this guy in my files, I intend to do it," Linnie said with a bullheaded look on her face.

A flush crept up Jeff's neck. He narrowed his eyes and compressed his lips. I honed in enough on his emotions to realize he was furiously angry.

"Goddamn it!" he yelled.

I jumped in surprise and Linnie fell back a step.

He blew out a breath and ran his hand through his hair. "Will you just once do what I tell you?" He didn't yell, but his tone was hard and cold as stone. "I don't want either of you to become a statistic. Take a vacation until we can catch this guy."

This was a new side of Jeff, and I remembered Linnie's sleeping pill induced comment from last night about warts. He pissed me off. I don't like being yelled at, and I certainly don't like being given orders.

"You've had eight years to catch him. What makes

you think you're going to do it any time soon?"

He turned to glare at me, and for a nanosecond I thought I saw hate in his eyes. Why not? I hated this maniac, too. Then, the look vanished.

He exhaled another deep breath and ran a hand over his face. "I'm sorry for yelling. It's just that this guy is always one step ahead of us. I'm worried about both of you. I dropped by to ask if you wanted to go to lunch. Guess that's not such a good idea, huh?"

Linnie placed her hand on his arm. "I think it's a wonderful idea. It'll give us all a chance to calm down."

I agreed and turned to leave.

Donald Duckworth stood in the doorway, his face ashen. "My God, I just heard about Janine."

"It's awful," I said. I couldn't begin to tell him how awful.

"But, I just saw her yesterday. Stopped by on my way home. Asked her out for dinner tonight. Someone said she was abducted from the parking garage."

"I'm Detective Jeff Hammond. Who are you and how well did you know Miss Henderson?"

"My name's Donald Duckworth. I work at Sanderson Engineering down the hall. Janine and I went out a couple of times. She was a nice lady and I enjoyed her company. Who could have done such a thing?"

"That's what we're trying to find out. What time did you leave yesterday?"

He looked startled. "Me? Gosh, I'm not sure. Around four or four-thirty."

"Did you see anything or anybody that looked out of the ordinary?"

"Not last night."

"Meaning?" Jeff's eyes hardened and his eyebrows drew together.

"Well, I get into the office early, and this morning I saw some guy going into Marilyn's office about seven o'clock."

We all gazed at one another. He'd seen the intruder and probable killer?

"Did he use a key to get in?" Linnie asked in a hushed tone.

"I didn't see. I just saw him as he entered. I thought maybe he had an early appointment. Miss Bellwood is sometimes here early, too."

"I don't suppose you got a look at his face," Jeff said.

Donald shook his head. "No, but he was wearing tan slacks, a baseball cap, and a black jacket."

"Damn," Jeff swore.

"He was about six feet tall, and I think he may have had blond hair," Donald continued.

Jeff's eyes narrowed. "How do you know that if he was wearing a baseball cap?"

"The bill was pulled down in the front. Left the back of his head exposed. Mind you, I just had a quick glance. I could be wrong."

"Thank you very much. May I have your address and phone number? I'd like to formally get your statement later."

While Jeff and Donald exchanged information, Linnie and I talked in undertones.

"My God, who'd have believed he'd see the killer," she said.

"Certainly not the killer. Guess his habit of long hours was something the bastard didn't know."

Duckworth left and Jeff returned. "Let's go get that lunch."

Linnie locked the office door. *Why bother? The killer still has Janine's keys.*

"I'll drive," Jeff offered when we reached the lobby. "How about Cannon's? It's quick and casual."

"Sounds good to me," Linnie said, fastening her seat belt.

"Me, too," I echoed.

Cannon's was close to Linnie's office. We found a table and ordered iced tea all around.

"Reed dropped by Sasha's this morning and brought us up to date about Janine. Is there anything new?" Linnie asked.

"Forensics found unidentified fibers on her clothes. I'm betting they'll come from the car. They also found hair and the same fibers on the coat we took from the homeless guy. We'll see what develops."

"What about the cap?" I inquired.

"Hasn't turned up yet. It will. I hope we can get something from it."

"Reed said the killer tampered with the seat belt," Linnie said. "How?"

"Jammed a pencil in the shoulder strap mechanism, and then broke it in half. We found the remains on the floor of the fourth level. Simple, but effective. What's the first thing a person does when they get in a car? Fasten the seat belt. And when it doesn't work, it's second nature to turn and find out why. The minute she did, he moved fast. It was over in seconds."

Linnie closed her eyes and shuddered. My stomach turned over. I picked up on the swirling emotions. Linnie's were deep sorrow, anger, and disgust mingled with acceptance. Jeff was harder to read, but I sensed an inner rage he tried to control.

The waitress brought our tea and we ordered food. Not overly hungry, Linnie and I selected salads while Jeff had the hot wings.

When she left, I asked, "Jeff, how did the guy get into the building? I thought the security company was watching all night."

"Hopewell was parked by the front door and another man kept watch out back."

"Well, one of them went to sleep," Linnie said, her voice tart.

"Possibly. I'm sure Brannon will talk to them. How long does it take to unlock a door, sneak in, find the files, and sneak out again?" he replied with a shrug. "Even if one of them did fall asleep, he'd never admit it."

He ran his hand over his chin. His eyes were bloodshot and lines grooved around his mouth.

"You look beat, Jeff," I said.

"I am. I'm working on two hours sleep. I bunked out on a couch in my captain's office. I went home this morning, showered, shaved, and changed clothes. Lord knows when I'll sleep again."

"Reed often has that haggard look, too. I guess it comes with being a cop."

"I don't see how you do it," Linnie said. "How can you stand to see dead bodies day in and day out?"

"It's tough. Some people burn out in a few years and request transfers. Others drink. A few eat their guns," Jeff admitted.

"Have you ever felt suicidal?"

He grinned. "Analyzing me, doc?"

"Maybe just a little."

"When the stress levels get too high, I go to the firing range and pump round after round into paper criminals. Sometimes, I don't quit until my hand is sore and my finger too cramped to pull the trigger."

"Good Lord," I said, appalled at his words. "That's a violent way of dealing with violence."

"Maybe, but it's healthier than booze and not nearly as permanent as shoving a gun in my mouth. You cope any way you can to survive."

"So do killers," Linnie commented.

"Let's change the subject," Jeff said abruptly. "I'm tired of murder, serial killers, and crime in general. How about a pleasant lunch subject?"

"I'll drink to that," Linnie said.

"Here, here." We raised our glasses, clinked them together, and then drank. "So, Jeff, how's your love life?"

He choked, and Linnie laughed. It sounded hollow.

"Well, it's been in the doldrums, but I'm confident things will pick up soon."

He cut a look to Linnie, who closed her eyes. "I see good fortune for you. Play your cards right and your dreams will come true," she intoned.

"Are you now a fortune teller?" he chuckled.

"I know all and see all."

I joined in the pseudo fun. "No, *that* is apparently my department."

His chuckle deepened into a laugh. "Where do you hide your crystal ball?"

I laughed along with them. *How can he sound so lighthearted in view of the circumstances? Must be a self-defense mechanism cops use to stay sane.*

The forced, silly banter continued until our food arrived. We spoke no more of murder.

****

Jeff dropped us at the front door of the office a little after twelve-thirty.

"Thanks, ladies. I'll be in touch, Marilyn."

We waved as he left, and then made our way to Linnie's office. I grimaced at the files on the desk. I had no desire to return to the work at hand, but sat down anyway.

From the discouraged look on her face, I sensed Linnie was on the same wavelength.

"I know we should go through these files, but I'm having a hard time focusing. Maybe it was a mistake to come in today. Let's go home. I'd like to visit Janine's parents up in Millington before I see Dr. Garland. Perhaps I can help them with their grief. We can tackle this later."

"I agree. Are you sure you don't want to stay with me? You're more than welcome."

She shook her head. "No, I'm sure. I'll be fine."

"Maybe I should take some of these files home with me."

"If you want. I'm hoping Jeff will come over later."

I gathered several file folders. Anything I'd say about taking it easy in the romance arena would fall on deaf ears. I didn't blame her. The next time Reed offered to sleep over, I sure as hell wouldn't make up either the sofa or the guest room.

We said goodbye in the parking lot. I chucked the files onto the passenger seat and had barely gotten behind the wheel when my cell rang.

"Can Marilyn do without you for the rest of the day?" Reed asked without saying hello.

"We both had a hard time concentrating and called it quits. I was about to head for home. Why?"

"I've got six possible sites on where this earthen dam could be located. I thought maybe you'd like to come with me. It's your vision. You'd be more likely to recognize the area than I would."

"Of course, I'll come."

"Good. Meet you at your place in twenty minutes."

He hung up without giving me a chance to confirm or saying goodbye.

I should have been irritated. Instead, my heart beat faster. Maybe he'd stay the night.

****

"So, where are we going?" I asked, snapping my seat belt secure. I shivered, unable to stop the image of Janine from popping into my head.

Reed backed out of my driveway before answering. "First stop is in Lakeland."

"Lakeland's pretty well developed. I saw lots of trees."

"This property has been owned by the same family for close to a hundred years. They sold some off to developers, but kept over eighty acres for their own use. Seems grandpa was an avid hunter and loved to fish. They've got three ponds. I called and got permission to drive on the land."

Reed threaded his way through traffic as we headed northeast while I pondered how to tell him of the latest news about our files. I edged my way into his emotions, detecting residual anger from the night before and hope that today would be the day he could put

Bridget Connor to rest. I also felt a certain amount of contentment, which my ego decided must have been due to my presence.

In that self-esteem boosting frame of mind, I plunged in head first. "Uh, Reed, there's something you should know."

"About what?"

I gave him the lowdown on our files and theories on how the killer could have gotten in. In reply, Reed fished his cell out of his pocket and dialed.

"Brannon, Reed McIntyre here. Did you talk to those security guards yet? Did either of them admit to taking a nap...I didn't think so. Did you take the files with you...Any prints...Let me know as soon as the lab gets back to you, but I wouldn't hold my breath. This guy's too smart to make a stupid mistake like that...By the way, was Janine Henderson's swipe card in her purse or car...That's how employees get in and out of the parking garage." He waited for what I considered an eternity for Brannon to answer. "Okay, thanks. If I were you, I'd pull tape from the entrance and parking level cameras again. We might catch a break."

He finally hung up.

"Let me guess, Janine's swipe card is missing, too," I said. "We should have thought of that this morning."

"You and Marilyn were still in a state of shock. Brannon didn't know about the swipe card system."

"But Jeff did."

"Then, he should have thought of it. When did you see Jeff?"

"He took Linnie and me to lunch. He thinks we should leave town for a while."

"He's talking like a friend and not a cop. We need Marilyn's expertise as a psychiatrist and your abilities."

"I suppose. He was furious when we both refused. I thought he was going to stroke out."

"That's interesting. In all the years I've known him, I never saw him lose his temper, even with the most vicious criminals," Reed said with a frown.

"I think he's more emotionally involved with Linnie than we realize."

"Jeff? He loves 'em and leaves 'em."

"Yeah, but Linnie's special."

He shook his head. "Jeff serious about a woman? That's out of character. Still it happens to the best of us."

I changed the subject. "Linnie said you'd been in to see her."

Reed stopped at a light and made a left turn. "That's right. I had a few issues to get off my chest. I may start seeing her on a regular basis again. Especially if I don't find this killer soon. It's been eight years. I'm tired of dancing to his tune."

He used the word "I" even though he hadn't been directly involved in the cases for ages. Obsessive or not, I didn't blame him. Janine's murder had hit home.

We made a right onto a gravel road and traveled another couple of hundred yards before turning left into a drive. Two large "No Trespassing, Private Property" signs were staked on either side of the blacktop entryway. It meandered through trees not thick enough to be called woods. We stopped in front of a two-story farmhouse.

"I'll let Mrs. Carver know we're here," he said. "I'll be right back."

He mounted the front steps and knocked on the door. A lady answered. Reed flipped out his badge and the woman nodded, gesturing to the right. Reed returned to the car.

"She said the ponds are located in this direction."

We found a narrow lane running through the property and drove slowly over the jolting ruts. An SUV or pick-up would have been a better choice of vehicle. Reed's car took a beating. I didn't think the killer would come this way. The terrain was too rough and open.

The first pond was small and the berm around it bare of trees. The second was larger, but a good fifty yards from the little road. Not even close to what I'd seen. The third pond was the largest, and while the trail did pass between the earthen dam and some woods, it still didn't look right. We got out and investigated anyway. After fifteen minutes of tromping through the underbrush, I recognized nothing.

"Well, that was a bust," I said in the car, refastening my seat belt.

The next two sites we viewed didn't match, either.

"Where do we go next?" I asked, growing weary.

"There's a place about ten miles away. It's part of a county forest preserve. There's more of a lake than a pond in the middle of it. It's isolated from the main roads."

I sneaked a glance at Reed's face. Given my jumping hormones, my curiosity level also rose. I needed to know more about his life.

"Tell me about yourself."

His eyebrows rose. "What do you want to know?"

"Where were you born? Do you have family

nearby? Brothers? Sisters? Pets? Where did you go to college?"

"Just full of questions, aren't you?"

"Yes."

He smiled. "I was born and raised in Holly Springs, Mississippi. My father was a cotton farmer. I've got two younger brothers, one a dentist in Hernando, and the other is the sheriff of Gladden County. I had a dog named Dawg when I was a kid. Cried like a baby when he died."

I had to chuckle. "How old were you?"

"Eighteen. Dawg was fifteen."

"Does law enforcement run in the family?"

"Baby brother is the only one who followed in my footsteps."

"Did you always want to be a cop?"

"Thought never entered my head until college. My roommate's father was a cop in Jackson. He talked about his work whenever I visited. Because of him I switched my major to criminal justice in my sophomore year at Ole Miss. When I graduated, I joined the Memphis police."

"None of the brothers took over the family farm?"

"No real interest. My mother passed away when I was ten, so when Dad died, we kids decided to sell. The proceeds helped put Rob through dental school. Bill used a chunk of his money to buy the election five years ago."

I stifled a laugh. "You're kidding, right?"

"Nope. He's a savvy politician. Outspent his opponent three to one and took office in a landslide. I contributed a few bucks to his efforts. It's nice to have a relative who's connected. If I need something out of

Mississippi, Bill makes a few phone calls, and I get it. Same goes for any needs he has in the Memphis area."

"Things like investigating possible serial killer victims?" I asked, no longer amused.

He didn't answer. He didn't need to. Now, I understood why often tight lipped Mississippi county cops allowed Reed access to investigations on their turf.

I wanted to ask more, but Reed pulled off the main highway onto another county road. We passed out of Lakeland. A series of turns led us into a more remote area of Shelby County. His GPS instructed us to take a right. The road, its reddish-brown soil compacted with old gravel, forced us to slow as we dodged potholes. It twisted and turned. The trees thickened on both sides of the car.

I held my breath. A cold, heavy sensation settled on my chest, while pulses of something I couldn't identify rippled along my skin. Neither my vision or hearing dimmed, but I instinctively knew this was the road.

"We're getting close," I told Reed.

"Are you sure?" He threw me a questioning glance.

"Oh, yes."

"The lake is just ahead."

We rounded a curve, and ahead of us on the left was a hill, maybe twenty feet high, covered with trees of various heights, just like in my vision. To the right, the woods stretched, deep and dark. The hair rose on my arms and the back of my neck.

"We're here."

Reed stopped the car, and then turned to me. "You don't have to come. I'll search. You don't have to put yourself through this."

I shook my head. "No, I have to go with you. I have to do this for Bridget, Kathy, and Janine."

We got out of the car. He stopped by the trunk and took out a shovel, then joined me.

"Ready?" he asked, shouldering the implement like a soldier would a rifle.

I nodded and we walked into the trees. The vegetation was thicker than in my vision, having grown in three years. Bushes clutched at my clothing. I worried that I had made a mistake, but the heavy cold and crawling skin still clung to me. I had to be right.

As though reading my mind, Reed said, "Are we close? Your vision took place at night. Does that make a difference?"

"I don't think so, but then how would I know? I've never done this before. I've got too many vibes telling me this is it."

There was no discernable path through the trees. I tried to remember if the killer had dodged and weaved while carrying Bridget's body as we did now. Of course, he'd had an advantage. Having already selected the burial site and digging the grave, he knew where he was going.

We stopped to get our bearings, and I slapped at the pesky spring insects buzzing around my ears.

"Well, I'll be damned," Reed said.

I peeked around his shoulder and drew in a deep breath. Ahead of us I saw three large trees—an oak and two hickories, one a shagbark. The area between them was covered in underbrush.

"The bushes look big and very green," I said, my stomach turning over.

"Maybe they've had help all these years," he

commented.

I gagged at the implication.

"Is this the spot you saw?"

"Yes." In a flash, I realized I had seen something similar a couple of days earlier. It looked vaguely like the clearing in the weird dream I'd had while asleep in Reed's car after finding Kathy's body.

Reed walked up to the nearest large bush and planted the shovel near its roots. The rains had been plentiful this spring, and the soil was loose. Within ten minutes he had unearthed the three biggest bushes, exposing an area roughly four feet wide and eight feet long.

I stood back, out of the way, and leaned against the oak tree with my arms clasped across my stomach. Sweat rolled down his face, and the back of his knit shirt clung to his body. He wiped the moisture from his brow with his arm, and then bent over, resting on the handle of the shovel.

"How deep did the killer bury her in your vision?"

"I'm not sure. Maybe three or four feet, but that seems awfully deep."

"Not if he didn't want her found. Animals would dig up something shallow."

"So, why throw Kathy in the river? Even I knew she'd surface."

He shook his head. "I don't know. Maybe he just didn't care about Kathy. Maybe he was afraid someone might have seen Bridget get into the car. The mall is a busy place. That's why the bastard dug the grave beforehand. Her disappearance faded from the news within a few days. The longer she went undiscovered, the safer he was."

"Maybe he left something behind on her body like hair or fibers."

"You saw her die. Did she fight back?"

"No, I don't think so. Once he started strangling her, I no longer saw, but felt. I suppose she could have scratched or gouged him. Would this much time in the ground destroy DNA?"

"I don't know, but if we find any, I'm sure it's compromised."

He picked up the shovel and dug. It didn't take him long to go down a foot. I shivered. The rectangular shape of the hole reminded me of a coffin—a coffin Bridget didn't have.

Reed continued to dig, only now inspecting every shovelful of soil. He'd scrape and occasionally sift through the dirt with his hands. At three feet, he had to jump into the hole.

"Is there anything I can do to help?" I asked. I felt useless standing alone, doing nothing.

"Would you recognize a human bone if you saw it?"

"I don't know. Maybe. I took an anthropology course in college."

"You can look through what I bring up."

I approached the hole. Reed was thigh deep inside. A hunk of dirt hit the ground at my feet. I stooped and pawed through it. Nothing but sticks and rocks. We worked in silence. Reed maneuvered the shovel in small precise movements, and then abruptly stopped.

"What have we here?" he said softly.

I peered over the mounds of dirt to stare at what looked like a tree root. He bent down and gently pulled it free.

"What is it?" I asked.

"This is a humerus, the big bone in the upper arm." He placed it on the edge of the hole.

I saw it clearly now—the knob at the end where it attached to the shoulder and the remains of the hinge where it connected to the elbow.

Reed was on his knees carefully brushing soil away. He uncovered the lower arm. The bones of the hand lay next to a pelvis encased in rotting denim. Working his way up, the remains of a pink T-shirt still clinging to the rib cage was revealed.

We had found Bridget Connor.

Chapter Thirteen

The spotlights glared on the open gravesite while the forensics team gathered evidence. A generator buzzed away up on the road shattering the otherwise still night.

Reed made little comment after finding Bridget. He crawled out of the hole and immediately called the police. Dusk had fallen by the time they arrived, hence the lights.

In a scene reminiscent of a few days earlier, I stood off to one side, out of the way while Bridget's remains were carefully lifted from the grave. The skeleton was largely intact, no doubt due to the clothing she wore. It takes a long time for denim to disappear, and if the T-shirt had any synthetic fibers, it would last forever. Bridget must have believed in all natural materials. Much of the shirt was gone. The pink and gray sneakers looked strange on the bones of her feet.

The soft tissue had long since turned to dust, but some of Bridget's long, brown hair was still visible on the skull. The rest had fallen when the scalp disintegrated and now lay beside her head.

The killer had dumped her in the grave with no conscience. She rested on her left side, her right arm caught on a root. When the cartilage had disappeared, the lower arm fell, making the humerus the first bone found.

Reed also kept his distance from the gravesite and talked with Detective Brannon. I didn't hear the conversation, but had no trouble opening the pipeline to their emotions.

Relief, anger, and sorrow all swirled in Reed. I read Brannon easily. He was disgusted and angry.

Reed finally joined me. "There's not much we can do around here." He touched my cheek. "Thank you for finding her. Now, maybe she really can rest in peace."

"Her family?" I asked.

"I'll call them as soon as we have a positive ID. I know its Bridget, but we have to do the tests and make sure. Damn, this is going to kill her mother. She always held out hope her daughter had been kidnapped. I even followed up on her suggestion of a white slavery ring."

"I guess thinking your loved one may be a sex slave is preferable to believing they're dead. At least the family will have closure and a grave where they can place flowers on her birthday. This always being right is a pain in the ass. How come Jeff isn't here?"

"Bridget wasn't his case. It was Brannon's." He cupped my elbow and turned me away from the spotlighted grave. "Come on, let's go home."

We wound our way back through the brush, now a path strewn with power cables. I opened the car door and more or less fell into the seat. I was exhausted. I had no idea how, or even if, I could control these visions. Linnie was right. I needed to call Dr. Silberstein.

"Want to stop somewhere for dinner?" Reed asked.

I shook my head. "No, I'd much rather go home and order in."

We didn't talk much on the ride home. What could we say? Although Bridget Connor had been found, her case was far from solved. Kathy and Bridget died because they trusted and believed in love. Janine was collateral damage. She died because the killer wanted a set of keys. I didn't just want him caught. I wanted him dead. Dead and buried in an unmarked grave, so no one would ever remember his name.

Our silence continued until we walked into the house. The time had come for me to tell Reed the whole truth about my visions.

"Is pizza all right with you?" he asked.

"It's fine. Reed, there's something I have to tell you first."

He gave me a strange look. "What? Is there more to Bridget's death than you let on?"

"No. It's something Linnie suggested a few days ago."

We sat on opposite ends of the sofa while I told him about Linnie's possession theory.

"Possession!"

"Linnie thinks Kathy linked into my mind in the restaurant and again in the dream. If she did; why not Bridget? I *felt* her inside me. I *felt* her die. And I viewed the burial through her eyes, as if her ghost hovered. Just like with Kathy."

Reed scowled. "Why didn't you tell me before?"

"You weren't ready to believe. Besides, how do you think I feel? It's not an easy thing to accept."

"Who else knows about this?"

"Just Linnie. It's not the kind of thing I want to advertise—assuming the theory is true."

"Had it ever happened before Kathy Watson?"

"No. Kathy upped the ante in my psychic abilities. I'm homing in on emotions. What does that make me? An empath?"

"I don't know. And Janine? Anything more there?"

"Janine died too quickly. No vision—just photos and an overwhelming sense something was wrong."

Reed frowned and ran his hand through his already mussed hair. "Are you saying Janine didn't have time to contact you? How did you get the pictures and the feeling something was wrong?"

"God, Reed, how should I know? I don't have all the answers to how this works," I replied wearily.

"Obviously not or you might have seen the killer's face."

"Well, excuse me all to hell, but I think I told you, I don't choose the visions. They choose me. I'm doing the best I can, and if you don't like it you can…"

The doorbell rang, saving us both from saying anything we'd regret. The stress levels had reached the breaking point in both of us. I opened the door to find Linnie and Jeff on the front porch.

"What are you doing here?" I asked, stepping back and motioning them inside.

"We drove by a little while ago on the way to my place, but you weren't home. We were just headed out to eat when we thought we'd swing by again. Want to join us?" Linnie asked.

"We were planning to order in a pizza," Reed commented. "Why not join us? We've had a rather nasty day."

He told them about finding Bridget's grave.

"So, you were right. She was murdered," Jeff muttered.

"How could you doubt it after what Sasha told you in my office the other day?" Linnie said.

"I guess I don't anymore. Give me the details, Reed."

The men sat while Linnie and I headed for the kitchen where I called in the order. Linnie took two beers out to the guys, and then rejoined me at the kitchen table, drinking wine.

"I'm sorry, Sasha. Today must have been awful. These things are coming fast and furious now. I wonder why."

"I don't know. I wish I'd paid more attention to investment banking that night at Le Bistro. If I had, I wouldn't be sitting here sick to my stomach and wondering when the next shoe's going to drop."

She sipped her wine and ran her finger around the edge of the glass. "It wouldn't have made any difference. Kathy would still be dead."

"But not Janine," I reminded her in a bitter voice. "I told Reed about the possession theory."

"What did he say?"

"He was upset I hadn't told him sooner. I said I couldn't explain it to him if I didn't understand it myself." I sipped from my glass. "I'm sick of talking about this. Let's talk about you and Jeff. You passed my house on the way to yours? The last time I saw you, you were on your way to Dr. Garland's."

Linnie smiled. "So I was. I spilled my guts, and had just gotten home when Jeff pulled in behind me. Would you believe he invited me out for ice cream?"

"Ice cream? You've got to be kidding," I exclaimed.

"He thought it might make me feel better. I found it

very sweet and charming. And the funny thing is; he was right. I do feel better. Or maybe I'm just accepting Janine's death. We drove past here on our way back home."

"When was this?"

"Around five."

"It's after eight. Do I dare ask what you did at your house for three hours?"

"Not what you think, dammit. We made out on the sofa, and I was ready to haul his ass into the bedroom when he called a halt to the proceedings."

"Why?"

"It seems I've hooked up with an old-fashioned kind of guy. He said we should wait a while longer."

"Jeff said that? Jeff, who's never met a woman he didn't like? He sounds like that nutty actor you dated. God, don't tell me he's gay."

"I brought up the other women. He said they were just flings and what he felt for me was deeper. He didn't want to spoil something wonderful with sex too soon." She sipped more wine and eyed me.

"And you bought it?"

"Why not? It makes sense. I've seen patients who've had severe commitment problems and all of them slept around. When the real thing hits them, they have a hard time believing it and adjusting."

Linnie's words bothered me. Any guy offered a full banquet rarely turned it down. When they did, it was because they'd just been fed.

"I think you're the one having a hard time believing it. Jeff's a nice guy and sexy as hell, but he's handing you a plate full of baloney." My best friend frowned, and I couldn't tell if I'd irritated her or burst her romantic bubble.

"What? No vision for me?" she said, arching her eyebrows. "I could use one about now."

"Sorry. I'm fresh out of visions, at least for tonight."

Linnie drained her glass and poured another. For some reason her question brought a cloud to my mind. I rubbed my forehead. I was surprised my mind functioned at all. Between last night and today, it had worked on overload.

I followed Linnie's actions, drinking my wine, and refilling the glass. Jeff walked into the room.

"Hey, you guys holding a gossip session?" he teased, opening the fridge and taking out another couple of beers. "If so, please treat me gently."

"We sliced and diced you, then hung you out to dry," Linnie quipped with a smile.

She rose and linked her arm through his. Jeff kissed her cheek, and they sauntered out of the kitchen. I took another sip of wine, mentally shrugging. He and Linnie seemed to be well-suited. Who was I to rain on their parade? I got up and followed.

Jeff sat in one of the chairs, Linnie planted on the floor at his feet. Reed still occupied the sofa, and I plunked myself next to him.

"So, did Reed bring you up to date on Bridget?" I asked.

"Pretty gruesome. You must be sick of finding bodies."

"I could do without it." I paused, thinking about something Reed had said by the gravesite. "Jeff, why didn't you investigate Bridget Connor's disappearance?"

"I wasn't assigned to it."

"Why not? You were on the first ones, weren't you?"

"Yes, but after Reed got shot, I partnered with another guy." Jeff shrugged. "It's not an unusual occurrence."

"Officially, I was no longer connected to the Memphis Police Department," Reed answered. "Some of the guys let me in on things when they find a body with similarities to my serial killer theory."

"But that makes no sense," I replied. "Jeff could have had valuable insight."

"Never said police department policies made sense," Jeff said.

The pizza arrived before we could pursue the discussion any further. While we ate, I turned an idea over in my mind. I was exhausted and my mind weary, but if I could find Eleanor, it would be one more family who could bury their daughter. The clothing and picture Reed had given me the other day did not evoke any visions then, but maybe now, with all that had happened I would be more open, more attuned to her.

I finished my pizza and polished off my Chianti. Maybe the wine helped. I'd been drinking the night of Kathy's and Bridget's visions. I poured another glass.

"Right, Sasha?"

Linnie's question brought me out of my thoughts. I pulled my attention back to my living room.

"I'm sorry. What did you say?"

She frowned. "Are you all right? You looked like you were in another world. You weren't, were you?" Her voice had an anxious quality to it, and her eyes widened.

"No. I was just thinking. Reed, do you have Eleanor's things with you?"

"No, they're at the office. Why?"

"I'd like to take another look at them."

"What's on your mind?" Jeff asked.

"Linnie, if I open my mind, if I invite a vision to appear, do you think it will come?"

"I have no idea. What are you suggesting?"

"I want you to hypnotize me. I'll have physical contact with the picture and clothing Reed has, and I'll open my mind. My resistance will be low. I'm tired and have had a lot to drink."

"Sasha, I'm not sure this is a good idea," she replied. "You told me your mind was tapped out. And mixing hypnosis with wine can be dangerous."

"How do you know? Have you ever tried it?" I asked.

"No, and now isn't the time to be a groundbreaker."

"What can it hurt?" Reed said. "She was right about Bridget. If she can find Eleanor, it'll be another step in nailing this guy."

She frowned and wrinkled her forehead. "I don't know *what* it can hurt or *what* the consequences could be."

"Linnie, in the end, it's my decision, isn't it?"

Silence answered my question. Linnie had a doubtful look on her face. Reed's expression was hopeful. Only Jeff remained inscrutable.

"Come on, Linnie. What's the worst that can happen? I'll babble and make no sense or see nothing."

She caught her lower lip between her teeth. "I won't do it here. I'll have to do it at the office in a controlled environment."

"Fine. Let's go do it." I rose, drained my glass, and refilled it.

"I don't think getting drunk is the answer to finding Eleanor," Reed commented.

Jeff gathered the empty beer bottles along with the pizza box and disappeared into the kitchen. When he returned, he bore a worried look.

"Sasha, are you sure you want to do this?" he asked.

"Of course. Why not?"

He shrugged. "I don't know. I just wonder if now's the time. You've been through hell the last twenty-four hours, longer if you count Kathy Watson."

"No. Now is the perfect time. I'm angry and determined."

Reed headed for the front door. "I'm going to get the clothing and photo. I'll meet you all at the office in half an hour."

He closed the door, leaving the three of us to stare at each other. It was an uneasy silence. I gulped my wine and took the glasses into the kitchen. Now that I'd made the decision, I was reluctant to leave the house. Linnie's concerns could be real. We were charting new psychic territory.

I returned to the living room and opened my mouth to say forget the whole idea when Eleanor's face in the photo popped into my mind. No, I couldn't let her down. She deserved to be found, too. I slung my purse over my shoulder.

"Let's go. I want to find Eleanor Gayle."

****

"Are you sure about this?" Linnie asked for the

tenth time since I made my request. She closed the blinds and plugged in the small fountain. Her fingers paused on the switch to the ceiling fan.

I settled in on the sofa. "Yes. I'm sure."

Reed extracted several items from a bag and handed them to me. The picture and the mini-skirt were the same as the other day, but a tank top and a pair of Daisy Duke's were new.

"What're these?" I asked.

"The clothes Eleanor wore the night she disappeared."

"I don't get it. Her body hasn't been found. How did you get the clothes?"

"The surveillance camera shows her wearing this outfit at the craps table at ten o'clock. We found them neatly folded on the dresser. The maid admitted she did it when she made up the room the next morning."

"So, Eleanor changed clothes before she left the hotel."

He nodded. "I thought maybe these would help, since it was closer to when she disappeared."

I held the clothing against my face and opened my mind. Excitement and anticipation transferred from the items to me. I saw no vision, but sensed her emotions.

"She may have met him at the craps table, but dice isn't her game. I don't think she stayed long," I told him.

"I reviewed those tapes dozens of times. She never sat near anybody at a BJ table who played craps."

My mind smelled garlic. "Was there film from the buffet?"

"She was granted a comp and ate around one in the morning. There are no cameras in the restaurant. He may have sought her out there. We interviewed personnel, but no one remembered if Eleanor was alone. They serve a lot of people on the weekends, even at one AM."

I took the rest of the clothing and bundled it all under my shirt, then held the photo in my left hand.

Jeff, silent until now, sat behind Linnie's desk, a frown on his face. "Are you sure about this, Sasha?"

"Yes. Let's start."

Linnie dimmed the lights and sat in a chair. Reed took the one next to her.

"Jeff, I want you and Reed to stay quiet, no matter what Sasha reveals while under hypnosis. I don't even want to hear you breathing. Understand?" Both men nodded. "Are you ready, Sasha?"

I closed my eyes and inhaled several deep breaths of the eucalyptus scent wafting from the dispensers. I also had a good buzz on from the wine. My muscles relaxed, and I tried to clear my mind of all thoughts. For the second time in a week, I listened to the swish of the fan's blades and felt the air touch my face. I heard the click of the tape recorder starting.

"Are you relaxed, Sasha? How do you feel?"

"Quiet and rested, even though it's been a tumultuous day."

"Good. Open your eyes and focus on the fan. Watch the blades turn."

I did as she said. She spoke in her usual soft monotone. It didn't take long for sounds to diminish and my eyes to grow heavy. I tumbled into a deep trance.

****

The emotions pummeled me as I slowly returned to

reality. Shock, rage, disgust, and contempt each took a turn. I heard the fan blades cutting through the air and shivered from the breeze. I opened my eyes and gazed around the room, confused and disoriented.

My right hand gripped my tank top and Eleanor's clothing beneath it. My left clutched the photo, now crumpled. I was a tad sick to my stomach, and my mouth was Dust Bowl dry. I relaxed my fingers, tossing the items onto the coffee table, and sat up cautiously. Then I looked at the audience.

Linnie's brow knit into a thoughtful expression. Reed frowned, and Jeff bore a blank look on his face.

"How did I do?" I asked.

"How do you feel?" Linnie countered.

I told her, and she brought me a bottle of water from the fridge. I drank half of it before coming up for air. She then brought the lights up, turning off the fountain and fan.

"So, did I say anything useful?"

"More than I expected," Reed replied.

"How long was I out?"

"About half an hour," Linnie said.

Most of the emotions I'd sensed when awakening had vanished, although disgust still lingered.

"What's wrong? Y'all act like I drilled a dry well." Their silence was unnerving.

"Don't you remember?" Jeff asked.

"No. I listen to the tape, and then Linnie and I discuss my session."

"When you listen, you'll see your sentences are disjointed. You're not *seeing*, but *feeling*," Linnie said.

"In other words, I'm more into emotions than events?"

"There are a few visuals."

"Replay the tape," Reed said.

"Let Sasha rest for a while," Linnie insisted.

"I'm fine. I want to hear."

She shrugged, punching the play button. We listened for several minutes, and then Linnie paused the tape.

"So, she *did* meet him in the restaurant," I said. "Do you think he stalked her in the casino or was it just a chance meeting?"

"He stalked her. I'm sure of that," Reed replied.

"Why leave the casino?" Linnie asked.

"He may have been registered at another hotel, and rather than use her room with the possibility of being interrupted by her friends, he enticed her to his," Jeff said, not looking up from Linnie's desk. He doodled on a pad of paper.

"Let's finish the tape," I told them.

When it was over, I sat back. Now, I understood the emotions that had hammered at me earlier.

"My God, was she killed in the parking lot?" I said.

"Very possible," Reed answered. "According to you, she was happy and anticipating a good time. We know she showered, changed, and left the room. Then she hits the parking lot and you unveil a brief moment of fright before things go blank."

Pressure built behind my eyes. I rubbed my forehead and took another swig of water.

"I don't think this is our guy," Jeff said suddenly.

"Why not?" Reed asked.

"Casinos. I hate 'em," he muttered. "They appeal to the lowest of the low. Women use them as pick-up joints. They wear clinging, low cut tops and miniskirts so short nothing is left to the imagination. Those impossible high heels make them look like hookers. Men get the wrong idea. How can women be surprised when men act on that impression?"

His outburst left me stunned. I glanced at Reed. His expression told me he'd never heard Jeff say something that judgmental.

"I don't believe you said that. How Neanderthal can you get?" Linnie demanded in a furious tone. "So she wanted a good time. So what? Are you saying Eleanor got what she deserved?"

Jeff tossed the pencil on her desk. "No. I'm saying casinos bring out the worst in people." He ran a hand through his hair and sighed. "No one deserves to die the way Eleanor did, but I'm not convinced this is the work of a serial killer. He probably incapacitated her, pushed her into his car, raped, and then killed her."

"So, this is an isolated incident that happens to come in the middle of a serial killing rampage?" Reed asked Jeff. His brow furrowed and his gaze sharpened on his former partner.

"Yes."

The pressure behind my eyes continued to build. It didn't hurt, but I closed my eyes anyway. Lord, I really wanted to sleep.

"Sasha, are you all right?" Linnie asked.

"Oh, God," I muttered. The sensation gripped me. I saw nothing. Only felt.

"Sasha!" Reed said.

I opened my eyes. The sensation vanished leaving me shaking and cold.

"She didn't die in the parking lot, but later. I don't know how. I didn't see anything, but I think she trusted him."

"Of course she trusted him. She wouldn't have left the casino if she hadn't," Reed said, waving his hand in an impatient gesture.

"No, no. She trusted him for other reasons." I moaned and clutched my head in my hands. "Maybe something he said or told her in the restaurant."

"Like, come to my room. There's a party?" Jeff said.

"I don't know."

"Anything on what happened after he killed her?" Reed asked.

I took several deep breaths and concentrated. "I see a building of some kind. It's abandoned." My shoulders slumped from the effort and my head drooped.

"That's it," Linnie declared, standing. "Sasha's had more than enough tonight. Reed, take her home."

Reed's arm supported me as we left the office.

"Call if you need me," Linnie said.

"I will."

"Are you going to be all right?" Reed asked, pulling out of the parking lot.

"Yeah. These sessions always leave me tired, but tonight was kinda rough. I'm not used to crowds."

"I don't want to burden you further, but do you think you can narrow down this building you saw?"

"Not right now. Maybe later."

"Did you sense it was very far from The Winning Touch?" he pressed.

I rubbed my forehead and thought. "I have no idea. But then, the killer would have chosen it beforehand, just like he dug Bridget's grave before killing her. You're not buying Jeff's theory of a random killing, are you?"

"Not for one moment."

"He could be right, you know."

Reed shook his head. "I was kind of surprised by his comments. Who would have thought Jeff Hammond to have such a Puritanical streak in him?"

I remembered Linnie's statement of earlier in the evening. "I didn't know he hated casinos."

"He always maintained they raised the crime rate and appealed to the baser instincts of their patrons. In a way, he's right. Greed and the chance to get rich quick with little effort can turn perfectly normal people into animals who will lie, cheat, and steal." We stopped at a red light, and he turned his gaze on me. "Have you ever had a vision right after hypnosis before?"

"Never, but then we're breaking new ground every day. And it wasn't actually a vision. I didn't see anything. I sensed it. Like I was in her head and at the same time, I wasn't. I can't explain."

The light changed. We drove in silence for a while and drained as I was, still tapped into his emotions.

"You're going to go look for abandoned buildings in Tunica County tomorrow, aren't you?" I said.

"Yep. I'll call my brother and see if he can give me a hand. He knows the area better than I."

"I want to go with you."

"I figured."

We pulled into my driveway, and I hesitated before opening the car door. An odd prickle slid over my skin. I was drop dead exhausted, and yet I wanted to make love with Reed McIntyre in the worst way.

I turned and laid my hand on his arm. "Nightcap?"

He took my hand, raising it to his lips. Heat raced

up my arm and suffused my body. My breath caught in my throat, and my heart pumped hard with heavy beats in my chest. The fire found a home in the pit of my stomach, sending out tongues of flame to wrap around my nerves.

"I'd better not," he answered. "I might not leave."

"I'm counting on that."

"Are you sure, Sasha?"

I pulled his head down to mine and let our lips produce magic. Tongues tangled, and our fingers clutched in each other's hair.

He finally pulled his mouth from mine. Without another word we got out of the car and into the house.

"Do you really want that nightcap?"

He shook his head. "No. I want you."

That was the only answer I needed. I leaped into his arms. What our mouths didn't touch, our hands did. Clothing melted away, littering the floor. We stumbled toward my bedroom. Reed tossed me onto the bed and shoved his slacks and boxers down his legs, then kicked them out of the way.

I was down to my underwear, which he quickly disposed of before settling next to me. He was hard and lean, his chest sculpted. My lips found the scars from his bullet wounds, and I shuddered at how close he'd come to death.

Then, I no longer thought. He latched onto my nipple, nibbling and sucking until I was little more than a squirming mass of flesh. His fingers slid down my belly to the junction of my thighs, massaging that tiny pinpoint of sensation. A spring coiled within me, hot and burning, ready to explode.

My hand encircled his erection, stroking in rhythm

to his mouth and fingers. He was hard as cement, and I touched the drop of wetness oozing from the tip. My finger swirled it around the head.

"God, Sasha," he groaned. He shoved my legs apart with his knee and nestled between them. "Wait. I have to get…"

I didn't let him finish. I reached down and positioned him where he should be.

"Now," I demanded and lifted my hips allowing him to slip in an inch.

"Sasha, I can't stop."

I wrapped my legs around his waist. He shuddered and with a hoarse cry plunged deep inside me. I wanted no gentle caresses or murmured words of endearment. I received none. We shouted with each lunge and thrust, our bodies separating, and then slamming back together.

The conflagration burned hotter. The spring coiled tighter and tighter until I shattered into a thousand shards. I screamed and thrust for all I was worth, the contractions sending currents of sharp pleasure to every cell in my body. My nails scored his back. Then Reed yelled and jammed deep, the strong, hot pulses of his orgasm prolonging mine.

Gradually, we drifted down from the heights. With a groan, Reed rolled off of me, collapsing on his side. I sucked in huge gulps of air. Neither of us spoke. Reed stroked my cheek, and then leaned over to kiss me. I ran my fingers through his hair, kissing him back.

I wanted the caresses now. I slid my hands over his chest, across his six pack abs, and around to his back. His lips found the pulse point in my neck and nibbled while his hand smoothed my waist and hip. His erection had not disappeared. It lay heavy and wet on my thigh.

"Reed," I whispered.

"Hush."

His lips traveled across my breast and fastened onto my nipple. The embers in my belly rekindled, the flames licking along my nerves. I gasped, letting the night spiral into indescribable delight.

Chapter Fourteen

Kathy paused at the edge of the stream of souls. Where the hell was this Bridget person? Had she slipped out through one of the holes? If so, then the chances of finding her were slim and none.

Someone bumped into her. She turned to stare at a man who glared back.

"Sorry, but keep it moving," he said.

His hair was long and he sported a goatee. From the clothes he wore, Kathy gauged his arrival in this other world sometime in the mid-seventies.

"Hey, I'm looking for someone," she snapped.

"Aren't we all?"

"No, no. Someone I met here. Her name is Bridget."

"Don't know any Bridget. Have you tried the park?"

Kathy had no idea what he was talking about. "Park? What park? Where?"

"Not that kind of park. More like a bus stop."

"Yeah, well, I haven't seen one of those either."

"You must be new," he muttered.

"I'm new, and I need to find Bridget. What's this bus stop thing?"

"It's where we go to wait for other souls to find us. Think of it as a bulletin board in a college dorm."

"Hey, you two! Go with the flow. You're backing up traffic," a voice called, floating past.

"Come on. I'll take you."

The seventies man touched her arm, and they re-entered the stream, swirling past several holes, some opening, others closing.

"What's the deal with these cockamamie holes?" she demanded.

"Whenever we're tired of the stream and want to return to earth, we punch through. Same with coming back."

"You mean, any time I want to exit, I can? How?"

"Pretend you're diving into a pool and go for it. The hole will stay open for a few seconds, and then close. If you're not in the right place or in the right era, try again."

"The right era?" Kathy remembered the field with the soldiers and swords.

"Before you go punching holes into reality, think of where you want to go and when. Keeps it simple."

Now he tells me. I could have used that information earlier.

Their journey ended at the entrance to a small—and for want of a better word—room. Kathy had spent so much time seeking her quarry from the stream on the left she'd never paid any attention to what was on her right. The man guided her through the portal.

"Here. Good luck."

"Thanks. I appreciate the help."

He nodded and disappeared into the stream.

Kathy gazed around the jammed enclosure. Restless spirits throbbed, sighing as though impatient to be found. Others rested quietly with serene expressions.

She spotted Bridget, one of the quiet ones, and drifted over.

"Hello," Bridget said with a smile. "I knew you'd find the park sooner or later."

"How long have you been waiting?"

Bridget shrugged. "Time doesn't exist here. It could be hours—days—months."

"Look, I've got a terrible problem, and I need some answers. Why do I have the feeling we're connected? Why did you thank me?"

"I understand your confusion. Yes, we are connected. And I thanked you for contacting someone who can help us."

"Sasha?"

"Is that her name?"

"Whoa, back up. How are we connected?" Kathy asked.

"We were both murdered by the same man."

Shock ricocheted through her. "Gerald? Gerald killed you, too?"

"I didn't know him as Gerald, but as Scott."

"Wait a minute. How did you know I was murdered?"

"I felt you arrive. I've felt others arrive, too, but they didn't linger. They passed on. I believe Scott has sent quite a few of us into the afterlife. You're the only one I connected with, though."

"I can't believe this," Kathy muttered. "Are you sure we're talking about the same guy? Describe Scott." Bridget's description matched Gerald. "Well, I'll be damned. We're the victims of a serial killer. I was stabbed. How about you?"

"Strangled. Did he drug your wine?"

"He must have, because I couldn't fight back. Funny thing is, at first I couldn't remember where he killed me. It was all blurry, but the longer I'm here the clearer the picture."

"I know. I had trouble viewing details when I arrived. Gradually, the vision improves. Maybe it's the drug wearing off or maybe things just happen slower in death."

"What do we do now?"

"You need to re-establish contact with our host. I met her a little while ago, but the thread was too slim to maintain," Bridget said.

"You said you felt other victims, but they passed on?"

"Yes, a woman named Susan, and another named Eleanor. They only paused for a moment, and then moved into the light, although I did sense tremendous anguish with Eleanor."

"How come you're still here?"

"He buried me. My body was never found. I can't rest until my family knows what became of me. Thanks to Sasha, that happened yesterday. Now, I can leave."

"Leave? Please, don't abandon me," Kathy begged, panic bubbling inside her.

Bridget shook her head. "I won't. I can't do much to help Scott gets what he deserves, but you can. I'm not leaving until our job is finished."

Kathy shrugged. "We may have a problem. Sasha was hypnotized, and I've had trouble getting back into her head. It's like a room with a locked door."

"Hypnotized? By whom?"

"Her shrink."

"Try Sasha again. With the drug wearing off you

might have more luck. If that doesn't work, go for the psychiatrist. There might be an avenue through her."

"I never thought of that," Kathy admitted. "Okay, I'll go back to earth or reality or whatever it's called. The guy who brought me here said all I had to do was punch through. Hope I don't spend the rest of eternity searching for the right place."

Bridget laughed. "Just have a clear picture in your mind of where you want to go. You'll get there. In the meantime, I'll wait here."

Kathy nodded and left the park, tossing her soul back into the stream. In her mind's eye, she visualized Sasha's living room, and then, clasping her hands in front of her, she launched herself at the shimmering wall to her right.

****

I slowly bit into my cinnamon toast. The aroma mixed with the sugary taste on my tongue. Reed sat across from me and smiled, drinking his second cup of coffee. I was sleepy, hungry, and in desperate need of more kisses.

"What are you thinking?" he asked.

"That we should go back to bed and take up where we left off."

He laughed. "Nothing I'd like more, but we have work to do." He fished his cell out of his pocket. "I'm calling my brother."

"I hate getting up at six. It's for the birds."

Reed chuckled as he scrolled down to the number he sought.

I finished the toast, and drained the last of my coffee. Last night's hypnosis still troubled me. I hadn't been able to get a handle on exactly what happened or where. I'd not really failed, but neither had I succeeded. What was worse, a darkness I didn't understand hovered at the edges of my mind like a warning.

"Ten? No problem. Will that give you enough time…Good. See you then." Reed hung up. "Bill says there are abandoned buildings all over Tunica, Tate, and Gladden Counties. Finding the right one will be a chore. He's going to get detailed maps of back roads within a twenty-five mile radius of The Winning Touch off the Internet. I doubt if our killer would chance going any further. We'll meet in the casino parking lot."

"Do I have time to grab a shower before we go?"

"Sure, there's no hurry. I have to go home and change. I'll come back in an hour."

I waved goodbye, and suddenly had a strong urge to call Linnie. I was surprised when she answered on the first ring.

"Wow, you're up with the birds this morning," I said.

"Yeah, well, having a shitty night's sleep helps. How are you? Recovered from the session yet?"

"I guess. What's on your agenda today?"

"The same as yesterday. I'm going over patient files until I can eliminate or confirm if the killer is one of them."

"Files. Nuts. I still have those I took yesterday in my car."

"Don't worry about them. You can bring them with you. Are you coming in?"

"Don't think so. Reed and I are going to search for abandoned buildings. We're leaving in a little while."

"He's there now?"

I hesitated, and then chuckled. "He was."

"So, you did it, huh? I'm jealous," her voice teased.

"You should be."

"That good?"

"Better. I'll tell you all about it soon."

Her sigh echoed in my ears as I hung up.

****

Even at ten in the morning, the parking lot of The Winning Touch was three-quarters full. Reed pulled into a space next to a white Tahoe. A man dressed in jeans and a black T-shirt lounged against the back bumper. Reed exited the car. He and the man gave each other a brief hug, surprising me. In spite of last night, I didn't think of Reed as the touchy-feely sort. I opened the car door and joined them.

"Sasha, this is my brother Bill McIntyre. Bill, Sasha Bellwood."

"Miss Bellwood, my pleasure." He shook my hand and smiled.

He was an inch or so shorter than Reed, but possessed the same eye and hair colors, and their features were similar, although Bill's were softer, not as sharp and craggy. Their body shapes were identical.

"I'm pleased to meet you, too."

He dropped my hand and reached into the front seat of the Tahoe, withdrawing several sheets of paper.

"These are the maps of the area. What type of structure are you looking for?"

"We're not sure," Reed answered. "But it would have to be off the beaten track. He went to a lot of trouble to conceal Bridget. Probably did the same with Eleanor."

"If he has half the intelligence you think, then he must realize he's in a pattern. You said he left some of

234

them in plain sight. Burying his victims breaks the pattern. Where do you want to start?"

"Sasha?" Reed asked.

I shrugged, staring at the maps as if for inspiration. "She may have died here in the parking lot or in the car soon after. If I was carrying a body in my car, I'd want to unload it as soon as I could."

"He'd have to get at least several miles away from the casinos and the traffic." Bill's finger jabbed at the map. "Let's start here."

We piled into the Tahoe, Bill and Reed up front with me in the back.

"If you see anything suspicious or familiar, sing out," Bill instructed.

"I will. I'm sorry you have to spend your Saturday hauling us all over Northwest Mississippi."

Reed laughed. "Are you kidding? The most excitement Gladden County ever gets is the occasional drunk driver or some poor soul who does thirty-five in a thirty. I assume you still have that speed trap in Winchester," Reed joked.

In the rearview mirror, I saw Bill grin.

"Of course it's there. How else do you think I afforded the Tahoe? And don't forget the trailer park. At least one drunk and disorderly every weekend."

Reed snorted. "Must be exciting handcuffing those sweaty, bare-chested rednecks who swear they only had two beers when the empty twelve-pack is on the trailer steps. And you call yourself a cop."

"Hey, some of those women are damned tough."

I'd never seen Reed like this. I listened to the friendly teasing between brothers, and wondered what had all but robbed him of a sense of humor. The murders? The job? A near-death experience? Would he laugh like this once he caught the killer? I fervently hoped so, and then focused my attention out the window. Bill drove at a moderate pace, and I had no trouble seeing the view on both sides of the car.

"How about that?" Reed asked.

I turned my head and stared at a structure about a quarter of a mile away.

"Let's go find out," Bill said, turning onto a gravel road.

We pulled into a dirt parking area. The sign on the building read, "Rogers' Gin".

Reed twisted around in his seat, looking at me with raised eyebrows. "Does this look familiar?"

"Not really, but I guess we should check it out."

The doors were locked, but we peered in through the dirty windows. Nothing appeared out of place.

"From the look of things, I'd say this is a working gin," Bill said. "Your killer wouldn't take the chance of hiding a body here. Too many people in and out during cotton harvest."

We returned to the car, resuming our search. Over the next three hours we explored the possibilities of two dilapidated barns, a grain elevator, and an abandoned train depot on the outskirts of Lennox, Mississippi. Even the railroad tracks had disappeared. The town wasn't far behind. It was Saturday and only a handful of cars parked on the one and only street.

We were now a good fifteen miles from The Winning Touch. I was discouraged. Bill and Reed had long ago given up the bantering. My failure and the silence in the car got on my nerves.

"So, Bill," I said to break up the sound of the tires

on pavement. "Are you married?"

Reed turned to stare. "Why do you want to know that?"

"Maybe she finds me irresistibly attractive. You jealous?"

Reed snorted, and I laughed. "I'm sorry. I guess it is kind of a personal question. I was just curious."

"I don't care. No, I'm not married—now."

"Oops, sorry again. Didn't mean to intrude."

"You didn't. I was married for three long-suffering years to Rita the Bitch. She was from Hernando. I'm still trying to figure out why the hell I married her. We had nothing in common."

"You didn't need anything in common. That woman was hot," Reed commented.

"That she was, but I work fourteen hour days. She didn't like that. Gladden County isn't exactly the center of sophisticated society, and she didn't like that. I like hunting and fishing. When the opportunity arose, I went."

"Let me guess—she didn't like it," I said. "Seems to me she didn't like a whole lot."

"She didn't. In the end, she didn't like me much, either. She packed her bags, went home to mama, and got a divorce. Can't say I was unhappy about it." We had found our way back to the main highway. "Anybody hungry?"

"I could eat a small cow," Reed said. "Sasha?"

"I'm starving."

"King's Point isn't too far away. There's a café on the edge of town. Serves up pretty good fare."

A few minutes later, we pulled into the gravel parking lot. The place was about two-thirds full, but we found a table near the front window.

Reed felt in his pocket and removed his cell phone, then made a face. "Damn, two missed calls. I was afraid being out here in the boonies would mess with reception. Order me a burger, fries, and iced tea. I'll be back."

The waitress appeared. Bill ordered while I read the menu before finally deciding on a club sandwich and tea. After she left, an awkward silence fell. Bill broke it.

"So, how did a psychic wind up with my brother?"

"I take it he's told you how we met."

He nodded. "I must say asking a total stranger to help find a dead body is one of the more original pick-up lines I've ever heard."

I sputtered with laughter. "I was horrified and told him to go to hell."

"I can imagine how he asked. Reed is not the most subtle of men. Don't hold it against him. He may be rough and abrupt, but my brother is damned decent. His passions run deep."

"He apologized after calling me a charlatan. Jeff said he was an okay guy and to forgive him."

The smile faded from Bill's face. "You know Jeff Hammond?"

"Yes. He came with Reed to talk to me about Bridget and Eleanor."

"I see."

The waitress brought our iced tea. I glanced through the window. Reed paced while on the phone. The tone of Bill's voice had caught my attention. I probed his mind gently.

"You don't like Jeff?"

He picked up his glass and gulped. "He's slick. I'm just glad I don't have a sister for him to hit on. And I still think he's the reason my brother was damned near killed."

I didn't need to see his face, or hear his voice to home in on his anger. I shifted uneasily in my chair.

"Why do you say that? According to Reed, Jeff did everything the way he should have."

"Yeah, well, Reed only knows what Jeff told the internal affairs guys. If you and your partner have a guy holed up in a house, you call for back up, and then take your positions. A good cop, even on the front porch, wouldn't allow himself to be seen or heard until his partner was safe. I think he was careless—sloppy."

I didn't know what to say. Jeff had struck me as being a good cop, which isn't to say he didn't make mistakes, but if Reed held no grudge, I couldn't see why Bill did.

"I'm sorry, Sasha. Reed defended him after the incident, and I can tell you like the guy."

I drank a long swig of tea. "He's kind of dating my best friend."

"Hope she has a bulletproof heart."

Before I could answer, Reed returned.

"Is everything all right?" I asked.

"Yeah. Got a report that we may have a break on another cold case I'm working. A liquor store was robbed and the clerk killed about two years ago. An informant may have new information."

Our food arrived, and we settled in to eat. I put Bill's animosity down to brotherly love, pushing it out of my mind. It was his problem. He had to deal with it.

I had to deal with finding Eleanor Gayle.

****

The next two hours saw more of the same search pattern. The net now spread out twenty miles from the casino, and I wondered if I had missed the boat.

Apparently, so did Reed. He pulled something out of his shirt pocket and handed it to me over the seat. It was Eleanor's photo, the one I'd crumpled last night.

"Here, Sasha. See if this helps."

I held the picture and traced the woman's features with my finger, then closed my eyes. I drew a blank. I neither saw nor felt anything. I breathed deep and concentrated harder. A faint shiver skittered up my arms. Something was there, trying to break through. Or did I feel it because I wanted to?

I opened my eyes. "I'm getting nothing."

"Why not? Last night you said you saw pictures."

"I know what I said last night. I can't help it if nothing is coming through now. I don't know why, so don't ask," I snapped.

I leaned my head back against the seat and stared at Eleanor's image.

Come on, girl. Talk to me. We want to help. We want to find you and put this creep in jail so he can never hurt anyone again.

I turned my head and gazed out the window. The cotton fields whizzed by, followed by the occasional house. Delta country is flat. The levee to the Mississippi paralleled the road we traveled. Bill slowed and turned onto a gravel lane, then turned several more times. I had no idea where we were, only that the levee was further away. I sighed and tried to choke back the rising guilt of failure. Then, in the distance, a structure caught my attention. My scalp prickled.

"What's that?" I asked in a sharp voice.

"What's what?" Bill replied.

I sat up and pointed toward the right. "Over there. See it?"

"Let's go find out," he said.

Bill took the next right, then a left. The gravel gave way to dirt.

"Looks like an old farmhouse," Reed commented.

"Why is it abandoned?"

"The property around here is owned by Big John Portman. He bought out a lot of small farmers. He didn't care about the houses, just the fields."

Weeds choked the rutted driveway, and off in the distance, I spotted the remains of an old barn. Vibes hummed along my nerves. "Guys, this doesn't look familiar, but it could be the place."

We got out of the car, standing knee-deep in weeds and creeping kudzu in what was once the front yard, and stared at the weathered farmhouse. Then, we slowly walked forward, mounted the steps, and entered.

Thick dust along with the stench of rotting wood and vegetation made me want to gag. It didn't take long to see we'd find nothing in here. No floor boards had been disturbed, and being so close to the river precluded any cellar.

The same could be said for the barn. It had collapsed long before Eleanor disappeared. Most of the outbuildings had also gone the way of the barn.

Still, the tingling of my nerves said something was odd about the place. I didn't want to call it quits yet.

"What's that back there?" Reed asked, pointing to the far side of the yard.

Several large pecan trees stood clustered next to a

241

smaller house, their leafy branches throwing protective shade over the structure.

We fought our way through the undergrowth and opened the door. It took me a minute to understand what I saw. I stared at the strange assortment of both adult and child sized furniture in the single room.

"It's a playhouse," I said. "The former owners must have had a little girl. Imagine having your own house to play grown-up in."

The tingles switched to chills racing up and down my arms. I shivered.

"This is an old slave cabin," Bill said. "Not too many left."

I licked my lips. Was I experiencing the sensations of past injustices? A chair and table stood in the middle of the floor. A cot graced another wall, as did a large armoire. A hole in the roof above it had allowed rain in. A key stuck out of the lock.

In a daze, I walked toward it, turned the key, and tugged at the door. It refused to budge. Years of moisture had warped the wood.

"Here, let me," Bill said, giving it a hard yank. The door opened with a screech of rusted hinges.

The smell had dissipated over the years. The three of us gazed at the skeleton on its knees, slumped against the side of the armoire. Blood stained the remains of the low cut, white blouse a dark brown.

"Oh, my God," Reed said.

"Jesus," Bill whispered, the comment more of a prayer than epithet.

My eyes followed theirs to the backside of the door. I gazed with horror at the deep grooves etched in the wood. I clapped my hand over my mouth and ran from the house.

Eleanor Gayle had been locked in that armoire, buried alive.

****

I stumbled into my foyer, exhaustion oozing from every pore. Reed caught my elbow, steadied, and then guided me into the living room and a seat on the sofa. I gripped my head in my hands while he rummaged through my liquor cabinet. He finally settled on vodka, handing me a glass. I bolted it down. The fiery bomb exploded in my stomach.

"Oh, my God, what a day," I murmured.

Bill had called the local authorities, and I was forced to re-live the finding of Bridget Connor. Pity for the poor woman in the armoire still stirred inside me. She looked so forlorn. Her clothing was intact. I guess the elements hadn't had a chance to do much damage.

The scarlet mini-skirt smoothed over her bones, and the blouse must have left little to the imagination. The bright red stiletto sandals were still strapped to the bones of her feet. There was no evidence of underwear. One gaudy, dangly earring was recovered from the floor of the armoire. But it was the tiny heart shaped locket, its chain ensnared in the cervical vertebrae, that made me cry. Had it been a gift from someone special? A father? A mother?

"Are you all right?" Reed asked in a low voice.

The ride home had been silent. He wouldn't talk, and I couldn't.

"Yeah. Did the killer intend to do that to her? Bury her alive?"

"I don't know. The blood on the blouse could have been from a blow to the head or from her actions trying

243

to escape."

"There's a lot about this I don't understand. If he hit her, he took a terrible chance of someone seeing him. I mean, even at three in the morning, a casino and its parking lot are active. And most have cameras. Can't have those big winners getting mugged fifty feet from the door."

Reed refilled his glass and quaffed it.

"We checked the tapes, but there were so many people coming and going it was hard to find just one woman. Plus, the quality wasn't all that good. Maybe he chloroformed her. A man with a staggering woman wouldn't attract attention, but a man hoisting a limp one would. Someone might remember. He could have whacked her on the head later."

I ran my hands through my hair and listened to my stomach grumble. The vodka awoke the hunger demons.

"What time is it?" I asked.

"Almost seven. Why?"

"I'm hungry. I know that sounds awful, but I can't help it. I've got a couple of steaks in the fridge."

"Not callous at all. Life goes on. I'll make a salad."

I made my way to the kitchen. The booze had also given me a small energy boost. While the steaks defrosted in the microwave, I called Linnie with the news. I caught her still in her office.

"Buried alive? Oh, my God. Can you imagine how long she must have screamed and pounded on that door, begging for help?"

The grooves made by her broken, crimson painted fingernails flashed through my mind. Yeah, I could. No one had heard in that isolated setting.

"We can't figure out if it was intended or if the killer thought she was dead. I guess we'll never know for sure. Did you find anything in your files?"

"Not a damned thing. I called Jeff a little while ago and told him so, too. He thinks I'm being hoodwinked. Said I wasn't being thorough enough. I told him to cram it up his ass. He pissed me off. I might be dumb about some things, but not my patients."

"What did he say?"

"Told me to calm down and take a Midol. Can you believe that! It's a good thing he's on duty tonight. I don't want to see him. He's not my favorite person at the moment," she grumbled.

"He'll show up tomorrow, full of charm and apologies, and you'll melt."

"Probably."

I paused for a moment. "Linnie, how do you think the killer got so many of these women to trust him?"

"I have no idea, but he must be damned good. Why?"

"I got to thinking on the drive home. Suppose our killer is an authority figure, like a cop. Janine would get into a car with a man if he flashed a badge."

Several moments of silence ensued. "Sasha, you may have something there. He wouldn't have to *be* a cop. He could impersonate one. A badge isn't hard to get. Maybe that's why Eleanor showed no fear. *Maybe* the killer never met up with her in the casino at all. *Maybe* he was trolling the parking lot."

"In a uniform, too. I'll run it by Reed. I'm making dinner for him."

"Lucky you. I'm just leaving. I've got a few more files I want to double check, but I'll do it at home."

Over dinner, I broached the idea to Reed.

"We thought of that, but could never prove it. Besides, too many of the victims described him as a new boyfriend," he replied.

"I forgot about that."

A frown furrowed his forehead. "But he *did* change his M.O. on manner of death. Maybe he decided to stop playing the boyfriend for a while."

Another thought flitted through my mind. "Would it be possible for me to see the files on the murdered women?"

He looked at me with a thoughtful expression. "You think you might be able to…see something?"

"I don't know, but it's worth a try. If a picture worked with Bridget and Eleanor, maybe the reports can trigger something."

"All right, I can do that. I shouldn't. It's against the rules, but I will." He reached across the table and raised my hand to his lips. "Sasha, I think whatever ability you have is real. I've never seen it put to practical use before. I believe you're going to help bring this killer to justice."

He believed. My heart thumped and my eyes welled with tears. In that moment, I realized I loved Reed McIntyre.

Before I could answer, his cell rang.

"Dammit! Why now?" he swore. "McIntyre here…Now? All right, I'll be there in twenty minutes…Yes, you interrupted me, but she understands." He gave me a slow smile that turned my bones to water. "Treat him like a king until I get there."

He hung up and rose. "Sorry, I have to go. An informant is about to make a statement. Will you be all right on your own tonight?"

"I'll be fine. Call if you get done before midnight."

I walked him to the door, waving as he drove away. I hand washed the dishes, dreaming about Reed and wondering if we had a future together.

****

Kathy hovered on Sasha's doorstep, undecided about what to do.

Is this woman never at home?

Armed with Bridget's information, Kathy wanted to get back into Sasha's head as soon as possible. Maybe she could even transfer Gerald's description.

But first, I need to find the silly woman.

The sun was low in the sky when Kathy decided to follow Bridget's advice. If she couldn't contact Sasha, then go for the shrink. She and Sasha had a connection, and if Kathy could get into the doctor's head, she might find a way around this stupid mental block.

Kathy launched herself into the wind, trying to remember the way to the office. After several wrong turns, she arrived just in time. Dr. Anderson was locking the office door, obviously on her way home.

She tucked herself behind the doctor and followed.

Chapter Fifteen

Kathy floated near a rocking chair next to the fireplace in Dr. Anderson's living room. If she could get into the doctor's head, she might be able to access Sasha. That damned hypnosis had screwed everything. There had to be a way past the blockage.

Gazing around the comfortable room, she smiled at the stuffed flamingo on the mantel. It just didn't fit with the traditional décor. Kathy deduced it must have special meaning, kind of like the Japanese fan her grandfather had bought in Tokyo during the Korean War. She kept it open, propped against the mirror on her dresser. Or rather, she had. She wondered who owned it now.

Kathy waited with uncharacteristic patience while Dr. Anderson ate. Food. Funny, she hadn't thought about food since she died. Now, the aroma of spaghetti and meatballs replete with garlic triggered the memory of how much she enjoyed eating. She assumed that since she wasn't hungry, her ability to taste had probably gone south. What a shame. She would miss butter pecan ice cream. And marshmallow sauce. And there was something about raspberry sherbet on a hot summer day that hit the spot.

God damn Gerald to hell for making me miss that.

Dr. Anderson finished her meal, and then shoved

the dishes into the dishwasher. But instead of plopping down in the nearest chair to watch TV, the doctor opened her briefcase and extracted several file folders. She sat at the dining room table, sipping a glass of wine and reading.

Well, damn.

She didn't want to enter the doctor's mind when it was cluttered with patient files. It might take longer to find Sasha, and Kathy had the feeling time had run out for yet another victim.

I wonder if they've discussed me yet. Do she and Sasha realize I was a patient? What irony. I found the one host with a link to my psychiatrist.

Or was this all part of some master plan? One from which neither she nor Sasha could deviate? Kathy had never been particularly religious or spiritual, but death and this dying young thing made her wonder.

The clock on the mantel striking the hour showed time was passing. It dawned on Kathy that she could now hear without being in someone's head.

Bridget must be right. Things happen slower when you're dead. Or maybe the drug is finally gone.

The doctor read file after file, making notes on a pad as she did. If a ghost could tap her foot, Kathy would. Finally, she closed the last file and sat chewing the tip of her pen, then shoved everything back into the briefcase.

About time. It's damn near midnight.

Dr. Anderson rose, stretched, and entered the kitchen. She returned to the living room bearing a glass of wine and curled up in the corner of the sofa. She took a sip, laying her head back, and breathed a deep sigh.

Impatient, Kathy decided now was the time to affect entrance. The doctor was tired, ready to relax. She projected herself forward and slipped into Dr. Anderson's head.

The doctor had stored a multitude of memories. She'd read a lot of files today, and it would take a while to find the route to Sasha, especially since the doctor's head was filled with thoughts of people named Jeff, Janine, and Eleanor. Eleanor? Bridget's Eleanor? Kathy wanted to stamp her foot in frustration. It would take hours to wade through everything.

The doorbell rang. Kathy used the distraction to sort through the faces and voices in Marilyn's mind. She didn't pay much attention until the doctor spoke.

"Good grief, what are you doing here?"

If ghosts could groan, Kathy would have done so. She wanted the doctor relaxed, not carrying on a conversation with a visitor. It would just clutter things up.

"I need to talk to you."

"Please, come in. I was just having a glass of wine. Could I get you one, too?"

"A glass of wine would be nice," a man's voice replied.

The voice sounded familiar—too familiar. By the time she pulled her fingers out of Dr. Anderson's mental files, Marilyn had already entered the kitchen and poured another glass, then returned to the living room with the bottle. Gazing from her host's eyes, a shock wave of horror washed over Kathy.

No! It's not possible! How does she know Gerald?

She wanted to flee the woman's mind and fast. Then, Kathy stared at the wine glass that had remained unattended for a few brief seconds.

Run! Run and get the hell out. Don't drink the wine.

She screamed and pounded in the doctor's head, but got nowhere. The man occupied Marilyn's thoughts.

The doctor placed Gerald's glass on the end table and resettled on the sofa. Gerald did the same, but did not touch the glass. The doctor drank.

Kathy frantically searched the images in Marilyn's mind. Could she stop a tragedy? She pawed through the morass of events cluttering the doctor's mind, praying to find an answer. Then, she saw it—Gerald in her office.

Oh, my God! Was *he* a patient? Had one of Dr. Anderson's patients killed her and Bridget? Kathy was aware the doctor and Gerald talked, but the thoughts racing through her consciousness overwhelmed and suppressed the words. What did it matter? Marilyn was in grave danger.

How do I stop this? Please, someone help me.

No one heard or came to her aid. Kathy's vision blurred and her movements slowed. Marilyn had drunk more wine. She ejected herself from the doctor's body and floated three feet off the ground near the end of the mantel.

Kathy sobbed. She couldn't stop anything from happening. Her hand clenched around the flamingo. In a scene horribly reminiscent of her own death, Gerald smiled and edged closer to his victim.

Kathy didn't want to watch, but couldn't tear her eyes away. *Help! Help! Please, somebody!* It was futile. No one could help now.

Gerald slid across the sofa to his victim's side. He gently removed the wine glass from her unresisting fingers, and using a handkerchief, wiped it clean of fingerprints. The doctor's eyes sagged half-closed. From her own experience, Kathy knew she struggled to stay awake as confusion numbed her mind.

"Sorry, doc, but you have to die. You all have to die," he whispered.

Fear and the realization something was wrong flitted across her face. His hands slipped around her throat. Now, Dr. Anderson recognized the danger. She pushed at him with a feeble gesture and staggered to her feet, managing to take two small wobbly steps away. Gerald leaped from the sofa and followed.

Scream! Scream for all you're worth!

She couldn't, of course, any more than Kathy had. Kathy screamed for her, over and over.

"No, you bastard!" Dr. Anderson's words slurred, barely above a whisper. She pushed at him again.

Caught by surprise, Gerald drew his lips back over his teeth. He grabbed her arm, slapping her across the face, and then closed his hands around her throat a second time. He laughed, but said nothing as his hands tightened. Dr. Anderson reached for his fingers, her movements awkward and slow. Kathy knew it wouldn't be long. His victim was already turning blue. Her knees had buckled.

Then, a car door slammed outside. Gerald froze like a statue. With his eyes slitted and a snarl on his lips, he squeezed one last time, flinging the doctor's body away. She dropped like a stone, hitting her head on the edge of the marble coffee table with a terrible crunching noise. Blood flowed. Gerald turned and ran for the back door. A few seconds later it banged shut. Kathy was left with a dying woman.

****

I awoke to the blinding flashes of blue and white strobe lights. My feet were freezing and my throat sore. Voices asked questions, but I remained mute unable to force words past my gasping sobs. I was drenched in sweat, and my heart labored as though I'd run a marathon. I leaned over, clutched my stomach, and then sank to my knees.

"Lady, are you all right?"

The strobe lights were attached to police cars, and two of them had stopped beside me. I was not in bed, but on the street. I gazed around, not recognizing the neighborhood. *Where the hell am I? How did I get here?*

I wore a flimsy silk nightgown. My feet were bare. God Almighty, I had sleepwalked.

"Lady, are you all right?" the man's voice asked again. At least he was flesh and blood and in front of me, not in my mind.

"I don't know. I think I was sleepwalking. Where am I?" My voice had a breathless quality.

"You're on Randolph just north of Columbia. Where do you live?"

Good Lord, I was over ten blocks from my house. I told the policeman my address, and then sat on the curb trying to pull myself together. I remembered nothing.

"Paramedics are on the way. Do you know your name?"

"Of course, I know my name. It's Sasha Bellwood and I haven't done this since I was in grade school." In the distance a siren keened. "How did you find me?"

"Are you kidding?" a second cop said. "Neighbors called saying a woman was walking down the street in a nightgown screaming."

"Screaming?" I struggled to my feet.

"Don't worry about it, ma'am. You're safe. I'm Officer White. Just have a seat. The paramedics will be here in a minute."

"What time is it?" A wave of dizziness forced me to sit again.

"Twelve-twenty."

The siren shut off. At the end of the street headlights rounded the corner. Several curious neighbors congregated on nearby front porches. The ambulance slid to a stop and the personnel got down to the business of checking me out.

"Blood pressure is a little elevated as is the pulse. Let's take a look at your feet." The EMT raised my foot. "You've got a few cuts, but nothing serious. Let's get you to The Med."

The Med is part of a huge medical complex located near downtown. It was where Elvis had been taken on the night of his fatal overdose. Accident victims ended up in the ER. It also houses a psychiatric wing. I knew exactly where I'd end up.

"No, that's all right. I don't need to go to the hospital. Just bandage me, and I'll call my doctor tomorrow."

"I suggest you let us take you. A doctor should look at the cuts," the paramedic tried.

I shook my head. "I'm fine, really. I've been under a lot of stress at the office. In fact, I was fired today. A friend of mine suggested primal screaming," I lied, faking a laugh. "I never expected it to come out during a sleepwalking episode."

"Is there anyone you'd like us to call?" Officer White asked. "Someone who can stay with you for the rest of the night?"

I needed and should have mentioned Linnie, but I wanted Reed. "Reed McIntyre." I gave them his cell number. *That* I could remember.

"Reed McIntyre? Former detective?"

"Yes. I was with him earlier. Do you know him?"

"We worked on a homicide together before he was shot. Damned good cop. Crying shame what happened to him. I hear he works unofficially for the department now," Officer White said, pulling out his cell phone and dialing.

During our conversation, the EMTs had disinfected and bandaged my feet. They helped me back up into a sitting position. Not counting the embarrassment, I felt almost normal.

The policeman ended his call and smiled. "Reed says he'll meet us at your place. I'll stay with you until he shows. Are you guys all done with her?"

The paramedics nodded, handing me a release form to sign. "She refuses to go to the hospital." He spoke to the officer first before turning his attention back to me. "Ma'am, make sure you see a doctor about those cuts tomorrow. They're superficial, but do it just to be on the safe side."

"Yes, I will. I promise." I scribbled my name.

I breathed a sigh of relief when they got into the rescue unit and drove away. Officer White helped me into his cruiser. The car was parked no more than twenty feet away, but whatever disinfectant the paramedics used had awakened my pain sensors. I limped. The policeman settled me into the back seat, and then closed the door. There was no door handle or window crank and for an awful moment I feared he was taking me to The Med anyway. My anxiety eased when he turned right at the next intersection instead of left.

We beat Reed to my house. During that time, I thanked Officer White for his assistance, and in order to avoid answering questions, fired them at him. By the time Reed arrived I knew all about the man's wife and four kids.

Reed opened my car door and peered inside. "Are you all right?" he asked.

I couldn't see his face clearly, but his voice had worry in it.

"Yes. I'm fine. I swear to God, I haven't done this in twenty years. I feel like a fool." I swung my legs out.

"Stay put." He pushed my legs back inside and turned to the officer. "If she sleepwalked, then she probably just strolled out the front door without locking it. Let's take a look around before we go back in."

He closed the door again, and the two of them did a search both inside and out. The front entry *was* unlocked. Several minutes passed before they returned. Reed opened the car door.

"Watch her feet," Officer White cautioned. "She's got some cuts. EMTs said to make sure she goes to a doctor tomorrow to get checked out."

"Will do, Gary. Nice to see you again. Thanks for bringing her home."

"No problem. If you need anything, give me a call."

The policeman slid behind the wheel while Reed pulled me upright, then swept me into his arms, and carried me into the house. He dumped me on the sofa, kissing my cheek before turning away. "Don't move. I'll be right back."

He returned in less than thirty seconds carrying a duffle bag. He tossed it by the coffee table and sat next to me.

"What's that?" I asked.

"I'm moving in. At least for the next couple of days. I should never have left you alone tonight. The past week has been hell on you. What brought this on? Eleanor?"

"I have no idea. I went to bed, fell asleep quickly, and the next thing I know, I'm ten blocks away with no memory of how or why I got there."

"Did you dream?"

"Not that I recall."

"You should never have gone on the search for Eleanor. Your mind's had about all it can take." He stood. "Can I get you anything?"

"Just a bottle of water."

He left and returned with my request. I drank greedily, emptying it in long swallows. He took it from my fingers and set it on the coffee table, then swept me into his arms again.

"Let's go to bed. Tomorrow we'll have those feet checked out."

"All right," I replied. I liked being carried by Reed. His arms conveyed a solid safety I needed more than I was willing to admit.

He settled me into bed, fussing with the pillows and covers before turning out the lights and undressing. He slid in next to me and rolled onto his side. His arm clamped me firmly to his body.

"Go to sleep," he murmured.

I yawned. "I'm sorry you were called so late at night. Were you in bed?"

"I just got home."

"Long night for you. Did your informant come through?"

"Yes. The interrogation ended about eleven and I stopped for a beer. Don't talk, Sasha. Sleep. I'm here if you need me."

I closed my eyes, snuggling closer to his body. That was fine with me.

****

Kathy followed what she would have done if alive. Rushing to Marilyn's side, she put her ear to the doctor's chest. She heard the faint beats.

Thank God. She's still alive.

The blood, however, was rapidly pooling by the doctor's head and bruises were popping out on her swollen neck. Already, she struggled to breathe.

Kathy needed to stop the blood. She reached for a pillow on the chair. Her hand passed through it as though it wasn't there.

Damn! There had to be a way to hold things. She'd seen it done in the movie *Ghost*. How had Patrick Swayzee finally mastered it? Didn't it have something to do with strong emotions? Well, Kathy was sure as hell angry.

She focused her attention on the pillow again and made a grab. Her fingers gripped, pulled it off the chair, and pressed it against Marilyn's wound. Now, to call 9-1-1. The land line was located on the end table. Refocusing her energy, Kathy grasped it and punched in the numbers.

"9-1-1 emergency," the operator answered.

Kathy knew the woman wouldn't hear her, so she made no attempt to reply. Instead she held the phone next to the doctor's lips and hoped the rattling breaths reached the operator's ear.

She waited, praying, with both instruments in her hands. The blood flow had slowed, but the breathing sounded worse.

Come on, come on. Where the hell are you guys? Then in the distance, sirens wailed. *Oh, thank God. Hang in there, doc. Help is on the way.*

The paramedics and police crashed through the unlocked front door. Kathy dropped the items and backed away to the fireplace.

One of the EMTs pulled the pillow away. A small chunk of something embedded in the doctor's scalp fell to the floor.

"She's stopped breathing!"

Kathy sobbed as the medics performed CPR.

"No good. Her throat's closing up. Get me a knife."

The EMT sliced into the doctor's throat and inserted a breathing tube. Slowly Marilyn's color changed from blue to a very pale pink.

"Better, but she's lost a lot of blood," one of the EMTs said.

"Front and back doors were unlocked," a cop said after touring the house. "Good thing she had the presence of mind to grab the pillow and call 9-1-1."

"Are you kidding? She hit the table like a rock. That piece of stone came from it. I can feel a slight depression around the wound. Might be a skull fracture. It was lights out in an instant," the paramedic said.

"Then who the hell did this and called?" the cop asked.

"I have no idea, but whoever it was saved her life."

I did it! I saved her from Gerald. A rush of pride swept over Kathy. *Even the dead can be useful.*

"If it weren't for those bruises around her throat, I'd say she got drunk, fell, and hit her head," one cop said, eying the overturned wine glass, the remains of its contents a puddle on the marble table top. "Think her attacker got scared and called?"

Pick up the glass, bozo. You won't get any fingerprints, but there has to be residue of the drug Gerald used. Take a sample of the spilled wine, too.

"I'll let forensics deal with the spillage and the glass. No sign of forced entry. I'd say the vic knew her assailant. Is she gonna make it, doc?"

"I don't know," he said, setting up the IV while his partner squeezed on a bag attached to the breathing tube. "She's breathing again, but the head wound is bad, real bad."

He rose from his knees and shouted, "Get the gurney in here. She's stable for the moment. Transport ASAP to the Med."

Kathy stayed behind as Dr. Anderson was wheeled from the house. She could help no more on that end, but maybe she could direct some energy to the policemen. A forensics team showed up. It wasn't nearly as dramatic or fast like *CSI*. The men and women meticulously gathered evidence, including the glass, spilled wine, and the marble chip. They also dusted every surface in the house for prints. She was impressed and had no idea it took so long.

How could she help? Had Gerald touched

anything? He'd avoided the wine glass his victim had set on the table and wiped his prints from hers. Kathy thought hard. Had he remembered to use the handkerchief when opening and closing the door? The car door slamming had panicked him. Did he get careless? And where did he go when he left? She didn't remember hearing the sound of a car leaving.

She threw her energy toward the policemen. *Talk to the neighbors. If he didn't park here, he must have parked nearby. Someone may have seen or heard something.*

"Start pounding on doors," the first policeman said to another. "Maybe someone heard or saw something."

"Already on it."

Kathy relaxed and collapsed onto the hearth. This thought projection thing worked! The clock on the mantel read almost two o'clock. So late? She was exhausted, her energy fading fast. Before it disappeared she had to make contact with Sasha. She had to let her know she could be next on the list.

Rather than use her remaining power for travel, Kathy concentrated, focusing hard to send the events of the last couple of hours to her elusive host's mind.

Come on, Sasha. Let me in.

****

The numbing cold covered me like a clammy blanket. I sat up, clutching my chest in an effort to calm my galloping heart. My breath crystallized into a light fog.

I had no idea what was happening, nor could I put it into words. My skin crawled and my gut clenched. I heard sobbing and voices in my head. The voices were indistinct.

261

Voices? Doesn't that have something to do with schizophrenia? Maybe Linnie's wrong. Maybe I am nuts.

I fought the urge to join the sobs. Then as suddenly as it all began, the voices faded, my stomach and heart rate returned to normal. The cold disappeared.

My actions awakened Reed. "Sasha?" His voice was drowsy.

I flopped back onto the pillows, pulling the covers up to my chin, and sobbed. Tears flowed down my temples and into my hair.

"Sasha?" he asked again sharply. He sat up and leaned over me. "Sasha, what's wrong?"

I couldn't talk. I cried harder and shivered.

"Goddammit, Sasha! Answer me! What the hell's the matter?" He knelt and placed his hands on my shoulders, giving me a hard shake.

I gulped and tried to regain control. "Dream. I had a dream."

"What kind of a dream?"

"I'm not sure."

"You're not making sense."

He released me, turning on the bedside lamp. His brow furrowed, and he looked scared.

"I know. I'm sorry. Give me a minute."

I hiccupped and swallowed the remaining tears, then heaved several cleansing breaths. I struggled to sit up, still shaking.

"I don't think it was a real dream. It was a bunch of disjointed pictures, some moving, some not. I heard someone crying and voices."

"Voices?"

I nodded. This could only mean one thing. If I

wasn't crazy, then something awful had happened.

"What did the voices say?"

Did *he* suspect I was crazy? "I don't know. They were muted, indistinct. I couldn't tell if they were men or women."

"What was happening in the dream?"

"It's all so jumbled."

He stroked a hand down my hair, and then gathered me into his arms. "Take a minute. Calm down before trying to remember."

I twisted my head from side to side hoping to eliminate the knot of tension from my neck. The warmth from Reed's arms seeped into my body. After several minutes, I relaxed, allowing my mind to wander back to the dream.

"Things are still jumbled, but I think the people I'm seeing are policemen."

"Police?"

"They're in uniforms. I sense the person sobbing is standing apart from the proceedings."

"What proceedings?"

"They're bending over something on the floor." I pulled away as I had a glimmer. "Oh, God. It's a body. Reed, I think Kathy Watson tried to contact me again."

"*What*? You mean there's been another murder?"

"Maybe. I don't know. God, why can't I see this clearly?"

He leaped to his feet and pulled on his slacks.

"Any idea where?"

I closed my eyes in concentration. The photo images cleared, and I recognized the living room. I gasped. Fear clamped around my chest, threatening to squeeze until my heart shattered in a thousand pieces. I couldn't breathe.

I screamed, lunging for my cell phone on the nightstand. In my panicked haste, I knocked it to the floor.

"Sasha!"

I ignored him and slid out of bed, scrambling on my hands and knees to retrieve the phone from under the bedskirt.

"Sasha, answer me!" He jerked me from the floor and once again shook me like a rag doll.

I had no problem tapping into his emotions. He was afraid—deeply afraid. But not half as afraid as I.

"It's Linnie! The house the cops are in is Linnie's!"

Chapter Sixteen

Reed didn't waste time asking stupid questions. He dropped to his knees, fished my cell out from under the bed, and handed it to me.

"Call her," he said, rising.

I shakily scrolled down my phone book. I hit the wrong button twice before finally connecting. It rang forever, and then went into voice mail.

"Hello, you've reached Dr. Marilyn Ander..."

I hung up. "She doesn't answer," I sobbed and dropped the phone again.

"Did you call her cell or her home?"

"Her cell."

He finished dressing, picked it up, and asked, "Which is her land line?"

"The second listing."

I knelt on the bed and sat back on my heels, my arms clasped across my stomach. I wanted to throw up. Reed, a frown on his face, punched the speed dial button.

"Who's this?" he barked a few seconds later.

He listened to whoever was on the other end, and I didn't need any psychic abilities to know something was very wrong. He would never have spoken to Linnie in that tone of voice.

"When?...You're sure?...Which hospital?"

I jumped off the bed and ran for the bathroom where I threw up and cried. I was still on my knees in front of the toilet when Reed walked in.

"She's dead, isn't she?"

"Not yet, but the son of a bitch sure as hell tried. She's in critical condition, hanging on by a thread, in the University of Tennessee Hospital at the Med. Come on, get dressed."

I brushed my teeth and grabbed the closest clothes, struggling to regain control of my emotions while I hurriedly dressed.

"What happened?"

"Tried to strangle her. Thought he must have succeeded. She fell and cracked her head on the coffee table. May have a fractured skull."

"How did he get in?"

"I didn't ask."

"Who'd you talk to?" I demanded to know, zipping my jeans and sliding my feet into a pair of ratty old canvas loafers.

"Brannon. He was there with forensics. He wants to talk to you. I told him to meet us at the hospital."

"Talk to me? What does that mean?"

"I don't know what it means. Hurry up," Reed ordered in a tense voice.

We raced out to the car and through the silent streets of Memphis. Madison Avenue was almost devoid of traffic and Reed ran all red lights.

"How did they find her?"

"Someone called 9-1-1. Saved her life. Whoever did it, disappeared."

"Why?"

"I have no idea."

We arrived, and Reed pulled into a restricted emergency room parking area. I jerked the door open, racing for the entrance before he had the key out of the ignition. I flew up to the reception desk.

"Dr. Marilyn Anderson. Where is she? Is she all right? Can I see her?" I spoke in short gasping breaths.

The woman at the desk stared with an inscrutable expression.

"And you are…?"

"Sasha Bellwood. I'm her friend."

She handed me a clipboard. "Add your name to the list and have a seat. We'll call you." She sounded bored and totally disinterested.

Her attitude pissed me off and the stress of the last several hours finally got to me. I snapped like a cheap rubber band. Leaning over, I slammed the clipboard on the desk.

"No! This is my friend, goddamn it, and I want to see her now! Where is she?"

The entire emergency room—about two-thirds full—went silent. Footsteps approached and Reed stood next to me, placing his arm around my shoulders.

"Calm down, Sasha." He turned to the receptionist and showed her his badge. "We're looking for Dr. Marilyn Anderson. I understand she was brought in about two hours ago."

"Get your friend under control or I'll call security," she said, glaring at me. "I'll check and see when you can go back."

Reed steered me toward a free chair in the corner of the waiting room. I shook like a leaf in a storm.

"Can I get you some coffee? A Coke?" he asked.

"No! Do I look like I need more caffeine? I want to

see Linnie."

"You will as soon as the doctors say you can. Now, get a hold of yourself."

I tried, but it was hard. My best friend was in critical condition just a few feet away beyond a pair of pneumatic doors, and I had to sit here twiddling my thumbs. I refused to look at the clock. It moved too slowly. I gazed around the room instead.

It was Saturday night, and the usual assortment of drunks who fell off a curb on Beale Street sat in the hard plastic chairs moaning and groaning. One man had a bloody towel wrapped around his hand and talked loudly on his cell phone. The conversation involved getting even with the son of a bitch who'd cut him. A woman, sporting a bloody lip, protested to her companion that if he wanted her to continue working, he had to find her a safer street.

After what seemed an eternity, the doors finally hissed opened. A doctor walked out and up to the receptionist who pointed in our direction. We rose as he approached.

"I'm Doctor Farmer. Are you the people here for Marilyn Anderson?"

"Yes. How is she?" I asked.

"Not good. Come on back."

We followed him through the doors and into a maze of corridors before stopping in front of a curtained cubicle. He pulled the fabric aside.

Linnie lay unmoving. IV needles invaded both arms, the tubes snaking along the sides of the bed. Wires connected to beeping machines crisscrossed the tubes. A respirator breathed through a hole in her throat, and bandages swathed her head.

"Oh, God," I moaned, turning my face into Reed's chest. I couldn't even cry.

"What can you tell us, doctor?" Reed asked.

"Her skull has three small, hairline fractures at the point of impact. Her hair is thick and prevented further damage."

I thanked God Linnie hadn't worn her usual French twist. By hanging loose, the strands had protected the side of her head.

"She lost a lot of blood, but we're getting that back into her. Her throat is badly bruised and swollen. The paramedics did a tracheotomy, so I don't think her brain was oxygen deprived. I won't know until she comes out of the coma. At the moment, brain activity is good and the swelling minimal. She's listed as critical, but stable."

"When you check her blood, see if there are any sedatives. I'm not sure what to look for, but it'll be fast acting and cause weakness and confusion. How long will she be under?"

"I don't know."

"What about that tube in her throat?" I asked, raising my face from Reed's chest.

"As soon as the swelling goes down, we can take it out. We'll be moving her upstairs to ICU in a little while. Until then, why don't you go to the cafeteria and get a cup of coffee? I'll send someone down for you after she's settled in."

Reed thanked the doctor and steered me out of the cubicle. "She's a fighter, Sasha. She won't give up. Her vitals are stable and that's important."

"She's also in a coma." I wiped my eyes on the bottom of my T-shirt and sniffed.

"Nature's way of self-preservation. I don't understand how it works, but it does."

In the cafeteria, I sat at a table trying to come to grips with what I'd seen and heard. I had to believe he was right and that Linnie was in no pain—just peacefully sleeping.

Reed emptied his change into the vending machines. At this hour of the morning the food line was closed, although clanging noises from the kitchen area suggested cooks had already begun breakfast. He set a steaming cup in front of me along with a cellophane wrapped muffin, and then sat down.

"Come on, honey. Try to eat."

When I made no move to unwrap the muffin, he did it for me. I sipped the coffee. It tasted like the cardboard container and was way too strong. I dumped in three creamers. It barely changed color. To please him, I broke off a smidgeon of the dry, unappetizing muffin and nibbled.

Two nurses walked in and headed for the machines. A second later, Detective Brannon joined us. He sat down and drank Reed's coffee, making a face.

"Stuff tastes like shit," he said. "Dr. Farmer told me where to find you."

"What can you tell us?" Reed asked.

"Not much more than you already know. There was a partial glass of wine overturned on the coffee table and a full one on the end table."

"Any prints?"

"Don't know yet, but forensics says the one on the coffee table looked like it had been wiped. They found only one set on the other glass. My guess is, the doctor's."

"Was the wine drugged?"

"Don't know that either. The wine bottle was on the other end table."

"What about the 9-1-1 call?" I asked Brannon.

"We have no idea. Whoever it was split before the paramedics got there."

"What about the doors?" Reed inquired.

"Both front and back unlocked."

"So, the caller could have found an unlocked or even an open door and decided to take advantage of the situation."

"You mean, a thief walked in?" I asked.

Reed shrugged. "It's possible. The thief doesn't see Marilyn on the floor right away. Maybe he's searching another room first. He enters the living room, finds her, and calls 9-1-1 because he doesn't want to be connected to a murder."

The image of a courtroom flashed in front of my eyes. "Oh, my God! Brian," I said, gasping.

"Who?" Reed and Brannon asked together.

"Brian Michaels. He and Linnie dated until he beat her senseless one night. He killed his next girlfriend and is supposed to be doing time on Parchman."

"I'll check and see if he's still there. Would she let him in?" Brannon said.

"Not unless she had a major league brain fart," I replied. "And he sure as hell wouldn't drink wine. He was strictly bourbon."

"If there was a second glass of wine, she could have been expecting company and gotten a surprise when she opened the door," Reed speculated. "Her attacker came in, she ran, and he caught her."

"You think the 9-1-1 caller was her guest who

panicked when he found her?" I said. "But why run?"

Reed shrugged. "If he, or she, was a patient, they might not want to talk to the cops."

"Would she entertain a patient? Have a glass of wine with them?" Brannon said to me.

"She's done it with me often enough. I suppose there could be others."

"You're a childhood friend. I doubt she'd set up a meeting with a patient in her home at midnight," Reed concluded.

"Maybe it was someone with an emergency who just showed up. She could have poured the wine for him."

Brannon shifted in his chair. "Whoever called also tried to stop her from bleeding out. Used a pillow from the sofa as a pressure bandage."

Clarke Pennington's face flashed in front of my eyes.

"Clarke Pennington," I exclaimed.

"Your boss? What's he got to do with this?" Reed asked.

"Linnie met him a couple of years ago. Hated him on sight, but when he discovered she and I were not only friends, but doctor-patient, too, he wouldn't let her alone. Called her day and night. Even showed up at her office a couple of times unannounced."

"What did he want?" Brannon said, taking another sip of coffee.

"Wanted to collaborate with her on a book. Probably using me as the subject matter. Linnie told him what he could do with himself. She said he was furious."

"Plus, you had an argument with him and quit the

other day," Reed said with a frown. "Would he have the balls to contact her and suggest her asking you to reconsider?"

"He might since he's full of himself."

Reed's frown deepened into a scowl. "But would Marilyn invite him in and offer a glass of wine?"

I shrugged. "I wouldn't think so, but he can be damned persuasive. He could have wheedled his way inside."

"I'll talk to him in the morning," Brannon replied. He pulled a notebook from his pocket. "Got a number where I can reach him?"

I rattled off the office and his private numbers while Brannon wrote.

"Forensics come up with anything else?" Reed inquired.

"Too soon," Brannon answered. "Funny thing, though. Both the pillow and the phone had this sticky substance on them."

"Sticky substance? What was it?" Reed's brow knit in puzzlement.

"Nobody knows, but it reminded me of that old-fashioned glue, rubber cement. Really weird."

"Rubber cement? Would that mask fingerprints?" I asked. Sticky? Residue? Something rattled around in the back of my mind, but I couldn't quite put my finger on it. I gave up. My mind was too weary to think.

Brannon shrugged. "I wouldn't think so, but criminals come up with something new every day. Forensics will check it out."

Brannon gulped more of Reed's coffee and grimaced. "We talked to some of the neighbors. One couple came home about midnight, but didn't see anything unusual. Another guy down the street says his dog kicked up a fuss around the same time. He looked out his back door and thought he heard someone moving, but isn't sure. Could have been leaves rustling in the breeze. By the way, I've ordered two guards for Dr. Anderson, twenty-four-seven."

"Good idea," Reed replied. "She's the first survivor."

Brannon turned to me. "Miss Bellwood, from what I understand, you're involved in this through some kind of psychic ability regarding the murder of Kathy Watson. Is that correct?"

"Yes." I told him the story from the beginning and the prevailing theories.

"We found a bunch of patient files in her briefcase. Did she say anything to you about a possible suspect?"

"No, just the opposite. When I talked to her earlier, she didn't think any of her patients were responsible."

"When was that?"

"Around seven, I guess. She was about to leave the office."

"Would she open the door to a patient?"

"I don't know. In spite of what I said a minute ago, I'm not sure a patient would know where she lives," I replied.

"He would if he followed her from the office," Reed interjected. "But even if it wasn't a patient, it could have been a patient's relative. Someone she didn't fear, assuming this isn't the work of the ex-boyfriend who may no longer be on Parchman."

"Or my former boss."

"You mean Mrs. Smith is the patient and Mr. Smith accompanies her to the weekly session, chats afterward, and then kills?" Brannon asked.

Reed shrugged. "It was just a thought."

I was about to ask a question when Dr. Farmer entered and strode over. I set my cup down with shaking fingers. The expression on his face was neutral. My stomach clenched and I focused on not letting my chin quiver. If Linnie was better, he'd have smiled. He'd also told us he'd send someone down, but he came instead. He had bad news. I knew it. I was afraid to ask. Reed wasn't.

"How is she, doc?"

"The same. We've got her set up in ICU. There's a policeman in the room with her and one stationed at the door. Only doctors, nurses, police, and Miss Bellwood will be allowed in."

"When can I see her?" I asked through stiff lips.

"Any time now."

"Can I stay in the room with her?"

Dr. Farmer shook his head. "You get ten minutes every two hours. That's a hard and fast rule. I don't even like having the cop with her. I suggest you use your ten minutes, and then go home. Come back in the morning. Visiting hours begin at noon and end at ten."

The doctor left, heading for the vending machines. Brannon stood.

"I'll go up with you. I want to talk to the officers on duty."

Reed scooped up my half-eaten muffin and untouched coffee cup, then tossed them into the trash.

Slick and modern, the ICU nurses' station was set up in the middle of the floor where they could monitor each patient's telemetry from a central location. It resembled mission control at NASA. Private, glass fronted ICU rooms surrounded the perimeter of the station. Two hallways led off in opposite directions. One had a sign showing the way to the restrooms, elevators, and waiting area. The other was self-explanatory—it led to an enormous elevator with the initials OR printed on the doors.

I walked past the guard seated in a chair next to the entryway and into Linnie's room with my heart in my throat. I didn't know what to expect, but in spite of the doctor's words, in the back of my mind I visualized her sitting up and smiling. Ridiculous, of course. She looked exactly the same as an hour ago.

Reed walked up behind me, placed a kiss on my temple, squeezed my shoulders, and said in a soft voice, "She's going to make it."

I wanted to believe him, but in her current position, doubts assailed me. Paper rustled from the corner behind one of the beeping machines. The other cop was sitting there, reading a magazine.

"Come on, Sasha. There's nothing more we can do here tonight. Let's go home."

I allowed him to steer me out of the depressing room. Brannon finished speaking with his man and joined us near the nurses' station.

"I've got a report to write. I'll be back in the morning. Go home and get some rest," he said.

"Do you honestly think I can *rest*?" I asked. "I don't care what the doctor says. I'm staying here until Linnie is awake and naming her attacker."

"Sasha, that could be weeks, maybe months," Reed protested. "You can't camp out in the waiting room that long."

I lifted my chin, ready to do battle. "And why

not?"

"It's an emotional black hole. Every day there's no change is another day to fall deeper into the pit. Ask my family. I was out for weeks. They went through hell."

"Well, I'm going through hell right now. How do you think I feel? If I hadn't come to her with that vision or crazy dream, she and Janine would never have been drawn into this mess."

"You can't blame yourself for that, Miss Bellwood," Detective Brannon said. "You had no idea what would happen."

"Is that a crack?" I asked in a furious tone.

"Sasha, Rick isn't maligning your abilities."

Reed ran a hand through his hair. The lines of his face were deeply etched with exhaustion. I didn't suppose I looked any better. Even Brannon's shoulders slumped.

Before I could apologize, the elevator doors opened and a distraught Jeff Hammond ran over. His hair stood wildly on end and his eyes were red and puffy, but whether from tears or lack of sleep I didn't know. They stared from a deathly white face. He stopped two feet away, grabbed my shoulders with hands of steel, and shook.

"Where is she? What happened? Is she still alive?" he shouted.

"Hey! This is a hospital. If you have a problem take it to the waiting room or into the lobby," a nurse seated at the station snapped.

Reed pulled Jeff away. He and Brannon pushed him down the corridor to the empty waiting area. I followed, rubbing my shoulders where his fingers had bitten.

I was calmer now, and for the first time since knowing Linnie was in trouble, could deal with the emotions of others.

Brannon was tired and irritated, mostly with Jeff, although I had a small slice of his attention, too. He was disgusted, but not particularly angry. He didn't really know Linnie and wasn't personally involved.

I easily read the anger in Reed, but fear dominated.

Both rage and extreme fear radiated from Jeff. The emotions slammed against my mind with the force of an F-5 tornado. He resembled a wild man on the exterior, but on the inside, it was ten times worse. He seethed like a witch's cauldron.

"Calm down, Jeff," Reed said. "Marilyn's in a coma. Her condition is critical, but stable."

Jeff staggered and sat abruptly on the vinyl couch. "Is she going to live?"

"We don't know yet."

Jeff covered his face with his hands. "God, if we hadn't had that silly argument this afternoon, I would have been with her. She wouldn't have let this maniac in. Do you know how I felt when I learned she'd been attacked? God Almighty, I thought she was dead."

"Jeff, I felt the same way a few minutes ago. It's not anybody's fault. Her doctor is down in the cafeteria. Let's go see if you can have a couple of minutes with her." Maybe helping Jeff would also help me.

Brannon placed a steady hand on Jeff's shoulder. "The doctor's hopeful, and so are we. I've got two guards on duty, one in the room and one by the door."

"You'd better! She's the only survivor. She can ID this son of a bitch," Jeff returned harshly.

"We know," I said, tugging at his arm. "Let's go

down to the cafeteria. I'll buy you a cup of coffee."

"I want to see Marilyn," he snapped. "I don't want any damned coffee."

"All right, but I do." I pulled him toward the door.

Brannon and Reed walked with us down the hall, halting at the entrance to Linnie's room. The policeman outside nodded. Jeff gazed through the windows with a hard, angry expression. His hands clenched and unclenched at his sides. Short, heavy breaths rasped from his nose.

Brannon spoke softly with Reed, and then headed toward the main elevators.

"I could use a cup of coffee, myself," Reed said.

Jeff turned and replied, "Do you mind if I talked privately to Sasha?"

Reed's eyebrows rose, but he didn't protest. He nodded and disappeared in the direction of the waiting area.

Jeff said nothing, turning from the windows, and with his hand cupping my elbow, he escorted me to the elevator. He said nothing on the ride down until we entered the cafeteria. Dr. Farmer was no longer there. A couple of interns sat at a table eating hot food. The serving line had opened. I glanced at my watch. It was almost five-thirty.

I headed for the coffee urn and filled two cups while Jeff sat at a table along the far wall. I returned, placing one in front of him.

"Jeff, you have to believe she's going to make it. Reed's right. Linnie's a fighter. She won't give up easily. Whoever did this has shot his last wad."

He sipped his coffee, gazed toward the hot food, and then rose. "Can I get you something to eat? I'm hungry."

The offer sounded off base, but as I'd learned over the past few days, people's reactions to tragedy and stress were sometimes strange.

"Yeah, sure. Couple of slices of bacon, scrambled eggs, and toast is fine."

He nodded, walked over, filled two plates, paid, and then rejoined me. I took a small bite of eggs, barely able to choke it down. Jeff shoveled his food in like he'd never eat again. I picked at mine. He didn't look at me until his plate was clean.

"Not hungry?" he asked.

I shook my head. He swapped out his empty plate with mine. I sipped my coffee. When he finished, he took the dishes to the conveyor belt running to the kitchen and refilled his cup.

"I guess my eating like a horse looks kind of strange," he said. "I can't help it. Whenever I'm scared or under a lot of stress, I eat. I polished off a twenty-two ounce steak the night Reed was shot."

He rested his elbows on the table and ran his hands over his face. I sensed he was bone tired, but the anger and fear had not abated much.

"I guess I don't have to tell you, I'm in love with Marilyn."

"You are?"

"I know I have a rep as a womanizer, but this hit like an earthquake. Still can't believe it." He banged his fist on the table. "Damn it, I should have been there for her. Sasha, I want you to tell me exactly what went down."

"Detective Brannon or the officers at the house would have more details than I do."

"I don't mean what the cops know. What did you see?"

"But I wasn't at the house, Jeff."

He raised his head, the anger turning his greenish eyes into emeralds. A twinge of fear darted through me. I'd hate to tangle with him in an official capacity. He may have given off a devil-may-care attitude, but underneath, he was stone-hard.

"I know that. Why did you call her at that time of night? What kind of vision did you have? Could you see the killer this time?"

I was tired. The night's events had me thinking in slow motion. I rubbed my forehead with my fingertips.

"I didn't have a vision, Jeff. I had a dream—a nightmare. I don't remember much about it. I just knew I had to call Linnie. I couldn't reach her on her cell and was so scared Reed called her house. He talked to Detective Brannon. That's how we found out she'd been attacked. We came here."

"So, it's a big goose egg. Nothing," he muttered. "That's it? You had a dream, but can't remember it?"

I stared into my coffee cup before raising it to my lips. I remembered. The images would be forever seared into my memory, but Jeff was too emotional to deal with it now, and I was sick of talking about it. The sleepwalking incident was none of his business. A sudden thought had me swallowing the strong brew in a gulp.

What if the two are related?

The cops said I was walking down the street screaming. I didn't remember any of that. Had Kathy Watson tried to contact me prior to the dream? Had *she* witnessed the attack? Was she the one responsible for saving my best friend's life?

I needed Linnie, but she was unavailable. I wondered how I'd react to someone else hypnotizing me.

"Sasha, what wrong? Are you hiding something from me?"

"What? Oh, no, sorry, Jeff. I'm so tired my brain is on half speed. No, I don't remember anything."

I didn't know why I lied. If the two incidents were connected, then I had to open my memory's door and put them together. Jeff would cause a problem with his constant questioning, like on the day Kathy's body was discovered.

"I'm the one who's sorry," Jeff said. "I didn't mean to snap. I just find it odd you have visions of these incidents and on one this important, you don't."

"Even if I had, I doubt it would have helped."

"You might have seen the killer's face this time."

"True. How did you learn about it?"

His fingers played around the rim of his cup. "I couldn't sleep," he said, not looking at me.

"I thought you were on duty tonight."

"I was. Got home a little after one. I had this feeling something was wrong. I couldn't get Marilyn or our argument out of my mind. I *had* to talk to her. I finally called the house and got a hold of an officer. He told me what happened."

"You're emotionally involved with Linnie. It's amazing how often emotions drive our actions."

"It's not the first time it's happened." He raised his eyes to mine. "I've had premonitions all my life."

"Premonitions?"

"Kind of like you," he replied, shrugging.

Amazement swept over me from head to foot. Jeff had psychic tendencies? And exactly how much like mine were his? What did he see or sense?

"Wait a minute. Are you telling me you have visions? Is that why you're open to psychics in police work?"

He nodded. "I know what it's like to have skeptics tear you apart. *That's* why I left Mobile and Birmingham. Unfortunately, not all my premonitions panned out. The night Reed was shot I knew something bad would happen. Before I could warn him, he'd disappeared around the house." He covered his face with his hands and stifled a sob. "Dear God, if I'd acted on what I felt tonight, Marilyn wouldn't be near death."

Before I could speak, Jeff jumped to his feet and fled the cafeteria.

Chapter Seventeen

"Jeff! Wait!"

I shoved my chair back and ran after him. By the time I reached the door, he'd disappeared. The hallway in front of the elevators was empty. I yanked open the door to the stairwell, racing up a flight where I burst into the lobby. He wasn't there either. I gave up and headed for the elevators, returning to ICU.

I stared through the glass of Linnie's cubicle. She looked the same. Machines beeped, and the respirator wheezed. The cops ignored me. I turned away and found Reed in the waiting room.

"Where's Jeff?"

"Gone." I flopped beside him on the vinyl couch. His arm wrapped around my shoulders, pulling me close.

"What did he want?"

"To assuage his guilt."

"His guilt?"

"About not being there for Linnie. They had an argument, and he thinks if he'd swallowed his pride, he'd have been with her, and nothing would have happened." I paused. "He also told me about his abilities."

"What abilities?"

"His psychic abilities. The premonitions."

Reed pulled back, staring with an amazed expression. "What are you talking about? What premonitions?"

I straightened. "Hasn't he ever told you? He said he's often had premonitions. He had a feeling something was wrong, but didn't act on it. That's why he feels guilty."

"Jeff? I don't believe it."

"He said it's happened before. Nothing specific—just feelings. He had one the night you were shot. I assumed you knew."

"It's the first I've heard about it. What else did he say?"

"That he knows all about skeptics and is sympathetic to me and psychics in general. Said he's been there, done that. That's why he left his other jobs. I guess his co-workers thought he was a flake. I can relate to that. It must be twice as hard if you're a cop."

"On the contrary. My views are often in the minority. A psychic detective might be an added bonus for any police department."

"Yet you objected to bringing psychics in on cases."

"Not really. I made my opinion clear on the subject, but to the best of my knowledge, no one insisted on consulting one."

I yawned, and he pulled me back into the shelter of his arm.

"Try to get some sleep. The next couple of days are going to be long."

I closed my eyes, but doubted I'd sleep.

****

Jeff reappeared the next afternoon. I was sitting

next to Linnie's bed, and looked up to see him peering through the glass. I waved him in.

"Hi, Sasha," he greeted with a sheepish look.

"Are you feeling better?"

"Are you?"

"Some."

"I'm sorry about running out on you, but I just couldn't…" He closed his eyes and took a deep breath.

"You don't have to explain, Jeff."

He smiled. "Thanks. I understand you're staying here overnight."

"Of course. I have to."

"You're a good friend. Linnie's lucky to have you. I asked to be assigned to the case, but got turned down. The lieutenant says I'm too closely involved. Don't worry, I'll keep my eyes and ears open for any…"

One of the machines interrupted its rhythmic beeping and blared an alarm. Startled, I swung my head in its direction. Linnie's heart rate and blood pressure had risen into the stratosphere. The intermittent buzzing scared me to death. *My* vital signs also rose. Two nurses dashed into the room.

"Out!"

Jeff grabbed my arm and hustled me into the hall. A doctor ran in while I plastered my face against the glass. I was too scared to do much more than watch. Jeff paced the floor behind me.

I couldn't hear what the doctor and nurses said, nor could I see the monitors. After what I thought was an eternity, the doctor came out.

"What happened? Is she all right?" I asked in a rush.

"She's fine. Her pulse and BP skyrocketed. What

were you doing when it happened?" he asked.

"Nothing. I was holding her hand and talking to her. Just nonsense. Then Jeff came in. We were talking when suddenly all hell broke loose."

The doctor frowned. "She could have been reacting to your voices."

"You mean she can hear us?" Jeff demanded.

"It's possible. She's not in a deep coma."

"So we stimulated a response?" I asked.

"Maybe. Keep talking to her whenever you visit. See if it happens again. Things may have spiked because her conscious mind is beginning to resurface. The familiar voices may have triggered the reaction. But for now, I'm going to ask you to leave. Let things settle down until the next two-hour window."

Jeff left the hospital, saying he'd return whenever he had a free moment. The frantic repeat of vital sign spikes did not happen again the rest of the day.

The next three days established a pattern. In defiance of everyone, I stayed at night. Reed brought a pillow and a blanket from my house and coffee in the mornings. The doctor on duty reported the night's progress. I then spent a few minutes reassuring myself he told the truth by staring at Linnie through the window. I rushed home to shower, change clothes, and do errands in time to return at noon. Sometimes Reed joined me, but the world moved on, and he had work to do. The cops were still on guard and no one attempted unauthorized entry to her room.

Reed didn't bring coffee on the morning of the fourth day. Instead, he had Dr. Farmer in tow.

"Good news, Miss Bellwood. The swelling in Dr. Anderson's throat has diminished to the point where I feel comfortable removing the respirator. Her brain activity has also increased."

"You mean she's coming out of the coma?" I asked.

"I didn't say that, but things are improving. I'm upgrading her from critical to serious."

"Which means you no longer need to stay here overnight," Reed added.

"Are you moving Linnie to a private room?"

"Not yet. I'll do that when she comes out of the coma," Dr. Farmer replied.

"Then I stay."

"Sasha, you can be more useful to Marilyn by not being here."

"What do you mean?"

"For starters, there's her office. I taped a sign on the door yesterday saying the office was temporarily closed and that someone would be in touch with Dr. Anderson's patients soon. She has no receptionist. Why don't you call them?"

"If they have a TV or can read, they must already know what's happened, but I see your point. It's polite and might save her practice. However, I won't be doing that at night."

"True, but there's no sense in exhausting yourself. It's a good idea to secure the office. I picked up her briefcase from her home a couple of days ago. She had a bunch of patient files in it. They should be locked up in a file cabinet."

Reed made a good case. I gave it one last shot. "I have some files from the office I was going to work on, too. Now might be a good time. She really is improving?" I begged of Dr. Farmer.

"She really is improving," he echoed in a reassuring tone. "Mr. McIntyre's right. You need the comfort of your bed, decent food, and a regular routine. I have your cell number. If there's any change, I'll call."

I surrendered in the face of common sense. "All right, you win."

The doctor allowed me in Linnie's room for a brief two minute stay. I held her hand, speaking as I always did.

"Hey, girl. It's me. I'm going to help out at the office for a while. Dr. Farmer says you're improving, and there's no need for me to stay overnight. He said he may take you off the respirator today and that your brain activity has increased, although that's always been marginal, right?" I laughed and squeezed her hand. Her heart rate increased by a few points, and while it wasn't the wild swing of a few days ago, I took it as a sign she heard. "You concentrate on getting well. I'll be back later."

Reed carried the blanket and pillow out to the car. "You're doing the right thing, Sasha," he said, opening the door for me. "I'll drop you off at your place. Would you like me to pick up dinner?"

"That sounds wonderful. Will you be staying?"

"I'm not leaving you alone at night. This guy killed Janine, almost killed Marilyn, and you could be next on the list. Promise me you'll lock yourself in, including at the office."

"I promise," I said, crossing my heart.

We stopped and had a quick breakfast, then headed for my place. Reed pulled into the drive, and then reached into the back seat for several large accordion files.

"These are the copies of the files you requested on the murder victims. Go through them and see if something stirs your abilities. And for God's sake, don't lose anything. I'm not supposed to take these files out of the office."

"All right. Are there any pictures?"

"Some, mostly crime scene photos. Sorry."

"I can stand it if they help. I feel like a slacker not being with Linnie. Suppose she has another reaction?"

"Reaction to what? Medication?"

With my concern for Linnie so deep, I'd forgotten to tell him.

"No. To my voice." I told him what had taken place a few days earlier. "Now, whenever I talk to her, I keep my eyes glued to the monitors. Sometimes she reacts."

"You say she responded while you and Jeff were talking? Has she responded to his voice when he visits?"

"I don't know. I'm sure I would have heard if she had. I don't even know if he's been back to see her. I guess it depends on his schedule. Do you think she can hear us?"

"I remember hearing things when I was in my coma, but damned if I can recall any of what I heard."

I shifted the awkward accordion files, fumbling for my key. Reed took it and unlocked my front door. He walked in first, and then stopped abruptly.

"Stay back!" he ordered.

Too late. I was already next to him. I'm sure a tornado ripping through my living room could have done more damage, but I didn't see how. The place was a mess.

Bookcases were overturned, the contents scattered across the floor, and furniture cushions had been tossed every which way. Pictures on the wall hung askew. The dining room breakfront was in disarray. The kitchen drawers had been dumped on the countertops. My bedroom was the worst. The mattress slanted at an angle half on, half off the bed. The nightstand and dresser drawers had been given a rough going over. Clothes were strewn everywhere.

I walked through the rooms in a daze while Reed called the police. They arrived, asking the usual questions.

"Do you keep any valuables—money, jewelry—in the house?" the officer said.

"No. I have a safety deposit box at the bank."

"There's no sign of forced entry. Do you keep a key outside in case you forget yours?"

"Under the flower pot on the front porch."

"That's the place *before* the first place a thief would look," Reed said.

I tossed him a stern look. I didn't need sarcasm now.

"Can you tell if anything's missing?" the cop asked.

"I'll have to go through this mess first."

"Her stereo and TV are still here," Reed said, looking around the living room.

"My laptop! I don't see my laptop."

"Where did you keep it?"

"On the dining room table."

"Anything on it a thief might want? Safe combinations, banking and investment account numbers or passwords?" the policeman inquired.

"No. I have an accountant and a lawyer who take care of all that." Then I remembered. "Oh crap, the files!"

I dashed outside to my car. The files still covered the passenger seat from where I'd chucked them days ago. I guess the thief hadn't been interested in my car.

The policeman asked a few more questions and left. Reed followed him onto the front porch, spoke for a moment, and then returned, closing the door.

"Forensics is here. With any luck, we might get some fingerprints, but don't hold your breath. Pack a few things. You can stay at my place."

"I'll be all right. The thief isn't likely to return."

"This was no thief. A pro would have taken your TV, stereo, and the sterling silver flatware I see in the breakfront. This was someone looking for something specific."

"Like what?" I said, perplexed.

"Like how much you know about Kathy Watson, Bridget Connor, and Eleanor Gayle."

A cold chill slithered up and down my spine. "The killer," I whispered.

He nodded, a grim look etching the lines deeper into his face. "I've already requested police protection. An officer will accompany you everywhere when I can't."

I felt sick to my stomach and couldn't keep the tears from my eyes. Reed slipped his arms around me, holding me close.

"I'm sorry, honey. Go pack. You can deal with this mess later."

"Sounds like a plan to me," I said with a shaky

attempt at humor. I packed a small bag and picked up the files from my car. Reed drove me to his home in Germantown.

The house on Ashley Way was a traditional three bedroom ranch. The front bushes were overgrown, hiding the painted tan bricks, but I chalked that up to a bachelor with little spare time. A brick walkway curved from the drive to the porch. A huge oak tree shaded the yard.

The interior was simple—a great room with a wet bar, a formal dining room, and an eat-in kitchen. The bedrooms and two baths lay on the opposite side of the house.

Through a back picture window, I spied a patio and sunlight sparkling off the clear waters of a pool.

"Reed, this is gorgeous."

"Thanks. Might be too big for just me, but it's comfortable."

I followed him down the hall to the bedrooms where he hesitated between the doors of what were obviously the master bedroom and the guest room. We'd passed a third room set up as an office.

He gazed into my eyes letting me make the decision. I pointed to the left and the master bedroom. He smiled, entered, and swung my bag onto the bed.

"Make yourself at home. Move anything of mine you have to. The officer should be here soon. I'll be home early. Do you still plan on going to the office?"

"Yes. I need to keep busy."

Reed pulled me into his arms. "I'm sorry this happened. As soon as forensics is finished going over your house, we'll go back and clean it up."

"Why would the killer think I had any information

on the murdered women at my house?"

"He could have been looking for a journal or a diary. Maybe he thought you kept notes."

"Is that why he took my laptop?"

"Possibly. It's the electronic age. Some people keep everything on their computers. And they aren't always careful about encrypting them."

The doorbell rang, and Reed left to answer. I assumed my protection had arrived. Voices murmured from the living room as I hung up a few pieces of clothing and shared the space in dresser drawers.

I still shook inside, but was determined not to let the incident alter my plans. I'd said I would help Linnie and by God, I intended to do it. I lifted my chin and joined the men.

"Sasha, this is Officer Simpson. He is your new best friend. Don't go anywhere without him."

"Gotcha. Pleased to meet you," I said, shaking his hand.

If the killer wanted to tangle with Officer Simpson, he had to be certifiable. The man stood a good six feet, five inches and weighed at least two hundred-fifty pounds. He had enormous shoulders and could crush beer cans between his forearms and biceps. His dark hair was clipped short, and I'd bet his sharp, brown eyes missed nothing. He wore jeans and a black, form-fitting T-shirt. Hell, I was intimidated, and I was the one being protected.

"Miss Bellwood, nice to meet you, too. I have a few ground rules. First, I drive. I've been trained in evasive maneuvers. Second, if we are anyplace other than this house, I am in the same room with you. If you have to use the facilities, I'm standing right outside the door. Third, we avoid as many public places as possible. That includes restaurants, bars, and shopping malls." He crossed his arms. "Okay?"

"No arguments from me."

"Good," Reed said. "It's after ten. Why don't you go to Marilyn's office and contact her patients? I'll bring dinner home."

"Italian, and not pizza," I demanded.

Officer Simpson opened my car door, and then slid behind the wheel of a black Chevy Trail Blazer. I waved at Reed as we pulled out of the drive. My chauffeur drove smoothly, cutting in and out of traffic, all the while keeping a close watch in the rearview mirror.

"What are you looking for?" I asked.

"Anything out of the ordinary. For instance, I'm taking a roundabout way to Dr. Anderson's office. Any car that's still following four blocks from there will get pulled over by the unmarked police car tailing *us*. The driver will be sternly questioned."

He had everything under control.

We parked in the visitor's area and walked in through the lobby. I unlocked the office door, taking down the sign Reed had placed there the day before, then flipped on the lights and shivered.

The room had a closed in feel to it. The flowers Janine brought every Monday were still in the vase on the table next to the chair, the dead blooms stiff as a corpse. I tossed them into the waste basket.

I entered Linnie's office and turned on the lights there, too. Suppressing another shiver, I made a pot of coffee. How many times had the two of us sat on her sofa, drinking coffee and chatting either before or after a session? Too many to count.

Papers and old appointment books littered the desk. For a moment, I wondered if the killer had searched her office, too, then remembered Linnie saying she'd had the locks changed. This was just Linnie being herself. Janine had kept things neat. I spied a few files on the credenza. Seeing them reminded me I'd forgotten to bring the files I had and her briefcase from Reed's. I made a mental note do it tomorrow.

I poured coffee for Officer Simpson and got down to business. Seated at Janine's desk, I phoned Dr. Corwin, the shrink who covered for Linnie, then called every patient in the appointment book for the next month, telling them the office was closed indefinitely. Most asked after Linnie and said they'd wait until she recovered to resume their visits or would consult Dr. Corwin.

As I sat stirring my fourth cup of coffee, a thought suddenly snapped into my mind. Donald Duckworth, who worked fourteen hour days, said he'd left early the night of Janine's murder. Why? It was out of character. Had he been the man in the car? Janine would have trusted him. Linnie would have opened the door for him. Plus, he could easily have made the acquaintance of the victims who'd been Linnie's patients. And for all we knew, he was a frequent visitor to the Tunica casinos. I needed to talk to Reed, fast. I dialed with trembling fingers.

"It's possible. You say he met Jeff the other day? Could be he's already questioned him. I'll find out."

He hung up and I resumed my duties.

My companion sat in the waiting area reading a book and refilling his coffee. He didn't speak and neither did I other than to order in lunch from a local deli.

Around three o'clock, I locked all the file drawers, and even remembered to change the message on the answering machine.

"Officer Simpson, I'm ready if you are. I feel silly saying Officer Simpson all the time. Do you have a first name—and please don't tell me it's Homer."

He chuckled. "It's Keith, Miss Bellwood."

"I'm Sasha. No need to stand on formality."

He smiled and closed his book. "Is everything secure?"

"All except Janine's desk."

I opened one of the drawers and found it empty. It was the same for the rest. Then in the corner beside the file cabinets I spied a couple of boxes. Linnie must have cleaned out Janine's things. I was about to leave when I turned and stared at the containers. Intuition told me to take them.

"Would you mind helping me carry those two boxes down to the car?"

He hefted both with no strain.

In the lobby, the security guard, Bob, opened the door for Keith. "How's Dr. Anderson, Miss Bellwood?"

"Hanging in there. She's in a coma, but the doctor gives her a good chance of pulling through."

"That's good. When she comes to, tell her goodbye. I enjoyed talking with her from time to time. Most people look right through the security guard, but if we met in the lobby or the hallway, she always said hello or had a nice comment."

I stared in surprise. "You're leaving? Don't tell me you've been let go. Not with all that's happened?"

He smiled, the corners of his light brown eyes crinkling. "No, nothing like that. I put in for a transfer. I do that every couple of years. Change of scenery. I'll be starting Monday at the First Bank of Memphis on Central. Besides, I'm taking two night courses at the University, so I can go straight from work."

"What kind of courses?" Bob hadn't struck me as being educationally ambitious.

"Forensics 101 For the Layman, and a creative writing class."

Now I was surprised. Bob the security guard as a writer? *Well, why not?*

"Never got the chance to go to college. Did a stint as a campus guard a few years ago. I was only there three weeks, but I loved the atmosphere. Thought I'd give it a whirl."

Keith cleared his throat, reminding me the boxes weren't exactly lightweight.

I held out my hand. "I've got to go, but I want to wish you good luck. Drop by and see Dr. Anderson sometime. She'll want a copy of your first book."

He shook my hand and laughed, his cheeks flushed. I turned and followed Keith to the car.

We stowed the boxes in the back and drove to the hospital where I caught the four o'clock visitation.

The respirator had been removed. She looked almost normal save for the bandages on her throat and around her head. I wanted to cry with relief. The nurse on duty said she was doing well.

"Has Detective Hammond been in today?"

"Oh, yes. He's here every day. Sometimes real early and at other times late at night."

"Your friend's going to make it," Officer Simpson

said on the drive back to Germantown.

"I think so, too. What'll happen now? I mean, she can identify the killer."

"If the killer has any sense, he's already lit out of town. With two men guarding her, he'd have to have brass ones to try anything."

"He has them, or he wouldn't have been this successful."

At Reed's, Officer Simpson settled on the sofa, and switched on the TV to ESPN. I didn't care. I needed a shower and a change of clothes.

I let the hot water beat on me until my muscles no longer felt like lumps of iron, and chose to wear a gauzy, yellow skirt with a white tank top. I wasn't sure who I wanted to impress. Reed wasn't impressionable.

The object of my thoughts arrived, handing me a grocery bag. While I unpacked it in the kitchen, Officer Simpson gave him a run-down of the day, and then left. A few minutes later, Reed, now wearing jeans and a light blue polo, joined me. He kissed my cheek, massaging the back of my neck.

"Tough day?" he asked.

"Tough enough. Most of her patients had already heard the news and were very supportive. How about you?"

He hesitated, and then said, "I'll tell you while we get dinner started."

"Did you get a hold of Jeff? Did he talk with Duckworth?"

"Yeah, several days ago. Duckworth claims to have misspoke. Said he wasn't heading home, but had just dropped by to talk and ask Janine out."

"He's changing his story?"

Reed shrugged. "It's possible. He was upset. Now, about dinner."

"What's on the menu?"

"Plain old spaghetti and meat sauce. You said no pizza and my Italian skills are that and spaghetti. Don't even know how to make decent meatballs."

He removed a frying pan from beneath a cabinet, set it on the stove, and dumped in the ground beef. He handed me an onion, some mushrooms, garlic, and a cutting board.

"Knives are next to the sink."

I peeled the onion while Reed stirred the browning hamburger. "So, how was your day?"

"Interesting. We got the tox report back on the wine. The bottle and the untouched glass on the end table were clear. The remains in Marilyn's glass and the puddle on the coffee table had traces of Rohyponal."

"What's that?"

"Also known as roofies."

"Isn't that a date rape drug?"

Reed nodded. "It can cause disorientation, slurred speech, loss of motor control, and drowsiness."

"Is it hard to get?" I chopped the onion, wiping tears from my burning eyes with a dishtowel.

"Not hard at all. Slip some into a glass of wine and it wouldn't take long for the victim to feel the effects." He paused, adding salt and pepper to the frying meat. "It disappears from the system pretty fast. So far, none has shown up in any of the victims. It'll take weeks before, or even if, we get anything back from Bridget or Eleanor."

I moved on from the odorous onion to slicing the mushrooms. "Well, we knew he drugged his victims, so

I'm not surprised to hear that."

"There wasn't as much in Marilyn as I expected. Maybe his supply was low, or she didn't drink much. Got that onion ready yet?"

I passed him the cutting board and he scraped the pieces into the ground beef, setting up an immediate sizzle. Within seconds the smell of cooking onions and mushrooms permeated the air. My stomach grumbled.

"Do the garlic next," he said.

I grabbed the bulb, broke off three cloves, peeled them, and proceeded to mince. He slid the ingredients into the pan, and I sniffed appreciatively at the mingling of the aromas. This time my stomach growled like an angry dog. Reed opened cans of diced tomatoes and tomato sauce, adding them to the mix. Oregano and basil followed.

"There's salad fixings in the fridge. Why don't you make those while I do up the pasta and garlic bread?"

I removed the makings from the crisper drawer and set them on the counter, glancing over at Reed. I sensed he wasn't telling me everything.

"Anything else I might want to know?" I asked, breaking the lettuce into chunks and tossing them into a bowl.

He filled a pot with water and set it on the stove before answering. From his body language I knew he struggled with how to tell me something. I didn't question him further, allowing him to take his time while grabbing the garlic bread from the freezer and setting the oven. Finally, he turned to face me.

"We know how the guy got into Linnie's office."

I stopped chopping tomatoes. Did I really want to hear this? I still felt guilty at not realizing Janine had been in danger sooner. I heaved a deep breath. Of course I had to know.

"How did the bastard do it?"

"He drove right into the parking garage using Janine's swipe card, went to the third floor, parked next to the stairwell, did his thing, and left."

"When?"

"Seven-ten the next morning. He left fifteen minutes later."

"And security didn't find that odd? Good Lord, a woman had been abducted from the garage and murdered the night before." My voice rose in outrage.

"Not at all. The hours of the engineering firm on the third floor are from seven-thirty in the morning 'til five-thirty in the evening Monday through Thursday. On Friday they knock off at eleven-thirty in the morning. He came in with the rest of the workers."

"Hat pulled low and jacket collar up, I suppose."

"You got it."

"And it confirms what Duckworth said about seeing a man enter Linnie's office around that time. Damn, why didn't any of us think about Janine's swipe card earlier?"

"Water under the bridge."

I finished the salads and set the table, my mind viewing the tape as it must have looked. The killer, disguised in some manner, drives up—probably in a stolen car—gains entry, parks, and uses Janine's keys to access the office. He knows which files to take and doesn't hurry. Janine's office isn't that large. Did he take the time to search Linnie's office, too? Perhaps.

My hands shook, and I clenched my teeth. I wanted to scream or kick something. Janine was dead. Linnie had damned near died. And all I could do was make a salad and set the table.

****

After dinner Reed left me watching TV while he worked on the computer. I still had the sense he was not telling all he knew, but didn't push it. At least, not now. I'd wait until morning and ask him then.

I gazed at the TV screen, but saw nothing. My mind tried to sort out the last few days, especially the night of Linnie's attack. I was convinced Kathy contacted me through the nightmare, but the sleepwalking episode had me baffled. I remembered nothing. That was unusual, and I was convinced the two were connected. It was important to remember. I sensed the entire case hinged on my memory.

Chapter Eighteen

I sat across the breakfast table from Reed, picking at my waffle and tapping into his intense inner turmoil. It had to do with the killer. I wondered why he wasn't sharing.

"Not hungry?" he asked.

I shook my head. "You were up until the wee hours of the morning. What were you doing?"

"Just checking out a few things online."

"Like what?"

He shrugged. "I'm researching several cases."

"The killer's victims?"

"No, the similarities of other murders in other cities. Serial killers move around. It's like a sixth sense."

"You mean like Ted Bundy or that guy who killed people living near the railroad tracks, and then hopped a freight out of town?"

"More or less."

"But didn't you or the detectives who took over after you were shot do that?"

"Not at first. Remember, I'm one of the few who insisted we had a serial killer on our hands. The diverse killing methods were sheer genius."

"Janine broke the pattern," I said slowly, pushing my plate away.

"Kathy Watson broke the pattern," Reed corrected. "She connected with you after death."

"And that gave him a new agenda." I paused, the skin along my arms prickling and rising in goosebumps. "Reed, *could* this guy be working in Linnie's office building?"

"Jeff said he would check it out. He's already talked with Duckworth. I imagine Brannon is doing the same. I'll ask both of them later." He glanced at his watch. "Damn, where's Simpson? I have to get to the station and make some phone calls."

His cell phone rang. He took the call, listened, spoke a terse thanks, and then hung up before turning to me.

"Sheriff's office got a call this morning. Seems co-workers were concerned about Donald Duckworth. They hadn't seen him in a few days. A Shelby County sheriff's deputy went to his house in Bartlett. Found him dead. Shot in the head. Been that way for at least three days."

I sat in stunned silence. "Was it random?"

"No sign of forced entry. Neighbors heard nothing. Might have used a silencer. I'd better call Jeff. My number one suspect just bit the big one."

I swept a hand through my hair. Another body. When would this nightmare end? If Duckworth wasn't the killer, then who?

"There's got to be someone who would arouse little or no suspicion if found wandering the hallways besides Duckworth," Reed said, his hand clenching the phone.

Then a scary thought occurred to me. "Reed, there is someone who knows the comings and goings of most of the employees, and wouldn't look strange wandering the hallways or stairwells on different floors."

"Who?"

"A security guard. The security guard, Bob, told me his hours are six in the morning until four in the afternoon."

"And like Duckworth, Janine would know him, trust him, and get into a car with him. But would Marilyn open the door and let him into her house?"

"Why not? She knew him and liked him. If he said he wanted to talk about Janine, she'd be eager to listen. And if he was wearing a jacket or windbreaker, Duckworth might have mistaken him for a…" I fumbled for the word… "a civilian. Plus, the tan slacks are part of a guard's uniform."

"But is he the boyfriend the victims mentioned?" Reed reminded me.

"Just because we don't see a killer smile or gorgeous eyes doesn't mean his victims didn't." I drew a deep, unsteady breath. "Reed, could we be dealing with two killers?"

"You mean the serial killer who murdered Bridget, Eleanor, and Kathy and someone else who nailed Janine, Duckworth, and attacked Marilyn? Someone from the building?" He spoke slowly, a frown etching the lines on his face deeper.

"It's a possibility, isn't it?" I drew in a sharp breath. "And last night the guard told me, he'd put in for a transfer. He also said something about being a campus guard once. Bridget was a college student."

"I'm calling Brannon. He needs to talk to this security guard."

Bob, the most unassuming person in the world,

might have killed Janine, but what the hell would have been his motive? Had he asked her out and been rebuffed? Maybe Janine thought it a joke and had laughed, sparking some kind of murderous rage. No, Janine might've been surprised, but would have handled it diplomatically.

And how would he have known Donald had seen him? Unless, of course, Donald talked at the office. Maybe even told Bob directly what he'd seen not realizing he was talking to the killer.

But was Bob connected to the other murders? I couldn't see how. I was convinced my theory of two killers was right.

Reed finished his conversation and hung up. "Brannon's going to check it out." He glanced at his watch. "Damn, I'm late. I've got some things to check on, too. I'll talk to Jeff later. Where's Simpson?"

I cleared the table, setting the dishes in the sink. My arms still tingled, and I rubbed them hoping to dispel the chill. I had an uneasy feeling things were about to pop, but I had no idea how. It was like looking at a Christmas gift, trying to divine what was inside by the shape of the package. Sometimes you knew, and sometimes you got a surprise. I didn't want any surprises. I'd had enough to last a lifetime.

The doorbell rang. "About time," Reed muttered.

I stood in the kitchen doorway while he let Keith in. They spoke for a few seconds, and then my bodyguard walked toward me. Today he wore brown cargo pants and a camouflage T-shirt.

"Good morning, Miss Bellwood."

"Good morning. And it's Sasha. Remember? Ready for a hard day of guarding?" I poured him a cup of coffee.

Reed reappeared, carrying a briefcase. "I'm off. Are you going to Marilyn's office today?"

"No reason to. I called everyone. There's nothing else to do. I may start on those files you gave me. I'll go see Linnie at noon."

"Be careful." He leaned over and kissed me. "Take good care of her, Keith."

"Don't worry, I will."

Reed left. Keith settled on the sofa and switched on ESPN. The announcers were giving recaps of the late night baseball games.

I washed the dishes, and then set the accordion folders on the kitchen table. I had four hours until the noontime visitation. I may as well make use of them.

I ignored the TV and pulled out the first file when my cell rang. I didn't recognize the number, but answered anyway, my mind occupied with Mary Alice Maghee.

"This is Sasha."

"Miss Bellwood, this is Dr. Farmer at UT Medical."

My attention snapped away from Mary Alice and a shot of pure adrenalin roared through me. I swallowed, trying not to tremble.

"Dr. Farmer, what's wrong? Is Linnie all right?" My voice wavered.

"Dr. Anderson is fine, but I'm calling to report that she had a bad night. I'm posting a twenty-four hour no visitors notice."

"Why? What happened? What do you mean by a bad night?" My mind conjured up a whole host of things that could be determined as bad. "Oh, my God, did the killer try something?"

"No, nothing like that. She's begun to move. Late last night, she tried to tear her IV's out and thrashed around so much we had to tie her hands to the bed rails."

I shivered, visualizing Linnie tossing and jerking like some demented rag doll.

"Does this mean she's coming out of the coma?"

"Possibly," Dr. Farmer replied in a cautious tone. "Her brain activity has increased, even though we had to sedate her."

"Have there been any more of those sky-high vital signs she had a few days ago?"

"No."

"Not even with Detective Hammond?"

"Negative. He was here at midnight, but didn't enter her room. He stood outside, talked to the guard, and inquired about her condition. The night nurse said he stayed maybe two minutes, and then left."

I hadn't talked to or seen Jeff in several days. I assumed he was busy. A spate of gang related drive-bys had kept Homicide active.

"Miss Bellwood, I have a favor to ask."

"Name it."

"It might help if when you come in tomorrow, you were to bring a few small items from her home. Personal things. Something familiar she can touch, hear or smell. Even unconscious patients respond. Familiar items help."

"Sure, I can do that."

"Nothing too big. We haven't got the room."

"I understand."

"Thanks. I'll see you tomorrow."

I hung up. The files could wait.

"Hey, Keith, want to drive me to Dr. Anderson's? The doctor says I should bring a few personal items to the hospital tomorrow."

"Sure." He turned off the TV, opened the front door, and scanned the street. "Looks clear. Let's go."

I scurried out to the Trail Blazer like an incognito rock star and buckled the seatbelt. The drive didn't take long. Keith got out, opening my door. I lingered in the car, not wanting to see where my best friend had almost died.

"Miss Bellwood?" he asked when I didn't move.

I sighed and released the seatbelt, but still hesitated.

"I know it'll be rough, but remember, Dr. Anderson is going to be all right."

"I know. It's just…"

I didn't finish the sentence. Instead, I sucked up my courage and exited the car.

Any silly hope I'd entertained that this was a random thing—Linnie didn't know her attacker; she'd left a door unlocked and someone had walked in, surprising her—was dashed the moment I stepped into the foyer.

Anger, no rage, and intense fear—the killer's—still hung in the airless room. My stomach cramped and I fought not to throw up. I ignored my trembling legs.

The plantation blinds were closed. I opened one. My shoulders slumped when I saw the gray-black residue of fingerprint powder on every conceivable surface. A hunk of carpet had been cut out next to the marble coffee table. Both the phone and the decorative sofa pillow were gone. I assumed they had been taken as evidence.

I quickly walked between the table and fireplace, not wanting to look at where Linnie had fallen.

The kitchen wasn't in any better shape. A basket of fruit sat in the middle of the table, flies buzzing around the over-ripe contents. The stink of rotting vegetation didn't help my shaky stomach.

I tossed the mess into the trash can under the sink. It also stank. I pulled it out, and then cleared the fridge of anything else that was limp or slimy. I'd return this weekend and give the place a good cleaning. Keith dumped the garbage into the trash can outside the back door.

I grabbed the empty fruit basket and marched into Linnie's bedroom. I had no idea what to take. Clothing was out of the question as was jewelry, although maybe her grandmother's ruby and pearl ring would be okay. I found it in her jewelry box, slipping it on my finger for safe keeping.

"What next?" I muttered, my gaze scanning the room.

I spotted a framed photo of Linnie and her late father on the nightstand and dumped it into the basket. Maybe it would help her when she came out of the coma.

The ring was touch; the picture sight. How about smell? I grabbed her favorite perfume from the dresser. Surely a dab on her wrists and behind the ears wouldn't interfere with hospital routine. It would certainly smell better than antiseptic.

In the dining room, I noticed her iPod on the table and added that to the basket along with a pair of headphones. Maybe the music would have a calming effect if she started thrashing around again.

"All done?" Keith asked, taking the basket from me.

"Just about. Dr. Farmer suggested familiar items, but now that I'm here, I can't decide what constitutes familiar."

We started back through the living room when I stopped and chuckled. Keith halted in front of the fireplace.

"What's so funny?"

I pointed to the mantel. "The flamingo. Add that. I want it to be the first thing she sees when she regains consciousness."

He grinned and dropped it on top of the headphones, then wiped his hand on his pants.

"That's it. Let's go home."

Keith set the basket on the back seat and we left. Suddenly, I felt better. I knew the flamingo would work. The next time I visited, I'd wrap her fingers around it. Linnie would understand.

****

Keith returned to ESPN, and I settled down at the kitchen table with Reed's files, opening Mary Alice Maghee's again. I read through the various statements by family members, neighbors, and friends. No visions or funny feelings surfaced. A manila envelope was in the back of the file. Unthinkingly, I opened it.

I bit off a gasp and stared at the crime scene photos. Murder on TV is sanitized. Reality is disgusting. The photos were in living color and not pleasant. The bicycle chain was wrapped twice around her throat, the links clearly imprinted on her skin. Her tongue protruded and her face was almost black with shades of blue, purple, and red.

I shoved them back into the envelope. They hadn't talked to me, and I saw no reason to look at them again.

I worked steadily through the files until noon when I stopped to make lunch for Keith and me. He'd switched to a local channel and watched the news. It contained the usual—another drive by on the north side, a carjacking, a jewelry store robbery, and miscellaneous city corruption. I left Keith chowing down on a ham sandwich and chips and retreated to the kitchen to eat. I didn't need murder and mayhem with lunch.

I was cleaning up when the doorbell rang, startling me. From the kitchen doorway, I watched Keith take a gun from one of the pockets of his cargo pants and look through the peephole. Apparently satisfied with what he saw, he put the gun away and opened the door. Detective Brannon stepped through.

"Is everything all right?" Keith asked.

"Fine as far as I know. Reed called a little while ago and told me to meet him here. He says he has a theory and wants Sasha's input."

"What input?" I said, coming into the room.

"I have no idea. He said he wanted to check out something and would meet us here. I *do* have news on the doc's ex-boyfriend, Brian Michaels. He was paroled two months ago. Good behavior. His P.O. talked to him on Monday. He has a job here in Memphis, but no alibi for Saturday night."

"Have you talked to him?"

"Not yet. He called in sick today and isn't at home. His car's gone, too."

"I guess if I'd tried to kill the woman who put me in prison, I'd bug out, especially if I'd left fingerprints behind," I said.

"So far, his prints haven't been identified. Yours were, though along with Reed's and Jeff's."

"Of course. I'm there all the time and Jeff is seeing her. Where did you find Reed's?"

"On one of the files in her briefcase," he told me. "Said he handed her some folders the last time he was in the office."

"Any unidentified on the front or back door knobs?"

"Most were too smudged to be of use. At least, you're narrowing the possibilities down. Too bad they're the wrong people."

Brannon shrugged and sat on the sofa. Keith had changed the channel. "What's on?"

"Game's about to start. Cards and Cubbies."

"Five bucks say the Cards take 'em."

"You're on. Chicago's on a four game winning streak and their ace is pitching today."

I left the two men to their baseball game. In the kitchen, I pulled the remaining files from the accordion folders and flipped through them, jotting the victims' names on a notepad. Everything was up to date, including Janine's. By the grace of God, Linnie was not a death statistic. Until she came out of the coma, I remained the last man standing who had a connection to Kathy. I leafed through the files again. Something wasn't right. I could swear one was missing.

"Nine names, nine files," I muttered. "Dammit, this isn't right. I know there was another victim."

Where had I gotten the impression of another name? I closed my eyes and fought through the mental sludge the last few days had deposited in my mind. I sighed. It was no use. I rose and paced until my gaze fell on a box in the corner with the words, "Janine's office things", printed on the lid in Linnie's handwriting. Keith had put them there the day before.

I don't know why, but I started sifting through the contents. I had no idea what I searched for. Janine had been big on "to do" lists. She kept a weekly one printed out from the computer, and a more detailed daily list on a notepad next to the telephone.

I read a couple of weeks' worth, and then put them aside. Nothing there piqued my interest. I rummaged among numerous scraps of paper with notes she'd written to herself, but found nothing.

Then in the bottom of the box I came across several steno pads. Janine must have used them in Linnie's personal correspondence.

I flipped through them, but found nothing of consequence. It was in the fourth notebook where I found the list—Mary Alice Maghee, Jennifer Graham, Melissa Tallmadge, Susan Parker, and Bridget Connor.

Melissa Tallmadge. I re-read my list. Her name wasn't on it, and there was no file. Why would Reed withhold a file? If I tried to connect with these victims, I needed all the information. Had he forgotten it? That didn't sound like the meticulous Reed I knew.

Suddenly, icy cold encased me. Goosebumps stood out on my arms, and I shivered. My chest compressed, making it hard to breathe. Was someone trying to contact me—someone who didn't quite know how to do it? Melissa? I clasped my arms around my stomach to keep from shaking. Could she be a victim whose body had never been found?

Come on, Sasha, get a hold of yourself. Who is

Melissa Tallmadge? I'm missing a vital clue. I just know it.

The upheaval of the past few days had forced my mind into other areas of concentration. I needed to focus.

Melissa? Is that you? Nothing. I tried again. *Melissa Tallmadge, are you trying to contact me?*

A vast darkness filled my senses. Empty, yet filled with anger. I wondered what Melissa was trying to tell me. For some reason, Reed popped into my mind. Was she trying to tell me something about him?

Then a horrible thought crossed my mind. Could Reed be the killer? Is that what she was attempting to say?

No! Don't even think such a thing!

My God, I was in love with the man, had slept with him. Surely, I would have sensed it if he'd murdered someone.

I tried to put things into a logical pattern. Reed was in charge of cold cases, but who was in charge of Reed? Could he have removed information from the files? And he *had* been Linnie's patient. In fact, he had just started seeing her again. He knew where things were kept. Had he taken the files from Linnie's office? Is that when his prints had been transferred to the file found at Linnie's house? Had he withheld Melissa's because of something it contained? Something I might connect to him? Had he slipped up and said something in casual conversation I would recall?

And Janine would have trusted him. She would have gotten into his car without a doubt or worry. And Linnie would have opened the door for him, maybe even poured him a glass of wine.

I closed my eyes again, trying to remember the night of Linnie's attack. Reed claimed to have finished his interrogation and gone to a bar. Had he? Or had he decided his psychiatrist might put two and two together and come up with his name?

I also recalled the icy rage rolling off of one of us at dinner the night Janine died. Reed? And to make matters worse, he'd been withdrawn and distracted the last couple of days.

My mind argued back. If he was the killer, why come to Linnie seeking help in finding the bodies? Why get close to me—the one person who could tap into his emotions?

In spite of the cold, I broke out in a sweat. Oh, God, it just couldn't be true. I rose from my knees, stumbling into the living room where Detective Brannon and Keith sat engrossed in the ball game.

I cleared my throat and tried to stop my teeth from chattering. "Detective Brannon, you worked on all the suspected serial killer cases, didn't you?"

"What? Yeah, all those after Reed was shot. I assisted before that." He didn't break concentration on the man at bat.

"You worked with Jeff and Reed?"

"Yeah. Jeff was never convinced it was a serial killer. I sided with Reed. After Reed left the force, I partnered with Ed Nobles. He wasn't convinced either. Yeah, another strike out!"

"I'm missing one of the files. There's only nine here."

"That's all we had."

"No, ten. I'm missing Melissa Tallmadge's file," I said. I was so cold I thought I'd turned into an ice sculpture.

A commercial came on, and he turned toward me, a frown on his face. "Who?"

"Melissa Tallmadge."

"Never had a vic by that name."

"Are you sure?" The cold receded. "I found the name in Janine's notes."

"What notes?"

I beckoned him into the dining room and handed him the steno pad. "See?"

"Yeah, Mary, Jennifer, Susan, and Bridget were all victims, but I've never heard of Melissa Tallmadge. Where did Janine get these names?"

"We thought maybe the killer was one of Linnie's patients, so we were cross referencing group therapy sessions."

"Maybe the list you have refers to something else."

I shook my head, and walked down the hall to Reed's office. I knew I wouldn't be able to pull up anything on his computer, but the desk was littered with papers. I searched through them. Nothing stirred my senses. I reached into the wastepaper basket and hauled out four crumpled sheets of paper. The second one contained four handwritten names. My fingers tightened. Melissa Tallmadge was the third. I didn't recognize the other three.

I returned to the living room.

"Detective Brannon, you need to see…"

The cold slammed into me with the power of a freight train. I staggered back against the wall. Brannon jumped from the sofa just in time to keep me from falling. Keith was right behind him.

A presence, so strong it took my breath away,

ripped the clutter from my mind. I saw the clearing where Kathy had died. Restraints—handcuffs?—tied a man's hands behind his back and around the trunk of a small tree. It was Reed. He struggled and out of eyesight, someone laughed. The image went fuzzy and finally faded.

"Reed!" I said with a gasp. "The killer has him."

"What? Are you sure? Where?" Brannon demanded in a harsh tone.

"The same place where he killed Kathy."

"We don't know where that was."

"I know!" I cried. "He's drugged, but he'll come back to me."

I took several cleansing breaths and opened my mind. *Come on, Reed. Come back. Show me where you are.*

He didn't answer. He may have passed out. I tried slipping into his mind, but got nowhere. I was blocked. By Reed?

"Come on, we have to find him," I said.

"Where do we look?"

"Go to where we found Kathy's body."

"But that's way up north," Brannon protested.

"Kathy was hauled out of the Frog River. My vision showed her being dumped in a river. The place where she was killed must be close by. Go to Frog River Park," I told Keith.

The three of us raced to the Trail Blazer. Keith drove with Brannon next to him and me in the back seat. Brannon called for back-up to meet us at the park entrance. I closed my eyes and concentrated. If Reed had been drugged, it was possible he'd slip in and out of consciousness.

I've heard it said that fear allows us to sometimes perform superhuman feats. Mine was trying to pull Reed's thoughts back into my mind. My heart pounded. All I could do was pray, "Please, Reed, don't die."

I stifled a sob, and my gaze fell on the silly pink flamingo in the basket from Linnie's. I needed the comfort now and picked it up. The plush pink fur was stiff with what felt like dried hair gel. I rolled the fur between my fingers, the substance disintegrating into dust. Where had I felt this before?

Then I remembered. The back door at my house had had the same residue on it a week or so ago. The library scene from the movie *Ghostbusters* flashed through my mind. The apparitions had left behind a thick, gooey mess. What was it called—ectoplasm? I held the flamingo closer. Kathy? My fingers tightened. I knew why I had sleepwalked.

Kathy *had* been with Linnie that night. The images were so horrific, I'd blocked them out. Not anymore. Somehow, she'd embedded what had happened into the flamingo, and now those images transferred to me.

Fear clawed at my gut, and I saw the face of the killer. Before I could say a word to Brannon and Keith, the sensation of being filled poured into me. It was Kathy, and she took control.

Sasha?

Hello, Kathy. Please, where's Reed? Lead me there.

I tried so hard to let you know about Dr. Anderson. It was Gerald. He did it.

I know, but now we have to find Reed. Where did you die? Is it near where we found you?

The drug's all gone now, and I can see. There's a

small clearing at the water's edge. When you go into the park, bear right. It's at the end of the road. A kind of cul de sac. That's where he parked. I was already fuzzy and he had to lead me down the path.

Kathy, go there. Wait for me.

Kathy Watson disappeared from my body.

"Take the first right in the park, and follow it to the end. The little clearing where Kathy died and Reed is being held isn't far down a path. Hurry!"

"Are you sure?" Brannon said.

"Yes, dammit. I'm not alone in this back seat."

His head whipped around, his eyes wide. Keith almost ran off the road, his gaze glued to the rearview mirror. He jerked the wheel back to the left.

"You're having a vision?" Brannon asked.

"A vision of what?" Keith demanded.

"Never mind, just hurry!"

Keith floored it. By the time we arrived, two patrol cars were there. Keith pulled up next to them, and Brannon rolled down his window.

"Follow us. We suspect a police officer is being held hostage. The kidnapper is armed."

We took off down the main drive, and then veered to the right. My heart pounded in my ears, and I shook so badly my bones rattled.

Reed, darling, we're coming. Hang in there. I love you. Please, don't die.

The narrow roadway twisted and turned through the trees. I bit my lip and prayed. Then a thought occurred to me.

"Stop! Pull over," I told Keith.

"What? Why?" Brannon asked.

"If we all go thrashing in there, Reed's a dead man.

He's bait. I'm the one the killer wants. He probably isn't aware Reed called you to meet him or that I have a bodyguard. Pull over, dammit," I said. The cul de sac loomed ahead. Reed's car was parked on the shoulder.

Keith pulled over. The two cruisers stopped behind us. I opened the door and got out.

"You can't go down there alone," Keith protested.

"I wasn't getting Reed's thoughts at the house. It was the killer contacting me. He stood near Reed and let me see. Give me ten minutes."

"Can you see the killer?" Brannon asked.

I told them.

"Are you sure?" he asked again.

"Yes, I'm sure."

"How does he know *you'd* know where to go?"

"I don't know. Maybe he thinks I know more than I do. Just trust me on this."

"I don't like it," Brannon muttered.

"I'm not too thrilled with it myself, but it's the best I can do. He's at the end of his rope—not as rational as he once was. Ten minutes, and be as quiet as you can."

I turned, and taking a deep breath, walked down the road. I found the path immediately. Maybe I should have said five minutes. I slowed my pace.

The little clearing was just as I had seen it the night Kathy died. My vision of Reed was also accurate. He sat against a tree; the same one Kathy had lain under. He had a gag in his mouth and was conscious. His eyes opened wide, and he made frantic noises in his throat while shaking his head from side to side.

I walked to the middle of the clearing. A rustling in the bushes in back of me caught my attention. Reed yanked and pulled against the handcuffs restraining him. I saw the fear in his eyes, but for once didn't attempt to tap in. Instead, I concentrated on the killer's emotions. Fear, triumph, anticipation, and lust enveloped me.

An arm snaked around my throat. My hands automatically reached up to grab the wrist. The barrel of a gun was pressed against my right temple. Hot breath tickled the back of my neck and a voice hissed in my ear.

"I knew you'd come."

I willed myself to remain calm. "Hello, Jeff."

Chapter Nineteen

A lot of emotions flew around that clearing. Despair and anger poured from Reed. Jeff's rage had intensified, coming close to consuming him. Oddly enough, mine were muted. I was scared, to be sure—my heart raced at ramming speed and my legs had the consistency of jelly—but I remained upright and in control.

I locked Reed's reactions into a corner of my mind and concentrated on Jeff. My use of his name surprised him. His arm squeezed and his gun hand twitched ever so slightly.

"How did you know it was me?"

"Kathy told me."

He laughed. It was the public Jeff Hammond—happy, devil-may-care, not a problem in the world, Jeff Hammond.

"Yeah, poor old Kathy. You know, if she hadn't crawled all over me wanting sex one night, she may have lived. But she was like all the rest—a slut who deserved to die."

He shoved me hard toward Reed. I stumbled and fell, then crawled over to sit next to him.

"You can take the gag off now. I got you here. That's what counts."

I worked the knot of the cotton strip until it

loosened. Reed rubbed his mouth against his upper arm to remove it. "You bastard!"

Jeff laughed again. "I knew you'd figure it out sooner or later. When you called and said you wanted to talk to me, I knew what the subject matter would be. So, I drugged a bottle of water. Then I pretended to open it fresh when I gave it to you. I have the dosages down pretty close now. I didn't want you so groggy you couldn't walk, and I sure as hell wasn't carrying you." He shifted his attention to me. "I contacted you, didn't I? I knew I could. I pretended to be Reed."

"You fooled me all right," I said. How long had I been here? Were the ten minutes up?

He looked back at Reed. "Gave me a turn when you told me you'd contacted a psychic. Thought maybe everything was all right when Sasha didn't come up with anything that first day in Marilyn's office. Then she told me about this vision when I saw her by the river the day Kathy was found. Still, Sasha couldn't identify me, so I thought maybe I was safe." He shook his head, a look of resignation on his face. "I really thought the body would make it to the Mississippi."

Reed fixed his gaze on his former partner. "Come on, Jeff, you can't get away with this. You've made too many mistakes. The tapes from the parking garage the day you killed Janine can be further enhanced. And I'm sure someone in the building will remember seeing you. I'll even bet the investigation of the drive-by ended at about the same time Dr. Anderson was attacked. By the way, doctors say she'll come out of her coma." He kept his voice calm and spoke in a monotone.

"I have that covered. As soon as I'm done with the two of you, I'll take care of her. I've watched the ICU.

Doctors come and go all the time, but how many people actually see them? The nurses sit at the monitors or are busy in the rooms. Not even the guards pay any attention when medical personnel breeze past them. The one never looks up from his girlie magazine. A little tinkering with the charts to make it look good and a syringe full of air into an IV tube, followed by a quick exit. She's dead and I'm safe."

"Security cameras, Jeff," Reed said.

"Fooled them before."

"You slipped up, didn't you?" I said in a soft voice. Where the hell were those cops? "You made a mistake that day in Linnie's office. Melissa Tallmadge."

"She was Birmingham. I knew the instant Janine repeated the names, I'd goofed. I had to eliminate all three of you."

"Why pick on Janine first?" I asked.

"Because she was the most vulnerable, the most trusting," Reed said with a sneer. "You sabotaged her car and offered to help when it refused to start."

Jeff shrugged. "I did what I had to do. It was easy. She never suspected a thing."

"You never cared about Linnie at all, did you?" I said.

"Actually, I did. Right up until she started with the sex thing. I knew she was borderline that first day in her office when she started flirting with all that coffee nonsense. I decide when to have sex, not the woman."

"Just like you did after you killed Kathy?" *Where the hell are Brannon and the posse? I can't keep him talking forever.*

"What are you talking about?" Jeff asked with a start.

"You pumped yourself dry in the river. I saw it in my vision. Kathy watched, too."

"I should have killed you first," he stated with a curled lip.

"But you didn't. And now you have to deal with what I may have told others."

I caught a flicker of movement along the path to my right. Finally! I also realized that if Brannon and the rest continued on their present course, Jeff would soon see them, too. A quick shift of the eyes was all he needed.

"I've got that taken care of," Jeff boasted.

My heart thumped wildly. I had to keep him distracted. He was in gloating mode now, convinced he had the upper hand. I closed my eyes and fed off his over-confidence.

"How?" Beside me, Reed drew in a sudden, quiet breath. His muscles tensed and I knew he'd seen what I had on the path.

"You never knew I sometimes collected trophies. Mostly impulse. Earrings, a necklace—things like that. Nothing anybody would miss. I keep them in the bottom of my dresser drawer. Or rather I did." He fished in his pocket and removed a clear plastic baggie. "I have use for them now." He shook it, the items inside jingling. "See?"

No, I didn't. What I saw was movement off toward my left. Brannon, Keith, and the rest must have split up. Good move. Jeff couldn't cover every direction.

"You're going to set me up," Reed said in a flat voice.

Jeff grinned. "Decided to do that the minute I realized Sasha was for real."

I spoke in a contemptuous tone to keep his attention focused on me. "So, that's why you kept insisting the killer was one of Linnie's patients. Plant the seed of suspicion in her mind. Only she never bought it. She checked it out, but never believed. Must have pissed you off."

"It did," he said.

"I caught your anger on numerous occasions, including the night of Janine's murder. We were at the restaurant and I tuned into someone's rage. I just wasn't sure whose. We were all arguing."

"I underestimated Marilyn. She was easy, but strong. A lot stronger than I realized. I thought she'd make the connection to Reed. I returned to the office after killing Janine and swiped those files. I hoped she would call the police and give them the information."

"And since I wasn't involved until Kathy's death that meant Reed would be the natural suspect."

"That's right. I had it all worked out except for Marilyn not doing as I anticipated."

"Why did you ransack my house and steal the laptop?"

"I took a chance. Kathy's file was detailed, but I had to know if you'd seen anything new, especially concerning Bridget. And then, you found Eleanor. I couldn't believe it. Your visions were growing stronger every day. I had to do something. It was only a matter of time before someone connected the dots."

My gaze fell on the Ziploc bag. "What's your plan now?"

Brannon dodged behind a tree twenty feet from the clearing. I didn't dare risk scanning the woods over Jeff's shoulder.

Hurry up for cryin' out loud.

"I can answer that," Reed said. "He'll probably kill you first, using my gun. He won't strangle you because he knows you'll fight. And stabbing is out. Too much blood. Some might get on his clothing. Once you're out of the way, he'll kill me. A head shot to make it look like suicide."

"And the jewelry will be tucked in your pocket. I'm really sorry. I like you, Reed. I always did."

"Yet, you tried to kill him once before," I said. Reed jerked and turned his head toward me, his eyes questioning. "Yes, the night you were shot."

"I was getting nervous. You just wouldn't let it go. I showed myself in the window knowing the perp would head out the back door before you were set. Almost worked."

"You son of a bitch. What kind of a cop are you?" he said.

"A good one," Jeff replied in an injured tone. "I was always a damn good cop." He shoved the baggie back into his pocket. "Well, I guess it's almost time. Sasha, move about ten feet to your right."

"No."

The gun centered on Reed's chest. "Do it or I'll kill him."

"So what? You're going to kill us anyway."

"Good girl, Sasha. Stay put," Reed told me. A sapling behind Jeff shivered. Someone was on the move.

"I said move, you bitch, or I swear I'll plug you now!" Jeff's breathing had accelerated and a sheen of sweat coated his forehead. Things were not going as he'd planned.

"No you won't. There'll be blood splatter on Reed. It'll screw up your plan." I hoped I was right.

"If you kill her here, you'll have to make me move in order to prove suicide. I'll fight. And forensics will find marks on my wrists from the handcuffs. You didn't think this one through, partner."

I cut my eyes slightly to the right. Brannon was moving behind another tree five feet away from the edge of the clearing.

Jeff caught my action. I felt a surge of fear and rage run through him. For the first time, he had an inkling he wasn't in complete control.

Then, one of the men in the woods stepped on a twig. The snap sounded like a gunshot. I jumped. Jeff didn't.

"Whoever's out there, drop your gun and show yourself. If you don't, I'll kill one of them. Your choice—a cop or a psychic."

"Give it up, Hammond," Brannon called from his cover. "You'll never get away with it."

"Sure I will. This is better than my plan. Everyone dies in a shootout. Except me, of course. I'll be the lone survivor."

He'd gone over the edge—totally delusional, thinking he could take down an unknown number of cops, and living in a world where he righted wrongs only he perceived. The problem was he would nail either me or Reed, maybe both of us, before biting the big one.

The gun wavered between us. His finger tightened on the trigger. In a futile gesture of self-defense, I put up my hands and held my breath.

Then, from out of nowhere, a thick column of

black smoke materialized in front of us.

****

Kathy drifted over the clearing desperate to help. She'd arrived to find Gerald standing guard over a man handcuffed to the very tree where she'd died. The prisoner's eyes were glazed and he acted drugged.

Of course he's drugged. This is what I looked like when the bastard killed me.

Gerald strode around the clearing, his gaze frequently cutting toward the path.

What's he doing?

The man stirred, struggling against his bonds. Gerald laughed and continued his tense pacing. The man slumped, and then shook his head.

The scene confused her. Gerald with a male victim? Why? *What's the purpose?*

She drifted closer to the bound man. Maybe his mind would be open to her. She slipped inside his head.

His thoughts were chaotic, shifting from scene to scene, most of which included Sasha. She had no problem reading his emotions.

He's a policeman. He's also in love with Sasha. He's terrified for her and furious with himself for being taken in by Jeff. Jeff? Not Gerald?

Of course. It made sense that the killer would use aliases. Bridget had told her that.

In a burst of enlightenment, she understood why this man was here. Gerald, the little bastard, wanted to lure Sasha to the clearing. He was going to kill them both.

I have to warn her.

Kathy pulled out of the man's head and tried to contact Sasha, but Sasha had her blocked. *No! Let me in.* Her plea went unanswered.

Suddenly, Gerald snapped his head to the left, his attention on the path. With a triumphant grin, he sidled behind a small tree and waited.

She sobbed when Sasha ran into the clearing toward the man. Sasha appeared calm and unsurprised when Gerald walked up behind her, placing a gun to her head. She sensed others nearby. Police? Sasha hadn't come alone! The ensuing conversation told Kathy, her mortal friend had things under control. It was the end of the road for Gerald. This time he wouldn't get away with killing.

Then, someone in the woods stepped on a twig, revealing their presence. Horror flowed through her as Gerald pointed the gun toward his captives.

No, by God! Enough was enough. Not one more life sacrificed for Gerald's warped sense of duty. She'd saved Dr. Anderson's life. Could she do it again?

You're the only one who can. The voice came from the edge of the clearing. She twisted her head and saw Bridget.

Help me!

I'll try, but I'm so weak.

Combine our energy. We have to act now! She saw Sasha raise her hands. *Hurry, Bridget! Dammit, help me!*

Bridget's power filled her like water in a bathtub. Her otherworld friend had more strength than she realized. Placing themselves between Gerald and Sasha, Kathy and Bridget let their fury take over.

****

My mouth dropped open. I wasn't sure what I saw. A sharp intake of breath from Reed convinced me I wasn't hallucinating. He'd seen whatever had appeared, too.

The column thickened, darkened, and tried to take human form. What looked like a head grew on top. Rudimentary arms and legs shot out.

Jeff screamed and jumped back. The apparition moved to the right away from them and the policemen in the woods. He swung the gun around and fired three times. The bullets passed through the cloud and slammed into the trees. A rage-filled face took shape on the head.

Somebody said, "Holy shit!", but I had no idea who. The arms lengthened, grew hands, and reached for Jeff. He stumbled backwards, firing again with the same results.

Tell the police not to shoot. We want him.

I recognized Kathy's voice and understood. This was the rage and hate of a murder victim in front of us. Then, I realized Kathy was not alone. Bridget was with her.

Brannon's gun was raised, ready to fire.

"Don't shoot!" I yelled.

Reed and I were in the line of fire. I had no idea if the projectiles could harm a rapidly materializing ghost.

By now all the cops were on the edge of the clearing with guns drawn and expressions varying from astonishment to disbelief. I spared a glance for Reed, slipping into his mind where I read acceptance and hope.

Another sobbing scream from Jeff brought my attention back to him, Kathy, and Bridget. He continued to back away, firing until his gun was empty. He threw it at the darkness. His face was frozen into a mask of horror, his handsome features twisted into a grotesque expression.

A second later, Kathy and Bridget leaped. The blackness enveloped Jeff. The appendages wrapped around his body and forced him to the ground.

He screamed. "Get it off me! Get it off me!"

No one stirred. We all stared, unable to move.

His arms and legs thrashed the ground as the column shrank and grew pitch black. His screams turned into choking gurgles, and his limbs slowly gave up the struggle until their movement ceased. The clearing went silent. Dead silent. No birds called. No insects chirped.

The black column of Kathy and Bridget rose, grew lighter in color, and finally disappeared like smoke in the wind.

Brannon and Keith slowly walked to the center of the clearing. The other cops followed. I rose, taking a few wobbling steps.

"Jesus," Brannon whispered. It sounded more like a prayer than blasphemy. "He's dead. Strangled."

"Exactly what did we witness?" Keith asked.

"I don't know, but it scared the piss out of me," one of the cops replied.

"How the hell do we write this one up?" another asked.

"Leave that to me," Brannon said. "Sasha, what was that?"

I looked at Jeff's body. The face was multihued with blue, purple and black blotches, and his teeth had bitten down on a protruding tongue. His throat bore the signs of constriction.

"Retribution," I replied.

"What?" he said.

"Vengeance, if you like. Jeff's past literally came back to haunt him."

"If it's not too much trouble, would one of you mind getting the goddamned key to these handcuffs out of his pocket and using it?"

I swiveled my head to Reed. I'd forgotten about him. I stooped, rummaging in Jeff's pockets until I found the key, and returned to Reed. I knelt next to him, opening his restraints. He groaned, rubbing his wrists, and then shoulders. Brannon helped me get him to his feet.

"Are you all right?" he asked.

"Yeah," Reed replied. "Just feel like a jerk for letting him get the upper hand. Even as I sat in his kitchen and drank the damned water I still didn't know."

"Why did you go to him?" I asked.

"I spent last night online, looking for similar cases in other cities. Dozens of women disappear from cities the size of Memphis every year. Some are found, some aren't. I searched Jackson, Baton Rouge, Shreveport, Louisville, Birmingham, and Mobile. I found several similar M.O s in all of them, but Birmingham and Mobile caught my interest.

"A Mobile woman was killed a couple of months before Jeff joined the force. And another woman, Melissa Tallmadge, died a few weeks after he left the Birmingham police, but before he moved here."

"So he didn't have psychic abilities," I said.

"That was bullshit."

"Why did you go see him by yourself?" the detective scolded. "That was foolish."

"I thought maybe he'd remember the cases. That's why I called him. I'd planned to ask a few questions about our early cases, the ones before I was shot, when I first suspected we might have a serial killer on our hands. Thought his perspective might help. I also wanted to know more about these psychic abilities he claimed to have. Afterward, I was going to talk to Sasha and re-read the files with both of you. I had a theory that something was in the files that we'd missed."

"He couldn't take a chance you might come up with the right answer, so he drugged your water, and used you to get to me. For a spur of the moment plan, it wasn't bad. It damn near worked."

"And none of us ever suspected," Brannon said in a soft voice.

"He was my partner for years, my friend, almost like a brother. I put it together the minute the room got fuzzy. I remember saying, 'It's you.' I didn't want to believe it. I wanted him to laugh and tell me I was nuts."

"We all missed it. The signs were there in plain sight. He was such a nice guy, always helpful and witty." Always helpful. The last person anyone would suspect. I thought of Janine.

Reed swayed, shook his head and muttered, "Damn drug is still with me."

"We better get you up the hill. Keith's calling this in. An ambulance will be here in a few minutes."

Two of the policemen assisted Reed while Brannon returned to Jeff's body. I turned and gave one last look around the clearing. On the far edge, beyond the scene in the center, I saw two shapes shimmering like heat rising from a hot surface. I recognized Kathy and

Bridget.

Thank you. You saved our lives.

Thank you for allowing us our revenge.

I raised my hand and waved. They waved back. The shimmers faded, and then disappeared.

I turned and continued up the path.

Chapter Twenty

It's been two weeks since that fateful day. I'm happy to say I've had no more visions, no more nightmares, and no possession. It's been a little dull.

After leaving the clearing, Reed argued with the paramedics, but went to the hospital anyway for an overnight stay.

I have no idea what Brannon wrote in his report. Three days later a newspaper obituary simply stated that Detective Jeffery Hammond had passed away in his sleep from a heart attack. The facts may have been kept from the public, but I know Reed, Brannon, Keith, and the other cops in the clearing were grilled by internal affairs for days. They even interviewed me.

In the end, the incident was labeled "closed" and the paperwork buried, probably in a locked box stashed up in someone's attic. For all I know everything had been incinerated.

"No way would anybody ever keep an official record of this," Reed commented one day at the breakfast table. "Can you imagine any of us explaining to the media that a couple of ghosts killed Jeff in revenge?"

"Plus, it doesn't look too good when one of your own turns out to be a serial killer."

"The entire department would look like fools,

including the Chief of Police. Trust me, he's nobody's fool."

"I heard he may run for mayor. This is the kind of thing that makes political fodder for the opposition."

"That, too," he agreed. "Especially in Memphis."

"On the other hand, Memphians have never shied away from electing crooks and weirdos."

With Jeff dead, all the police protection had been dismissed, including those men guarding Linnie. The doctors had extended the ten-minute visiting restriction to thirty minutes for me. For the next week, I sat in her room and read aloud. Linnie loved vampires, so she got a steady diet of them.

One afternoon, I paused for a few minutes and downed a bottle of water. My throat was parched.

"So, what are you waiting for? How does the hero save the heroine?" she said in a croaking voice.

Naturally, I came unglued, jumped to my feet, and ran from the ICU cubicle screaming for Dr. Farmer, much to the annoyance of the nurses and the relatives of other patients.

By the time he arrived, Linnie was struggling to sit up. "Jeff!" she said, gasping. "Jeff's the killer."

"We know, Linnie. Take it easy."

She collapsed back onto her pillows.

"Miss Bellwood, if you would be so kind as to leave the room, I'll examine my patient," Dr. Farmer said with a smile.

I left, but stood behind the window to get a good view and called Reed with the news. The next day, she was subjected to a battery of tests before being moved into a private room. It took a few more days for her memory to come back completely. Reed and I brought her up to speed on events, including my sleepwalking, the flamingo incident, and the bizarre happenings in the clearing.

"I'd have given a million bucks to see that," she said.

"No you wouldn't. It's not something the human mind was ever meant to see," Reed said.

"I hope I never sense rage like that again." I sighed. "Kathy gave me a ringside seat to your attack. My mind refused to see it. If I had, Jeff would have been arrested that night. Instead, I wandered the streets, screaming."

"As Reed said, some things just aren't meant to be seen by the human mind." Linnie picked at a loose thread on the blanket. "I'd spent the entire day going over my patient files again, and so help me God, I couldn't see how any of them were killers. I was relaxing with a glass of wine when the doorbell rang. It was Jeff. He had this shamefaced expression and mumbled an apology. He looked like a little kid who lied about the baseball breaking the window. I can't believe I bought it. I freaking bought it!"

"We all did, Linnie."

"I was his partner," Reed said. "Think how I feel. I waltzed right into his lair."

"He was good," she muttered. "Damned good. Are you sure Kathy saved my life?"

I nodded. "She used a sofa pillow to slow the blood and managed to dial 9-1-1. I don't know how. Then, she contacted me through a dream. That's how I knew you were in danger. Scared the hell out of me."

"Didn't do me any favors, either," Reed interjected.

Linnie frowned. "You know, looking back on it, I wonder if she was trying to connect with me that night, too. The longer Jeff was with me, the more uncomfortable I felt. I can't explain it. I'd already drunk some of the wine and it was like this inner voice kept screaming at me to run. Unfortunately, by the time I decided to obey, the drug took effect." She shivered, touching the bruises on her neck. "I can still feel his hands around my throat."

"I guess we'll never know exactly how she accomplished what she did," Reed added. "I'm not even sure I want to."

Dr. Farmer walked into the room and read her chart, making a couple of notations.

"So, when can I go home?" Linnie asked.

"How about this weekend? I'd like to keep you another couple of days. You still have a fractured skull."

"But my brains aren't scrambled."

"Having any headaches?" He held her wrist and took a pulse.

"Now and then." Linnie squirmed, looking away, a sure sign she was lying.

"Uh-huh." The doctor smiled and dropped her wrist. He didn't believe her any more than I did. "Saturday afternoon at the earliest, and after I get the results from the tests I've ordered for Friday."

"But that's three days away."

"Humor me." He looked at Reed and me. "I'm afraid I'm going to have to kick you out for tonight. Visiting hours are almost over."

I gathered my purse and kissed her on the cheek. "I'll see you tomorrow."

"You better be here. I want another vampire reading," she called out as we left.

****

Dr. Farmer called Friday evening to say Linnie's tests had come out fine and he'd release her the following afternoon. The hairline fractures were healing. The pressure exerted on her throat hadn't left any permanent damage. Her speaking voice had almost returned to normal.

I spent Saturday morning cleaning up at Linnie's. The fingerprint powder was a pain in the ass, as I had discovered on cleaning my house after the ransacking, but I finally got most of it. Reed dropped by with his brother Bill in tow, bringing in several sacks of groceries. He also brought a five-by-seven area rug for under the coffee table to hide the missing carpet forensics had cut out.

We finished at two o'clock, just in time to leave for the hospital. Bill offered to stay behind and start dinner. Linnie had requested lasagna, garlic bread, salad, and wine. I wasn't sure the latter was on Dr. Farmer's list of approved menu items and told her so.

"Blow him. I want good Chianti and don't see how a couple of glasses will hurt. Besides, red wine taken in moderation is good for the heart," she stated.

Can't argue with medical science.

****

"Home, sweet, home," Linnie murmured, stepping over the threshold. "What's that terrific smell?"

"I believe you requested lasagna with all the trimmings," I reminded her.

She inhaled, smiled, and then walked into the living room. Her gaze swung immediately to the seating area. She had no memory of her head striking the coffee table, but Linnie stopped, catching her lower lip between her teeth.

"Nice rug," was her only comment.

"Forensics had to take a carpet sample," Reed explained.

She drew a shaky breath and walked over where she'd fallen to sit in her favorite corner of the sofa. At that moment, Bill entered from the kitchen carrying four glasses of iced tea on a tray. He set it on the table and offered one to Linnie with a smile.

"Thanks," she said. "And you are?"

"Marilyn, this is my brother, Bill. He's the sheriff down in Gladden County."

"He's also our chef for the evening," I added.

She leaned back and sipped the tea. "Well, if the food is as perfect as the tea, I won't complain. And the name is Linnie. Only very special people get to call me that." She tossed a smile at Bill. "That includes you, Reed."

"Thanks," he said dryly, throwing me a glance with a raised eyebrow.

Linnie kicked off her shoes and tucked her feet up under her. "You know I have a whole theory on personality and iced tea."

"Oh, no," I said with a groan. She was out of the hospital a whole thirty minutes and already flirting.

"She's well on the road to recovery," Reed said.

Bill lounged in his chair and gulped half the contents of his glass. "Do you now? I have a few theories of my own. Sippers are cautious and like to prolong the good times. Gulpers throw caution to the wind, eager to move on to the next adventure. And real men don't use sugar or lemon. They like it straight and to the point."

I burst into a laugh. "Linnie, you've just been out theorized."

She grinned. "I guess I have. Who coached you?"

"That would be me," a chuckling Reed replied.

"He mentioned your little game this morning. I like it. Do your theories extend to Italian food?"

"Not yet, but I'm sure I can come up with something."

Reed gulped his unadulterated iced tea and said, "Bill's here because he brought me some reports on Eleanor Gayle."

"And?" I said.

"Can't be completely sure, but she probably died from dehydration. We found several deep lacerations along with pieces of bark embedded in what was left of her scalp. He whacked her several times with a log or a branch and shoved her into the armoire," Bill said.

"Only she wasn't dead. She came to, but was too weak to break down the door, so she scratched and clawed trying to escape. I wonder if Jeff knew she was alive when he shoved her inside," I said in a bitter tone. "Did he drug her in the parking lot?"

"We'll never know the answer to either, but my guess is yes, probably with chloroform," Reed concluded. "I've been researching Jeff. He was busy for years before he came to Memphis."

"So, his killing spree didn't begin eight years ago?" Linnie asked.

"No. I got a hold of his uncle down in Lockerville. Jeff's parents didn't die in a fire like he told Sasha. When he was six, his father murdered his mother. He beat, and then strangled her. To finish off the job, he hacked her into pieces and buried each piece in the back yard. Jeff told the uncle he witnessed it."

"Oh, my God," Linnie said. "The apple certainly didn't fall far from the tree, did it? I hope his old man's rotting in jail."

"Nope. Was never arrested. He told everybody, his wife left him. It was his bad luck to have a sister-in-law who hated his guts and didn't believe him. It took her three years to finally get the local cops to dig up the yard. They found enough evidence to seal his fate, but before they could slap the cuffs on him, he blew his brains out, in full view of his son."

Bill rose and went into the kitchen, returning with a pitcher of tea. He refilled the glasses while Reed continued.

"Jeff went to live with his uncle. According to him, the kid was always spouting off about how women were a pain in the ass and if his old lady hadn't nagged the hell out of his father, she'd be alive and kicking."

"Sounds like the father worked on the kid," Bill said.

"The uncle started to worry when Jeff reached puberty. He found mutilated animals behind the barn. Kept telling himself the mice and rats were the work of the farm cats, but he knew he had a problem when the cats and other animals started showing up. He took Jeff to a psychologist. He stopped going after a year."

"Not enough time," Linnie said. "Something like that takes years to unearth."

"Then, the body of a twelve year old girl was found near a creek about a mile from the farm. She'd been strangled. Jeff knew her from school. They rode the

345

same bus. No one suspected Jeff, except his uncle who remembered seeing Jeff with the girl a few days earlier, but he had no evidence."

"How old was Jeff?" I asked.

"Fourteen. Another girl was murdered in the same manner four years later on graduation night. Jeff had been dating her, and this time the police questioned him. The report said Jeff was crying and distraught, but claimed he'd left her at her house around midnight. There was no evidence to assume otherwise."

"And that was before DNA became such a helpful tool for police," Bill added.

I remembered Jeff's reactions at the hospital. He was distraught, almost over the top. His rage and fear that night stemmed not from concern for his supposed girlfriend, but from the fact Linnie was still alive. His actions in the cafeteria later must have struck an unconscious chord. I was glad I hadn't revealed my dream to him.

"That's when the uncle handed Jeff a check for five grand, telling him it was a graduation present and to find a better life in a large city. Lockerville didn't offer a lot in opportunity."

"So, the uncle just foisted his problem child off on an unsuspecting public. Jerk," Bill muttered.

"The uncle was scared to death of his nephew," Reed replied.

"He made it sound so pitiful, an orphan and an uncle who couldn't wait to get rid of him," I said.

"Guaranteed to pull at your sympathetic heartstrings," Linnie commented. "He just told me he was orphaned at an early age."

"He was probably afraid you'd see through the

dramatics. He must have buffaloed the child psychologist, too," Bill added.

"Well, he sure knew how to manipulate and charm," she replied, taking a long swallow of iced tea. "The son of a bitch."

"He was in Mobile just long enough to join the police force. Being a cop gave him access to all kinds of information on murders, including the ones he committed. I unearthed two unsolved cases dealing with strangulation in the year he was there.

"Jeff wisely moved on to Birmingham. I found two more cold cases with the same MO."

"Including Melissa Tallmadge?" I said.

"Who's Melissa Tallmadge?" Bill asked.

I told him about the slip up Jeff had made at Linnie's office that day.

"And the ironic thing is, none of us paid any attention to it. I'm sure Janine never gave it another thought," Linnie said, shaking her head.

"Our computer people are checking Jeff's hard drive. The day of Janine's murder, he was seeking information on her through DMV," Reed told us.

"So, that's how he knew which car was hers," I commented.

"It also explains how he knew her age and vital statistics off the top of his head when he called in the abduction," he continued.

"A small detail and we all missed it," Linnie remembered.

"We were all upset and distracted," I told her.

"Even though he'd seen Janine a few times, he couldn't possibly have known her age and exact height and weight," Reed said. "Bank records show he stopped at the grocery store before returning to Linnie's office. He paid with a debit card. Sometimes the smallest things trip you up. He used it every time he bought groceries."

"I'll bet one of his purchases was a goddamned potato," Linnie said. "He probably stopped by a thrift store and bought a trench coat and a baseball cap, too."

"He then parked in the Kroger lot, walked back to the office building, and strolled in the front doors. After killing Janine and dumping her body, he abandoned the car, got in his own, and picked you up for dinner," Reed said.

"His past caught up with him fast," Bill added.

Reed nodded. "Too fast for him to cope. We found Janine's keys and swipe card in the baggie he intended to plant on me. The missing files were in his house. I'm sure they would have shown up at my place."

"By that time, I'd had the vision of Bridget's death and gravesite. He panicked."

"So why not kill you first?" Bill wondered.

"Janine was the easiest," Reed told him. "Sweet, vulnerable, trusting. Her death would distract Linnie, and Linnie's death would put Sasha right where he wanted her. Unable to focus."

"Fucking bastard," Linnie muttered. "By insisting the killer was one of my patients, he set the stage to throw suspicion on Reed and keep me from concentrating on what he said and did."

"It must have made sense to him. I suppose he killed Duckworth, too," I said.

Reed nodded. "We also found an unregistered twenty-two when we searched his house. Ballistics matched it to the bullet that killed Duckworth. I guess that, too, would have found its way into my possession."

"Must have scared the crap out of him when a total stranger said he saw someone entering Linnie's office the morning after Janine's murder. It was Duckworth's bad luck to tell what he saw to Jeff. If he'd dropped by ten minutes earlier, he'd have told Brannon."

I drank from my glass to ease a dry throat. Just talking about all of this scared me. *What a difference a few minutes can make in our lives.*

"And even though the description Duckworth gave was generic, Jeff couldn't take a chance he might remember more, so he had to die, too," Linnie murmured.

"And the victim, expecting to make a statement to a cop, would open the door and let him in. Probably at night. Duckworth must not have known police procedure would have demanded he make the statement at the station," Bill added.

"Why did Jeff skip out in Birmingham?" I asked. "Sounds like fertile territory."

"Serial killers often change locations. They know that sooner or later, they'll make a mistake." Reed ran his hand through his hair. "Captain Bridges told me Jeff had tendered his resignation the day before I was shot. He rescinded it the day after."

"So, my gut instincts were right. He was trying to get you killed," Bill said.

"I was stirring up the serial killer waters. Several detectives thought I could be right, including Brannon."

"Yet Jeff made it sound like you were obsessive and unstable. Your attitude toward me when we first met fueled that assumption. You let me know in no uncertain terms what you thought of psychics."

"I'll admit I came on strong, but I was frustrated."

"A lust murderer," Linnie said.

"A what?" I asked.

"Jeff was a lust murderer—an organized one, too. I surfed the internet about serial killers. I've treated all kinds of problems, but never anything criminal.

"At any rate, that's the category Jeff fit. He was organized, highly intelligent, made friends easily, and could charm the birds off the trees. Ted Bundy was like that."

"That explains why Jeff was always the new boyfriend," Reed acknowledged.

"But why did he kill?" I asked.

"Stress," she replied. "The stress builds and builds until they have to kill. He was smart enough to vary his methods, but the timings were predictable."

"Two to three year intervals and often in pairs," Reed confirmed.

"Add to it his obvious sexual hang-ups. Any woman in a mini-skirt was a slut, not fit to live," I said. "We should have picked up on that in your office the night I tried to contact Eleanor. He described what she wore. The rage I often felt was Jeff's, but I connected it to the situation at hand, not his personality."

"How could we have all been so blind?" Linnie cried.

"I realize now that the visions I had at dinner weren't from Janine, but Jeff. He'd just murdered a woman and couldn't control his emotions or his thoughts."

"Plus, he was angry with me," she said.

"It also explains why he was late picking you up,"

Reed informed her.

"And since he was a cop investigating some of the murders, he was in a position to lose any evidence that might be available. Who knows how long he would have gotten away with killing if it hadn't been for Sasha," she said.

"No," I answered softly. "Not me. Kathy Watson. A psychic window opened and she leaped through to contact me. If it hadn't been for a boring date…" I let the sentence trail off. We all knew what I meant. "I feel wretched for having suspected Bob."

"Damn near everyone in the building was a suspect," Reed said.

"Yes, but that sweet man?"

"Honey, Ted Bundy was a sweet man, too," Linnie drawled.

Reed finished his tea. "By the way, I talked with Brannon this morning. They found Brian Michaels."

"Brian! What the hell does that scumbag have to do with this?" Linnie demanded.

"He was paroled two months ago. I thought he might have had revenge on his mind," I told her.

"Who's Brian Michaels?" Bill wanted to know.

"Where was he?" I asked Reed.

"He heard about the attempted murder, figured he'd head the suspect list, panicked, and took off for his sister's in Jackson."

"Who's Brian Michaels?" Bill repeated.

"An abusive ex-boyfriend of mine. I lived in Olive Branch at that time and helped put him down on Parchman. The authorities were supposed to let me know when he got out. Guess it must have slipped their minds." Linnie spoke in a crisp tone.

The phone rang, startling all of us.

"Let the machine get it," Linnie said. "I'm in no mood to talk to well-meaning friends."

The answering machine clicked on. "Dr. Anderson, Clarke Pennington again. I've left several messages. Please call me back. It's regarding Sasha. I need your help."

"Are you kidding me?" I said when he'd hung up.

Linnie reached over and erased the tape. "He started calling the day you quit. I ignore the little creep."

The dinging oven timer brought us back to more pleasant thoughts, like dinner.

"That will be the lasagna," Bill said, rising and heading for the kitchen.

"Dinner so soon?" Linnie asked.

"Your doctor said you are to have an early night with little or no excitement," I told her.

"Screw him. I'm tired of vegetating. I was in a coma. Remember?"

How could I forget? On the other hand, she had a point. The only excitement she'd experienced in the last few weeks was that wild vital signs display. Personally, I think she reacted to Jeff's voice and tried to warn me of the danger. Linnie had no recollection of having been aware of external stimuli.

"Come and get it," Bill called from the dining room.

He pulled out Linnie's chair and seated her.

"Wow. A gentleman and a cook. Do you do windows by any chance?" she teased.

"If asked nicely—maybe," he said.

The meal was delicious, but the conversation

revolved around the flirting innuendoes between Bill and Linnie. A spark had been struck. Reed and I cleaned up, giving the two of them a chance to continue their banter.

"Should I be asking you your brother's intentions?"

Reed grinned. "Probably disgraceful. I think he likes her—a lot."

We finished the dishes and re-entered the living room. In spite of her protestations, Linnie looked tired.

"You should be in bed," I told her.

"It's not even six-thirty. Give me a break. Quit hovering. I'll be fine."

"Are you sure you don't want me to stay with you tonight?" She'd pooh-poohed this idea earlier, too.

"No. No one is going to break in and kill me. Jeff is dead." Her determined expression softened. "Thanks for the concern, but I can handle this."

"Reed, why don't you and Sasha take off and have fun? I'll stay here a little while longer, if Linnie doesn't mind," Bill offered.

"Fine with me," she said. "I play a mean game of double solitaire."

I chuckled. "Beware, Bill. She cheats."

"Good. So do I."

Reed laughed and we left. Neither of them noticed.

****

Reed's idea of going somewhere for a little fun was my place. A beer for him and a glass of wine for me hit the spot. We cuddled on the sofa.

"You know, you don't seem as rude and lacking in social graces as you once did. I must be a good teacher."

"Naw, I'm still the same rough-hewn guy. You just

don't notice because you're in love with me."

Jeez, was I that transparent? "I am? And how would you know that?"

"I'm tuned into you."

"Oh? Are you now the psychic?"

"I'm tuned in because I'm in love with you."

My heart lurched and my breath caught somewhere between my lungs and throat.

"You are?" I'd wanted to sound smart and sophisticated, but I'm afraid it came out as wistful.

He kissed my nose. "Yeah. I am. You got to me that first night at the coffee shop. I wanted to know more about you and worse yet, to see you again. Kind of scared me."

"I'll bet, me being a psychic and all."

"Figured you might have something going for you at Giovanni's. You told me about the vision and used Kathy's name. While you were in the ladies room I kept telling myself it was just a coincidence. Decided you were on the up and up when you did the Bridget thing. You had to be telling the truth. I became a true believer when we found the grave." He kissed me again, long and hard, ratcheting up my body heat. "So, are you going to admit it or not?"

"Admit what?" I was a little dazed from his lips and my raging hormones.

"That you love me."

I deliberately tapped into his emotions. His love mingled with an uncertainty that he'd made a fool out of himself. I put him out of his misery.

"Of course I love you. I realized it the night you said you believed in my abilities. I was terrified when I knew you were in Jeff's clutches as bait." Under no circumstances would I ever reveal I'd had thoughts he might be the killer.

"Not half as scared as I was when you bolted into that clearing."

I sipped some wine. "This whole experience has taught me something."

"What's that?"

"I have no business keeping my abilities to myself. From now on, if the police want my assistance, I'll help. And that includes your cold cases."

"You may help me right out of a job."

"I doubt it. Man's cruelty to man is bigger than my power."

"I suppose you're right. Unfortunately, there'll always be cold cases." He nuzzled my neck.

His actions reawakened my hormones, but I needed to get back to this love thing. "Okay, so we love each other. What now?"

He drew in a deep breath. "Are you suggesting the next logical step?"

I leaned forward, setting my glass on the table. "Marriage? I don't know."

"I do. In my world, love and marriage go together."

"This psychic invasion has left me with a lot of unanswered questions. I'm not sure I can deal with a permanent relationship yet."

He blew the breath out. "The whole experience has me questioning things, too. For years I focused on a serial killer. Now that Jeff is dead, that focus is gone. It's like coming down from a drug high. I feel disconnected, lost."

"Are you going to see Linnie professionally again?"

He finished his beer. "I think so. Maybe I need some kind of closure."

"I love you. I want to marry you, but think we both need to get our heads on straight."

"Let's call this an engagement."

"Do I get a ring?"

"Of course." He kissed my temple. "You could move in with me. See how that works out."

"I guess I can put a few things in your closet."

Reed grinned and kissed me lightly again. "I'd like that." He sobered and stroked my cheek with his finger. "I love you, Sasha. So much so, that I can't envision my life without you."

"Same here. Marriage scares me."

"I think marriage and forever scare most people. But it's something we accept because we love."

I choked back a throat full of tears and pulled his lips down to mine. The kiss was hot, wet, and stirred my hormones to the max. I slipped into his mind. His imagination was active with original sexual pleasures.

I broke off the kiss. "I am not standing on my head."

He rose to his feet, towering over me. "Why you devil! You've been in my mind, haven't you?"

"Just a little," I said with a laugh.

He reached down, pulled me to my feet, and proceeded to kiss me breathless.

"Ground rule number one for any relationship. No mind intrusion. It's not fair when only one can play."

"Maybe you can develop into a psychic." I tugged his ear lobe playfully.

"God forbid!"

His lips covered mine again. I forgot about psychic

abilities and mind intrusions. Besides, what he didn't know wouldn't hurt him. I concentrated on other more important matters, like Reed and the pleasure we were about to enjoy.

Suzanne Rossi

A word about the author...

Suzanne was born and raised in Indianapolis, Indiana, but has had the pleasure of living in several states throughout her adult life.

During her college years at Ball State University she majored in history, and was the only student in the dorm who actually enjoyed writing term papers.

She has two grown sons and is blessed with seven grandchildren, five boys and two girls.

Currently, she and her husband live in Ft. Lauderdale, Florida along with dogs Lucky and Liza, taking advantage of year-round warm weather, the beach, and all that goes with it.

She loves sharing her fantasies with readers and looks forward to meeting her fans.

Thank you for purchasing
this publication of The Wild Rose Press, Inc.

If you enjoyed the story, we would appreciate your
letting others know by leaving a review.

For other wonderful stories,
please visit our on-line bookstore at
www.thewildrosepress.com.

For questions or more information
contact us at
info@thewildrosepress.com.

The Wild Rose Press, Inc.
www.thewildrosepress.com

Stay current with The Wild Rose Press, Inc.

Like us on Facebook

https://www.facebook.com/TheWildRosePress

And Follow us on Twitter
https://twitter.com/WildRosePress